2 8

A BLESSING IN DISGUISE

Also by Elvi Rhodes

Opal
Doctor Rose
Ruth Appleby
The Golden Girls
Madeleine
The House of Bonneau
Summer Promise and Other Stories
Cara's Land
The Rainbow through the Rain
The Bright One
The Mountain
Portrait of Chloe
Spring Music
Midsummer Meeting
The Birthday Party
Mulberry Lane

A BLESSING IN DISGUISE

ELVI RHODES

BANTAM PRESS

LONDON · NEW YORK · TORONTO · SYDNEY · AUCKLAND

TRANSWORLD PUBLISHERS
61–63 Uxbridge Road, London W5 5SA
a division of The Random House Group Ltd

RANDOM HOUSE AUSTRALIA (PTY) LTD
20 Alfred Street, Milsons Point, Sydney,
New South Wales 2061, Australia

RANDOM HOUSE NEW ZEALAND LTD
18 Poland Road, Glenfield, Auckland 10, New Zealand

RANDOM HOUSE SOUTH AFRICA (PTY) LTD
Endulini, 5a Jubilee Road, Parktown 2193, South Africa

Published 2003 by Bantam Press
a division of Transworld Publishers

A catalogue record for this book is available from the British Library.
ISBN 0593 051041

Typeset in 11/13pt Plantin by
Kestrel Data, Exeter, Devon.

Printed and bound in Great Britain by
Mackays of Chatham plc, Chatham, Kent.

1 3 5 7 9 10 8 6 4 2

This book is offered with love to the people of
St Margaret's Church, Rottingdean, in gratitude
for their friendship.

Acknowledgements

First to my son, Stephen, and to Fr. Martin Morgan, Vicar of St Margaret's Church, Rottingdean, and friend, who each, when I asked them separately what I should write about, immediately replied, 'The Church of course.' So I did.

Every week Stephen discussed the book with me, on the phone from New York, always encouraging me. Fr. Morgan, out of his long and wide experience as a parish priest, helped me at every turn to get things right, and when I went wrong steered me back.

Several other people helped me in many ways. Olwen Holmes, my friend for many years and deeply experienced in church matters, read and discussed with me as the book went along – all in lengthy long-distance phone calls.

Mary Irvine, my agent and friend, encouraged me, as always, every step of the way.

The Revd Christine Wilson took time from her busy life as a parish priest to tell me what it was like. Her viewpoint was invaluable. She prevented me from straying on to the wrong path.

Shirley Hall, my secretary and friend, kept her cool through countless drafts and redrafts.

Tony Brenton, Information Officer at the National Canine Defence League, together with the staff of its Shoreham Rescue

Centre, showed me and told me everything about adopting a dog from them.

Sandie Coleman, wise Head Teacher of St Margaret's Church of England Primary School, gave me insight into how caring a school could be.

Elizabeth Morgan, daughter of the Vicarage, wrote down her memories of what it was like when she was a ten-year-old moving into a new school. Elizabeth was my research assistant for a few years before, alas, I lost her to university.

All these people smoothed my path and I can hardly thank them enough.

The characters and places in this book are purely fictitious. Thurston, and St Mary's Church, exist only in my imagination.

A BLESSING IN DISGUISE

ONE

When the organist starts the hymn I rise to my feet and leave my seat. Providing I'm not found guilty of doing anything truly terrible this seat will be mine for as long as I choose to remain in Thurston. I don't know how long that will be, though I rang the bell ten times at my institution. Tradition says you ring the bell to indicate how many years you intend to remain in the parish, but whether I'll stay so long remains to be seen.

I have to walk from my seat to the pulpit, which is no more than a few metres away but suddenly seems like a mile. I hope I appear to be walking steadily, with measured tread, head held high, pleased to be here, which I am, even though at the moment my legs feel like cotton wool.

The pulpit staircase is awkwardly curved; eight steps, each one worn and hollowed from the thousands of times feet have climbed them in the last two hundred and fifty years, though the pulpit is not as old as some other parts of the church. How many of the priests who climbed them felt as nervous as I do right now? Standing in the pulpit, raised high above the congregation, looking down on them.

'It's a position of which I don't approve,' I said (more than once) to Father Humphrey, my boss at Holy Trinity in Clipton. 'I prefer to be on a level with the congregation rather than looking down from six feet above contradiction. I don't agree with priests being set above everyone, either physically or in any other way.

He didn't agree. Well, he wouldn't.

'Well, at least we can *see* you, up there!' he said. He was referring to my height – five feet two in heels – but I reckoned there was more to it than that. There are people who prefer their clergy to be a mite exalted, a comfortable distance from them, and that, from another point of view, was how Father Humphrey liked it for himself. Set apart, elevated.

I take no notes with me into the pulpit. I'm more comfortable speaking without them – Father Humphrey once said, 'You never prepare anything, do you?' Black mark!

The trouble is, today I don't know what's expected of me. What I have to say now will be what I've said before; it's the same message but will it need new packaging for this congregation?

What they will get, what I plan to speak about, is the love of God. I know my homily should be based on the Gospel for the day but what Gospel reading can't be turned around at some point to the love of God? At Holy Trinity I was only allowed to preach at the Eucharist once a month, so I always managed to make it the love of God. I want to tell them also that the Christian faith is not a hunger lunch, it is a banquet. But do they want to hear that?

'It is *not* always what people want!' Father Humphrey complained. 'You make everything sound too easy.'

I suppose he was right, that's not always what people want. There are those who would rather hear themselves and the rest of the congregation roundly berated for their shortcomings, who enjoy being castigated as miserable sinners, feel better for it, but I'd decided at the beginning, from the time I'd made up my mind I wanted to be a priest, that they weren't going to get that from me no matter where I served. And at Holy Trinity, Clipton, they could get that from Father Humphrey. With knobs on!

Today is not my first appearance in St Mary's but at my institution, less than a week ago, the Bishop preached, though I – another quaint custom – was allowed to give out the notices for the following Sunday. Which is what I've arrived at now, presiding at my first Eucharist here, which I must remember not to refer to as the Mass, as we did at Holy Trinity. Some Anglicans are deeply touchy about the names of things and Mass is thought to be papist – though it is perfectly acceptable, the done thing at Christmas, for one and all, including those who will arrive straight from celebrating at the pub for their yearly visit to church, to refer to it as Midnight Mass.

First of all now I look down at my family. There they are, sitting in the very front pew. When I told my family that places had been reserved for them at the front, and they'd be conducted to them, my father said, 'I don't like the sound of that. You know I don't like to be conspicuous, Venus!'

When it comes to churchgoing my Dad is of the old Church of England school. 'Come early to get a good seat at the back.' However, he has had no choice. He and my mother, together with my daughter Becky and my mother-in-law Ann, have been ceremoniously conducted to the seats which have been reserved for them.

Becky's lips are compressed in a thin, tight line, turned down at the corners. Her head is bent so that her dark fringe hides her eyes. She is refusing to look at me. She is refusing to look anywhere except at the ground. My ten-year-old daughter is not a happy bunny. It saddens me, it saddens me so much, but it comes as no surprise.

She never wanted to come to Thurston, not for one minute. 'I'll hate it!' she cried. 'I know I will!' We had passionate tears, tantrums, scenes which have left me shaking, given me sleepless nights. 'I won't go!' she said. 'I will *not* go! You can't make me! I'll go and live with Granny and Grandpa!' But at ten years old you don't have the choice, do you? The taller people decide everything. They *can* make you. And I was not about to change my resolve.

It's not strange that she didn't want to leave Clipton. Life there wasn't a bed of roses for Becky any more than it was for me; on the contrary, it had been a place of unbelievable sorrow and I knew that she felt, along with everything else, as if she was deserting her father.

Now I find myself gripping the edge of the pulpit, stiffening the muscles in my face and opening my eyes wide, willing them not to fill with tears as I look at my family. Or what is left of my family. Philip, my rock, my prop and stay, my lover and the love of my life, is not there. On this day of all days, the culmination of all those years of study and training for what I have known, with absolute certainty, I wanted to be and to do for the rest of my life. 'It has nothing to do with ambition,' I told him. 'I don't want to rise higher. I don't want to be an Archdeacon, or someone important in a cathedral. All I want is, one day, to be a parish priest. To have my own people, God's people, of course, but entrusted to me.' And now the day is here, but Philip is not.

And will not be. Not now, not ever. Or at least not in the flesh. I hope, I truly believe, that he is here in the spirit, but there are times when in the spirit is not enough, and this is certainly one of them. I want him here and now; I want him to look up at me, to meet my eyes, give me a small wink, and then his broad smile. And afterwards I want him to go home with me, back to my new Vicarage, to chew over the day's events, and then to go to bed with me. Going to bed without him is one of the hardest parts, but who can I talk to about that? God, you might say, but I have to tell you that if God gives me an answer to that one it's never loud enough for me to hear.

I want Philip's strength, his assurance that all is well and all will be well. That I *will* win.

I didn't always have that assurance from him. It didn't come quickly or easily. 'I always assumed,' he said, 'that when Becky started school you'd take a job, probably part time. I didn't expect you to say at home. I thought the idea was that you'd go back to being a librarian, or perhaps work in a bookshop.' But I knew what I wanted to do, and was sure I *would* do. 'I've told you,' I said, 'and I'm totally certain about it, that I wish – if I am found to be suitable – to be ordained into the Church of England.' It came as a bombshell to him.

'But why?' he demanded. 'Venus, for heaven's sake why? I don't understand! Where has all this come from? Have you really thought about it? About what it will do to our lives? And Becky! What about Becky?' She was at nursery school then.

The questions had come thick and fast and I wasn't always

able to answer them adequately. I just knew it was what I had to do. I was totally certain and I suppose my certainty made me selfish.

My mother agreed entirely with Philip and she was even more confused.

'What's it all about?' she'd said. 'You certainly don't get this tendency from me, nor from your father. There's nothing like it on either side of the family. Except . . .' she paused, suddenly remembering, 'there was your father's Uncle George who was a missionary in Africa, but not C of E. He was a Baptist. And we only saw him the once, when he came home on leave. You can't have been more than four then.' She shook her head doubtfully.

'I do remember Great-uncle George,' I told her. 'He took a large white handkerchief out of his pocket and tied knots in it so that they looked like animals. Then he somehow made them into shadows on the wall, moving as if they were alive. He said it was how he amused little children in Africa.'

'That can't be it,' my mother said testily. 'Animal shadows on the wall can't account for your madness and I don't know what can!'

'I'm not in the least bit mad,' I said.

In the end she reluctantly came round, my father trailing compliantly after her. But what was more important, so did Philip. One day when he came home from work he said, 'Seeing that you're not to be moved an inch, and much more because, although I still don't fully understand, I love you, I've made the decision to support you.'

I was overcome. I rushed into his arms and burst into tears. 'I promise you'll be happy!' I said. 'We'll all be happy!'

It was not a giving-in on his part, it was a positive decision. He was never a weak man. And being Philip he did what he'd promised, right through my training, my time as a deacon and eventually my ordination to the priesthood. He never failed me, not once. He was always there when I needed him. He looked after Becky at the times neither I nor my mother was able to do so. He listened to the new problems which confronted me. On the few occasions when I needed to – I am not the crying sort – he let me cry on his shoulder. And at night he held me in his arms and we made love as if nothing or no-one else in the world existed.

But now, when I need him as never before, he isn't here.

Deliberately, I turn away from the sight of my family before it proves too much for me. The church is rather more than half full, and almost all of them are strangers to me. I spot the churchwardens, Henry Nugent and Richard Proctor whom I do know. I have met with them many times since the idea of St Mary's was put to me. They, more than anyone else, have been my link with the parish. I reckon Henry is in his seventies. Thick white hair, a round face, bright blue eyes. He has the good looks of a man who would be perfect for a grandfather in a TV ad. Indeed I know he is a devoted grandfather.

'I've been waiting for the new Vicar,' he told me, 'hanging on until I could hand in my cards. I've been a churchwarden here for fifteen years, good years, but it's time to finish.' He's right about that. It's something I won't encourage. I don't mean Henry personally, I mean fifteen years in the job.

Richard Proctor is different. I guess he's in his early forties. He's quite attractive in a dark, bearded sort of way, doesn't say much, keeps to the point, asks the right questions, listens to the answers and makes notes. He's a solicitor in Brampton. I don't feel I know him as well as I know Henry. Though I've met with him several times now I know next-to-nothing of his personal circumstances except that he's not married. In Henry Nugent's case I was invited to their house, met the family. Molly Nugent is a nice woman. They have, I'd guess, a happy family life.

What I *did* gather without it ever being stated was that neither of the men liked me very much, or to be fairer to them, I wasn't what they were looking for. They'd both been polite, expressed sympathy with my circumstances, but the enthusiasm to have me was muted, even though St Mary's has been struggling without an incumbent for nine months and Henry wanted out. I did wonder if they thought I'd bring too many personal problems with me, though I purposely hadn't dwelt on them.

On that first clandestine visit I'd made to Thurston, soon after the Bishop had sounded me out about a possible living there, I rated it an attractive and lively-looking village, not unlike

Hampton where I had been a deacon at St James's, and where I'd been happy. The population of Thurston is around two to three thousand, mostly, I'm told, middle-class except for a small council estate on the outskirts. There's a post office, which also sells milk, a newsagent, more than its fair share of antique shops and estate agents, plus a few other shops, a church primary school, two pubs. According to the timetable posted in the shelter, the bus goes every half-hour to Brampton, the nearest town and railway station, but if the report in the parish magazine which I picked up in the church is true, the bus service is threatened with withdrawal or severe cutting since too few people use it. 'Most people these days have cars,' I was told.

The church is attractive and, in spite of the fact that it's several centuries old, seems in reasonable repair, though it's a bit dusty and shabby inside. Perhaps the long interregnum was simply because there aren't enough priests to go round, though there's a commonly held view that the diocese deliberately prolongs interregnums to save money on the incumbent's salary. Meanwhile the parish has to make do with whatever help it can get from other parishes. If there are any other reasons for St Mary's, I expect they'll come to light. I did wonder, when I'd finally been offered the post, if Bishop Charles, realizing in the end that something had to be done, had put the pressure on St Mary's to have me. Last Chance Saloon, boys, even if it *is* a woman! And indeed, hadn't the Bishop put gentle pressure on me to take the appointment if it was offered?

That, I like to think, is out of his kindness and concern for me, and not only because of Philip but because I had not got on well with the Reverend Humphrey Payne, whose curate I became at Holy Trinity when I was priested. It would take a saint to get on with Father Humphrey and I'm not all that into saints, though Teresa of Avila is all right. A tough cookie that one! She would have eaten the Reverend Humphrey alive and spit out his bones. In the Bishop's view – I had discovered this in the way that totally confidential matters eventually filter down to the lower ranks – I had done my job at Holy Trinity well but he, knowing Humphrey Payne's view on women in holy orders, would never have appointed me there. My appointment had been made shortly before Bishop Charles (we are all into first names now, even with bishops) took over. 'It is not,' the Bishop was quoted as saying, 'that I myself am wildly enthusiastic about women in the priesthood, but given that they are now a fact of life I shall see, as far as I can, that they are treated fairly; not given preferential treatment, but equal chances. It is my job to look after the clergy in my diocese and that I shall do, irrespective of gender.'

You may ask why Humphrey Payne, being so against women in the priesthood, had accepted me into his parish in the first place. The reason was that having decided after a struggle with his conscience not to go over to Rome but to stay in the Church of England he then, as another and important matter of conscience, had to remain obedient to his bishop. Duty was done, but I don't suppose he could ever have actually welcomed me.

Looking down at St Mary's congregation now, it's larger than I'd expected from the parish profile I'd been given. Have some of them come out of curiosity, to take a look at the new Vicar but not to be seen in church again unless they venture here for the Harvest Festival or the Christmas Carol Service? I suppose the advent of a new Vicar, following one who'd been here for twenty-seven years, is an event in the life of any village.

And had some stayed away because they couldn't cope with the thought of me, a woman? I knew that had been the case with some of the laity at Holy Trinity (and they didn't even have to contend with loyalty to the Bishop). Others had coped because I was only the Curate, which didn't quite count. There was always the Vicar on hand to do the proper jobs like giving communion or officiating at funerals or weddings. At a push, he allowed that it was OK for the Curate to do a few baptisms. All the same, I like to think that by the end of my stint at Holy Trinity there were those who had come to terms with having a woman in Holy Orders. Some, I know, actually liked me.

So what about *these* people, here? What do they want of me? What do they expect? I am on display – I feel totally vulnerable. Will they laugh if I crack a joke, or is their church (theirs as much as mine) not the place for levity? I see before me faces I wouldn't mind having dinner with, and others which would serve as ice packs. But I remind myself that I am here to proclaim the word of God, the good news of the gospel, and not only on this first occasion. I will offend some – not intentionally, but I'm not here to puff people up with platitudes and half truths, though I *am* here to encourage.

The hymn is drawing to a close. One thing I can say for this lot, they're quite good at singing. I join in, though it is not my forte. 'Thus provided, pardoned, guided,' we sing, 'Nothing can our peace destroy.' I hope they are right.

I stretch out my hands and rest them on the ledge which runs around the pulpit a few inches below the top so that, hopefully, no-one will see they are trembling. I take a deep breath, count up to five. Here goes! I shall probably be marked out of ten for this sermon.

I remember what a wise priest once told me. 'Preaching is like prospecting for oil. If you haven't struck it in the first two minutes, stop boring.'

'In the name of the Father . . .' I begin. Never have I meant it more.

TWO

The service is over. No-one stood up and denounced me, no-one marched out, though I did notice that not all those who were in the pews came up to the altar to receive communion. Several remained in their seats. You do notice things like that. And a great deal more besides.

And now I'm standing in the porch, flanked by the church-wardens, all three of us making farewells. These people look reasonable sorts; some smile and some don't but no sign of horns or tails. I hope I look confident. I am normally a confident person, sure of myself. If I hadn't been how would I ever have got as far as this? How would I have survived, right from the beginning, right from the freezing winter's morning when I had to wait thirty minutes for a train which was delayed because of ice on the points – or some such reason – and I presented myself late for my first interview, frozen to the marrow and dying for a cup of very hot coffee, which was not forthcoming. The Director of Ordinands didn't acknowledge my apologies. Instead he looked at his watch and said, 'Well, we'd better get on with it, hadn't we?' The words he didn't say were written on his face: 'Trust a woman to be late!' It was all the more maddening because I'm normally punctual to the minute.

That was only the first of several interviews, meetings, tests, before I was even accepted for a theological college. Not one of

20

them, even when the interviewer was basically polite, welcomed me. I was clearly not wanted, I was a chore the rules said had to be dealt with. Nor was I any more welcome when at last, after delays and procrastinations – I swear someone sat on my file, or hid it – I was finally admitted to theological college where I was pleased to find three other women on the same course. One of them was married; only I had a child and there were certainly no concessions for that. The feeling was that I should be at home, looking after her.

But I made it, in fact I did well. I coped with the studying, the reading – often far into the night – the various tests, the obstacles. My goal was crystal clear and it was not so much a goal as a calling, loud and clear, there was no way I wouldn't answer it. And at the worst of times there was Philip to go home to, and Becky. The students who were married were allowed to live out.

So why, having come through everything so far and now standing here at the door of my own church, do I feel apprehensive, panicky even? Perhaps it was the sermon? The minute it was over, even before I walked down the pulpit steps, I knew all the things I'd left out and the things I'd put in and maybe shouldn't have. Oh well, that's what hindsight does for you! Too late now. There's no going back on it. And no way will I show that I'm the least bit nervous because, as a matter of fact, I'm looking forward to meeting all these people again, getting to know them. God has given them to me and it's up to him to give me a helping hand, which of course I know he will. I'm not doing this on my own. I shall be OK.

Actually, though we are all saying good-bye, except those who slide out without a word, I know I'm sure to meet some of these people a few minutes from now since there are refreshments to be had in the parish hall and if they're anything like as good as those laid on after the institution then they'll be worth staying for. 'You'll learn quite soon,' Richard Proctor told me on that occasion, 'that the people of St Mary's are particularly good at social functions, whether public or private!'

When everyone has left the church, except for the sidesmen who are tidying up, I set off with the churchwardens across the churchyard to the parish hall. A light rain is falling. 'We'd have liked to have had the hall built adjacent to the church,' Henry Nugent says. 'Walking across the churchyard in the winter, when the weather's really bad, isn't pleasant. But we couldn't because of the graves. We had to build on the nearest bit of spare land.'

'I thought something could be done about graves,' I say.

Henry shakes his head. 'Not without a lot of fuss and palaver. Some of these are very old, hundreds of years in fact. Make the wrong move, get valid objections, and before you could say "in loving memory" you could find yourself up before a consistory court.'

I have already heard about consistory courts. The thought of them can keep church officials, especially incumbents, awake at night, sweating. Stories are always in circulation about how an objection from a single parishioner about a seemingly small matter, let alone anything as sensitive as graves, when taken through the court had resulted in financial ruin for the church in question. Henry Nugent shudders now at the thought.

A gratifying number of people are gathered in the hall, gratifying if they're waiting to meet me. Maybe it's just the baked meats but I prefer to think not. Most of them are standing, juggling with cups of coffee, plates, glasses of wine, but some are seated at tables around the room. Each table is covered with a checked cloth and boasts a small vase of fresh flowers artistically arranged. 'Ah!' I say, 'very pretty! A nice feminine touch!'

'Oh no,' Henry says. 'Eric always does the flowers.'

A buffet has been laid out on a long table down the side of the room and a queue is forming there.

'Let me get you some wine,' Richard Proctor offers. 'Or would you rather have coffee?'

'Wine please! Red,' I tell him. And off he goes.

There was wine at the collation a few evenings ago. I'd been pleased then, and am again now, by this evidence of civilization. The last hour has certainly been, not really an ordeal, but testing. A glass of wine will be welcome before I start on the next phase, that of speaking to as many people as I can, with the impossible task of remembering all their names. A few I might remember from the collation but there I was also involved with friends from

Holy Trinity who had come to give me a good send-off in my new job.

Standing at Henry Nugent's side, waiting for Richard to return, I look around the room, searching for my family though I am sure someone or other will have taken charge of them. I spot them at a table at the far end of the room, in conversation with two women. I wave and, having seen me, they wave back – all except Becky who, though I know she's aware of me, deliberately turns away.

Richard returns with the wine. 'I didn't bring you anything to eat,' he says. 'I thought you'd rather choose for yourself.'

'Later,' I tell him.

Henry Nugent catches sight of someone halfway across the room. 'Ah! There's Bill Carstairs. Will you excuse me for a minute?'

'Why don't we move around?' Richard suggests. 'I'll introduce you to people, put names to faces.'

I'm bad at remembering names. I wish I knew an infallible way of doing it. Someone once explained to me a method which they swore had always worked for them. You try to fix an image on to the person you're meeting, something which will be a reminder next time you meet. I tried it. Mr Hyland, the man's name was. High Land, I thought. Mountain. And he was tall. So the next time I met him I called him Mr Hill!

We begin to move. I abandon my wine, the better to shake hands.

'Ah!' says Richard, coming to a sudden halt. 'Here's a lady you must meet. Mrs Rose Barker. Rose has been secretary to the PCC since before I came to live in Thurston. She was away when you met some of the church council on your previous visit.'

Rose Barker is a small, thin lady, of my own height, or even shorter. She is elderly, plain of feature, sallow skinned and dressed from head almost to foot in a shapeless black garment. Anything less like a rose I have seldom seen, so the method isn't going to work on her. What about Barker? Think of a dog's bark. A small, yappy dog.

'I'm delighted to meet you,' Rose Barker says in a voice so beautiful, so mellifluous, that she makes the everyday greeting sound like poetry. 'And what an unusual name you have! Venus! How did you come by it – or does everyone ask you that?'

'Lots of people do. I tell them they must blame my mother. It was her choice.'

'I suppose it was,' Rose says. 'But she must have had a special reason – not that it isn't a lovely name, of course. And in a way it suits you. A pocket Venus, though. Not a great big Venus de Milo with no arms. And you're very pretty. How incongruous it would have been if I'd been named Venus!' She laughs heartily at the thought. Even her hearty laugh is like music. 'So tell me, what *was* the reason?'

I take a deep breath. I have gone through this before and no doubt will again. Perhaps I should write an account for the parish magazine. 'Well –' I begin, 'and she won't mind me telling you this though whether you'll find it believable is another matter – three years after my parents were married there was no sign of baby coming along, for which, her doctor said, no reason could be found. My mother was deeply unhappy about this, on the verge of what used to be called a nervous breakdown, so in an effort to cheer her up my father took her on a holiday. He chose Rome and Florence because she had always loved art galleries, and in Florence they went almost every day to the Uffizi. And there, to her surprise and even more to my father's, she fell madly in love with Botticelli's "Birth of Venus".'

'I know the one,' Rose Barker said. 'Very beautiful!'

'Yes. Well, after the first time they went there every day. My mother would stand in front of it, just looking and looking. When it came to the last day she could hardly bear to leave it. Standing there, taking her last fill of it, she swore to my father that if she ever were to have a child it would be named Venus. Then to her amazement, a month after she returned home she found herself pregnant. So there was never any doubt what my name would be.'

'Lucky she didn't have a son!' Rose Barker says.

'Quite!' I say. 'She might well have named him Botticelli, which would have been shortened to "Botty". Anyway, she never had another child, nor did she ever regret naming me Venus though I've gone through life hating it.'

24

'Poor you!' Rose Barker says. 'But what a lovely story. Is your mother here? I must meet her.'

And when you do, I think, you are in for a big surprise. I love my mother dearly, I wouldn't change her for any other mother in the world, but she is, honest to God, the most down-to-earth, matter-of-fact person you could ever meet. Her obsession with the Botticelli Venus was possibly the one romantic episode in her life. I put it down to the fact that she was already, but unknowingly, pregnant when she was in Florence. The dates fit. Pregnant women get weird ideas. I think she went a bit funny. She certainly hasn't had a strange notion since, nor one even the least bit unconventional.

I point her out. 'She's over there. In the far corner, with the rest of my family.' It was the most obvious place for my father to choose.

'Then I'll go and have a word with them,' Rose Barker says. 'Good-bye for now!' Her voice makes that sound like a benediction.

I turn to Richard.

'Look, I mustn't monopolize you. Why not leave me to it? I'll just wander around and speak to whoever I come across. I'm not the least bit shy. Honestly, I'll be quite happy.'

I don't need him to shepherd me. I'd much rather make my own way, speak to people at random, not have them chosen for me. Also I'm pretty certain Richard is merely doing his duty.

Another thing, Richard would introduce me mainly to the hierarchy and I don't want that. I don't like hierarchy, anywhere or at any time. I shall meet them all in any case, but here's my chance to speak to just anyone, find out who they are, why they're here today, what particular part, if any, they play in the village. Pick up a bit of village gossip. My ministry here, as I see it, is not only to those who come to church. To my mind it includes everyone in Thurston, whether of my creed, some other creed or no creed at all. Indeed some of the last will almost certainly turn out to be the most interesting. But some won't approve of me, and not only because I'm a woman. For a priest it's an occupational hazard. Nor will they hesitate to tell me

25

why, and that will come from people in the church as well as outside it.

Anyone can be as rude as they like to the clergy. Oh yes, it's par for the course! They can tell you, whether you want to know or not, how they disapprove of your beliefs, because they know better. They *know* God doesn't exist. They can criticize the way you dress – walking around the parish in a cassock, fancy vestments on a Sunday. Jesus didn't wear embroidered stoles, did he? Anything is game. And of course the clergy can never be rude back because no-one entitled to wear a dog collar can be rude. It's not in the job description, is it? But I can cope with that. I don't argue, even though I think I might have some of the answers on the tip of my tongue, because I've never believed that the Christian faith was spread by argument.

So I move away from Richard – and is it my imagination that he looks relieved? – and the first person I bump into, literally, is a woman of indeterminate age and appearance. A sort of beige woman.

'Whoops!'

'My fault!' she says. She has a nice smile which shows off teeth perfect enough to be American. 'My husband says I do it all the time. I mean walk around in a dream, not necessarily bump into people.'

'And you are . . . ? I'm sorry, I don't know names yet.'

'Trudy Santer. I run the Sunday School.'

'How wonderful!'

'Not really. I only do it because there's no-one else. You see it used to be done by the Vicar's wife. I mean the former Vicar's wife. Before that, when we had a curate, it was naturally done by him.'

It would be. It was one of the jobs I did at Holy Trinity, largely because Humphrey Payne didn't know what to do with me, with my sore handicap of being a woman. Running the Sunday School, visiting the elderly chronic sick, organizing the Women's Group and taking the occasional funeral of some obscure, non-attending parishioner whom the Vicar had not known in life and was not interested in in death had been the bedrock of my duties.

26

'So I'm hoping you'll take an interest in the Sunday School here,' Mrs Santer says, which I translate as she has high hopes that I'll take it on.

I give her my widest smile, but it can't compete with hers because my teeth are not as expensively maintained.

'Of *course* I'll be interested,' I assure her, with truth. 'Work with the young is one of my passions. It's very important. But I'm a great believer in the laity doing all the things for which they're equally well fitted. I expect this is a busy parish so I'll need all the help people like you can give me. And I'll be grateful for it.'

Her smile falters a little. 'I had thought . . .' she begins.

'We must have a talk about it later,' I say. 'When we have more time. I'd really like to know what you're doing. But if you'll excuse me for now . . .'

'Of course!' she agrees.

I move on, then pause at a table where a man and four women are sitting. 'May I join you?' I ask.

'Please do,' one of them says.

'Can I get you something to drink?' the man asks. 'Coffee, or wine? Something to eat?'

'Nothing to eat,' I tell him. 'A glass of wine would be lovely. I did start out with one but after one sip I seem to have lost it. Now, I'm going to ask all your names but I tell you here and now, I'll probably forget them. So you won't hesitate to remind me next time we meet, will you?'

'I'm Carla Brown,' one of the women says. She is plump and confident-looking. 'I don't particularly do anything. I don't even come to church much, but I thought I'd make an effort today. That's my husband who's gone to get the wine. He's Walter.'

I turn to an elderly woman who is sitting very upright at the end of the table, behind a plate piled high with tomato sandwiches and sausage rolls. I tell myself that this lady is most likely an old dear who lives alone and is turning this occasion into her Sunday lunch. 'And you are . . . ?' I ask politely.

'I am Miss Frazer. Miss Amelia Frazer,' she replies in the finest cut-glass tones.

'The *Honourable* Miss Frazer,' a woman beside her says in a suitably deferential voice. 'With a zed.'

'And have you lived in Thurston long, Miss Frazer?' I enquire.

'I was born here,' she replies. 'The Frazers have lived in Thurston since William the Conqueror gave the land on which the village, the church, and indeed the foundations of the house I inhabit, are built to my ancestor, Cedric de Frazer.'

'Goodness!' I say – which sounds inadequate. 'You must know every bit of local history!'

She concedes with a slight nod. 'I make it my business, as well as my pleasure.'

'And you must have known several incumbents here?'

'Five,' she says. 'Of whom the last Vicar was quite the finest. I am older than he, and in his twenty-seven years as Vicar of St Mary's I was able to guide him in the traditions of Thurston and of St Mary's. It was something he always appreciated. Yes, his retirement was a great loss to all of us. A great loss! Indeed, the Reverend John Marks was a true saint!'

There is a silent pause in which I am more or less waiting for someone to say 'Amen', then the woman beside her says 'Excuse me' and rushes away in the direction of the loo. Miss Frazer herself breaks the short silence.

'And let me tell you here and now, it has to be said and I shall not shirk it, I do not approve of you. It is not personal since I don't know you, except that I know you made the choice, but I do not in any way approve of women priests. Women priests are an abomination unto the Lord! If I had still been on the Parochial Church Council, from which, and now to my regret, I resigned a year ago, I would hope and believe this appointment would not have gone through!'

I don't reply immediately and it's probably that which makes Carla Brown decide I am at a loss for words. I'm not lost for words. I'm not even wounded or thrown because I'd known it would come from one quarter or another. I decide to let Miss Frazer have her full say – I'm sure there's more to come – before I respond, and even then it won't be with an argument. That would be a waste of time.

28

'I think that's uncalled for,' Carla Brown says bravely. 'In any case, I don't see what difference it makes – man or woman!'

Miss Frazer gives her a freezing look.

'I wouldn't expect you to,' she says. 'You are ignorant of the traditions of the Church. What would *you* know of the apostolic succession? Jesus was not a woman and he did not appoint women. His apostles were men, chosen by him not only to found the Church but to carry it down through the ages. As long as the world shall last.'

I long to tell her that there are those, one or two of them known to me, who like to think that God *is* woman, but that would be too provoking. All the same, I can't stand by and let her insult Carla, who has tried to come to my rescue. What she's just said to Carla *is* personal, meant to put her down.

'I'm interested in your views, Miss Frazer,' I say, exceedingly pleasantly (though not truthfully), 'and also in Carla's' (I give her a real smile), 'and of course you both have a perfect right to express them.'

'I don't need you to tell me that,' Miss Frazer says. 'And express them I shall!'

'Again your choice . . .' I begin, but she interrupts me.

'But *you* will never drive *me* out of St Mary's. It is after all my parish church. My forebears were instrumental in building it and my family have worshipped here for generations, so *I* am not the one to be driven out. You might well find, I am sure you will, that there are others who hold the same opinions as I do. It is quite possible that they will be driven away, but you will find I am made of sterner stuff. And now, having said what I came into this hall to say, I shall leave.' Which she does. Her departure is followed by a few moments of complete silence, which is then broken by Carla Brown.

'Stupid old bat!' she says furiously. 'But don't let her upset you!'

Of course she hasn't upset me. These, to her, are intended to be stab wounds, rapier wounds, but to me they are little more than pinpricks. I've heard it all before. The woman who left us (I *must* ask her name) returns, looking decidedly pale.

'Where is Miss Frazer?' she asks.

'She had to leave,' Carla says, lying fluently. 'She remembered an urgent appointment.'

'How strange,' the lady says, 'she never said anything to me.'

Nothing is said of the short scene she has missed and she asks nothing more. I think at the moment she has her own physical difficulties. Something she ate.

It's possible some people will leave St Mary's. It's not unusual when a woman priest takes over. I've heard all the horror stories. I shall face it as it comes. I don't expect members of the congregation to leave in droves, but even the loss of one would be sad. Of course it would! Even Miss Frazer's departure would, though it would make life easier for me. But she won't leave, will she? She will stay if only to torment me, and to win others to her cause.

People do leave churches, and for a wide variety of reasons. They don't like the new hymns, the sermons are too long or too short, the church is too cold or too hot, the services time badly with a favourite television programme, or they are church tasters who enjoy trying new places. Sometimes they come back, sometimes not. Every parish priest knows this.

'By the way,' Carla says, 'what *do* we call you? Some used to call the last Vicar Father John. Not me though. That's for the Romans.'

The others look at me expectantly. I rather think they're glad to have the subject changed.

'You can take your choice,' I tell them. 'You can call me Vicar, or you can call me Mrs Stanton, or you can call me by my first name, which is Venus. Whatever!'

'So is Venus OK?'

'Absolutely!'

For the thousandth time I wish my mother had been besotted by someone with a more usual name. There must have been several such in the Uffizi. Mary, Elizabeth, Anne. Probably all of them saints. Cecilia would have been nice.

'One thing is certain,' Carla Brown says. 'No-one's going to call you Mother Venus!'

'Too right!' I agree. That's certainly one of the differences between men and women priests. Father Humphrey but not Mother Venus.

Walter Brown returns with the wine. I sip it gratefully then say, 'Well, it's been lovely meeting you all. I'm really looking forward to getting to know you better.' Then I move away, as usual leaving my wine glass behind.

THREE

I'm debating now whether or not I'll take a minute to have a word with my family, especially with Becky, when a woman walking towards me comes to a dead stop in front of me.

'Good-morning!' she says.

She is a few inches taller than I am, dressed in a well-cut grey suit with a mauve silk scarf draped immaculately around her neck – something I can never do. I spend ages getting every last fold exactly right and ten minutes later it's all over the place again. She has tawny-red hair, so well cut that I know that whatever she went through it would fall back into exactly the right place, green glass dangly earrings and an interesting face. Not exactly pretty, but attractive. High cheekbones, broad brow. I guess she's about the same age as me, somewhere in her mid-thirties.

'Good-morning,' I reply. 'And you . . . ?'

'I'm Sonia Leyton,' she says before I can finish the question. 'Your local GP. Nigel Baines is the other partner in the practice.'

'It's good to meet you,' I tell her. 'I was going to come along to see you in the next day or two to ask if my daughter and I could register with you. Becky is ten.'

'Sure you can,' she says. 'Since you live in the village and you're who you are, that's fine. Otherwise our list is completely full. We need a third doctor but we haven't the room and we've had no luck in getting new premises in Thurston.'

'I didn't see you in church,' I tell her – and then feel awkward, as if I'm reprimanding her.

'I was there. Hiding behind a pillar. Not that I'm usually there. I'm not sure whether I'd call myself an agnostic or just plain lazy. I'm not all that keen on institutionalized religion. But I wanted to meet you. Parish priests and local doctors should know each other, don't you think?'

We chat for a few minutes and then she looks at her watch and says, 'I'll have to leave. Sunday or no Sunday I have a couple of hospital visits to make. And I've no doubt you're just as busy.'

'I am at the moment. Though it's a funny thing that everyone thinks Sunday is the Vicar's busiest day and it seldom is. I have far more to do on other days of the week. On Sundays I mainly do what other parishioners do, which is go to church. And they're going on their day off.'

'Do you take a day off?' she asks.

'I try to. I shall see how things work out here and then if I can I'll settle on a regular day – barring emergencies, of course. If anything crops up then I'm on duty. Like you, I suppose.'

'True. But you should try. We all should.'

I hold out my hand. 'Good-bye for now, Doctor Leyton.'

'Sonia,' she replies. 'Pop in during the week. Bring Becky with you.'

I go to join my family.

'I'm bored!' Becky says. 'When can we go?'

'I'll have to stay a little longer,' I tell her. 'Why not walk around with me and meet a few people?'

'Are you joking?' she says. 'Definitely not!'

'Why don't Becky and Ann and Grandpa and I go back to the Vicarage?' my mother suggests. 'I can be getting on with the lunch.' My mother has undertaken to make all the meals this weekend. She and Dad go back to Clipton on Wednesday. I shall miss her. I shall miss my mother-in-law too.

I watch my family depart, my parents and my mother-in-law smiling at people as they pass them on the way to the door. Becky with never a sideways glance. 'She's not really like this!' I want to say to all these people she's deliberately snubbing. 'Please excuse her! She can be a very nice child.' But when was the last time? I want to run after her, to put my arm around her, plead with her, try to comfort her, but I must stay here just a little longer. In any case she would rebuff me, I know she would. She's got that to a fine art.

'I won't be long!' I call after her. Not a flicker, not a sign that she has even heard me, though I know she has. I carry on and, like the Ancient Mariner, I stop the next person in my path, who looks surprised at being suddenly accosted. 'I'm the new Vicar,' I say, as if I weren't dressed for the part, as if she hasn't seen me standing up there in the pulpit. 'And you are . . . ?'

'Elsie Jones,' she informs me. 'I run the Brownies.'

'How nice!' I say. 'I love the Brownies.'

Wasn't my own Becky a Brownie? Keen as mustard. Never missed a meeting, took all the tests, gained all the badges. But it tailed off when her father was ill, and after he died it stopped altogether and nothing took its place.

'I hope you'll drop in and see us,' Elsie Jones says. 'Tuesdays, five o'clock!'

'Oh I will!' I promise. And I will.

We chat for a few minutes – she has two children, a son and a daughter both younger than Becky. Naturally, one is a Brownie and the other a Cub Scout. Her husband is a paint salesman, his territory Sussex and Surrey. He doesn't come to church but he's quite pleased that she does, and if it's needed for the church he will always get us paint at a discount. 'Well, I hope to meet him some time,' I tell her – and then I pass on. I speak to a few more people and they all seem friendly enough, no more Miss Frazers among them, at least not with the ones I encounter. I think they are probably curious about me, what I'm like, whether things will be different. I suppose that's natural given that the previous Vicar was here all those years and most of them won't have known anyone else. I am an unknown species. By now there's a general drifting away and I suppose I could do the same, though first of all I must let my churchwardens know. I see no sign of Henry Nugent but Richard is at the other side of the room and I make my way towards him.

34

'I think I must leave,' I tell him. 'My mother-in-law's going home soon and I want to have a little time with her. Actually, I've met quite a few people. Very interesting.'

'Good!' Richard says. 'Don't forget, will you, there's a Eucharist at eight p.m. on Tuesday.' It has already been explained to me that this was instigated by the former Vicar, not because he himself particularly wanted it, he didn't go much on weekday services, but at the firm request of a parishioner and for the benefit of those who couldn't get to church on Sundays, who were working in Brampton, or even London, during the week and didn't get home very early in the evening. It had never gone down really well. The said parishioner had since moved away.

'And you'll remember that the monthly finance meeting is on Wednesday evening,' Richard says. 'We have that here.'

'Ah!' I say. 'Well, I'm afraid some of these things will have to change. Tuesday this week I can do because my parents will still be here, but next Wednesday I can't possibly. As you know, I have a ten-year-old daughter and even if she knew people here, which she doesn't, I'm not prepared to leave her alone in the house in the evenings. So next Wednesday you'll all have to come to the Vicarage. After that we'll have to work something out. The problem will be the same for most evening meetings. I'm sure I've mentioned this before.'

He gives me one of those looks described as impassive, though I know exactly what he's thinking. He's thinking, this is what you get with a woman Vicar. If we had a man . . . Clearly, he can't envisage a man being a single parent, and I suppose if he was, and he happened to be the Vicar, half the women in the parish would rush to his aid. They would bring shepherd's pies they'd just happened to have made that morning which he would only have to pop in the microwave. They would bring fruit cakes, pots of home-made marmalade, mango chutney. They would offer to iron his shirts, they would draw up a roster for sitting in. Probably fight to get on it.

But hold on girl, I chide myself, they might do a roster for you. Give it time. Not that they would ever bring me shepherd's pie and marmalade. Real women knock up that sort of thing themselves between making the beds and putting a wash on and before cleaning the windows.

'I see,' Richard says. 'Yes, I do see. Perhaps you could get someone to stay in the house with your daughter?'

I shake my head. 'Not too often, and not yet,' I tell him. 'Not until both of us get to know more people.'

'Very well,' Richard says. 'In the meantime I'll let the other members of the Finance Committee know. Wednesday at the Vicarage. Is eight o'clock convenient?' He sounds quite amiable.

'Fine!'

I don't like committees, though naturally I'm used to them. The difference now is that I'll be expected to chair most of them, whether I know anything about the subject or not. And indisputably the one I like least is the Finance Committee. Over the last few years I have worked hard to hide the fact that I hardly know which way up to read a balance sheet, let alone make any sense of it. However, I can guess what the finance meeting at St Mary's will be about. We will discuss how deep in debt we are or, rather, how far we fall short of the money we need for the upkeep of the church, not to mention the quota we have to pay to the diocese. There will be the usual crop of grumbles about the quota because everyone hates paying it. We shall hear the large amount it will cost to repair the bits of the chancel roof where the rain is coming in again and the fact that the lighting must be overhauled or one of these days someone will get a nasty, possibly fatal, shock. We shall discuss ways of raising the money, shying away from asking for more generous direct giving as if it was an indelicate suggestion, and then go into the realms of the Christmas bazaar. Is November too soon? Is December too late? Who will do which stalls (this will turn out to be the same as whoever did them last year)? Shall we run a Grand Raffle (as opposed to just a raffle)? Who shall we ask for prizes (which will also be the same as last year)? Then a few more Bring-and-Buy Sales will be mooted and agreed, at which I am quite certain that, even though I have yet to experience one at St Mary's, many of the same articles will be given, sold, and brought back to the next one for resale. At Holy Trinity there was a vase in a particularly hideous design of a yellow spotted fish which I noticed in every sale during my time there and eventually bought at a knock-down price so that I could throw it away. Yes, I know exactly what the Finance Committee meeting will be like.

I had naively thought that after I was ordained my job would be to take the word of God to the people. I would be visiting the sick, comforting the dying, assisting at the Eucharist, explaining the scriptures, possibly even saving a soul or two. I had put from me the thought that once I had my own living I would also be elevated to Chief Fund-raiser, a role for which I am about as fitted as a lame man, blindfolded, is to walking a tightrope.

I leave the hall and make for the Vicarage – how long before I will call it 'home'? The day has turned chilly, there is an autumnal nip in the air and the leaves on the sycamores in the churchyard are turning yellow and brown. The first strong wind will scatter them on the ground. The Vicarage is no more than five minutes' walk away, built in Victorian times in the road next to the church. It is large, with lots of rooms and high, artistically moulded ceilings. On the whole this pleases me – I never did like living in a modern semi – but Becky and I, after Wednesday when we will be on our own, will rattle around in it.

I turn my key in the lock and walk in. 'Hello!' I cry. My mother pops out of the kitchen at the far end of the hall.

'Hello!' she cries. 'Dinner won't be long. Are you going to have a sherry?'

My mother is from Yorkshire. When my father retired they moved south so as to be closer to me. A meal in the middle of the day is dinner, and in the evening supper. The word lunch is not in my mother's vocabulary. Sherry is my mother's tipple.

'No thank you,' I answer. 'I've started two half glasses of wine. I don't know what happened to either of them in the end. Do you want any help? Where is everybody? Where's Becky?'

'She's in her room, with the door shut. Ann is packing, Dad's gone down to the newsagent's.' He will be buying the *Sunday Express*.

'Shall I lay the table?' I ask.

'It's done,' she says.

'Then I'll go up and see Becky,' I tell her.

'I wouldn't if I were you,' my mother counsels. 'I'd leave her be for the moment.'

I flop down on a kitchen chair and take off my dog collar.

'How long is this going to last?' I ask.

My mother opens the oven door, takes out the meat dish and proceeds to turn over the potatoes. A comforting smell of roasting beef fills the kitchen.

'I don't know, love,' she replies as she puts the dish back in the oven, closes the door and turns the heat up high to bake the Yorkshire puddings which she will do, not under the meat, but in loaf tins. They will rise up and call her blessed, they will be golden and crispy on the outside and soft within. They will be served before the main course, smothered in onion gravy. If I were to say grace it would be before eating my mother's Yorkshire puddings.

'Life's hard for the lass at the moment,' my mother says. She is quite right, but her words catch me on the raw.

'It's not all that easy for me!' I say briskly.

'I know that, love,' she says. 'Don't imagine I didn't think what was in your mind this morning. But it's certainly worse for Becky.'

'And how do you work that out?' I demand.

'Easily,' she says. 'And so can you. It was your choice to come here – oh, I know you didn't choose what went before, but you did choose to come to Thurston. You've got all the excitement of a new job, new challenges – and we all know how you like new challenges. You always have, ever since you were a little girl. Always ready to throw yourself into something new. It used to worry both me and your Dad, though it usually worked out all right in the end. But Becky's not like that. She doesn't have your push and go. She likes things settled. And right now she's the one who's had to give up everything. You've got to bear that in mind.'

'I know, Ma! I will, and don't think I'm not sorry for her. I want to help – but how?' How terrible that sounds! Me, a priest of God and I don't know how to help my own daughter!

'You'd do best right now to leave her be,' my mother repeats.

'When I'm ready to dish up you can go and fetch her. In the meantime, why don't you take a turn round the garden?'

The garden at the back of the house is large, mostly lawn and shrubs, a lot of them evergreens. Not much colour. I shall change that. I enjoy gardening. The lawn is quite well kept and I hope I'm right in seeming to remember that a man, I think the man who looks after the churchyard, cuts the grass at the Vicarage.

At the bottom of the garden, beyond the mown lawn, there is a fence, and beyond that what I suppose it would be polite to call a wild garden, which sounds better than abandoned and neglected, which it is bound to have been since the Vicarage hasn't been lived in for several months. When I came earlier it was full of wildflowers – buttercups, daisies, dandelions, red sorrel – and looked quite pretty. Now, the flowers being over, abandoned is the right word. In the wall which borders it at the bottom there is a rickety gate, leading to a path which climbs up to the Downs. I would like to explore this right now but very soon the Yorkshire puddings will be ready and one does not keep Yorkshire puddings waiting. On the contrary, my mother will insist that we are seated at the table before she will bring them in. Time, tide and Yorkshire puddings wait for no man.

I walk around a little longer then, impatient, I go back inside the house and, ignoring my mother's advice, climb the stairs to Becky's room. My knock on the door receives no answer, so I open it a crack and say, 'Lunch is ready, darling!' Brightly, I say it, as though there is a clear blue sky between us. Still no answer. Deflated for the moment, I go downstairs. However, I am fairly confident that Becky will soon follow. She has a healthy appetite and it is unlikely, however black her mood, that it will include starving herself. And indeed it doesn't. With perfect timing she slips into her place five seconds before my mother enters, bearing the puddings aloft as if preceded by a fanfare.

Ann is already seated at the table.

'You'll excuse me if I leave straight after lunch, won't you?' she says. 'I brought work home with me and I haven't even touched it.'

Ann is secretary to a professor of mathematics at the University of Clipton, which used to be Clipton Technical College before

39

they all became universities. She is a dear friend as well as my mother-in-law. And of course we have shared in the same bereavement, though to lose a husband and to lose a son are two different things and probably no-one who hasn't gone through either can understand them.

'I thought everything went well this morning,' Ann says. 'Philip would have been proud of you!'

There is a poem, 'Slowly, the dead steal back into our speech' – I'm ashamed that I can't remember the author – but Ann has never hesitated to say Philip's name, usually in a matter-of-fact way. She is braver than I am and she is also right. He is never excluded.

Becky eats a hearty meal, her plate is clean, though she is as mute as a nun under a vow of silence.

'I thought you and I might explore the path up to the Downs this afternoon,' I suggest.

She gives a single shake of her head, turning me down flat without having to speak to me, and the moment the meal is over she goes back to her room.

When we have cleared away Ann brings her suitcase down and I see her to her car.

'Bear up!' she says, giving me a hug and a kiss. 'It can't last.'

I am not so sure.

I join my mother in the kitchen, where she is washing up. This is totally unnecessary since I have a perfectly good dishwasher but she does not trust it to do the job properly. I offer to help her with this self-inflicted chore but she turns me down.

'In that case,' I say, 'will you mind if I go for a little walk – or perhaps you'd like to come with me?'

'I won't if you don't mind,' she says. 'As you know, I usually put my feet up on a Sunday afternoon. You should do the same. Your Dad's already well away.' Indeed he is; we can hear his rhythmical snores, fortunately muted by the distance between the kitchen and the sitting room.

'I could do with some exercise,' I tell her. 'I won't go far, won't be long.' The truth is, I want to be on my own. Since the company of the two people I love most in the world is not available to me I don't want any other.

40

I walk down to the bottom of the garden, go through the little gate, and take the path up to the Downs. ('Why do they call them downs when they go up?' Becky once asked me when she was small – another of the many questions to which I couldn't give a satisfactory answer.) When we lived in Clipton the sea, on a clear day, was visible from the top of the Downs. In Thurston we are just that bit too far inland, but nevertheless the view is good. I look down on the village, noting how snugly it's contained in its hollow, the narrow High Street running in a straight line to join the Brampton road at the south end; the church – *my* church – in the centre, the Ewe Lamb and the Queen's Head, the two pubs, at either end. There is almost no sprawl of houses beyond the edge of the village, where it gives way to fields. Thurston, I'm told, has always been an agricultural village and from here I can see that it's still surrounded by farmland, though whether there are as many farms as there once were I don't yet know. There are cornfields, where the grain has been harvested, leaving a golden stubble, and other areas already planted with winter crops. Very little of the ground is level and I doubt if the harvesting will be easy, though being a townie I can't judge these things.

Philip would have liked this. Will I ever settle without him? Should I have come here? But the Bishop was right, I couldn't have stayed where I was.

The afternoon is cool and there are very few people about. A man comes towards me, followed by a Labrador. He gives me a nod as he passes me on the narrow path – the man, not his dog. I don't recall having seen him in the congregation. I walk around for twenty minutes or so, keeping to the main path though there are others which branch off it. I will explore those another time. Also, though what good it will do me I don't know, I want to be back with Becky. I can't bear the thought of her alone in her bedroom. I turn around and retrace my steps – there is no sign of the man or his dog – and twenty minutes later here I am, back at the Vicarage.

Dad is awake, doing the crossword, my mother has made a pot of tea and there is my daughter eating a jammy scone. Her stomach could be my salvation. Thinking of Becky I ask

41

myself yet again, have I done the right thing in coming here?

'You've just come at the right time!' my mother says, which seems a strange answer to the question I haven't put into words. She pours me a cup of tea. 'Oh, and there was a telephone call for you. A Doctor Leyton. I've written her number down. She says will you give her a ring. She sounded pleasant. Will she be your doctor?'

'Yes, she said she'd fit us both in. I'll ring her.'

'It was just to suggest,' Sonia Leyton says when I do so, 'that if it suits you it might be a good idea if you were to call tomorrow. We'll be through surgery at about half eleven. I'll introduce you to Nigel.'

'That will suit me fine,' I tell her. 'I'm seeing the Headmistress at ten o'clock, with Becky. I'll come along to you afterwards.'

At my mother's beckoning I follow her into the kitchen.

'I've been having a chat with Becky,' she says. 'She's all for going back with me and your Dad. I've told her it's not on.'

'Quite right!' I agree. 'That's definitely out of the question.'

A little later I go up to Becky's room. The radio is going at top volume and I have to shout over it.

'I have to go to Evensong now . . .'

'I won't go!' Becky says.

'Fine by me. As you know, you don't have to. You never have. All I expect is for you to go to church on Sunday mornings, just as you always have done. It won't be any different.'

'Oh yes it will!' she flares. 'Everything will be different! I don't know anyone. I don't want to know anyone! Why do you have to be a Vicar? Who wants to have a Vicar for a mother?'

FOUR

Monday morning, and since my most important job today is to go with Becky to the school, both of us to meet the Headmistress, I am not wearing my clerical collar. First things first, and this morning I am not so much the Vicar of St Mary's as Becky's Mum so I am dressed accordingly; blue jeans, trainers, and a thick red sweater my mother knitted for me. She is a dab hand at knitting, always has some on the go though usually these days to sell to send money to some good cause. She would feel more fulfilled if she had a clutch of grandchildren to make woolly garments for. Becky is most definitely not into home knits. They are not cool. Her attire today is almost the same as mine except that instead of the sweater she wears a trendy jacket declaring her loyalty to Manchester United. If the rest of the school are Liverpool supporters – and I have no idea about this but I fear the worst – she will be even deeper into what she sees as enemy country. It is not in her nature to change her ideas to suit someone else – not unlike me I suppose, which is why when our goals happen to be different there is no halfway meeting place – so she will be out on a limb again.

St Mary's Church of England Primary School is a ten-minute walk from the Vicarage. It was built in the early part of the twentieth century on land given by the one-time Lord of the Manor, though the present buildings are not more than twenty-five years old, since the first ones more or less fell down. We are due to meet the Headmistress, Mrs Evelyn Sharp, at ten o'clock and I have practically had to take a gun to Becky to get her out of the Vicarage. Heaven knows what it will be like come next Monday, the day she starts in earnest. 'She'll be all right by then!' my mother says, with what I think is misplaced confidence.

The security at the school is tight. We have to ring the bell and state our business, through a grille, to a disembodied voice. After a longish pause, the door is answered, by which time it would not surprise me if we were submitted to a body search. Sad to think that these precautions are necessary, but I know they are, which is why I refuse to leave Becky alone in the house in order to attend an evening meeting. I expect I shall be the same even when she's older. There is a stream of callers at any Vicarage, many of them difficult, some decidedly strange, and they can be threatening, especially when you won't give them what they want, which is usually not a cheese sandwich and a cup of tea but hard cash. She's a sensible child, not at all fearful, but I wouldn't like her to have to deal with them.

Once inside the school it is not at all like a fortress, it is all light and colour, with children's paintings and vividly illustrated poems pinned up everywhere; mobiles hanging from the ceiling. The secretary takes us down two corridors to Mrs Sharp's room and the Headmistress comes out from behind her desk to greet us. She is tall, has dark, wavy hair, a bright smile and a gap between her two front teeth, which makes me think – the gappy teeth, that is – how well she will match with some of the children.

'How nice to meet you both,' she says, holding out her hand first to me and then to Becky, who suffers herself to be touched without actually flinching, but looks down at her feet and says nothing.

'Shall we sit down?' Mrs Sharp invites, and we move to three low chairs set informally around a small table away from the desk. I approve of that. 'I'm sorry I wasn't in church yesterday, Mrs Stanton,' she continues. 'I was away for the weekend, though in fact I don't attend St Mary's regularly because I live over the far side of Brampton. But I would have been there yesterday to welcome you.'

There are papers on the table, which Mrs Sharp shuffles through before selecting one. 'Well, Becky,' she says, 'I had a nice letter about you from your school in Clipton, from Mrs Porter. She was your Headmistress, wasn't she?'

She doesn't wait for an answer. Just as well.

'She tells me you are a bright girl, that you worked hard and you were friendly. So it seems to me you'll fit in well at St Mary's. You'll be in Year Five when you start here next Monday. I'm sorry you couldn't be here for the beginning of term but I'm sure you'll soon catch up. Who knows, you might be ahead!' Mrs Sharp has a voice which is at one and the same time both businesslike and soothing. I can imagine her dealing exceptionally well with playground disasters. However, Becky is unmoved.

Mrs Sharp hands the letter to me so that I can get the whole story while she tries, with little success, to chat with Becky. What the Head at Clipton has also said is that since her father's death Becky has become a difficult child whom some of the staff have found hard to handle, though they understand why. She hopes allowances will be made for her and that she will be sympathetically treated. 'You can be sure of that,' Mrs Sharp says to me as I hand back the letter.

'So have you bought your uniform yet?' she asks Becky, who shakes her head.

'We're going into Brampton for it tomorrow afternoon,' I tell Mrs Sharp.

'Good! It's a rather pretty shade of blue this year. We change colours every two years so you don't get bored with it. And don't forget, Becky, you can wear any combination you like, as long as it's the school uniform. You can wear the shirt with or without the sweater or the sweater without the shirt, or the pleated skirt or the plain. Whatever takes your fancy on the day.'

A bell rings, loud enough to waken all Thurston.

'Break time!' Mrs Sharp announces. 'So Becky, why don't we go into the playground and I'll introduce you to your class teacher? Mr Beagle his name is.'

45

She ushers us out into the playground, espies Mr Beagle who is keeping an eye on a group of boys and girls kicking a ball about, and summons him.

'This is Mrs Stanton, our new Vicar and, more to the point at this moment, the mother of Becky who, as you already know, will be in Year Five from next Monday.'

Mr Beagle shakes my hand with a grip so firm that I wonder if he has broken one or more of the small bones, then turns to look straight at my daughter and says 'Hi, Becky!' His look is so direct that she can hardly avoid it and before she can control herself I hear her saying 'Hi!' Not with any enthusiasm of course, but she has actually spoken. She has not totally lost her voice from lack of use. Well done, Mr Beagle!

'Why don't you introduce Becky to a couple of people?' Mrs Sharp suggests to him. 'Just for a minute or two.'

He looks at Becky. 'Yes or no?' he asks. 'The choice is yours!'

She is faced with a question she must answer and, to my astonishment, she gives a faint nod, which Mr Beagle chooses to treat as a wholehearted 'yes', and off they go. As they walk away, against his height – he is tall and broad – she looks small and vulnerable and my heart aches for her.

'Don't worry, she'll be all right. We'll look after her,' Mrs Sharp assures me. 'I'll keep an eye on her myself. And if any problems do crop up please let me know and I'll deal with them. We're a happy school on the whole and I don't see why Becky shouldn't enjoy herself once she's got to know people.' Then, changing the subject, she says, 'I'd like to talk to you some time about the school vis-à-vis the church. I have a few ideas in mind, a few things I thought we might do, if you're in agreement. In spite of being a church school we've never had as much involvement as I could wish with St Mary's.'

'I'd like that,' I tell her. 'We didn't have a church school in my last parish so you'll have a lot to teach me.' Then the bell rings and the break is over. Mr Beagle delivers Becky back to me and a few minutes later she and I leave.

★   ★   ★

46

'So there you are!' says my mother when we return, as if we were a lost parcel she'd been looking for. 'Would you like a cup of coffee, love? What about you, Becky?'

Becky's answer is to disappear up the stairs. My mother shakes her head and makes the sound usually written as 'tut tut'.

'Dad and I will take her out this afternoon,' she promises. 'We'll drive into Brampton, look at the shops, have an ice cream. At least it'll make a change.'

I feel like asking if, while she's there, she could exchange Becky, swap her for an all-smiling, all-talking model. What I actually say is 'Thank you. Yes, I would like a cup of coffee but I mustn't dawdle, I have to be at the surgery at eleven-thirty.'

'It won't take a minute, love,' my mother says. 'Dad has gone off to wander round the village. He'll be back for his dinner. Will you? Shepherd's pie. Shall you go into Brampton with us?'

'I think the Brampton trip would be smoother without me,' I say. 'And I'd like to take the time to have a really good look at things in the church. Open drawers, peer into cupboards, find out where everything's kept. Of course I've been shown, but I'd like to go over it on my own.'

I swallow the coffee and eat a Shrewsbury biscuit my mother's made – I shall miss her when she returns to Clipton but at least I'll lose a bit of weight, no longer being tempted by her baking – and now I'm on my way to the surgery, which turns out to be in a largish semi in Downs Way, a road which leads off the north end of the High Street. The small reception area opens off the hall. One elderly woman is still waiting there. I go to the desk and give my name to the receptionist, an efficient-looking, middle-aged woman sitting in front of a computer.

'Ah yes!' she says. 'Doctor Leyton is expecting you. She has a patient with her at the moment but she shouldn't be long. Would you like to take a seat?'

I take a seat three chairs away from the elderly lady, not wishing to crowd her, and I smile at her. Until I'm more sure of myself I suppose I shall smile at everyone, just in case they attend St Mary's, and if they don't know who I am they'll think I'm barmy. The lady immediately turns to speak to me.

'Are you waiting to see Doctor Leyton?'

'I am.'

'I thought you must be. She has someone with her. Mrs Gregory with her little girl. I'm here for Doctor Baines. They say Doctor Leyton is very good but I'd rather have a man. I don't know what's the matter with the little Gregory girl. She looked very pale. Probably something she ate. I'm here with my legs.' She pauses for breath, clearly waiting to know which bit of me I am here with, but before I can enlighten her what I assume is Mrs Gregory, accompanied by a child who is decidedly pale and looks as if she might at any minute throw up on the grey carpeted floor, emerges from what must be Doctor Leyton's room. The receptionist nods at me, which I take as a signal to go in. Neither Mrs Gregory nor the elderly lady with the legs has shown any recognition of me so I take it they are not members of my flock – though members of the flock is an expression I don't normally allow myself to use, assuming that it makes them no higher than sheep while I am something superior. Shepherd, or perhaps a nice black-and-white collie dog?

I knock, and enter. Sonia Leyton smiles at me, a sort of lopsided smile which lights up her face but doesn't entirely disguise the fact that she looks tired, shadowy and a bit puffy around the eyes.

'Come and sit down, Venus,' she says. 'Would you like some coffee?'

'Thank you, no, I had some just before I left home,' I say. 'My parents are staying with me at the moment. My mother gives me tea or coffee every hour on the hour.'

There's a cafetière on a side table and she moves across and pours herself a cup from it. 'I think I keep going on it,' she admits, 'which is not a thing I'd advise any of my patients to do. Doctors do a great many things they wouldn't advise their patients to do.'

'Priests are much the same,' I tell her. 'Have you had a busy morning?'

She stirs sugar into her coffee, but no milk, and takes a couple of gulps.

'The usual. We're always busy, being just the two of us.'

'And you can't get another doctor, I think you said?'

48

'Oh, I daresay we could,' she answers. 'But as I told you yesterday, we don't have the room. We'd need another consulting room. I suppose it might look as though we would have, but you see I also live here. I have a bedroom, a living room and a kitchen, so there's no spare space unless I were to move out, which at the moment I don't want to. Nigel doesn't live here, of course. I'll introduce you to Nigel in a few minutes.'

'He had a patient waiting,' I tell her.

'Mrs Thwaites with her legs. Whoops! Sorry, I shouldn't have said that. Most unprofessional!'

'She did actually tell me herself,' I assure her. 'I mean that it was her legs. I'm sure she'd have told me more if I'd waited longer.'

'She would indeed. But Nigel's very good with her. He has a way with elderly ladies. And most elderly ladies seem to prefer a male doctor, which always surprises me. You'd think the opposite would be true. Modesty and all that. Though it shouldn't surprise me. My grandmother was a doctor . . .'

'Your *grandmother*?' I can't believe it.

'Oh yes!' Sonia says. 'She was one of the really early ones. She qualified in the nineteen twenties. She knew what opposition was all right. It dogged her most of her professional life. Very few people wanted women doctors then. Now I suppose it's only the Mrs Thwaiteses of this world who don't.'

'Perhaps the same will happen about women priests,' I say. She raises her eyebrows in a question. She has expressive eyebrows, but I don't pursue the question. 'And did anyone else in your family go into medicine?' I ask.

'No-one else at all,' Sonia says cheerfully. 'No-one in my mother's generation, and neither of my two brothers. They're both university lecturers. No, it had to wait for me. But I caught it early. When I was small I had a family of dolls and my fantasy was that they were usually ill – measles or some exotic life-threatening disease or they had multiple injuries from a car smash. My dolls were always in bandages or splints. And there was Gran – she was in her seventies by this time – deeply interested in all this, discussing the symptoms with me, deciding on the treatment. And of course she and I between us cured them all.'

49

'Not like real life?' I find myself saying.

'No, not like real life,' Sonia agrees. 'But more than Gran was able to cure in her day. Who was your GP in Clipton?' she asks, changing the subject. 'It was Clipton, wasn't it?'

'Yes. Doctor Henry Mackintosh. He was very good to me, especially when Philip was ill, and after he died. And Becky liked him.'

'That's good! How long since your husband died?'

'Just over a year.' Sometimes I feel so raw that it might have happened only yesterday. At other times . . . well . . .

'It's still early days,' she says. 'What was it?'

'Leukaemia. It was so sudden. It seemed to come out of the blue. He was very tired a lot of the time but we didn't take that seriously, not until he started vomiting. When it was diagnosed he had all the treatments: injections, blood transfusions, drugs – but the illness was always two steps ahead.'

'Wasn't a transplant – bone marrow – suggested?' she asked.

'Oh yes! But we couldn't find a matching donor. And the time was so short, I mean from beginning to end. I didn't . . .' I hesitate.

'You didn't have time to get used to it,' Sonia prompted. 'That's often the way with terminal illnesses which advance quickly. There's no space in which to adjust, either for the patient or the family. Strange though it may seem, it's sometimes easier to deal with a long illness – at least for the one left it is. So you made a swift move into another job?'

'Another parish,' I correct her. 'It's the same job, just as yours would be if you moved to another practice. Though in another place and with other people.'

What I had wanted in Clipton after Philip's death was to be wrapped in a warm blanket of love and, except with a few people, it hadn't happened. It wasn't that they were purposely unkind, or even unthinking. I learnt by experience, though I don't know if it's always the case, that after a bereavement a lot of otherwise quite nice people take a step backwards, especially if it's been an untoward death; unexpected, someone too young, someone who had seemed healthy. You see it when children, of whatever age, die before the parent. My mother-in-law felt that keenly in people's attitudes towards her after Philip died. They would cross the road to avoid speaking to her, I suppose they didn't know what to say. It's a happening against nature and other people find it too much to cope with, as if one's misfortune might be infectious.

'If my mother died,' Ann once said to me (her mother, aged ninety-seven, is still going strong, driving the nurses mad, in a rest home), 'that would be normal and people would have no inhibitions in speaking to me about it. As it is . . .' I knew exactly what she meant.

'There were a number of reasons I left Clipton,' I tell Sonia. 'I think, even if Philip hadn't been taken ill, we'd have done so fairly soon. As it was, everything seemed to come together at once. And here I am.'

'And here you are!' Sonia echoes. 'And I hope you're going to be happy in Thurston.'

'I would be happier if my daughter were,' I tell her. 'At the moment Becky hates every stick and stone of it! Do you have children?' I had noticed that she was wearing a wedding ring.

'No,' she says. 'And I'm divorced.' From the way she says it I know that's the beginning and end of the subject. No questions to be asked, no information to be given.

'The situation for Becky isn't simple,' Sonia says, though gently. 'Moving to another area is often difficult for a child. You're leaving your life behind, possibly the only life you know. I remember my parents moved, only to the other side of the city, when I was twelve years old. It was three years after Gran had died, and I hadn't stopped missing her. It felt like the end of the world to me. I cried for weeks. And then I made a friend and, although I never forgot Gran, I recovered. I was as happy as a lark from then on. And for Becky it's a double whammy. Her father's death must have hurt her deeply.'

'Oh, it did!' I agree. 'She adored him. They adored each other.'

'Children sometimes feel partly responsible when a parent dies,' Sonia said. 'They wonder if it was something they did, especially if they've been naughty. But why am I telling you this?

I don't have a child. You do. Presumptuous of me. You know more about parenting than I do. Mine's all theory.'

'Not at all,' I tell her. 'Having one child doesn't make me an expert. I knew the theory too. I read all the books, I thought I was going to be a model mother. Well let me tell you, the theory doesn't always work. It's mostly trial and error. You just have to meet everything as it comes. And I don't mean I haven't been happy with Becky. Of course I have! I love her very much.'

'Go on giving her that, and time. It'll do more for her than doctor's medicine. But I don't have to tell you that either.'

She gives me her lovely, lopsided smile again, which cheers me up, then she says, 'I reckon Nigel will have finished with Mrs Thwaites's legs by now. I'll give him a call.'

She picks up the phone, says 'Are you clear? Good! Then come in and meet the new Vicar.'

He is tall and thin. For a second or two, he stands in the doorway before coming into the room. His hair, strangely, is also red, but golden-red, two or three shades lighter than Sonia's, and would be curly if it weren't so close-cropped. He has the bright blue eyes which often go with red hair. He is a Viking, I decide. Or his forebears were. Or perhaps he's Irish.

'Venus Stanton,' Sonia says. 'Nigel Baines.'

He holds out his hand. 'Pleased to meet you,' he says. Baines isn't an Irish name, at least as far as I know it isn't, but his accent is as Irish as the shamrock. His voice is deeper than I expect it to be, and musical, I think he might be good at singing. His accent must come from his mother's side and I guess it means he won't be one of my particular congregation, a fact which he immediately confirms.

'I go to St Patrick's,' he says. 'Though we get on quite well with your lot. I think there's a group at St Pat's which does things together with St Mary's. Not that I'm part of it.'

St Patrick's is the Roman Catholic church at the far end of Thurston. It's new as churches go, not more than fifty years old, and comparatively small, though I've been told it has a good congregation because it draws from two nearby villages – well, not so much villages as large private housing estates which have sprung up in recent years, neither with a Catholic church of its own let alone a priest to run it. They are worse off than we are.

He takes the only other empty chair, a low one, and leans back in it, his legs stretched out in front of him.

'So! Are you going to settle down all right in Thurston?' he enquires amiably.

'Oh, I think so!' I tell him. 'It's early days yet, but I don't see why not. I reckon there's quite a bit to be done, and I look forward to that, but I won't push it. People have to get used to me.'

He nods agreement. 'Well, let's face it, you are quite a bit different from your predecessor – including being the wrong sex.'

'The *wrong* sex?'

He throws up his hands. 'Sorry! I didn't mean it like that. I just meant . . . anyway, we're always hearing there'll be women priests in my church within the next five years, though they've been saying that for the last ten years.'

'I hear it too,' I tell him. I don't want to rub it in that we're well ahead; we've taken the plunge, even if the water does sometimes turn out to be icy cold.

He rises to his feet, the lowness of the chair meaning that he has to sort of unfold himself.

'Sorry I have to rush. I've got visits. Nice meeting you. I'm sure I'll see you around. Thurston's a small place.' He waves a hand and leaves.

'You must come to supper,' Sonia says. 'I'll arrange something. Probably not church people, but you'll get to know them anyway.'

FIVE

There are four people at the Tuesday evening service, three women and one old man, thin as a rake, with rounded shoulders and a permanently bowed head. I notice he sits in his pew, doesn't kneel at all. I understand completely why he doesn't, and I sympathize. The pews are hard, narrow, the backs at a ninety degree angle to the seats, no chance of leaning. They are uncomfortable enough even to sit in, but when it comes to kneeling there is insufficient room to accommodate anyone's legs from knee to ankle, except those of a child or a dwarf. I know this because I knelt in a pew on one occasion before I became the Vicar. I only just fitted in and, as you know, I am not tall. I came to the conclusion that previous generations of worshippers at St Mary's were tiny little people. Seventeenth-century elves and goblins (I *think* that's when the pews were put in).

I decide he cannot be one of those who has rushed from his workplace in Brampton, jumped on the number twenty-two bus, jumped off again and hurried up the High Street to be on time for his weekly communion. Much more likely he is one of those, and they are not uncommon, who likes to practise his religion quietly, in the presence of as few of his fellow Christians as possible. Privacy is his thing. If so, this service is perfect for him. He would find the ten o'clock Sunday Eucharist, with its mixture of ages and types, quite unacceptable. As for the Peace

54

celebration, everybody shaking hands, some (*quelle horreur!*) actually embracing or even kissing. It would finish him off. Of course he has every right to his views, to his own almost solitary way of worshipping, and, though I might not agree with him, I must respect them. I shall speak to him on his way out, though my guess is that he might prefer me not to. I've discovered that there are churchgoing Christians who do not like priests, who would just as soon not have one, except that there are things he or she can do that cannot be done by the laity. Those are the things priests should stick to. I shall not make the mistake I made in my early days, of welcoming this man to his own church, because it's as much his as mine. He could very well turn around and tell me he's been coming here for fifty years.

I shall also try to speak with the three women, especially the two I haven't seen before. The third one is Miss Frazer and I would be happy to avoid her.

I go through the Mass (and I really must remember not to use that word out loud). The four of them make their responses, though almost inaudibly so that at times I wonder if I'm talking to myself. 'Holy, holy, holy,' they mutter. 'Heaven and earth are full of your glory.'

I stretch out my hands over the bread and wine as I consecrate them.

'Take, eat . . .' I hold the host high before them. Then I take the chalice. 'Drink this, all of you . . .'

The familiar words are to me newly minted every time I say them. Every time as if it was the first time. I am never other than awestruck by what I'm saying, doing. It is always a new wonder.

I hold the paten and the chalice in an invitation to the communicants to approach and partake. Perhaps above everything else this sharing of the bread and wine is for me the high point of the whole Mass. At this moment I hold everyone in the congregation up to God, as well as those in my heart who I know have need of him. The fact that there are only four people in this congregation makes no difference at all. I hold up each one of them separately, and all four of them together as if they were one, as I would if they were a hundred or a thousand. Don't ask me how this is possible in the seconds it takes. I don't know. I only know it is. It is a mystery.

All four rise to their feet and walk slowly forward, the man almost tottering. They kneel at the altar rail, the man with such difficulty. I'd like to tell him it's OK to stand but I guess he'd feel that would be less reverent, he must be on his knees. Miss Frazer is the third in the short row, her hands now cupped, ready to receive. It is not until I stand immediately in front of her, the wafer in my fingers ready to give it to her, that she lowers her hands, tucks them away by her sides and – but not before giving me a look of pure hatred – averts her face. It's all over in about five dreadful seconds. As I move on to the fourth person I try to keep calm inside me, but I am shaking. I feel sick. It is not so much me she has refused, she has rejected and has refused God himself, and in the most insulting way she could devise. She must know what she has done. She has planned this. She has spat in his face.

I think that what people who insult or reject God through one of his priests, actually making use of a priest for their purpose, do not realize is the strength of the love which priests have for God. It is real, living, passionate love. God, to his priests, comes first. He is paramount. Would people who reject God in this manner do the same to the loved ones of the priests: mothers, wives, children? Unlikely. And if they did they would expect retaliation, but they will get no retaliation, no come-back if they spit in the face of the one the priest loves above all others. They will not comprehend the hurt. Perhaps that ignorance and the lack of understanding is the only excuse there is.

All four return to their separate pews. I have no idea whether they saw what took place. I consume the wafer I had consecrated for her.

Shaken though I am – and when I raise my hand to give the final blessing it is visibly trembling – I still have every intention of being at the door first so that I can catch the others. Miss Frazer rushes away, pleased with herself. She will not wish to speak with me, nor I with her.

No! Wait a minute! Of course I want to speak with her. I am enraged. I can feel, almost physically, the bile rising in my throat.

I want to let it all out, my fury, my hurt at this bloody woman, to hurl words at her which have possibly never assailed her ears before – and seldom passed my lips, either. But I can't. I'm a priest, I've just celebrated the Mass, I'm in church. God is here, present. So are others, and I won't cause a scandal by letting go in front of them.

How wrong I am – I mean in thinking that she won't wish to speak to me. I hurry to reach the door first but Miss Frazer is well ahead of the others and she has every intention of confronting me. Alas, while she stands there the other three worshippers seize their opportunities to slide past with no more than a nod, and I watch them walk down the path. Miss Frazer and I look at each other like two adversaries squaring up for a fight. She is the first to speak.

'I hope,' she says briskly, without any preliminaries, 'you are not going to close down this service because of the numbers. "Where two or three are gathered together . . ." as you well know. Your predecessor set great store by this small oasis in the middle of a busy week.'

Is the woman crazy? Has she no idea what she has done? Does she care in the least? As well as sick to the heart I am filled with fury, spilling over, which is definitely not the right frame of mind after celebrating Holy Communion. So I take a deep breath and determine with God's help, to keep calm.

'Is that so?' I ask. 'It's not at all what I have heard. But I shall think about it, Miss Frazer, as I shall about many other things. I'm not going to do anything in a hurry.'

'Very wise,' she says. 'It wouldn't do at all! Not at St Mary's.'

And then I can't keep it back any longer. I look her straight in the face.

'Miss Frazer,' I ask, 'why did you do what you did?'

She looks back at me. Her eyes are like grey steel.

'You know why I did it. For me to take the Lord's Supper from the hands of a woman, a so-called priest, would be a blasphemy. A total blasphemy!'

'I am not a "so-called" priest,' I say evenly. I will not allow myself even to raise my voice, nor, I know, will she. 'I am a true priest of God. My orders are valid. I am consecrated by the

Bishop to celebrate the Mass.' Even as I say it I'm sure she's aware that the former bishop of this diocese, at the time I was ordained, refused to ordain women. I had to go to another diocese.

'Mass is not a word I care to use,' she interrupts.

'Choose your own word,' I tell her. 'I'm still consecrated to offer it and what you have done is not only an affront to me – that hardly matters – you have refused God himself, at the very moment he offers himself to you. What has God done to you that you do this to him?'

'I could say – ' the reply comes back from her as swift as an arrow – 'that he has sent a woman masquerading as a priest into our midst, I could say that if it were not that I believe it was the devil who sent you!'

I shall get nowhere with her. The arguments will go round and round.

'So,' I ask, 'if that's how you feel why don't you go to St Saviour's in Brampton where the priest is a man? And why do what you are doing so publicly?'

'I have no wish to attend St Saviour's,' Miss Frazer says. 'As I have told you before I have worshipped at St Mary's all my life. And I did what I did publicly because I believe it to be my duty. St Mary's has temporarily lost its way. But it will find it again. I am, so far, only one voice – or at least the only one to be heard out loud – but I shall do my small part to guide it back.'

'You will not drive me out,' I tell her. 'You'll never do that.'

'We shall see,' she says – then turns and walks away. Two or three yards down the path she turns round. No doubt she has one parting shot.

'By the way,' she says as if nothing the least bit untoward has happened in the last few minutes, 'I hope you're going to do something about the state of the churchyard. It's been disgracefully neglected over the last few months. In my father's day he would have sent his own gardener down rather than see the grass in its present state, but alas, I no longer have a full-time gardener. Just a man for two hours a week.'

I can hardly believe her! Is she off her head? And if that's the case will it make her easier or more difficult to deal with?

'I understood there was someone who looked after the grass in the churchyard?' I make a great effort to speak in as normal a voice as I can produce, though I want to scream.

'There is,' she says, 'but he's only part time, they say they can't afford any more, and no-one seems to know *what* time or when. In my opinion he needs closer supervision. We must always respect the dead. I'm sure you agree?'

'Respect the dead!' I cry. 'What about the living? What about you respecting me? Whether you like it or not I'm your parish priest. But you – you don't even have respect for God!'

'I don't acknowledge you!' she says. 'And I never will!'

'Then I shall manage without your acknowledgement!' I tell her.

She gives me a venomous look. 'And you have not heard the last of this, Mrs Stanton – and I refuse to call you Vicar. Oh no! You have not heard the last of it!'

She walks a few more yards and then turns round again. Now she has to shout because of the distance.

'And don't dismiss the matter of the graveyard!' she says. 'A church is judged by its graveyard!'

This time the words, the forbidden words, do rise to my lips, but I draw them back just in time. I realize in the same second that if I don't she'll have good cause to report me to the Bishop. Or more likely higher. She strikes me as a woman who would never hesitate to write to the Archbishop of Canterbury.

I watch until she is out of sight. I notice she limps a little. Then I go back into the church.

I kneel at the altar rail in the side chapel where the light is permanently lit in front of the reserved sacrament, and say my night prayers. For a few moments I shall try to put Miss Frazer out of my mind. There are so many people to pray for: Becky, my parents, Ann, Philip – though I've been taught, but sometimes when I'm low I find it difficult to believe, that those we've known in life and who are now in heaven are praying for us. When I can believe it, but even sometimes when I can't, it brings Philip closer. Next I pray, as I always would, for the people who've been at this evening's service, which has to include Miss Frazer by name. Always pray for those one finds difficult, I was once told, *not*, I hasten to add, asking that they will necessarily be converted to one's own point of view but that one might learn to understand them. I reckon that either of those options will be a real challenge for God. And then I turn my thoughts and I pray for those who have no shelter on this chilly autumn night and I pray for the deeply troubled world we live in. Lastly I pray for myself. I give God my love and I ask him to give me courage and patience.

After a few more minutes I get to my feet, go into the vestry and turn out all the lights except the one which is never turned out, and I leave. The main door to the church is made of oak, a faithful replica of the one which stood for centuries until it had to be replaced, and is so massive that I find it hard to manoeuvre, and the key is so large that carrying it around will eventually wear a hole in my pocket.

It's quite dark when I leave the church, and raining, a nasty penetrating drizzle. I must learn to leave a spare umbrella in the vestry, something I always did at Holy Trinity. I pass the pub, the Ewe Lamb, which lies between the Vicarage and the church on the other side of the road. It's brightly lit and there is the sound of music, someone playing the piano rather well. It really looks inviting; I am half inclined to plunge in and drown my sorrows in a large gin-and-tonic, but at present my sorrows are too deep for that. One of these evenings – or maybe, thinking of Becky, it will have to be a lunchtime – I will pop in, just to say 'hello' and perhaps, who knows, meet a few more of my parishioners. Sometimes the people inside the pub are friendlier than those who would never darken its doors.

Nearing the Vicarage I note that the light is on in my study, which is at the front of the house. This is surprising because my mother doesn't go into my study except perhaps to run the vacuum around or flick a duster, and then only after asking me if she may. I think she believes it to be consecrated ground. I walk into the house, shake the rain off my coat, and call out, 'Hello! I'm home!' In the best of worlds my daughter would appear from wherever she was with a smile on her face and cheerful words on her lips. 'Hello, Mummy!' There is, of course, no sign of Becky – knowing my return was imminent she has probably retreated again – but my mother appears at once, and from the study. She takes my arm and propels me into the dining room, speaking urgently but quietly.

'You've got a visitor!' she says. ' "The Vicar's not at home at the moment," I told her. I said she must come back some other time, or phone you. I wasn't for letting her into the house at all but she pushed straight past me, so I took her into the study and stayed with her. I didn't fancy leaving her there on her own.'

'Right,' I say. 'I'll go and see what she wants.'

'The other thing is . . .' my mother begins . . . but before she can tell me what the other thing is the sound of a baby's cry comes from my study. A young baby, I can tell that, but nothing wrong with its lungs.

I look at my mother.

'I couldn't keep her out,' she repeats. 'But in any case it's raining. What else could I do?'

'Don't worry, you did the right thing,' I assure her. 'I'll sort it out!'

Those were brave words, I was to think not many minutes later.

'Good-evening!' I say as I walk in. The woman is sitting on the edge of the sofa, holding the baby which continues to cry. I raise my voice above it. 'I'm the Vicar! And you are?' She is quite young, twentyish. Pretty, with long dark curly hair, red lips and a tanned skin.

I can tell at once by the look she gives me that I am not what she'd expected, that I'm a disappointment. I daresay she'd expected some saintly-looking, compassionate man and here am I, a small woman with windblown hair, dressed in a long black cassock and no doubt looking suspiciously at her. My mother has used the words 'the Vicar' instead of 'my daughter'.

'What's your name?' I ask, I hope gently. The baby has momentarily stopped crying and I don't want to frighten it, do I?

She is reluctant to tell me.

'Emmeline,' she says in the end.

'What a pretty name!' I remark. 'And your baby's name? How old is she?' (He?)

'Gloria. Three months.'

I'm not sure why, but I smell something not quite right about this, and I don't only mean the baby, which is a malodorous addition. Little Gloria is in urgent need of a change of nappy.

'So what can I do for you, Emmeline?' I ask. 'What do you want?'

The answer comes with the speed of light, no hanging about. 'Money! Me and the baby have nowhere to sleep and we haven't eaten all day and I need the money to get a bed for the night. So please . . . ?'

'First things first!' I tell her. 'I think before we do anything else Gloria needs changing. She'd be more comfortable. And after that you can feed her while I get you something to eat.' One good thing, at three months Gloria will still be breast-fed, or is she already on to meat and two veg from a little jar? 'Do you have a spare nappy?' I ask. 'I expect you always carry one. I know I did when my little girl was a baby.'

Emmeline looks at me as if I'm speaking Chinese. 'If you'll just give me the money, ten pounds would do it,' she says. 'I'll be off and out of your way. I don't want to bother you.'

'No bother!' I say, moving to the door, opening it, calling out to my mother, who immediately comes running, no doubt she's been hovering close by on tenterhooks with curiosity.

'Mother,' I say, 'the baby needs a clean nappy. I know we don't have nappies but could you find a towel and cut it up? And some soap and water and a flannel.' Nothing in my training ever mentioned that I should keep a supply of nappies in the linen cupboard and baby food in the larder.

'At once!' my mother says, all her skill as a one-time voluntary hospital worker coming to the fore.

I am left with Emmeline and Gloria, and I try not to go too near, but fortunately my mother is back in no time at all and applies herself to the baby, talking all the while. 'Ooh! what a nice old mess you're in! Let's wash this dirty little botty shall we?' And so on.

Did Father Humphrey Payne ever have to go through this at Holy Trinity, I wonder? Of course not! If faced with it he would simply have lifted the phone and called for one of his parish slaves (female) and she would have been around in a trice (just as your mother was, a small voice niggles at me).

While this is going on I try to converse with Emmeline, but get nowhere. All she wants is to be off, preferably with the money; if no money, then without, and better luck somewhere else.

Eventually my mother says, 'There! Who's a lovely clean girl, then!' and I say to Emmeline, 'Now you can feed the baby and while you're doing that we'll get you a nice cheese sandwich . . .'

'I don't like cheese,' Emmeline says.

'Have we some ham left, Mother?' I ask.

'Yes dear,' she says. 'Do you like mustard?' she asks Emmeline politely. 'Or perhaps not if you're breast-feeding?'

'I'm not. She's on the bottle!' Emmeline says quickly.

'Oh! Well I don't think . . . We don't have a feeding bottle. But not to worry,' my mother says. 'I'll nip down to the chemist's . . .'

'And in the meantime I'll ring Social Services and see if they can get you somewhere to sleep,' I tell Emmeline.

'Oh, I don't want the Social!' she protests. 'They're no good!'

'I can't have you with nowhere to sleep,' I say firmly, picking up the phone. 'Let alone little Gloria.'

'I'll make do with five pounds,' she says desperately. But I am already being put through to Social Services.

'What did you say the woman's name was?' I'm asked.

'Emmeline. Just a minute, I'll ask her for her last name.'

'Don't bother!' the woman at the other end says. 'It's Field-house. Emmeline Fieldhouse. Did she ask for ten pounds and then drop it to five?'

'That's right. But there *is* the baby to think of.'

'Is the baby Gloria or Peter?'

'Gloria. How do you . . . ?'

'Peter is her cousin's baby, Gloria is her sister's. She borrows them.'

'No wonder she couldn't breast-feed her.'

'What did you say?'

'Nothing!'

'Hang on to her, Vicar,' the woman says. 'We'll send someone to collect her and deliver her back where she belongs.'

'Which is where?' I enquire.

'With the Travellers. They're camped this week at the top of Thurston Hill. Travellers, not gypsies. Emmeline is known the length and breadth of three counties, though I don't remember that we've ever picked her up from your Vicarage before.'

Full marks to them, they collect her pronto. I slip two pound coins in Emmeline's pocket as she leaves and my mother gives her a block of Cadbury's milk chocolate. 'But not for the baby,' she warns. 'It's too rich.'

When they've gone my mother and I move to the sitting room, which is otherwise empty.

'Where's Dad?' I ask.

'He thought he'd take a walk down to the pub as it's our last evening here. Just for an hour or so, he said.'

So I could have popped in to the Ewe Lamb and my father would have been there to greet me. It would have been a pleasant introduction. On the other hand, my mother would have been left to deal with Emmeline so it's as well I didn't.

'And I take it Becky is in her room?'

'Actually, she's gone to bed,' my mother says. 'Oh, Venus love, I'm really worried about her! She's such an unhappy little girl.'

'I know. And I'm not a deliriously happy woman,' I reply. 'But what more can I do?'

'She's on all the time about coming back to Clipton with me and her grandpa . . .'

'I've already told her that's impossible,' I interrupt. 'She has to live here, with me. You know that.'

'Of course I do, love. But I wondered . . .' She pauses.

'Well?'

'Do you think she could go back with us tomorrow . . . ?'

'I've already said . . .'

My mother holds up her hand, and when my mother holds up her hand, perhaps because she seldom does, you stop and listen. My Dad knows that, I know it, Philip knew it. I think my mother has succeeded so far with Becky because she's listened without ever holding up her hand and stopping her. That's how grandparents are. Indulgent, open to persuasion,

64

but I am only a daughter so I wait for my mother to have her say.

'If she could go back with us tomorrow and stay just until the weekend – she doesn't have to start school until Monday – I think it would help her a lot, give her a bit of a breather. And you too.'

'You think I'm being hard on her, don't you?' I'm aware I'm sounding aggrieved but it's partly because I really don't know what to do. 'It's an acute stage for me as well as for Becky, you know.'

My mother shakes her head.

'I'm sorry, love, but however bad it is for you, it's worse for Becky. You have an incentive for coming here. You made the choice. Even if you didn't think it was going to be perfect you knew you would make something of it. Becky's too young to think that. She had no choice, she was made to come, and she's left everything behind – her friends, her school and – don't forget – her father. She can't think of him as being here in this place.'

'How could I forget?' And hadn't I heard more or less the same thing from Sonia Leyton yesterday?

'Of course you can't. But Becky's a child. Everything's in the present. Her world is here and now, she can't believe that things will get better. Oh dear, I don't know whether I'm saying any of this properly. I'm not clever like you. I can't find the words!' My mother's face is lined with anxiety. Suddenly I feel terribly guilty about her.

'Don't worry . . .' I begin – but she interrupts me.

'Venus love, just sit down for a minute and think about it. Please!'

I must have heard my mother say that a hundred times in my life. Venus love, sit down for a minute and think about it. Quite often it works.

'I'll make a cup of tea,' she says, and disappears into the kitchen. So I do as I'm told and sit and think.

When she returns with the tea I say, 'All right! You win!'

'It isn't a battle,' she says.

'Well at times it feels like it! Anyway, she can go with you tomorrow and stay until the weekend. I'd like her to come back on Saturday evening. And how's she going to get back? Am I to come and fetch her, or what? I could do that, I suppose.'

'No, love. It's better if your Dad and I bring her back, that's if you can put up with us for another weekend. If you could it might actually help Becky to see that not everything in her life is upside down, that some things haven't changed and won't change.'

There's a short silence between us, and then I say, 'You're right, Mum.'

Actually, I think, I could go further than that. Much as I would miss her, I suppose Becky could spend parts of her school holidays with her grandparents; half-term, which is coming up soon. Christmas, summer, and so on. Why haven't I seen this before? Answer: because I wanted her to myself; I wanted her to fit in with my ways. I wanted my ideas to be her ideas.

'Then why don't you go up and tell her?' my mother suggests. 'She might still be awake.'

She isn't awake. She's fast asleep. There are tear stains on her cheeks and her expression, even in sleep, is troubled. I sit by the bed and stroke her hair and her face, feeling an absolute cow. I don't mean to wake her, but I'm pleased when she stirs, and opens her eyes and sees me.

'It's all right,' I tell her. 'You can go with Grandma and Grandpa in the morning, I'll see you at the weekend. And don't worry, it's all going to work out. You'll see!'

Still more than half asleep, but clearly taking in something of what I've said, she gives me a small smile. Then she closes her eyes and is back in the Land of Nod.

I think I might actually have got something right!

I stay a little while in case she wakens again, thinking about the evening. Thankfully Emmeline and the baby, and then Becky, helped to keep Miss Frazer out of my mind for a little while, but when I go to bed what then? Becky doesn't waken again. I go downstairs. Half-an-hour later the phone rings. It's Sonia Leyton.

'Look,' she says, 'I know it's frightfully short notice and you mightn't be able to get anyone to stay with Becky, but I did wonder if you could make it for supper on Friday, here? But never mind if you can't, there'll be other times.'

'Oh, but I can!' I tell her. 'Becky's going to her grandparents.'

'Fine!' Sonia says. 'Around seven-thirty, then? Just a few of us!'

SIX

What shall I wear? It's already Friday, the dinner's this evening and I'm in a bit of a tizz because I still haven't decided. Some people seem to be surprised that, being what I am, I'm interested in fashion. I do believe they think I wear clothes simply to keep out the cold. Not true! But what *do* people wear when they go out to dinner in Thurston? Velvet trousers, smart tops? Skirts – long or short? Skimpy little dresses with spaghetti straps – well I don't have any of those, do I? A little black number? Common sense tells me that the dress code here will be much the same as it was in Clipton which, if it was referred to at all, was described as 'smart casual', whatever that means.

'Does that mean I have to wear a suit?' Philip would ask. He wasn't into suits. On the other hand, he didn't like to be different.

Smart casual is more easily defined for men than for women, I reckon. They can let go and wear a fancy shirt. Sometimes in Clipton the men's clothes would be more flashy than the women's. I guess for the women smart casual rules out jeans and tee shirts at one end and strapless ball gowns at the other, but take your pick of the whole range in between.

My choice is limited by what's in my wardrobe, which at the moment is not a lot and most of it's dated. In the last year or two I've got out of the habit of going out to meals. As Philip's illness progressed the only company he wanted was his family, and after he died I think people were wary about inviting me. Women friends would ask me to tea (I don't do tea) but seldom to dinner parties. Perhaps there was a feeling – it's not un-common – that a recently widowed, moderately attractive woman would have an eye on their husbands. Certainly not true in my case. How could anyone compare to Philip? I daresay they also thought I might be depressing company, that if someone said the wrong thing I might dissolve into tears at the table. I wouldn't have, and there were times when I'd have liked to have been asked out. Why do people think that mourning is best done on one's own?

So, I'm looking forward to this evening. New job, new friends, and a start, albeit with some trepidation, on a new part of my life here in Thurston.

I could go into Brampton right now and buy something new to wear. I could treat myself. I have a burial of ashes in the memorial garden at one o'clock, and I'm having my hair done at Sandra's in the village at two-thirty, but there's nothing to stop me nipping into Brampton this morning.

No sooner thought of than done, and I am driving along the Brampton road in my little Fiat, which is the first new car I've ever had and the pride of my life. Philip and I had been buying a house, with a mortgage plus a legacy from his favourite aunt, so when I accepted the living here, with its Vicarage, I sold the house, paid off the mortgage and invested most of what was left for Becky's future education. One day she will want to go to university. But not all of it. I bought Becky a new bicycle and treated myself to a car and a Toshiba laptop.

I park by the town hall, which isn't far from the shopping mall. There is no shortage of clothes shops in Brampton: Gap, Next, Monsoon (a bit pricey for me?), Top Shop. I wander around two or three, without seeing anything which takes my fancy. In the third a pleasant assistant approaches me and says, 'Can I be of any help, Madam?' This is so unusual that I decide that either I appear lost or I look like a shoplifter. I explain what I'm looking for. 'I see,' she says. 'And what kind of thing do you usually wear?'

'A cassock,' say I without thinking.

She is totally uncomprehending, but she no longer thinks I'm a shoplifter, just a madwoman.

It is true that I spend a lot of my time wearing my cassock. It's comfortable, it defines my role as the parish priest – normally one wears it only when walking around one's own parish. In the summer a cotton one can be cool because one need wear little underneath it; in the winter it can conceal several layers of clothing, as indeed it conceals my own bulges which I intend to do something about once I'm settled in. It is unisex, it is always stylish. The only reason I would one day like to rise to the height of a Canon in the Church is that their black cassocks are trimmed with deep pink piping, with small matching buttons all the way down the front and on the cuffs. Possibly this is the chief reward for being a Canon? So I am not knocking the cassock but that doesn't mean I don't like to dress up in pretty clothes and wear a jewel or two. My long drop earrings and the pearl necklace which Philip gave me as a wedding present would not look well with my cassock.

'I'll leave you to it, then, shall I?' the shop assistant says. 'I'm here if you want me.'

I eventually pick out four outfits which I take to the fitting-room, which I discover to my horror is communal! There are half-a-dozen women in there in various states of undress, two with nothing on their top half and not more than a strategic few square inches below. They are aged around seventeen to twenty, all size eight or at the most ten, with firm bottoms and high breasts which require no help from underwired bras. Not an inch of spare flesh to be seen anywhere. They have no compunction about displaying their lovely taut bodies. Why should they have? Beside them, size fourteen, I want to hide mine, but there being no escape from it, I strip down to my pants and bra and try not to look at the ample flesh which hides the fact that somewhere I actually do have ribs. And is my bosom beginning to sag? Is it? I grab at the first garment to hand in order to cover myself up. Not that anyone cares. They take not the slightest notice of me, bless their kind hearts. They are all looking at the vision of themselves in the cruelly (for me) revealing mirrors which are so positioned that one can see oneself front, back and sides, all at the same time.

The first thing I try on is a shift dress, knee-length, low-necked, in a sort of toffee colour, which has the benefit of a matching jacket which will be useful if bare arms and décolleté necklines are not *de rigueur* for the kind of place I shall find myself. I don't like it. Next a green, fine wool, no-nonsense dress: elbow-length sleeves, A-line skirt, belted at the waist. A suitable dress for a Vicar, but I'm not going as a Vicar, I'm going as myself, Venus Stanton. So I don't even bother to try that on. The third is a long, rather full-skirted, blue polyester affair, with ruffles at the neck and hem. Ankle-length skirts, with any fullness, which this has, make me look as though I have no legs. I look like a table lamp. Why on earth did I take it off the rail? The last is a two-piece in a pale lilac linen, ankle-length but bias cut; a scoop neckline with pretty beading around the neck. It costs far more than I can afford, and being linen it will crease every time I move and will need constant ironing. Nevertheless, this is the one I shall buy. It fits like a dream and the colour suits me. I climb back into my jeans and jacket and go out to the cash desk, taking a deep breath as I hand over my credit card.

I am back in church, five minutes before I am due to meet with the ashes-burying family. All goes well there and they seem to derive comfort, as families often do, by laying their father's remains to rest in a place they can visit when they so wish.

'Your hair's come up well!' Sandra the hairdresser tells me an hour or so later and, looking at myself in the mirror I agree. It's a lightish brown, but Sandra has put a blonde rinse on it which has brought up a few highlights. I wear it chin length, sometimes a bit longer, to remain feminine looking when I'm wearing what you might call my uniform. At my ordination, all the ordinands of both sexes, being similarly attired from head to foot, were most easily distinguished by their hair styles. The men's hair then was longer, curlier, more bouffant. Now the men are all-over close cropped, a Number Three, a Number Two, or even a Number One, and don't look half as fetching.

I pop back to the church, deciding to have a word with the

71

voluntary verger. The voluntary vergers – more often referred to as the voluntary virgins – are a band of true saints. Between them they are in the church for several hours a day, most days of the year, simply so that visitors to Thurston, of whom there are a good number because it's a pretty village, can come in and look around. And hopefully leave something in the donations box. They – the vergers – bring their knitting, or the crossword or a book with them. I suppose it can be a boring two hours if not many people come. To my surprise and pleasure Carla Brown is doing this shift.

'Hello,' I say. 'Nice to see you! I didn't notice you when I was in earlier.'

'I was a bit late,' she admits. 'I had to take Jack to be clipped.'

For a moment I think she means her husband to the village barber, but surely his name is Walter? And then I notice a white poodle lying beneath the pew. Very close-cropped, he is; his pink flesh showing through. Definitely a Number One.

'He always comes here with me,' Carla explains. 'He seems to like it, I can't think why!'

'Have you had many visitors?' I ask.

'Not really. It's getting a bit late in the year. I had three Japanese. I think they might have been speaking English but I couldn't understand a word. Your hair looks nice, Venus. Are you going somewhere special?'

'Thank you! Actually I'm going to supper with Doctor Leyton.'

I have not yet learnt that in Thurston you never say exactly whose house you are going to in case the person you're talking to might think she should have been invited, and hasn't been. This, as you can imagine, can lead to complications.

'Oh, she's a nice lady, Doctor Leyton, though I have Doctor Baines myself. Have you met him? He's quite a dish!' she says with enthusiasm.

'Yes I have. He seems nice,' I agree.

'Yes. It's a pity he's one of the St Patrick's lot!'

'If you want to leave,' I tell her, 'I'll lock the church. It's nearly time anyway.'

'Well, if you're sure,' she says.

She closes her book and stands up and I see that she's been sitting on a cushion.

'Oh!' I say. 'How sensible! These pews are hard, aren't they?'

'I always bring my cushion,' Carla says. 'Otherwise you go home with a numb bottom.'

Back at the Vicarage it seems strange without Becky and my parents. I do miss them. My mother has phoned each day but so far I haven't spoken with Becky. I could be mistaken, but I've decided it's best to let my daughter come round in her own time. No pressure, but I hope it won't be too long. It's a weight on my heart. Apparently everything's OK and they'll be back in Thurston Saturday evening. I tell Mum I'm going out to supper this evening and she's pleased. I also tell her about my new purchase.

I have to say, taking a last critical look at myself before leaving for Sonia's, that I don't look half bad. I've piled on more make-up than I do when I'm walking around the parish. Blusher, eye-shadow, mascara – which I hope won't smudge or park itself in blobs on the end of my eyelashes. I go around the house, switching off some lights, leaving others strategically on, then, checking that my mobile phone is in my handbag, I leave the house in a tingle of excitement.

Now that I have my own parish, and new responsibilities, whenever I leave the Vicarage I take my mobile with me, with the Vicarage phone switched through to it. People need to be able to contact me in an emergency. Because I might be called out I take my car. I hope I won't be called out.

I am the last to arrive, but that's better than being the first.

'How nice to see you!' Sonia greets me. 'Did you walk here?' She takes my jacket and hangs it on a peg in the hall.

'I'm sorry I'm late,' I apologize.

'Oh, you're not,' she assures me. 'Do come and meet every-one.'

She shows me into the living room where a sofa and some comfortable-looking armchairs, most of them occupied, are grouped at one end and a dining table is laid at the other. I'm glad to see the fire is switched on. I'm a bit chilly.

There are four other people in the room, three of them men who rise to their feet, the other is Evelyn Sharp.

'This is Venus Stanton,' Sonia says. 'She's the new Vicar at St Mary's. You do already know a couple of people here, Venus,' she says to me.

I smile an acknowledgement at Becky's headmistress and then at Nigel Baines. 'Hello, Venus!' he says.

That's a good start if it means that people aren't going to address me as 'Vicar' all evening. Is that because they're not church folk – or as far as I know they're not?

The man sitting next to Mrs Sharp says, 'I'm Colin Sharp, though usually described as Mrs Sharp's husband!'

'And I,' says the last man, 'am Mark Dover.' He takes my hand in a rather lingering grip. He doesn't say where he fits into this gathering, I suppose that's for me to find out in due course.

'Now, what would everyone like to drink?' Sonia asks. 'Venus?'

'A glass of wine, if I may.'

'Sure!' Sonia says. She asks everyone else then she turns to Nigel. 'Nigel, can I leave all that to you while I finish off a few things in the kitchen?'

So we sit there pleasantly chatting for twenty minutes or so while Sonia darts in and out. I learn that Colin Sharp is something in computers and has a small company in Brampton and that Mark Dover is a painter with a studio halfway up Fenton Hill.

I chose well on the dress front. Evelyn Sharp is wearing a floral silk dress, knee length, rather nice green suede shoes with pointed toes and kitten heels, and lots of make-up. She looks most attractive, not at all like a headmistress – whatever that means. Sonia is wearing a well-cut pants suit in dark blue, fine wool. My outfit slots in nicely between theirs, attractive, but not overdone. The men? Colin Sharp, a dark suit, white shirt, jazzy tie; Nigel Baines looking elegantly casual in well-cut beige trousers and a yellowish linen jacket over a brown-and-white striped shirt, no tie; Mark Dover in black velvet trousers, cream shirt, silk, also no tie. His clothes complement his thick black hair, which is longer than that of the other men, and his smooth olive skin. His hands, though scrubbed clean, are a little paint stained, especially around the cuticles. All in all we are a colourful group.

Sonia comes in from the kitchen. 'OK,' she says. 'Shall we eat?' We move to the other end of the room.

I am seated between Colin Sharp and Nigel Baines, with Mark Dover opposite. How clever of Sonia, and in my experience how unusual, to have equal numbers of men and women, not to mention that two of them – as far as I know – are unmarried. I suppose they could be gay. I haven't worked out where she fits in vis-à-vis Mark and Nigel, but possibly nowhere. Nigel is a colleague; Mark could be, probably is, just an old friend.

The first course is already on the table, a concoction of mixed salad leaves, fresh peaches, mozzarella and prosciutto with a lemony dressing. I am a third of the way through mine, everyone is chattering happily, when my mobile rings. The conversation dies away as I take it out of my handbag and listen to the cool voice of the nurse on the other end. 'Right!' I say. 'I'll come at once. Mary Parker, Spring Ward.'

I switch off and turn to the others, who are waiting to hear what it's all about.

'I'm sorry,' I say, 'I'll have to leave. Brampton Hospital. A lady who apparently lives in this parish. A serious heart attack. Quite ill, and she wants a priest. Her family are there. They told her to ring St Mary's Vicarage. I must go. I'm terribly sorry!'

'Of course you must!' Sonia says.

'There's a hospital chaplain,' Nigel interrupts.

'Apparently he's not available,' I tell him.

'Then I'll take you,' Nigel says.

'Oh no!' I protest. 'I don't want to interrupt your evening still further. I feel bad about this.'

'No need to,' Sonia says. 'We're both doctors, we know all about interrupted evenings. And it'll be much better if Nigel takes you. He knows the hospital. I don't suppose you do as yet.'

'I also know where to park,' Nigel says. 'It can be the very devil if you don't. Come on, Venus. Let's go!'

He's out of the door while Sonia is helping me on with my coat and when I go out he's in his car with the engine switched on. I suppose it *will* be quicker than going in mine, with him having to direct me every yard of the way.

'I'll pick up my car as and when,' I call out to Sonia, who is standing on the top step.

'Oh, but you must come back here if you possibly can. You might not be long. I'll save you both some food.'

She's right. I might not be long. On the other hand I could be a couple of hours. It depends what the family want or whether the medics want me out of the way. 'I'll ring you from the hospital,' I call out to Sonia as we drive away.

Nigel is a fast driver and doesn't say much but I'm glad of his company, and especially glad when we arrive since the car park looks totally full, but he knows exactly where we can find a place. He parks swiftly and neatly, switches off the engine, and says, 'I'll come in with you.'

'No need,' I say, though it would be warmer for him than sitting in the car.

Nigel grins. 'I really think I'd better,' he says. 'They don't know you. You'll not be what they're expecting. If I may say so, you don't look in the least like a Vicar, especially in that charming get-up! You might need me to vouch for you!'

'Oh, I'm sure I'll be OK!' I tell him.

We go through the swing door and present ourselves at the desk.

'Hello, Doctor Baines,' the receptionist says. Then she gives me a doubtful look. Am I a patient he's bringing in, or am I a girlfriend he doesn't want to leave?

'Hello, Hazel,' Nigel says. 'This lady is the Vicar of St Mary's, Thurston. She's been called to a patient in Spring Ward, a Mrs Mary Parker.'

Hazel consults the notes on her desk.

'Oh yes, we're expecting the Reverend Venus Stanton.' She looks at me again, as if she thinks I might be working an illegal entry.

'That's right!' I tell her.

'I must say . . .' she begins, taking in my clothes, my make-up, my hairdo.

'I told her she might need me to vouch for her,' Nigel says, laughing. 'It's OK. She's who she says she is! Shall I show her the way to Spring Ward?'

'If you wouldn't mind, Doctor Baines,' she says. 'We're short-staffed – as ever.' I get the feeling she'd have been loth to let me wander around unaccompanied.

We walk along a corridor, take the lift, get out at the second floor, and the short corridor to Spring Ward is in front of us. Staff Nurse walks towards us.

'Hello, Doctor Baines,' she says. 'I'm not expecting you, am I?'

'No, not me,' he says. 'This lady is the Vicar of St Mary's, Thurston.'

She looks, for the moment, thrown – much as the receptionist did.

'Can I leave my coat with you?' I ask. 'It's deliciously warm in here.'

When I take off my jacket I see her note my dress.

'I was at a dinner party,' I explain.

'Oh! What a shame!' she says – and then she's all professional efficiency again. 'Mrs Parker is quite ill. She had a heart attack at home and her family called the ambulance. She's been seen by a doctor. She's very poorly. I hope you can do something for her.'

'I'll do whatever I can,' I promise.

Mrs Parker's bed is right by the entrance to the ward. Floral-patterned curtains are drawn around the drama of life, and possibly death, which is taking place behind them, cutting it off from the patients in the ward. Staff Nurse ushers me through the curtains and immediately draws them close again.

'This lady is the Vicar of Thurston,' she says. 'I'll leave her with you for a little while. I'll be quite close if you want me.'

The man and woman sitting by the bedside, at a guess they're the patient's husband and possibly her daughter, give me a brief nod. They show no surprise at how I'm dressed. They have more important things on their minds.

Mrs Parker looks terrible. Her face is waxy, a yellowy colour. She is propped up in bed with tubes and wires attached to her. Her eyes, blue-lidded, are closed.

'It's the new lady Vicar, Mum!' the young woman says. 'You wanted to see the Vicar, didn't you?'

Mrs Parker's eyelids move fractionally. I know she's aware, even though she hasn't the strength to speak. I know that hearing is the last of the senses to go.

'Mum isn't a churchgoer,' the daughter says. 'None of us are, but she was insistent she wanted to see you.' She herself seems puzzled as to why.

'That's all right,' I say.

Mrs Parker is now trying hard to say something. Her lips move but almost no sound comes out. The daughter bends her ear to her mother's lips, then looks up at me.

'I think she says "Sunday School" and then "Married",' the daughter says. 'That's all I can make out.'

'That'll be it!' Mr Parker speaks for the first time. 'She used to go to church at one time. She was a Sunday School teacher when I first knew her. And we were married in church. It's a long time ago.'

So far I've been standing but now I move to take the empty chair by the head of the bed, which I suspect Staff Nurse put there for me. I sit down and I put my hands over Mrs Parker's, which are together on the sheet. They are as cold as ice. There are things I would do if I felt that they would be what this lady wanted – I would anoint her with the holy oil, I would, if she wished, hear her confession, I would give her the last rites, but in my opinion this is not what she wants from me. I look at her husband and her daughter. 'Shall we say the Lord's Prayer, all of us together?' I ask. So we do. Mrs Parker can't join in but I know she hears us. Then I lay my hands on the top of her head, after which I make the sign of the cross and I give her a blessing, using the old one which isn't heard as often nowadays but I guess she will have known it. It's what God said to Moses.

'The Lord bless you and keep you;
The Lord make his face to shine upon you,
and be gracious to you;
The Lord lift up his countenance upon you,
and give you peace.'

★

78

We sit in silence for a few minutes, then I speak into her ear.

'I'm wondering what hymns you sang when you were a Sunday School teacher. Did you sing "All Things Bright and Beautiful"?'

Again, I can tell by the faint flicker of her eyelids that she's trying to say 'Yes'.

'Then we'll sing a bit of it for you!' I tell her.

And we do. Quite quietly, the three of us. Very badly too. We are not exactly a choir of angels. And when we're almost through Staff Nurse comes in, and finding us singing she joins in, again very quietly, but she has a lovely voice. At the end she says, 'The doctor is here to see Mrs Parker. I'll have to ask you . . .'

'I'm on my way,' I tell her. Then I turn to Mr Parker and the daughter. 'I'll ring you in the morning. If you want me before then let me know and I'll be with you. Don't hesitate!'

Then, since the doctor is waiting, I leave the ward quickly. Nigel is waiting on a seat in the corridor. 'All right?' he asks.

I nod, and as we walk back to the car he says nothing more, for which I'm pleased. I know this visit is no different from many others I've done, and yet it is, because in the very short space in which I'm with the dying person – and I'm pretty sure Mary Parker is dying – that person becomes the most important individual, not just one of several. No-one else impinges. The only thing I can think of which is equally awesome to being in the presence of a soul close to leaving this world is being there at the moment a baby is born into it.

Ten minutes later, we are back at the house and Sonia is opening the door to us. I'd looked at the clock in the car and realized we've been away only slightly more than half an hour, and yet it seems a little lifetime set apart and as Sonia opens the door I feel as though I was stepping from one world into another.

'Was everything all right?' she asked. 'Were you in time?'

'I was,' I tell her. 'I don't think she'll be with us tomorrow.'

Everyone is still sitting at the table and Nigel and I resume our places. No-one asks me anything. They are obviously still only part way through the main course. Everything is bright – no, not bright because we are in candlelight, but warm and welcoming.

'Yours is keeping hot in the oven,' Sonia says. 'That's the beauty of a casserole, isn't it? Are you hungry?'

Curiously enough, I am. I feel as though sustenance for the body will repair my spirit. It's a very superior casserole – *Boeuf Bourguignonne* I would say. I tuck into it and notice that Nigel is doing the same, and I accept the glass of rather nice Bordeaux which Sonia pours for me. 'If you're worried about driving, one of us will take you home,' she says. But I had less than a glass of the white wine before supper so I'm not. Since some people are apparently having seconds of the casserole, both Nigel and I manage to empty our plates without keeping the rest waiting.

The pudding which follows is pure heaven, a sort of vanilla-flavoured, creamy, chocolaty crème brûlée with a golden caramel topping.

'This is wonderful,' I tell Sonia.

'Thank you,' Sonia says. 'I can't take all the credit. It's a Jamie Oliver recipe. I'm deep into Jamie Oliver.' There follows a ten-minute tribute to Jamie Oliver from all, especially from the women who agree that he's the kind of boy one would like to have for a son. Everything by now seems back to normal, as of course it should. Sonia and Nigel, being doctors, know all about moving from one life to another without detriment to either.

Afterwards, we remain at the table, talking. They are an articulate lot. The conversation ranges from the latest film – which the Sharps and Mark have seen, and mildly disagree about, but the rest of us haven't; it's an age since I went to the cinema – to this summer's holidays. Mark has been painting in Venice. 'I love Venice,' I tell him. 'I went there once with my husband. The islands – Burano and Torcello; and the buildings, the paintings . . .' And then I come to a sudden stop. It was my last holiday with Philip. We left Becky with my parents while we went on a four-day trip, which was all Philip could cope with. Now I remember it so vividly that for the moment I can't go on, and I think this might also have something to do with my visit to Mary Parker.

'Then I must show you my paintings some time,' Mark says in a calm voice, after only the briefest pause.

I recover myself. I think Sonia must have told them about

Philip before I arrived since no-one asks one question more about the holiday. And from there, though I don't quite know how, we move on to politics. I gather that we are all to the left, though there are differing opinions about Tony Blair. I'd marked Evelyn Sharp down as a Tory, I don't know why. She certainly isn't. No-one, and let me tell you this is unusual, makes a point of telling me that they're not a Christian, and *why* they're not, expecting me to come back at them with a speech for the defence. No-one makes an apology for not attending church (with the usual addition that it was what they were brought up to and perhaps they should mend their ways). I've heard it all before and thank goodness they don't give it to me. They're a nice bunch.

Then the conversation takes another turn and Colin Sharp says, 'So are you going to enjoy being Vicar of St Mary's?'

I come down to earth with a bump. Since Tuesday what Miss Frazer did has never been out of my mind – until this evening. I have risen with it in the morning and taken it to bed with me at night. I have relived every second of those scenes in the church and the church porch. I know it's wrong to brood on it and I do try not to. I have heard of similar things happening to other women priests and, though I've sympathized with them and been angry with those who did such things to them, I have never envisaged how much it hurt, how great the shock could be. I know I should leave it to God – as the old hymn says, 'Take it to the Lord in prayer' – and that I've done. The trouble is that God doesn't answer instantly and I am impatient. Where is it going to end, I want to know? And how and when?

'I hope so,' I say. 'I do like what I've seen of the village. I expect to settle down quite quickly.' No use telling them what's troubling me. Nice as they are, intelligent as they are, I couldn't expect them to understand.

Then, out of habit, I look at my watch and see it's ten past eleven. Evelyn Sharp sees me doing this and says: 'Are you worried about Becky, is it time for your sitter to leave?'

'Actually no, not on this occasion.' I explain that Becky's with my parents.

Evelyn looks surprised.

81

'She'll be back tomorrow,' I tell her. 'And in school on Monday morning.'

'Good!' she says. 'We'll look after her. But bring her yourself as it's her first day.'

Soon after this there's a general, though not rushed, movement towards leaving, but this is then delayed until after midnight as other topics are discussed.

'I'll give you a lift home, Venus,' Mark Dover says eventually.

'Actually,' Nigel chips in, 'I have to go past the Vicarage. I could drop you.'

'How kind of both of you,' I tell them, and remind them that, in fact, I have my car!

SEVEN

When I wake on Saturday morning a shaft of sunlight is penetrating the gap in the middle where the curtains don't quite meet and making a narrow path across the floor. They were not made for this window. I brought them with me from Clipton and as soon as I can afford to I must buy, or make, some which will fit. But the fact that the sun is lighting up the bedroom means not only that it's a nice day but it's later than I thought. I've overslept, no doubt because I deliberately allowed myself the luxury of not setting the alarm. As far as I know, but with one telephone call it could all go awry, I have a free day. No services, no wedding booked – the wedding season is more or less over – no other appointments, and Becky and my parents aren't due until around five. Tomorrow's sermon is in my head and I might or might not make a few notes.

So I will have a leisurely breakfast and then I will do some shopping in the village.

My mother did all the shopping while she was here. 'You needn't worry about it,' she said. 'I shall drive into Brampton and go to Sainsbury's. Sainsbury's is what I'm used to. I suppose it's much like the one in Clipton. I like everything under one roof and they always have a car park.'

'That's fine,' I told her, 'but since I'm the parish priest I must shop in the village as much as I can.'

'You do that, love!' she said. 'In the meantime I'll stock up a few things from Sainsbury's.'

I don't yet know which shops I should go to. There are two butchers, so I suppose I should try to split my purchases between them, or visit them turn and turn about? Ditto the two greengrocers. All in all it will be a delicate operation. However, I intend to ring Sonia Leyton to thank her for last evening so I could ask her advice about the shops. I wonder if she has a Saturday morning surgery?

I ring immediately after breakfast.

'There is a surgery, but only for emergencies,' the receptionist says. 'This morning Doctor Baines is taking it. Would you like to speak to him?' I would actually, but I resist the temptation.

'It's not an emergency,' I tell her. 'I just want a word with Doctor Leyton on a private matter. Would it be possible for me to have her private number? I'm Venus Stanton, the new Vicar.'

That seems to be a good enough password and she gives me the number.

'It was a lovely evening,' I tell Sonia. 'Thank you so much for inviting me.'

'It was a pleasure to have you,' she assures me.

I enquire about the shops. 'I think I should shop in the village as far as I can,' I say.

'Oh absolutely!' she agrees. 'Well, let's see. Manson's is a good butcher, but Joss Barker also sells fresh fish – there's no other fish shop in Thurston – and his sausages and cold meats are good. The Manson family have been here for years but Joss Barker came only about three years ago. He's a bit more up to date. As for the greengrocers, Chalmers' – he's down by the crossroads – has the best selection of fruit and vegetables, more adventurous, but Winterton's delivers, which can be a boon.' She gives me a quick resumé of the other food shops. 'And you'll discover we don't have a bookshop and not much in the way of stationery so you can go to W.H. Smith's in Brampton with a clear conscience. There's the library, of course. Open three days a week, of which one is Saturday. I don't remember the other two. I don't get much time for reading and most of it's medical journals.'

'Well, thanks for the info,' I say. 'It's very useful. And thank you again for last evening.'

I hope I do see some of them again before too long. Evelyn Sharp I shall see at school from time to time, starting with Monday morning when I take Becky. Nigel Baines lives in Thurston and Mark Dover not very far away so I might meet up with them in the village. I'm looking forward to the time, hopefully not far off, when I'll walk down the High Street and be constantly waylaid by people I know.

The shopping goes OK. It being Saturday I don't walk around in my cassock. I've always liked to keep Saturdays as home and family days, so on this occasion no-one, unless they've already been to church, knows I'm the new Vicar and I shan't be announcing it in the shops. In Manson's I buy a shoulder of lamb for tomorrow's lunch and in Barker's some haddock for this evening's supper, also some delicious-looking boiled ham which Mr Barker tells me he has cooked himself. Joss Barker looks too young to be running a butcher's shop, cooking hams. Why do I expect a butcher to be middle-aged, ruddy complexioned, and on the plump side? Mr Manson certainly fills the bill, but not Joss Barker.

As Chalmers' is farther down the street I leave it for another day and go into Winterton's. By the time I've finished I'm piled high with shopping and Mr Winterton (I presume) says shall he deliver it for me?

'Thanks for the offer but I don't have far to go, only to the Vicarage,' I tell him.

'Oh! So you're the new Vicar, are you?' he says pleasantly. 'Well, welcome to you, and thank you for coming in. Are you sure I can't send the stuff up for you?'

'Quite sure, but thank you. And don't you hesitate to pop in and see me at St Mary's!' I say lightly.

He grins at my cheek. 'Stranger things have happened! In fact we've got a new granddaughter, so we'll be bringing her to have her done.' That's what they often say when they want the child baptized. I've become used to answering the phone and hearing

85

'Can I have my baby done?' What I want to reply is, 'Yes Madam. Rare, medium or well-done?' But so far I've bitten it back. I love 'doing' babies.

'Give me a ring,' I say to Mr Winterton. 'I'll be delighted to do it. Perhaps it will be my first baptism in my new parish. Always rather special, that!'

I haven't gone more than half-a-dozen yards up the High Street, on my way back to the Vicarage, when I almost literally bump into Mark Dover. If he hadn't put up a hand to stop me I would have done so because I am peering in my short-sighted way across the street at a woman I think might be Carla Brown – but isn't.

'Hey!' Mark says. 'Good-morning, Venus! You look as though you're in a tearing hurry to get somewhere!'

'Hello!' I say. 'I'm sorry if I nearly knocked you down. I wasn't looking where I was going.'

'So where are you going?' he asks.

'Back to the Vicarage. I've been doing some shopping.' What else, since I'm carrying three plastic bags full of food. 'My parents are bringing my daughter back this evening. I have to cook.'

'Then if they're not arriving until evening and it's now only eleven in the morning you'll have time for a coffee?' Mark says reasonably. 'After which I'll carry your bags back home for you.'

'I'd enjoy coffee,' I tell him. 'But you needn't act as bag carrier. Where does one go for coffee?' I suppose I should let him carry the bags back and then make coffee at the Vicarage, but I don't.

'Gander's, the baker's, has a room at the back. Or there's the Black Cat Café.'

'You choose,' I say.

'On the whole,' he says, 'the baker's. They do very good fruit buns, and cream cakes to die for.'

He strikes me as far too sophisticated to eat cream cakes in the village bakery, but perhaps it's the thing to do. He takes my bags and we walk down the road.

'You're right,' I tell him fifteen minutes later, biting into a chocolate éclair. 'This is exceptionally good!'

'It being Saturday,' he says, 'you're allowed a second one. Now tell me, how are you getting on in Thurston? You didn't say much last night. Are the natives being kind to you?'

'I'm getting on well,' I tell him. 'And yes, people are very kind.' I have no intention of mentioning Miss Frazer. Somehow, charming though he is, I don't think he'd be interested. He'd be one of those who would find it trivial.

'I'm looking forward to my daughter returning this evening,' I say. 'Do you have children?'

'No,' he says. 'And I'm not married.' There is a slight pause before he says, 'I almost was once. We were engaged, but it clearly wasn't going to work, so it was called off.'

Poor man, I think. Engaged to be married, everything arranged. Left at the altar. The love of his life and he's never met anyone else though it must have happened a few years ago since I reckon he's about my age. I smile sympathetically. 'Hard luck!' I say. Not my place to press for details.

He nods. 'Yes, I suppose it was hard on her. She was a very nice woman but I realized just in time that she wasn't for me. Poor Susan, she took it badly at the time, but she got over it. In fact she married someone else within the year.'

What he means is, he jilted her. She was the one who was left in the lurch. And he makes it sound so reasonable, as if he was doing her a favour.

'In fact,' he confirms my thinking, 'I did her a favour. She wouldn't have been happy with me.'

Perhaps he does himself an injustice, I think, giving him the benefit of the doubt because he does seem a very nice man. Charming, in fact. 'Perhaps you're not the marrying kind,' I suggest, which sounds banal, and in any case this conversation is getting a bit personal for two people who hardly know each other.

'Oh, I don't know about that,' he says. 'I won't say I've totally given up on the idea!'

We each have another cup of coffee and chat a little longer. He's easy to talk to. Then I say, 'I'd better be going.' 'If you must,' he says, and I say, 'I really must. It was lovely. Thank you very much.'

'It was a pleasure,' he says. 'I'm often in the village on Saturday mornings. I shall look out for you. And you must come and see my paintings.' He doesn't say when. And I, I decide, must make a date to have the Friday night people to a meal at the Vicarage, when I can get around to it. Or should I ask people from church first? And I wonder who from the church I might invite.

I refuse Mark's renewed offer to carry my shopping back to the Vicarage, and we part company outside the bakery.

I haven't been home more than five minutes when the phone rings. It's Mary Parker's daughter, whose name is Josie French.

'Mum died at five o'clock this morning,' she says. 'Very peacefully. Dad and I are both grateful for what you did. I know it was a comfort to her.'

'I'm glad she died peacefully,' I say. 'We'll pray for her in church tomorrow morning. If you want me to do her funeral service, please tell the undertaker. I'd be pleased to help. But let me know because I'd like to come to see you beforehand. Give me a ring.'

'I'm sure we'll want that,' she replies. 'I must just check with my Dad. He's very upset at the moment, can't bring himself round to dealing with things.'

I'm always sorry for men who are left. They seem to cope with it less well than women.

After that my thoughts turn to Becky. I had thought of giving her her favourite meal this evening, to welcome her back. Haute cuisine it is *not*. What she likes best is beefburgers and chips, and not good, wholesome beefburgers made by my own fair hands from the best quality, low fat, mince. Oh no! She likes quarter pounders, picked out of the freezer section of the food shop. 'Succulent beef, a touch of onion, a hint of seasoning. Tasty and nourishing. Cook from frozen.' A hint of seasoning or not, she will smother the whole plateful in tomato ketchup. This will be followed by ice cream, three flavours. This is what Becky likes, bless her heart, but it is not what she'll be getting today because it is anathema to my father. It will give him indigestion and keep him awake all night. We are having haddock. I will get no Brownie points from Becky for that.

I also think, as I put a few flowers from the garden in her room (which she will probably not even acknowledge) that perhaps I'll redecorate the room, which is neutral and dull, letting Becky choose the colours, perhaps running to new curtains and a brighter duvet cover. Will that cheer her up? Who knows?

Having put away my shopping, I take time out to glance at the local newspaper, the *Brampton Echo*, and it's while I'm skimming through its pages that I come across the headline 'DOG HELPS CHILDREN OF DIVORCED PARENTS'. I start to read it, expecting some fascinating tale of heroism, of a member of the canine breed jumping into the rushing river and bringing the child back to land, or rescuing them from a burning building, but no – it's a report of a piece of recent research which says that *ownership* of a dog has been proved to be of great help to a child, especially an only child, who is traumatized by the divorce of its parents, a child who is, it says, in a way bereaved. Indeed, it goes on to say, the same thing might equally apply to a child who has lost a parent by death, though in this case the research has not extended so far.

I sit there thinking. This could well be true. It has never occurred to me before, perhaps because my mind doesn't run on dogs – or cats for that matter. It's not that I dislike them, they just haven't entered my thinking; we never had either when I was a child and I don't remember that I ever wanted one. My chief unfulfilled longing was for roller skates. The article says that dogs are better for the purpose than cats because they rely more on their owner, thus giving her more responsibility for them, whereas cats are independent and don't need their owner as much.

I shan't mention this to Becky right away. I have to judge how both she and I might respond to a dog in the house. I'm not kidding myself that, even though it would be Becky's dog, I wouldn't share the responsibility. Not a hope of that! But when it comes to keeping a dog, do I know the first thing about it? I do not! I shall have to find out much more before I breathe a word to Becky.

The library! They'll have books on dogs. How to choose them, feed them, train them. And didn't Sonia say the library was open on Saturdays? So I jump to my feet and rush out of the house. The library is not more than five minutes' walk away.

'I'm looking for books on dogs,' I tell the librarian, a thin girl with spectacles and a nice smile.

'Dogs? Any special breed?'

'No. Just dogs in general. Buying, training, feeding. All that sort of thing.' I'm a long way from thinking of special breeds.

'There's a whole shelf of books on dogs,' she says, and comes out from behind her counter to take me to it. 'You can take out two books. Are you a member? I don't think . . .'

'Not yet, but I could be. I live in the village. I'm the new Vicar.'

'Oh!' she says. 'I read in the parish magazine that you were coming. 'I'm afraid . . .' (Here it comes.) '. . . I'm afraid I don't go to church, but I do always read the parish magazine.' She gives me another of her nice smiles and leaves me to it.

There is a wide choice: training, behaviour, choice of breed, feeding, illnesses of, psychology of. I narrow it down to three but I can't decide which two, and, a stroke of luck, the librarian joins me.

'Can you find what you want?' she enquires.

'It's just that I can't decide which two out of these three,' I say.

'Oh,' she says with hardly a pause, 'I suppose as you're the Vicar I can let you take three – as long as you don't keep them after the date, at least not without renewing them.'

How nice! Special privileges for the clergy! We didn't have that in Clipton.

Back at the Vicarage I make myself a cheese sandwich and settle down with the three books: *The Right Dog for You, Choosing Your Dog* and *A Dog in Your Home*. I shall read *A Dog in Your Home* first. No point in us choosing a dog until I've decided whether it's feasible to own one at all. And then, even as I start to read the first page, I remind myself that Becky starts school on Monday morning. A whole new life to face there, so I'm not sure that this is a good time to think about dogs. So I shall hide the books away and say nothing until we see how school goes before I breathe a word. And in the meantime I might come across a dog owner I can talk to in the parish. There must be dozens of them – and I expect they'll all recommend their own breed, but no matter.

Halfway through chapter two of *A Dog in Your Home* the telephone rings. In the week I've been here I've had surprisingly few calls, for a parish priest that is. I suppose people are waiting until they've met me, seen what I'm like.

'St Mary's,' I say. 'Can I help you?'

'I hope so,' a woman says. 'We'd like to have our baby done.'

Well, that had to come too! I bite back what I'd like to reply and ask, 'Do you live in the parish?'

'Yes,' she says. 'But I'm afraid we don't come to church. Well, not often.'

I'm no longer surprised by the fact that couples who haven't seen the inside of a church since the day they were married in one want to have their babies baptized, though I'm not always sure why they do. Does it go along with inoculations against various childhood infections? Measles, whooping cough and so on? Is it a precaution, superstition, against bad luck? Or is it an opportunity to dress up, adults as well as the infant, and have a bit of a party afterwards? Well, nothing wrong with that. It *is* a cause for a celebration, and if I'm invited to the party I always try to put in an appearance.

'Why don't you both come along to the Vicarage and see me?' I say. 'Have you chosen the godparents?' I hope they haven't because I'm going to tell them the ongoing duties and responsibilities of godparents, if only in order to deflect them from selecting the godparents who will give the best birthday presents to the child.

'Actually we have,' she says. 'My brother and his wife and my husband's sister and her husband.'

'Then I'd also like them to come along to the Vicarage with you,' I tell her. 'Could they do that? It's quite important.'

She thinks they could, most of them if not all. Her brother works shifts. I take a few details and we fix a meeting for next Wednesday evening. Perhaps I shall keep all Wednesday evenings free to see couples wanting to be married and/or have their children baptized, sometimes both things at the same time.

It's not all that unusual for the man and woman being married to have their child as a bridesmaid. Better late than never!

'Right, Mrs Mortimer,' I say. 'I look forward to meeting you and your husband – and the other members of your family – on Wednesday. Ring me if there's anything else you want to know in the meantime.'

Mr Winterton will have to get his skates on if he wants his grandchild's baptism to be my first at St Mary's. I hope I'm going to have a load of baptisms.

I return to my book. It all seems daunting, so much to do for a dog, and will I have time for it? Let's face it, I don't know how reliable Becky will be and in any case she's too young to take all the responsibility.

I'm so looking forward to seeing her again. Four hours to go before they're due. I do hope she's going to be happy here, in Thurston. And at this point I long, once again, so intensely, for Philip. Apart from the fact that *I* need him and want him, so does Becky. What Becky needs is a father, not a bloody dog! The thought strikes me so hard, so incapable of a solution, that I lose my cool and throw the book across the room. (A library book, and if it's damaged I shall have to explain why, and pay for it.) And then I feel guilty again, this time as if I've abused a so far non-existent dog!

I rescue the book, luckily no worse for its flight across the room and hard landing. I feel like apologizing to the beautiful Labrador on the front cover for my unkind thoughts. What I decide now is that I'll ditch the books for this afternoon and go out into the garden. Anyone who gardens will tell you that it brings healing, and at this moment I need healing. That soppy poem which says one is nearer to God's heart in a garden is just possibly true.

On the other hand, I ask myself an hour later when I'm down on my knees, digging them out with a trowel, what was God thinking of when he made all these weeds which, if I do nothing about them, will take over my entire garden? Answer: possibly giving me the great sense of satisfaction which is mine when I survey the border which runs down one side of the garden weed-free and clean, the soil newly turned, and the large black plastic bag full of the stuff I've pulled out. But why have to go through trouble to reach satisfaction? I know there are answers to this deeply philosophical question somewhere, and if I could work out one or two they'd be the subject for at least a couple of sermons, but right now it's four o'clock and I shall have to go indoors, scrub the soil out from under my fingernails and get ready for Becky and my parents.

They arrive on the dot of five.

'Lovely to see you, Venus love,' my mother says. My father nods and smiles. Becky says nothing, nor does she smile.

She doesn't immediately retire to her room but she tends to cling to her grandmother. However, she seems to enjoy the meal even though it's not beefburgers, and if she doesn't say much my mother makes up for her since she talks twenty to the dozen all the time.

'We've had a lovely time, haven't we, Becky? We've done some shopping, and we've been to the cinema, and we've played no end of games of cards. Everything's gone very well!'

And then at eight o'clock Becky takes herself off to bed and not long afterwards my mother says, 'I think I'll follow suit!'

'You look tired,' I say. 'You've been wearing yourself out, trying to please Becky. It's lovely of you.'

Dad decides to go down to the Ewe Lamb and for a moment I wonder whether I'll go with him, but decide I won't. I too will have an early night.

I can't get to sleep. In a way, though I've pushed the thought from me, I'm dreading tomorrow – which is all wrong for me because I love Sunday – but I know the reason I'm dreading it is Miss Frazer. What will she do? Will she stay away? I don't think so, I don't think she's going to let this thing drop too easily, if at all. And when she comes will she remain in her seat or will she come up to the altar? If she does, if I see her approaching, I will expect trouble. And if she does refuse to receive will it be done quietly, something between the two of us, or will she make it as public as she can? Will she go all out to involve others? I don't know, do I? And if she does the latter I don't know what effect it will have. It could be devastating – though that is something anyone who has no connections with the church would find it difficult to believe. What is of great importance to one person can be no more than a triviality to another. So some woman refused Communion? So what?

The Honourable Miss Frazer could cause a great deal of trouble if she is powerful enough, but that's another thing I don't know, whether she is looked up to, respected, or whether she's seen as an old bat. There are most likely several opinions of her and if at the Eucharist, at the very height of the action, with others gathered around, she does as she did on Tuesday, then it could grow in no time at all to a split in the parish which is something any incumbent totally dreads. And it wouldn't need a fifty-fifty split to have an effect. Half-a-dozen determined and vociferous opponents could do it, especially as this is a parish which didn't really want a woman priest.

I tell myself I'm being neurotic, and probably I am, but there's nothing I can do about it. It's in God's hands (though he's Miss Frazer's God as well as mine). I must keep calm, and have trust. By the grace of God it might not happen, and if it does then I shall have to decide what to do about it. For now, I must simply put the thought from me.

The last thing I see before me before I fall asleep is a vision of Miss Frazer's hate-filled face.

EIGHT

Sunday is here. I didn't in the end sleep well last night, though it was lovely having Becky home and I am always happy to have my parents. My mother is a practical and calming person, my father is a man who takes everything as it comes. Now that he's retired he has time to read his chosen newspapers cover to cover, and does: everything from the hot news on the front page right through to the racing predictions on the back, from which he picks his horse for the day and sometimes goes to the betting shop to back it. 'He always ends up losing,' my mother says, 'but no matter, he has his fun!'

I've taken the eight o'clock service.

'How many were there?' my mother asks as I walk in.

'Fourteen. Not bad for a chilly morning,' I tell her. In fact they were quite pleasant as they were leaving, though not effusive, and they didn't linger. How long will it take to get to know them if this is the only contact I have?

A heavenly smell of breakfast pervades the Vicarage. Breakfast is another of my mother's traditions, not to be broken except in times of worldwide crisis.

'You've just come in at the right time,' my mother says. 'One egg or two?'

'One please. Turned over and fried both sides.' I can't bear runny eggs.

My mother gives me a direct look.

'Venus Stanton! Are you telling me how you like your eggs done? Do you think I haven't been doing them for more than thirty years?'

'Sorry, Mum!' I tell her.

'I should think so!' she says, with one expert hand cracking the shell and dropping the contents into the frying pan.

Bacon and egg, fried bread, tomato, a sausage, and today mushrooms in addition. I love it, especially when my mother cooks it and just lays it on the table in front of me.

'This is heaven, Nan!' Becky says. 'But of course we only have it when you're here, even though it is my favourite meal.'

'Because I don't have time to fit it in between two services,' I chip in. 'Anyway, I didn't know it was your favourite meal. How long has that been the case?' She's seizing the chance to wind me up, and she doesn't even have to speak to me to do it.

'Where should we sit when we come to church?' my mother enquires.

'Anywhere you like,' I tell her. 'I don't suppose there'll be any lack of room.' Becky, I know, should sit with the Sunday School children near the front. Unless there's something special on they go across to the hall for the middle bit of the service then come back later to join in, and receive a blessing, but I've told Becky she needn't do this when her grandparents are here, she can sit with them – at which she seems relieved.

I hurry away again after breakfast. It's not that I'm running late, but I want to spend a few minutes in church on my own before I have to cope with Miss Frazer's arrival. You could say it's a lack of trust on my part, and in any case everyone else I'll meet with this morning is of equal importance with Miss Frazer, but I can't kill my apprehension. So back in church I sit for a few minutes in the Lady Chapel, trying to empty my mind of any fears, after which I leave to vest for the service. An ordinary Sunday, so it's a green stole and I shall wear the one which was given to me by some of the people of Holy Trinity as a leaving present. That done, I stand at the door waiting to greet the people who are just beginning to arrive.

There's definitely not a rush, more of a steady trickle. I doubt if, in the end, there'll be as many here as there were last Sunday. But, heavenly bliss, I recognize a few people and actually remember one or two names.

'Hello, Mrs Jones!' I say. 'Everything all right with the Brownies? I haven't forgotten I'm going to pop in to see you. It's just that it's been a busy first week.'

And then, later on, there's Rose Barker, she of the melodious voice. She is wearing a grey suit of which my mother would say 'It fits where it touches!' and a squashy black felt hat, but who thinks of any of that when she opens her mouth and says, 'What a beautiful morning!' – because suddenly it is, at least until she passes out of sight into the church. Then after a while comes a slight rush, well not really a rush, just four or five people hurrying up the path because it's almost ten o'clock. I know perfectly well that these are the people who will hurry up the path, out of breath, at the last minute every Sunday, and frequently after the last minute. I just know. I've met them in every church I've ever been in. If I moved this service to half-past ten they would still be late. Or eleven o'clock or even noon, likewise. They dance to their own time. You can set the clock by them as long as you remember to set it late. Apart from that they will turn out to be friendly, charming people.

There is still no sign of Miss Frazer. I wouldn't have thought of her as being unpunctual but on the other hand she could be one of those persons who, aware of their own importance, would think it untoward if they were to arrive at the same time as the common herd. Miss Frazer will probably wait until everyone is seated and I am in my place before making an entrance. There are those priests who would not have the temerity to start the first line of the first hymn until their counterpart of Miss Frazer (not necessarily a woman) is seated. Let me tell you, I am not one of them.

I am about to leave the door – if she comes, she comes – when I see what I think of as Miss Frazer's satellite, the drab little woman who was sitting at the table with her last Sunday and who I have discovered is a widow by the name of Thora Bateman, rushing at great speed up the path. By the time she reaches me she is panting like an exhausted dog for water.

'I'm sorry!' she gasps. 'I'm sorry I'm late! It's Miss Frazer. She's ill!'

'Nothing trivial, I hope!' are the words which spring instantly to mind, though all I say is 'Oh dear!'

'I don't think it's anything serious,' Mrs Bateman says. 'Not really serious. A nasty chest cold, perhaps even the start of flu. She said she's been awake half the night, coughing.'

There is some justice in the world. While I've lain awake in apprehension she's been denied her sleep because of a nasty cough!

'She's certainly not fit to venture out,' Mrs Bateman adds. So now, since it *is* only a cold, I can allow myself to think, swiftly, 'The Lord's name be praised!' followed by, 'God moves in a mysterious way, His wonders to perform!'

'We'd better go in,' I say. 'We're late.'

The service goes as smoothly as silk. There aren't as many people as last Sunday, but possibly this is nearer the norm. Sitting with the Nugents are what I take to be two of their grandchildren. They have long blonde hair and bright, mischievous faces and throughout my sermon they giggle at picture books they have brought with them. We pray for Mary Parker and her family. My family sits in the side aisle – trust my father! Becky looks bored to death throughout and doesn't join in any of the responses or the singing. Clearly she is at war with the Church of England as well as with her mother.

When it's time to give communion and I stand there, watching the people come up to the altar to receive, I can't help feeling that I have been given a deliverance. Delivered from the hand of the enemy, probably a very wrong thought at this moment and I don't allow it to linger. In any case I know it's only a temporary deliverance; I will have to face whatever awaits me sooner or later. But not just now, and I thank God.

When the service is over my parents and Becky elect to go home straight away. I know my mother would be pleased to go in to coffee and meet people but it is not my father's scene and still less, at any rate for the moment, Becky's. I think how pleasant it would be if she would accompany me, if I could take her round and introduce her to people, show her off. '. . . And this is my daughter, Becky.' It's not to be, certainly not this week. So I tell my family I won't be too long and now I am standing outside the church, bidding farewells. It's chilly and I'm glad I'm well padded under my cassock. Henry Nugent introduces me to his granddaughters. 'This is Fiona, she's six, and Victoria, she's four.'

'I shall be five on Wednesday,' Victoria says.

'But you're not five yet, you're still only four!' Fiona corrects her, and is rewarded with a dirty look from Victoria.

'Their father is my middle son, Clive,' Henry says. There is no sign of Clive, or of Mrs Clive. 'Shall we go across for coffee, Vicar?' he adds.

I guess he will always call me 'Vicar', not because he's un-friendly but because he can't get his tongue around 'Venus'. Would it help if my name was Mabel?

'You go ahead, I'll be there in a minute or two,' I promise. I can see Thora Bateman hovering, looking anxious.

'I don't know whether I should go into coffee or whether I should go straight back,' she twitters. 'I do enjoy going for coffee but Miss Frazer might be needing me.' (Does anyone call Miss Frazer by her Christian name?) 'She has no-one coming in on Sundays.'

'Oh, I'm sure she wouldn't begrudge you a cup of coffee on a cold morning,' I say. 'Besides, you'll be able to tell her just who was here. I'm sure she'll want to know *that*.'

Thora Bateman seizes the excuse. 'You're right,' she says. 'She will!' Then she makes a bold decision. 'Well, just a quick cup!'

We walk together across to the parish hall.

'Are you feeling better?' I enquire. 'I thought perhaps you weren't too well last Sunday.'

'I have a rather delicate stomach,' she says primly. Then she starts on again about Miss Frazer, how good she is really, what she's done for the church, etc., and I, remembering that Mrs Bateman wasn't there on Tuesday evening and has no idea what Miss Frazer did then, try to think of something polite to say in reply. There must be something, like 'I believe she's very fond of her dogs,' but I fail to find it. Anyway, if she has a dog I expect it will be a small, snappy one which bites everyone's ankles or a

99

large, lion-sized one which scares the living daylights out of all callers. Either way, it's sure to be a thoroughbred of impeccable pedigree.

I reach the hall door not having said another word, but there's no need to. Mrs Bateman is rattling away twenty to the dozen.

As soon as we walk into the hall I am grabbed by Carla Brown who is sitting at the table nearest the door.

'There's a seat here, Venus!' she says. 'Walter, get the Vicar's coffee. No wine on an ordinary Sunday, I'm afraid!'

There is another vacant seat at the same table, which Thora Bateman promptly takes, though I notice Walter isn't commanded to fetch coffee for her. I rather feel that Carla has appointed herself my guardian. I could do worse.

'It's not often I'm in church two Sundays in succession,' Carla says. 'Walter will vouch for that.'

There are two others at the table, both women. Carla, breaking through Thora Bateman's dramatic description of Miss Frazer's symptoms, which are beginning to sound like double pneumonia, introduces them to me. Joyce and Alice Dean are twin sisters, I guess in their forties, and as well as being as alike as two peas in a pod, they say 'Pleased to meet you, Vicar!' in unison. After which Thora Bateman rounds off her description of Miss Frazer's ills and launches on a panegyric of her wonderful qualities as a person.

'She's a wonderful supporter of St Mary's,' she informs us, though I have the feeling everyone else knows the recital by heart. 'She gave the new altar in the Lady Chapel, and those beautiful silver candlesticks which stand on it. And then there was the repair of the organ, that cost a pretty penny!' (I have plans, in the fullness of time, to augment the organ, or use it perhaps alternately, with a newly formed music group – keyboard, guitar, recorder, possibly even drums – but I am keeping quiet about that for the moment. It isn't that I dislike the organ or that Mr Blatchford isn't a very competent organist, and of course I shall consult him at every step and turn, but a variety of music would be good.)

'And then . . .' continues Thora Bateman '. . . there's the

100

Sunday School outing every summer. It was started by her late father, Lord Frazer, you know. And if it weren't for Miss Frazer's generous contribution it simply couldn't continue. What St Mary's would do without her I really can't imagine!'

Carla looks at me, her face expressionless except for the raising of her eyebrows, and then I am mercifully rescued by Henry Nugent who wishes to tell me that the matter of the boiler must be resolved. It is playing up again, he thinks we should have a special meeting about it because he fears it might mean quite a heavy expenditure to put it right. 'But we can't have people shivering in their pews, can we?' he says. 'They just won't come in that case!'

Thora Bateman, having reached a temporary pause in her narrative, looks at her watch and gives a little squeal.

'Good heavens, just look at the time! Miss Frazer will wonder where I've got to!'

So that was Sunday. It could have been worse, or some of it could. The afternoon was pleasant enough. I spent quite a bit of it in the garden, even though it was chilly. The more you get the garden in order at this time of the year, the better it all is when the spring comes. If you haven't eradicated the weeds they keep hidden under the soil until spring arrives, when they burst out all over the place, as if invigorated by their long rest. I wished, as I gardened, that I knew what bulbs were buried there. It would be a bit late now to plant daffodils, which I love, but tulips would be OK and I thought that maybe I'd take an hour off on Monday, after I'd delivered Becky to school, to go to the garden centre and buy some.

My mother came out to join me, but not to garden. She doesn't do gardens. She is queen of her house, Dad is king of his garden.

'I think you've been out here long enough,' she said. 'Anyway, I've made a pot of tea and after that your Dad and me will have to be off. He'd like to get home before dark, though it never used to bother him driving at night.' She doesn't actually mean 'a pot of tea', she will have made a whole spread. Sandwiches, scones, cake.

'Oh Ma!' I said. 'Do you think you could persuade him to stay a bit longer for once? I have to take Evensong and I'm not happy about leaving Becky on her own even if it is only for an hour. As for taking her with me . . .'

'Of course we will!' she agreed. 'If Dad doesn't want to drive, then I will.'

From next week, when the clocks go back, Evensong is in the afternoon right through to next spring.

So I rushed back from Evensong – six people only, and I hardly stopped to speak with any of them – after which my parents departed and Becky and I were left to spend the evening together. I thanked heaven for television. As yet, Becky doesn't have her own in her bedroom, so since she wanted to watch it she had to suffer my presence. When the programme we were watching finished I said, 'It's nine o'clock, love, and you still have to have your hair washed and get everything ready for school in the morning.' Possibly at ten years old she should be capable of washing her own hair but it's something she's always been happy for me to do, so I did it and she suffered me to. Needless to say, there wasn't much conversation between us, though there's not a lot of time for talk when your head's being held over the wash basin and water poured over you.

Becky has lovely hair: thick, dark, glossy, and with a natural wave in it. It is exactly like her father's, as so much about her is. Wielding the hairdryer I ran my fingers through it, coaxing the waves into place. The feel of it was so like Philip's that for a moment I couldn't go on. I didn't realize that I'd paused, and was holding the dryer on one place, until she shrieked, 'You're burning me! You're burning me!'

I quickly pulled the hairdryer away, turned the heat down to low and held it against her head again to cool it down. It was all over in no time at all, but she was furious. She pushed me out of the way, ran out of the bathroom and across the landing to her bedroom, slamming the door shut behind her. I waited a minute or so, then I knocked on the door.

'I'm sorry, Becky! I'm truly sorry! Please let me in. I want to see you tucked up in bed.'

'I can put myself to bed!' she called out. 'I don't need you!'

102

But I need you, my darling, I thought. Of course I could have opened the door and walked in on her but I decided not to.

'Wouldn't you like some cocoa?' I asked. 'I'll bring it up to you.'

I waited, but there was no answer. In the end I said: 'Well, call out if you want anything. And don't forget to say your prayers. Good-night, darling!' Then I went downstairs.

An hour later I went back upstairs. I stood outside her door and said her name softly, but there was no reply, so I opened the door and tiptoed into her bedroom. She was under the duvet, fast asleep, her hair spread out over the pillow. In sleep she looked totally peaceful, as if nothing in the world could ever worry her. I would like that to be true.

And now it's Monday, and school looms. A momentous day for Becky, as I am only too well aware. As a special treat, and remembering yesterday's conversation about cooked breakfasts, I have made one: bacon, egg, tomatoes. Becky sits at the table, pale-faced and silent, but the silence is of a subtly different nature from the one she's been imposing on me so far. How can I tell it's different? I'm not sure, except that it isn't accompanied by hostile looks and from time to time she actually catches my eye and I see in her eyes a little girl who is apprehensive rather than angry. What's more, her cooked breakfast – the one she declared yesterday to be her favourite meal – is there in front of her and she's not eating it, simply moving it around the plate until in the end she pushes it away.

'It's all right,' I say. 'You don't have to eat it if you don't want to, at least not this once. I've packed sandwiches for your lunch until we find out what the school dinner arrangements are. You might be allowed to eat one at break time if you're hungry. You'll have to see about that. And now I think we'd better set off. You don't want to be late on your first day, do you?'

She is wearing her school uniform. She's chosen a combination of pleated skirt, blouse and sweater and I must say she looks rather nice. I help her on with her jacket and, lo and behold, she doesn't push me away, though in fact I'd rather put up with that than having my little girl look so sad.

'Cheer up, darling!' I say. 'I'm sure it's going to be all right! You'll soon settle in. You've met Mrs Sharp and Mr Beagle and you liked them both, didn't you? Most people are quite nice when you get to know them.'

For a fleeting second I wonder if this could possibly apply to Miss Frazer, just supposing I ever did get to know her. And then I push her out of my mind. This is Becky's time, no-one else's.

'Would you like me to come and meet you from school this afternoon?' I ask.

'No!' she says quickly. 'That's only for the babies.'

'OK,' I agree. 'But come straight home. I'll be in. I'll be waiting to hear all about it.'

We leave. There's no more conversation during the short walk to the school. When we arrive the children are all out in the playground, running around, shouting and laughing, which I comfort myself is a good sign. There is a teacher on playground duty and I present myself and Becky to her.

'I think you need to see Mrs Sharp,' she says – so we go into the school and find Evelyn Sharp in her room. She is very welcoming to both of us and presently she says, 'Mr Beagle is in his classroom. Why don't I take Becky to him? If you'd like to wait here I'll be back in two minutes.'

I do feel sad as she leads Becky away, which is silly really. It isn't as if she's a tiny tot and it's her very first day at school – an occasion I suppose all parents remember. She's ten years old, bright and intelligent and relates well to people. Or used to.

Evelyn Sharp returns.

'Don't worry, Venus,' she says. 'She'll be OK. Jim Beagle is a very nice man as well as a good teacher. He'll look after her. Would you like a cup of coffee?' I tell her I would.

'The thing is,' I say as we drink our coffee, 'most of the other children have come up together through the school. They've known each other for a few years.'

She nods agreement. 'I can't deny that that does make life easier, but give her a little time and she'll cope with it. Most children are adaptable. Honestly, Venus, we'll do everything we can to help her.'

'I'm sure you will,' I say, 'and I'm grateful.'

'While you're here,' she says, 'I'd like to talk to you about school assembly. Your predecessor used to take an assembly at the beginning of each term, and then one at the end of the school year. Apart from that the church and the school had very little contact with one another. I was never totally happy with that, I felt there should be much more involvement, but I was fairly new at the time – it's only three years since I came to Thurston – so I didn't push it. And the previous Vicar was elderly and probably had too much to do already.'

'So what do you have in mind?' I ask.

'Nothing very specific, I haven't thought out the details. In any case a lot of that would be up to you. I just know I'd like a closer contact between the school and the church. It is after all a church school. It was founded as such in the nineteenth century. It's all there in the records.'

Could it be, unfortunately it could, that it was Miss Frazer's grandfather who was involved in founding the school? If so, I am on a sticky wicket!

'For instance,' Evelyn says, 'I would have liked it if the Vicar had come into the school from time to time, got to know the children, have the children know him. But perhaps you think that's asking too much?'

'No I don't,' I assure her. 'But it would have to be structured to a certain extent. You couldn't do with me suddenly appearing in the middle of lessons, upsetting the curriculum.'

'Of course not,' she agrees. 'We'd have to discuss it – and with the other teachers, naturally.'

'Well, I'll be happy to do that. Just let me know when.'

The telephone rings and she answers it. 'In a few moments,' she says.

I stand up. 'I'll be off. I expect you're busy. Thank you for everything, especially for understanding about Becky.'

NINE

What a nice woman Evelyn Sharp is, I decide as I walk down
School Lane on my way back to the Vicarage. I think she'll be a
good friend. And I'm interested in what she said about forming
closer links between the church and the school. It makes a lot of
sense. The only thing is, will it be good for Becky to have her
mother in and out of the school? Children of the Vicarage don't
always have a good time at school. Too much is expected of
them. St Mary's, however, is the only one she could go to, so
we'll just have to work through it, Becky and I, though I daresay
it will be harder for her than for me. She'll be at the receiving
end.

'There are one or two very good private schools in the area,'
Henry Nugent said earlier when I questioned him about education. 'Highly recommended.'

'I daresay,' I'd said. 'But I'm afraid my stipend won't stretch
to the fees.'

'You might get a reduction of some sort,' Henry said. 'Clergy
families sometimes do.'

I'd shaken my head. 'In any case, I'm a strong believer in State
education,' I told him. 'I always have been.' I don't think my
political leanings, of which I'd made no secret, went down well,
but Henry is a polite man.

'Of course,' he said. 'Of course! And if you decide to send

106

Becky to St Mary's I'm sure you'll find she'll do very well there. We have a splendid Headmistress!'

Which has turned out to be true, hasn't it? At any rate the last bit.

Monday is the day I'm going to make my regular day off, a usual practice with clergy in parishes and I did tell the church-wardens I would follow this practice. 'Not that my day off will be sacrosanct,' I assured them. 'If there's something I need to do on that day, visits or meetings, or a funeral – whatever – then that will come first.' I wasn't being noble. It's the way it works. You're on call. If you're one of those rare Vicars who has a curate then some things can be shared, but not if you're on your own. Then you're on call twenty-four hours a day.

This brings me back to a problem which has been niggling at me and which, though I've been here for two weeks, I've so far done nothing to resolve, and I absolutely must. And the problem is this. What do I do if I'm called out in the evening when I'm at home with Becky? Or, worse still, if it's in the middle of the night? Either way, it's not likely to be the sort of situation where Becky could accompany me. It will be an emergency, or the person calling me will see it as an emergency, which amounts to the same thing. In Clipton, apart from the fact that I was only the curate and therefore not the first to be called upon, I had friends, neighbours, parents who would step in when they were needed, and in the short time I've been in Thurston I've been cushioned by the fact that my parents have been here so much, but I can't put off making proper plans any longer. What I want is someone who'll be agreeable to come and sit in with Becky when needed, and at short notice, and of course someone Becky would get on with, which in her present state of mind will *not* be easy. So I resolve to do something about it here and now, and what I do is I sit down and dial Henry Nugent's number. The Vicar's first cry for help is usually to the churchwardens. Richard Proctor will be at work in his office in Brampton, but in any case Henry is the senior warden, added to which he's more likely to be sympathetic.

His wife, Molly, answers the phone.

'It's Venus. Do you think I could have a word with Henry?'

107

'Of course!' she says. 'He's in the garden. I'll give him a shout.'

I can't imagine Molly Nugent shouting for anyone. She's one of those patient, calm, soft-spoken women. Unruffled. However, whatever she does now it's effective because Henry is on the line in two minutes flat.

'Good-morning, Vicar! What can I do for you?' he asks.

I tell him my problem. 'And why I haven't done something about this before I can't imagine,' I say. (Actually it had come up in my interviews before I was appointed, but was never thoroughly gone into.)

'Naturally,' I say now, 'I'm not thinking I'm going to be called out every night, or even often.'

'I doubt you will be,' Henry says. 'I don't think your predecessor was, much.'

'But it could happen. And with no warning. So what am I going to do? I just need someone I can rely on to come in and be with Becky. A woman.'

'Yes,' he agreed. 'It would have to be a woman.' There is a short pause and then he says, 'But I'll tell you what I think your best bet might be, certainly until we get something more permanent sorted out, and that's my Molly.'

'Molly?' Molly Nugent has never occurred to me. 'Is that the sort of thing she'd do? Isn't she awfully busy?' I ask.

'If you want something doing, ask a busy person,' Henry says. 'I'm sure you know that as well as I do. Anyway, apart from the fact that we live near, she's well qualified. She's brought up her own children and now she's into grandchildren. She gets on well with the young. She was a teacher, you know. Shall I have a word with her and ring you back?'

'Well, that would be wonderful,' I agree. 'I don't yet know many people I could ask. I'd thought about Carla Brown, though I don't know her circumstances and I certainly don't know if she'd want to do it. But don't press Molly too hard!'

'I won't,' he promises. 'Anyway, I'll ring you back. Will you be in?'

'I plan to go to the garden centre,' I say. 'I want to perk up the garden a bit.'

'Not before time,' Henry agrees, 'though we mustn't blame your predecessor too much. He had arthritis, he couldn't do much in the garden.'

While I'm waiting I start to write my list for the garden centre. I know I want bulbs. Tulips, crocuses, a few hyacinths, chionodoxa, muscari and so on. I'd also like some shrubs, especially flowering or colourful ones, but it's going to be a question of money. In Clipton we gave each other cuttings, or divided plants and handed them around to friends, and I expect this will happen here in due course. I shall put out feelers. For now I would like a *Viburnum fragrans*. I've always had one, wherever I've had a garden. It flowers profusely on its bare branches from November to Spring, which is when the leaves come; and one small flowering twig brought into the house in the middle of winter scents a whole room.

At the end of my list I add a soil-testing kit because I've made some awful bloomers in my time, before I knew a thing about soil. Rhododendrons and azaleas planted in the chalky soil have died the death in double quick time – I probably murdered them. Gorgeous red Japanese maples withered away, camellias refused to flower. In my ignorance, in those first days I thought that I had only to buy a healthy-looking specimen, plant it well, water it and feed it, and I would have a garden like a royal park.

I'm just adding fertilizer and plant labels to the list when the phone rings. It's Molly Nugent.

'Hello, Venus!' she says in her cheerful voice. 'Yes, I'll be pleased to help out as and when needed. At least I will in the short term, until you can get a more permanent arrangement. I think I'd better come around to sort it out, don't you? I don't really know Becky, nor she me, and I think we should get to know each other. She doesn't want to feel she's being left with a stranger, does she?'

'That's true,' I agree. I don't tell her I wish her luck in getting to know Becky. In any case Becky might be fine with Molly Nugent. Or shall I say as fine as with anyone chosen for her, by me. 'This is very good of you, Molly! When would you like to come?'

'I think fairly soon, don't you? I can't come today, though.

109

There's a WI meeting this afternoon and this evening I'm babysitting the grandchildren. What about tomorrow?'

'Tomorrow would be fine. Could you come early evening? Oh, but there's the Tuesday Eucharist at eight o'clock? In fact . . .'

'Would you like me to stay on with her while you take that?' she asks.

'That would be wonderful!' I tell her. 'It takes about thirty minutes as you know. Becky was away with my parents last Tuesday, so it didn't arise.' In fact I'm going to have to do something about Tuesday evenings and I'm not sure what. I'm weighing four people coming to a mid-week service which will last less than thirty minutes against my daughter's needs and I don't know what the answer is, except that a single parent who's a woman priest is not, once again, the ideal combination. But I didn't set out to be a single parent, did I?

'I can guess what you're thinking,' Molly says. 'You'd best have a word with Henry about that. Anyway, I'll be with you tomorrow, say around quarter-past seven, and I'll stay until you get back. Does Becky like games – I mean board games, Monopoly and suchlike?'

'She might,' I say. 'She used to.' But who knows now?

'I'll bring something or other and we'll see,' Molly promises. 'My daughter will know what the latest craze is.'

Fenton Hill Garden Centre is – surprise, surprise! – at the top of Fenton Hill where the ground levels out into a plateau. Carla Brown recommended it to me. 'It's quite good,' she said. 'A bit pricey but the quality's good. And some of the staff are quite knowledgeable.' So, list in my pocket, I get into my lovely little car, drive down Church Lane and turn right into the High Street, pass the end of Sonia's road, picturing her with a busy Monday morning surgery, and drive forward, which quickly leads me to Fenton Hill. It's a steep hill with houses on both sides to begin with, before they give way to open fields. It's a lovely October morning, bright and sunny, and, apart from the fact that my mobile's in my handbag should I be needed, I'm free! The conversation with Molly Nugent, though I can't kid myself it's going to solve everything at once, has cheered me up, *SO* – I'm going to enjoy the next hour or two. And as I drive up the hill, I start to sing. A hymn, admittedly, but a fast, cheerful one with a strong beat. I shall introduce it to St Mary's. 'Teach me to dance to the beat of your heart.' I doubt they sing it already. The kids will love it.

I'm still singing when I turn into the car park, which is half empty – I suppose because it's a Monday. There are loads of trolleys, neatly stacked together in a long row, and the one I take actually has four wheels which all go in the same direction. I buy the dull things first; fertilizer, soil-testing kit, plant labels, before allowing myself the heady experience of the bulb and then the plant sections. Packet after packet of spring bulbs find their way into my trolley, all of them with exquisite, highly-coloured photographs of how I can expect these dull little brown shapes inside the packet to eventually end up in my garden, and I don't for one minute disbelieve the photographs, partly because when it comes to gardens I'm an optimist but also because it's a miracle I've seen happen time and time again. In fact, give me an ordinary daffodil bulb, dull and dead-looking, and I'll give you a sermon on the Resurrection. Though not at the moment because, having bought extravagantly, I'm going to tear myself away. I'm off to look at the shrubs.

To my great delight I do find a *Viburnum fragrans*, also a *Cornus Westonbirt*, which in plain English is a dogwood which will cheer up a bit of the garden in the sharpest winter weather with its brilliant red stems. And then I think of the cost of all this and turn my trolley firmly in the direction of the checkout but, walking down the aisle with my attention caught by a display of terracotta pots of all shapes and sizes, I literally cannon into, nay, lock trolleys with, guess who? Mark Dover!

'Good-morning, Venus!' he says. 'Are you and I destined to bump into each other like characters in a romantic novel, or is it a crime story and do you have some sort of plan to mow me down?'

'I'm sorry!' I say. 'I was taken by these pots. They're rather nice, aren't they?'

'They are,' he agrees, 'though I doubt you have room for even the smallest one in your trolley.'

'You're right,' I tell him. 'Or on my credit card! That's why I'm making for the checkout.'

'I'm going in the same direction,' he says. 'In my case because every single thing in my trolley means another job in the next day or two. Sometimes I think I'll have my garden concreted over.'

'You don't like gardening?'

'Not over-much,' he admits.

We push our trolleys along together, not unlike the companionable way new mothers, side by side, push their babies in the park.

'Do you have a large garden?' I enquire.

'Large-*ish*,' Mark says. 'Why not come and see it? You might be able to give me some labour-saving advice.'

'I'd really love to, some time,' I tell him. 'See it I mean.' It's true. I like seeing other people's gardens. They so often reflect the owner, both in what they are and what they're not.

'I don't mean some time,' he says. 'I mean now. Why don't you come home with me now?'

'Now?' I say, as if I didn't understand English.

'Yes, now. I remember that at Sonia's you mentioned Mondays as probably being your free day, also you said you'd come and look at my paintings.'

'I said "some time".'

'This is some time,' he says.

Why not? I'm thinking. He's a very pleasant man. 'Then thank you,' I say. 'I'd love to!'

I sign my credit card chit, trying not to wince at the total, and we go out into the car park. As it happens, his car is parked quite close to mine. It's a black BMW, almost new, so he can't be a painter starving in a garret.

'It's not far,' he says. 'A matter of minutes. Follow me!'

His house is beautifully situated, standing alone not far below the crest of the hill, the soft grey of its flint walls blending into the landscape as if it had grown there. A gateway – the gate is open – gives on to a short, curved drive which ends in a terrace in front of the house. When I get out of my car I look ahead at the view. There, at the bottom of the long hill, is the village, well tucked in. St Mary's is clearly visible but the Vicarage is cut off by trees. I can see the school and I wonder how Becky is doing. I shall be glad to see her when she gets home. Looking around here there are a few other houses, not by any means closing in on this one, but not far away. I wonder if Miss Frazer lives in this area, and then I wonder why I don't already know that if she's so important, after which I stop thinking about her because Mark says, 'Let's go in. We can look at the garden afterwards if you want to. It's not madly interesting.'

We step into the hall, which is large, square, and well-furnished. The furniture, I note, is not the kind you go to the store and buy, it's the kind you inherit. It's mostly dark, standing out against the white walls, and each piece, which doesn't match any other piece, has that look of having been lovingly polished over the years.

'Come through to the kitchen,' Mark says.

The kitchen is in stark contrast. Nothing old-fashioned here. Stainless steel tops, gleaming Aga in red, black-and-white tiled floor, gadgets everywhere – blenders, bread machines, state-of-the-art steamers – filling the shelves and hanging from the ceiling. A pretty penny all this will have cost.

'Would you like some coffee – or perhaps a drink?' Mark says. 'In fact, it's more or less time for lunch. How about some soup, or bread and cheese – or both? And a glass of beer? Do you drink beer?'

'Sometimes,' I say. 'But really, I didn't come for lunch. I came to see your garden and your paintings.'

'And so you shall,' he says. 'I take it you do eat lunch? You're not one of those women who exist all day on black coffee and a leaf of lettuce?'

'Definitely not!' I assure him. 'I have a healthy appetite!'

'Good! So you would be having lunch, so why not here and now?'

No reason at all, I think. All I have to do is get back in time for Becky and the red-framed clock on the wall says it's only twelve twenty-five, so why am I hesitating?

'Well, that would be rather nice,' I say.

He takes a carton of soup out of the refrigerator, carrot and coriander, heats it up and serves it with fresh bread which has a

113

subtle flavour of sun-dried tomatoes and basil, and also sets out a cheese board. Then he opens two cans of beer.

'A feast!' I tell him. 'My compliments to the chef!'

'Well I did make the bread,' he says. 'If you can call chucking the ingredients into the bread machine and operating a couple of switches making it.'

After we've eaten I say, 'I really would like to see some of your paintings, if that's all right.'

'Sure!' he says. 'I don't hang many in the house, as perhaps you've noticed, but I have a studio out at the back. When my mother was alive she hated the smell of oil paints and turpentine, said it pervaded the whole house, which of course was true, but I love it. So I had this place built at the bottom of the garden. It works well.'

From what he said I had in mind a sort of garden shed, but this is much more than that. Solidly built, with huge windows, one built into the roof, and blending into the garden because there are shrubs around and climbing plants up the walls. A clematis, one of them, though past its flowering stage and now hung with clusters of fluffy white fruits. As he unlocks and opens the door I realize he's right about the smell. It pervades the air but I quite like it. There are canvases everywhere, hanging on the walls and resting on easels, stacked around, but what strikes me most is the blaze of colour. Reds, yellows, blues, and blends of primary colours: orange, magenta, vibrant purple, pinks, greens. I am – what's the word? – assaulted by colour. But not assaulted, because the experience is pleasant. And pleasant is too mild a word, too milk-and-water, I am stimulated, up-lifted!

'Wow!' I cry. Which sounds inadequate. 'Is that what most people say?' I ask him.

'More or less,' he admits, laughing.

I don't think I've heard him laugh before. It's a pleasant sound. Not a guffaw, more of a chuckle, as if he's really enjoying the experience.

'Though as a matter of fact,' he adds, 'not all that many people come in here. It's my workplace, and I work alone. Sometimes I bring them if there might be a commission involved, if they want

to see samples of my work – especially if they live in the neigh-
bourhood, which makes it convenient for them. But on the whole
I prefer people to see my work hanging, in exhibitions and so on.
They get a better idea of what I do.'

'You have exhibitions?' Why am I surprised – though I'm less
surprised now that I've seen some of the paintings around.
Perhaps because he doesn't come over as important. Perhaps
because I've seen him eating cream cakes in the village baker's?

'Sure!' he says.

'Where? I mean . . .'

'Several places. I have one of my own work about once a year,
in London. Then I have paintings hung in other exhibitions,
mostly in London because I'm more or less tied up with a
London gallery; some in other places – Bath, Brighton, the West
Country, Edinburgh.'

So why have I never heard of him? Because I don't read the
right things, that's why! A painter wouldn't be mentioned in a
political article, or a headline in the *Church Times*, or in one of
the fashion magazines I buy from time to time. But why didn't
Sonia say anything? Perhaps because he's a patient, or a long-
time friend. I suppose you don't define friends by what they do,
more by what they are to you.

'Perhaps you might like to come to an exhibition some time?'
Mark says. 'I have one in London in December.'

'Thank you! I'd love to!' I tell him.

We look around and talk a bit more about the paintings,
though he doesn't have much to say about them individually
except occasionally, 'I painted that in France' or some such. I
suppose that's reasonable. You wouldn't expect a singer to
talk about her singing or an author to talk about his books.
It's there in the work. It's not to be explained. And I discover
as we do chat that what he really enjoys most is painting
portraits.

'Though I don't have many to show you,' he says. 'They're
mostly with the people I painted.'

'Commissioned, I suppose?'

'Very often, though in fact I much prefer to choose my own
subject rather than be asked to paint some important man or his

wife. Actually . . .' He pauses, and I realize he's looking at me quite intently. '. . . Actually, I'd like to paint you.'

'Me?' I'm truly surprised.

'Yes,' he says. 'You have an interesting face.'

When people say you have an interesting face they mean you're not beautiful, or even pretty. Or you could be quite plain.

'Thank you,' I reply. 'But I'm afraid I couldn't commission you, not even to do a very small portrait.' And I reckon by what I see here that he works large.

'I wasn't suggesting that,' he says. 'No way! I'm just saying I'd like to paint you. Come to think of it I could paint you in your uniform. That would be different. I've never painted a Vicar!'

I'm not totally amused by this.

'Really? And when you say my uniform do you mean my full glory on Easter Day – white-and-gold chasuble and stole – or my everyday black cassock?' I ask.

'Oh, the latter!' he answers quickly. 'A black cassock would be perfect. You would stand out against it, the emphasis would be on you. I don't much like painting fancy uniforms. They can take over from the subject. Anyway, think about it!'

I am, though I'm not going to say so, highly flattered. No-one has ever before wanted to paint my portrait.

Presently I look at my watch and it's a quarter to three.

'I must go!' I say. 'I want to be home well before Becky arrives. Thank you very much, it's been so interesting. And thank you for my lunch.'

He sees me to my car. 'I meant what I said,' he says. 'And also about the exhibition. I'll let you have the details of that.'

Back at home I turn up the heating and then I start to make a lasagne, which is another one of Becky's favourite meals. I would like to walk down to school and meet her but I won't because she mightn't like it. I don't want to make a fuss of her in front of the other children, but when the bell rings just after half-past three I rush to open the door.

She stands there, her face pale and troubled.

'Hello darling!' I say, my arms held wide. 'How did it go? Come and tell me all about it!'

She pushes past me.

'It was horrid! I knew it would be! Why do we have to live here? Why can't we go back to Clipton?' She's not yet crying but her voice is full of tears and pain.

TEN

I follow Becky into the sitting room where she throws her schoolbag on to the floor and herself into an armchair. I think she's chosen the chair deliberately. If she sat on the sofa, which is nearest, I would certainly sit beside her. I long to put my arms around her, which is not what she would want.

'So what went wrong, darling?' I ask. 'Please tell me!'

'Everything!' she says. 'They're horrid! The girls are horrid, the boys are horrid, the teacher is horrid!'

'Mr Beagle, horrid? I can't believe that. He seemed such a nice man, and you liked him when you met him, didn't you?' I say.

She glares at me as if I'm too stupid to understand – what in fact she hasn't told me.

'It wasn't Mr Beagle. He's got flu. It was Mrs Hayes, and she's a cow!'

'So please tell me, love, what happened?' I ask.

'I don't want to tell you! You wouldn't understand!'

Those three words are ones which no parent ever wants to hear. 'You wouldn't understand.' Aren't we the wise ones? Aren't we the ones who know all the answers, know how to guide the young things? But at the moment I feel totally inadequate, perhaps because I'm pretty sure this young thing is not going to confide in me.

'Well, I just might. You could try me,' I offer.

'It's no use trying *you*,' she says bitterly. 'It's all your fault!'

That doesn't surprise me. I am definitely the fly in the ointment. 'So what have I done now?' I ask with as much patience as I can muster. 'Tell me!'

'You know what you've done! If you weren't a Vicar we wouldn't be here and if we were here and you weren't a Vicar it wouldn't be as bad except that we'd never have come here in the first place and in any case you're not a proper one but it would be just as bad if you were!'

The words rush out of her, after which she sits further back in the chair, her eyes filled with a mixture of pain and anger. I know someone has said something stupid, and immediately, I'm as angry as she is. I could march straight down to the school and bang a few heads together. But I'm not going to. It might make me feel better but it would do Becky no favour at all.

'Not a proper what?' I ask as calmly as I can.

But she has had her say and she's not going to favour me with another word. Her lips are as tightly closed as if they'd been zipped together.

'Not a proper what?' I repeat. 'Do you mean I'm not a proper Vicar? Is that what someone has said? If it is, they're quite wrong. I am a proper priest, God has made me so and I will always be so. Anyone who says otherwise is wrong. I was made a priest when you were still a very small girl. I don't suppose you can remember when I wasn't one.'

I'm used to this accusation, as is everyone else of my ilk, though it's well over ten years since some of the women were ordained priests. We are used to reading it in the newspapers – it can give renewed life to a letters page any time anyone decides to stir the embers. I have heard it on the radio, the television, on the street. I have heard it from men and from women, and not infrequently, from my fellow priests of the opposite sex. I know that often it's a conviction sincerely held, though conviction and prejudice can be close bedfellows. But I have not heard it from a child before, so now it is being handed on to another generation.

'So we can't change that,' I say. 'But a priest is not all I am.

I'm a woman. When Daddy was alive I was a wife, and I wish I still was. Don't think I don't miss Daddy! And I'm your mother and you're my daughter and the dearest person in the world to me. I can't bear to see you unhappy. I'd do anything I could for your happiness, you know I would, but I can't ever stop being a priest any more than you can stop being you.'

There is a silence between us, which Becky breaks.

'Why did you have to be a priest *here*?' It's as much an accusation as a question.

'Because,' I tell her, 'it seemed to me to be what God wanted me to do. I have to listen to God. Priests do.'

'I *hate* God!' she says.

'I'm sorry to hear that,' I tell her. 'But it's your choice. He doesn't hate you. Are you hungry?'

I did well to make lasagne. Becky eats two hearty helpings, followed by a Marks & Spencer's sticky toffee pudding. A stodgy meal, not the healthiest in the world, but stodge, I've found, and not only for little girls but for grown women, has healing properties for aching hearts which can't be found in a bunch of watercress. It also loosens Becky's tongue.

'Mrs Hayes is stupid,' she says, finishing the last crumb of pudding.

'Really?' I ask. 'Why?'

'She said,' and here she puts on a voice which I presume is Mrs Hayes's, '. . ."Now Becky, your mother is a Vicar, so I'm sure you can tell us the names of all the people St Paul sent letters to?"'

'And what did you say?'

'I said, "No I can't, Mrs Hayes. Can you?"'

'Oh, my goodness!' I say. 'That was *rather* rude!'

'I know!' Becky says in a satisfied voice.

When bedtime comes I read to her. She's quite capable of reading herself but sometimes I choose to do this as a special treat and I reckon this evening is one for a such a treat. I read Harry Potter, which I enjoy as much as she does so it's no chore, and I read for quite a long time but eventually, struggle against it as she does, sleep overcomes Becky. I close the book and sit there for a minute just looking at her. I would do anything for my daughter, yet these days I seem to be the cause of all her troubles, even though for an hour or two she seems to have shifted the blame on to God. Well, I suppose he can bear it! He must be used to it.

On the other hand, I think as I switch off the light and tiptoe out of the bedroom and back down the stairs, *would* I do anything for her? So far I seem to have gone my own way and she has had to run beside or behind me. I've always thought I was taking her along the right road, and I know that when she's older she'll branch off in her own direction and I shall let her do that. I most certainly will.

I wish, for the thousandth time, that Philip was here. He would know the answers. He was much wiser than I am.

Next morning Becky goes off to school, albeit unwillingly. I am standing in the window, watching her go down the road, when the phone rings. It's Cliff Preston, who is the local funeral director. I met him last Saturday, after Mary Parker's family had been in touch with him. Mary is to be cremated on Thursday. This will be my first funeral in the parish and I'm glad I was able to be with her for that short time before she died.

'Good-morning, Vicar!' he says brightly. (I am to discover that in spite of his profession he is the most cheerful of men.) 'Another funeral for you! It never rains but what it pours! A Mr Leigh, fourteen Branksome Close, died in the night. God rest his soul.'

'I'm sorry to hear that,' I say.

'He's been ill a long time. It was a release.'

'I don't think I know him. Should I?'

'Not unless anyone told you. They're in the parish but they haven't been to church for years, his wife said. However, she wants a service in St Mary's and for him to be buried in the churchyard.'

'No problem!' I tell him. 'There isn't anything which might be, is there?'

'Nothing at all,' Cliff says. 'They haven't got a grave so it'll be a new one.'

'OK. I'll sort that out with you,' I say.

They don't sound like the kind of people who've been marking out a special place in their minds for years: top of the hill, six yards from the east wall, which I usually suspect is where the couple in question did a significant bit of their courting. I don't delve into that. I have a duty to look after the churchyard, keep it orderly, not graves dotted here and there haphazardly, like almonds in a trifle, and that's what I'll do. I've already discovered that Thurston people – and not only those who go to church – are proud of their churchyard, and so they should be. It's well laid out, with trees, lawns, seats – and everything beautifully maintained (at great cost to St Mary's), peaceful and – I use the word thoughtfully – pleasant.

'So, date and time,' Cliff says. 'What suits you?'

This is music to my ears! Here is a man who doesn't make all the arrangements to suit himself and then tells me where I must fit in.

'As it happens,' I say, ' – and I suppose it's because I'm so new – I don't have a lot in my diary. Does the family have a preference?'

'Well,' he says, 'the widow would like it next Monday. I must say, she seems a bit lost. She has relatives from the North who are coming to stay with her over the weekend but they'd like to get back as soon as possible after that because they have jobs to go to. But I suppose Monday is your day off?'

'That doesn't matter,' I assure him. 'Monday will be fine. So if you'll give me the phone number I'll give Mrs Leigh a call and make the rest of the arrangements.'

It is Cliff's job to carry out his part of the funeral but mine to arrange the service and, I hope, in this case as with the Parkers, to do what I can for the family. It's one of the times in my life when I can feel really and truly of use. It matters nothing to me whether the family have been churchgoers or not. Perhaps in the latter case they have more need of me than otherwise.

I call Mrs Leigh as soon as I've finished talking to Cliff.

'I'm so sorry to hear about your husband, Mrs Leigh,' I say. 'How are you? Do you have someone with you? Do you have someone to stay? Your daughter Marilyn? Oh, that's good. Well,

122

Mr Preston has been in touch with me and we'll do all we can to help. For instance, Monday morning is fine for the funeral, and before then I'll take you and your daughter to show you just where the grave will be.'

She seems relieved by that.

'I'll want to come and see you,' I say. 'You can tell me then just what you want – any special music, readings and so on – but I'll give you time to think about it, discuss it with your daughter. What about Thursday morning? Would that suit?'

'That will be all right,' she says. 'And Marilyn will be here.'

I arrange to be with her around ten-thirty. 'But if there's anything you want to talk to me about before then,' I tell her, 'or if you just want me to come round and see you, then ring me. Any time.'

She sounds a reasonable sort of woman, a bit shaky in the voice, a bit incoherent at times, but who wouldn't be? Aside from the grief, if her husband's been ill for a long time I haven't the slightest doubt that she'll be bone tired and short of sleep. I know I was.

I can't say I enjoy a good funeral, 'enjoy' is the wrong word, though sometimes I can feel I've helped, so there's a certain satisfaction, but when I was at Holy Trinity I knew a woman who did enjoy them. Mrs Fanshaw was quite elderly by the time I got to know her and she'd seen off several friends and relatives, and even mere acquaintances – she never missed a funeral. Which was why, she once confided in me, that although she had no intention of giving up buying new clothes should she wish to do so, she always stuck to black because it came in so handy.

An hour or so later I meet with Cliff in the churchyard and we sort out where the grave will be. A nice position, it will catch the morning sun. 'I've arranged to see Mrs Leigh on Thursday morning,' I tell him. 'She sounds a very reasonable woman.'

'I thought so,' he says. 'I think she's looking for advice, but I don't think there'll be any difficulties there, not unless she has awkward relatives.' Which, as he knows and I know, because we've both experienced many funerals, she could have.

'I had this woman last week,' he goes on. 'She was in the

Chapel of Rest, funeral due next day, and her sister came to see me. "Do you think we could have Lucy's nightdress back before you bury her?" she asked. I thought she wanted it as a very special memento, but I should have known better. "You see she'd only got it from Marks & Spencer's a few days ago," she explained, "so it's as good as new. It won't fit me but if I take it back I'll get a refund." '

He laughs heartily. I daresay it's episodes like this which keep him so cheerful. I don't have any difficulty in believing the story; I could match it with several of my own.

At that moment my mobile rings. It's Molly Nugent.

'Do you mind if I come round a little bit later this evening? Something's cropped up – nothing serious, but it would suit me if I came slightly later. Is that OK?'

'Absolutely!' I tell her. 'I don't have to leave the Vicarage before ten-to-eight, so I'll have a bit of time with you and Becky, and then I'll be back soon after half-past.'

It will in fact suit me better. I'd like some time with Becky after school. If she comes home worried again it will give us time to talk about it well before Molly arrives, if she will talk, that is.

'Do you have children?' I ask Cliff as I put my phone back in my pocket. I know he's married, his wife helps him in the business. I met her briefly and thought she seemed a nice woman.

'I have a son at university,' he says. 'Doing Modern Languages. He seems to be doing well enough.'

'And is he going to follow in your footsteps?'

Cliff shakes his head. 'I'm sorry to say he's not. What he *is* going to do I don't know, and for that matter nor does he. Says he wants to travel. You don't do that in my job. I've lived in Thurston all my life, and my father before me. He inherited the business from *his* father and I started with my father straight from school, learning everything there was to learn. Then he handed it over to me when the time came, though he worked until he was well in his seventies. He built it up a lot.'

I wonder, vaguely, how one builds up an undertaking business. You can't actually get more people to die, can you? Then, having checked on the final details of the Leigh plot, we turn to walk down through the churchyard and he answers what I haven't liked to ask.

'There used to be two funeral directors in Thurston – we're all funeral directors now, but my father would have called himself an undertaker – and I can't say we were ever on bad terms, but there was a lot of rivalry, especially about who would get what I'd call the big funerals. My father buried Lord Frazer, we won that one.'

'So you know Miss Frazer?' I asked.

'Oh yes!' he says. 'Who doesn't? She used to teach me in Sunday School. She was very strict, frightened the life out of me sometimes. We had to learn the catechism, and all the prayers, and know who was who in the Old Testament – she was more for the Old than the New and I reckon she knew most of it by heart. Put me off for life, I can tell you. You'll have noticed you don't see me in church.'

'I had noticed,' I say.

'But then she had her good points, she used to take us – the whole Sunday School – on this trip every summer. We'd go to Eastbourne. Of course we kids would have liked to have gone to Brighton but she reckoned Brighton was common.'

'But there's only one funeral business in Thurston now, isn't there?' I ask.

'Oh yes,' Cliff says. 'We won in the end. The other fellow sold up two or three years ago. I think we had the edge, the family having been here so long.'

By this time we are standing at the parting of the ways. His business is at the bottom of the High Street and I'm going back to the Vicarage.

'Are you disappointed your son isn't going into the business?' I ask him.

He nods his head. 'Oh, I am indeed! "Preston and Son" it's said on the sign, ever since my grandfather's time. It can't stay like that, can it?'

'Cheer up, Cliff,' I tell him. 'You've a lot of years to go yet!'

'That's true,' he agrees. 'And by the time I pop my clogs then

125

they might have thought up totally different ways of doing things!' He's smiling again.

I haven't been in the house more than a minute when the phone rings again, and this time it's Mark Dover.

'Hi!' he says. 'You left your scarf behind.'

'My scarf?'

'Navy silk?'

'Well, yes. That sounds like mine, but I hadn't even missed it. I don't remember taking it off,' I say.

'Perhaps when you took off your jacket before lunch?' he suggests.

And then I remember. I did take my jacket off, and I put the scarf in the pocket. It must have fallen out. Being silk it's very lightweight, weighs practically nothing. I might never have missed it until I'd wanted it again.

'I'm sorry,' I tell him. 'Anyway, not to worry. I'll get it back some time or other. There's no hurry.'

'Oh, that's all right,' he says. 'I'll be down in the village in the next day or two. I'll bring it to the Vicarage.'

'That's kind of you,' I say. 'But please don't come specially – though if I'm not in you can push it through the letter box. Anyway, thank you for ringing, and thank you again for my lunch!'

When Becky comes in from school I take one look at her face and I know immediately that things are still not right, far from it. She is pale, unsmiling, and there is a new tightness about her which seems to extend to her whole body. It's a tightness which is holding something in, afraid to let go. And to my shame and chagrin I do not know how to deal with it, what to do for the best. Do I ask questions, probe if necessary, or do I keep quiet, act as though everything is normal? As if I hadn't noticed? If she had come into the house angry, furious with something or someone, or just with life itself, if she had hurled at me a selection of the swear words children seem to know as soon as they can talk, or if she'd burst into tears, then I'd know what to say next. But she doesn't. This is something different. She is hiding herself. So I decide, since I don't know what's for the

126

best, to act as though none of it was obvious, while hoping that she will spill it out.

'Hello, darling!' I say, almost casually. 'How was school today?'

'As usual,' she says, not looking at me. Then she switches on the television and sits herself down in front of it as if it was the only thing in the world which mattered. It happens to be a cookery programme, people rushing around preparing things against a stopwatch, and I know her interest in cookery programmes, even though she enjoys food, is non-existent.

'I thought we'd have an early supper,' I say, 'since Mrs Nugent is coming round later. But would you like a snack now?'

'I'm not hungry,' she says, her eyes firmly fixed on the screen where a man is chopping onions at great speed.

I told her last night that Mrs Nugent would be coming round to stay with her for a short time while I went to church, and she seemed to accept it. At least she didn't make a fuss. She's not unused to such arrangements, though not usually with someone she doesn't know.

'So what sort of a day did you have?' I venture. 'Did anything special happen?'

'Nope!' she says, without for one second taking her eyes off the television. And that, I am given to understand by her manner, is the end of that. So I take myself off to the kitchen and set about preparing ahead for supper. From time to time I slip back into the living room on some pretext or another but always she's glued to the television. In fact, after the cookery she sits, without bothering to change channels, through a quiz, an animal programme, 'Neighbours', and is still there when the six o'clock news comes on and I call her to the table. She eats hardly anything, which adds to my worry.

Molly Nugent arrives, a bit later than we'd arranged, full of apologies.

'I had this woman with me,' she explains. 'She just wouldn't go. In the end I had to tell her I was going out. Anyway, here I am now. I brought Junior Scrabble in the end because I haven't managed to see my daughter. If you haven't played it before I'm sure you'll soon learn. It's quite good, actually.'

I have to leave, but they seem to be getting on amicably. Molly has a flow of interesting talk – she is such a nice woman – and all Becky has to do is listen, which she is doing.

'Back in forty minutes!' I tell them.

I arrive at the church early enough to open up, switch on the lights, and still leave myself with time to say my prayers before anyone is likely to arrive. I desperately need that time of quiet, not because it's been an especially full day, I've known many far busier, but because at the back of my mind I've been worrying about this evening, dreading it. It's never been quite out of my mind. Even while I was so concerned about Becky – and still am – I couldn't quite keep Miss Frazer at bay. And now, in a very few minutes, I shall have to face her.

I try to clear my mind, to leave it free for God, and having done that as best I can I think of those who need his help. I pray for the souls of Mr Leigh and Mary Parker and for their families in their grief. I can never say to anyone, 'I know just how you feel,' because it wouldn't be true; we can never quite know another person's feelings, but at least I know how it feels to be widowed, so I can feel close to Mrs Leigh there. And poor Mr Parker. Possibly worse for him. I pray for Becky, my poor little Becky – I wish I knew *her* feelings and what it is which troubles her – and I ask for enlightenment. I pray for the people who will attend this service, including Miss Frazer. I ask for understanding and patience, and even while I'm doing so I'm thinking that where Miss Frazer is concerned this is likely to be an ongoing prayer. God will see the end, but I can't.

And then I hear them coming in, and by the time I'm on my feet they're sitting in the pews – separate pews, of course, I don't suppose they ever sit together – the two women, the elderly man, but there is no Miss Frazer!

'We'll wait a few minutes,' I tell them, 'just in case anyone else comes.' I suppose all three of them know who I mean, but no-one says a word.

I do wait, but Miss Frazer doesn't arrive. At the end of the service they glide away down the path like three ghosts. They bid me 'good-night' quite pleasantly, none of them mentioning Miss Frazer, and as far as I can tell they don't speak to each other. I can only think that Miss Frazer's cold is worse and that she's not well enough to come. Can I, with a clear conscience, thank God for this deliverance? I'm not sure.

ELEVEN

It's Thursday morning and I'm seeing Becky off to school. It's stalemate as far as Becky and I are concerned. When I returned from church on Tuesday evening she seemed to be getting on well with Molly Nugent – they were in the middle of a game of Scrabble – and there was a better feeling in the room.

'I'll stay to finish it,' Molly said. 'We've not long started this one and I won the last but I've a feeling Becky is going to wipe the floor with me this time.' She turned to Becky. 'You've picked it up remarkably quickly,' she said. 'Are you sure you've never played before?'

'Quite sure!' Becky said.

'I can confirm she hasn't played it before,' I told Molly. 'She must be lucky.'

'Oh, it's not only luck,' Molly said. 'You have to have skill as well.'

Becky did win the game, and by a wide margin. It seemed to cheer her up. Nevertheless, as soon as Molly left she chose to go to bed, and in the preparations for bedtime she had nothing to say, though I felt she was less hostile than worried.

'You would tell me if there was anything wrong, wouldn't you?' I asked. She was brushing her teeth and pretended not to hear me.

Afterwards, in my own bed, I lay awake worring, wondering

what to do. Should I have a word with Evelyn Sharp? If so, I thought, I'd not tell Becky. But I don't want to be one of those over-anxious mothers who are always on at the teachers for one thing or another. Is my child doing well? Does she need extra help with her reading? She's very bright, should she be stretched more? And so on. I prefer to leave it to the teachers to get on with the teaching and make the judgements.

Even so, I think this morning as I hover around Becky, making sure she's got everything she needs, that it isn't a matter of teaching – at least I don't think it is. Mrs Hayes is a supply teacher and it's more likely she just got off on the wrong foot with Becky, possibly partly Becky's fault. In the mood she's been in since she came to Thurston she can't be any teacher's dream pupil. All the same, I'll be glad when Mr Beagle gets over his flu.

'It's going to rain,' I say. 'I think you should wear your mac.'

'I'm not going to!' Becky says. 'If it rains I get wet. So what?'

'Don't be silly,' I say. 'You could get a nasty chill!'

'That would be OK,' Becky snaps as she flounces out of the house, 'I wouldn't have to go to school!'

I'm due at the Leighs' for the bereavement visit at ten-thirty, so when Becky's left I phone Mrs Leigh to check that she's expecting me. She says yes, she is.

'How are you?' I ask.

'I'm all right,' she says in a low voice. 'Marilyn's with me. I'll see you at half-past ten. Number fourteen is halfway up the Close on the left.'

There's no telling how long the visit will take. It could be as little as half-an-hour – which is unlikely – or last for two hours. I was an hour with the Parkers. It's for as long as Mrs Leigh needs me. I don't want to rush her, nor do I want to outstay my welcome. There are people who don't want a priest around the house for too long, especially if they've never had much contact with the clergy. Once the business part is settled they find it difficult to keep the conversation going. They seem to have the idea that they must talk only about God, the church, and perhaps the weather. The weather is soon disposed of and what is there left to say about God and the church if weddings and funerals are one's only contact?

Branksome Close is about fifteen minutes' walk away, to the east of the village, a group of red brick bungalows probably built in the seventies. Mrs Leigh is looking out for me, I see the curtain twitch as I approach, and by the time I get to the front door she is holding it open.

I follow her into a small hall and through a doorway on the left into the front room of the house. It has the feeling of not being used much: everything spotless, cushions immaculate, as though no-one ever leaned against them, a framed landscape over the fireplace, a vase of artificial poppies on the windowsill. A young woman, I reckon she's about my age, is sitting on the sofa.

'This is my daughter, Marilyn,' Mrs Leigh says.

We shake hands, I sink into one of the armchairs – they are large and deep, the sort which go back a long way and envelop one and, me being short, this doesn't suit me. I know I shall soon have to inch myself forward and perch uncomfortably on the edge.

'I'm so sorry to hear of your loss,' I say. 'I understand Mr Leigh had been ill for some time.'

'More than a year,' Mrs Leigh says. 'It was expected, and it was what was best for Ronnie, but it doesn't make it any easier when the time comes.'

'I know,' I tell her. And I do know, but this isn't the time to explain why. I learnt at the beginning that when one's grief is new and raw and oh, so painful, there isn't room in the heart or the head to think about anyone else's. So now I leave it at those two words: 'I know', and I expect she'll think, how can she?

'Well now,' I say, 'there are a few questions I need to ask, I have some forms to fill in. So shall we deal with those first and then we can go on to whatever else you'd like to talk to me about. The service, hymns and so on.'

Both women nod agreement. So far Marilyn hasn't said a word.

'So what was Mr Leigh's full name?' I enquire.

'Maurice Leigh,' his widow says.

'His full name?' I repeat.

'That was it. Maurice was his only name. Maurice Leigh.'

'But I thought . . . you called him "Ronnie", didn't you?'

132

'Oh yes,' she says. 'That's right! We always called him Ronnie. He'd been called Ronnie from a little baby.'

Now it's not new to me that the name which will go on the certificate is not the one by which the man was known to his family and friends. He can acquire a nickname at any time of life, quite often from his friends, sometimes from the job he does, but how does a man whose legal name is Maurice come to be called Ronnie almost from birth? Maurice to Ronnie is a big jump.

'I see,' I say – which I don't at all. 'And how did that happen? When he was a baby, you say?'

'Six weeks old,' she confirms. 'I've never known him as other than Ronnie, but my mother-in-law told me the story.'

'Which was . . . ?'

'Well, she wasn't all that well after the baby was born, and his birth had to be registered so she asked her husband to go and do this, and he agreed. She was dead set on the name Ronald – there was a film star, Ronald Colman, she admired. Unfortunately, on his way to the registrar's he – Ronnie's dad – met up with a drinking pal who insisted that first they should call in at the pub and wet the baby's head. From the way my mother-in-law told it,' Mrs Leigh says, 'they drank enough to bath the baby, never mind wet its head. Anyway, the pal says, "What are you going to call the lad?" "Ronald," says the baby's father. "Oh, that's no name for a little lad!" says the pal. "Call him Maurice – my late father's name, and none better! Finest name in the world!"

'So they drank to that a few times more,' Mrs Leigh says, 'and the pal went with the baby's father, and somehow the baby was registered as Maurice.'

'And what did the baby's mother say to that?' I enquire.

'She told me she was fit to kill him!' Mrs Leigh says. 'And if she'd had the strength she thought she would have. But the baby was never spoken of as Maurice; not once, not by anyone, not ever. Till the day he died he was Ronnie!'

'Well,' I say, 'I'm glad you've told me this. I always like to find out if the person has been known by some other name, usually a nickname, and if at the funeral I'd referred to your husband as Maurice . . .'

'No-one would have known who you were talking about. They'd think you were burying the wrong man!' Mrs Leigh says.

She's very amenable about the rest.

'Harold – that's Ronnie's brother – will say a few words about Ronnie, if that's all right?'

'Of course it is!' I tell her. 'About five minutes is usually the best length.' It's advice I always give before a funeral now because I am still haunted by the memory of the one at St Saviour's where I hadn't done so and the speaker was still in full flow after fifty minutes. I could see people looking at their watches. Fortunately, he paused for breath and I was quick enough to rise to my feet and say, 'Let us pray!'

Mrs Leigh has no ideas about what to have for a reading so I recommend Corinthians, which almost everyone can relate to, especially if the word 'love' is used instead of 'charity'. And I'm thankful she doesn't suggest that poem which says the deceased is not dead, he's only in the next room. I happen to think it's not true, it's a false promise. If only Philip *were* in the next room. If only . . . ! Well, I won't go on, but I do feel strongly about it.

'So what about the music – hymns and so on?' I ask. 'Was there something your husband particularly liked?'

This can be a tricky area. I once did a funeral at the crematorium in Clipton where the requested music was 'Smoke Gets in Your Eyes'. Frank Sinatra singing 'I Did It My Way' is a common request but I try to be as accommodating as I can.

'Ronnie wasn't one for music,' Mrs Leigh says. 'He was tone deaf. But he liked "Abide with Me" because they had it at the cup finals. He loved his football. And I've chosen two more hymns if that's all right.'

I reckon the hymns she's chosen are familiar ones she can remember from way back: 'All Things Bright and Beautiful' (that will be twice for me in less than a week since the Parkers have chosen it because we sang it at the hospital) and 'The King of Love My Shepherd Is'. I wish I'd had a fiver for every time I've had 'The King of Love . . .' at a funeral.

She says that Mr Preston has already shown her where the grave will be.

'We went down to the village to visit the Chapel of Rest and he happened to be there, so he took us across to the churchyard. We were very pleased with the position and I think Ronnie would have been.'

Marilyn nods assent.

'He's a very kind man, Mr Preston,' Mrs Leigh says. 'You're both very kind! Would you like a cup of tea, Vicar? Marilyn would make one in a jiffy.'

Marilyn half rises from the sofa, and I say, 'Thank you, but I won't at the moment, Mrs Leigh. But don't forget that if you think of anything else, or if you just want me to drop in for a chat, give me a ring.'

'Thank you, Vicar,' she says. 'I will.' Then she suddenly looks embarrassed. 'There *is* one thing . . . I just wonder how much I'll owe you, I mean for the church and everything. And would it be all right if I didn't pay you until I got the insurance money?'

'Oh, of course!' I say. 'Sort all that out with Mr Preston. He'll pass on whatever's due to the church. Don't worry about it, Mrs Leigh.'

I decided yesterday that I would give up the Tuesday Eucharist and I phoned Henry Nugent to discuss it with him.

'It doesn't seem to make sense to me to keep it going for the same people week after week,' I said. 'And I don't mean exactly give it up. I'll do it on Tuesday mornings instead. They're all four retired people so I expect they could manage the mornings as easily as the evenings. Indeed it should be better, with the winter coming on.'

'I agree with you,' Henry said. 'It's never served the purpose for which it started. Of course there'll be complaints – some of them from people who don't go anyway!'

'Then I'll have to cope with them, won't I?' I said. 'I'll write to the regulars. I don't doubt Miss Frazer will make an almighty fuss.'

'Sure to!' Henry said. 'But she'll have the choice of Tuesday morning, Thursday morning and Sundays.' (Which will give her three opportunities a week of refusing to take communion at my hands, I thought.)

135

'It'll have to go before the PCC, of course,' said Henry. 'But I'm sure there won't be any difficulty there.'

The Parochial Church Council has the right to approve just about everything to do with the church, indeed they and the churchwardens are legally responsible for a great deal of it, especially in the realms of money. We have a meeting every other month and there's one due on Friday evening, which it's already been agreed will be held at the Vicarage so that I needn't make arrangements about Becky.

'Anyway,' I said to Henry, 'I think people might prefer coming to the Vicarage rather than having the meeting in the parish hall.'

'Oh, certainly!' he said. 'They like a glimpse into someone else's home. It's human nature. And very few people got a glimpse inside this one, over the years. I did, and Richard did, us being churchwardens, but not many others.'

There's a school of thought which says that the Vicarage should be a private place for the Vicar and his family, and there's truth in that, but I believe it should also be a place where any parishioner should feel they'll be welcome if need arises.

I've been looking forward to meeting the couple who wanted to have their baby baptized, not Mr Winterton's grandchild but Mr and Mrs Mortimer and the godparents, but she phoned me to say she wouldn't be able to come, she hadn't been at all well, so could they come the next Wednesday? This suits me very well because I want to talk to the PCC on Friday about changing the times and the form of baptisms, bringing them more into the open, into the Sunday morning congregation, and I'm hoping the Mortimers might be a family who would agree to this. We shall see.

And now as I'm walking back from Mrs Leigh's I think about Becky again – she's never far from my mind – and I wonder should I encourage her to ask some friends from school back to the house? Would it make her happier? I know it's early days but really I'm getting desperate about her unhappiness. I feel that I should know what to do about it, I'm her mother, for heaven's sake! And then I decide that when I get back home I'll phone my mother and ask her advice. And when I've done that, I remind myself, there's a load of post to see to, yesterday's as well as today's. A lot of it's from the diocese. Reports to be read, notices of meetings (there's a Chapter meeting next week which it's my duty to attend), financial statements – there's usually something to do with finance though like every other church we have our own money problems here at St Mary's. There's a letter from a friend in Clipton who suggests coming to see me, and a couple more letters which came just before I left home and I haven't opened them yet. Neither of them are stamped, they've been popped through the door and I think they might be from parishioners. I hope they are, whether they're good or bad. It will show they think I'm alive, and available.

Back in the Vicarage I'm in the middle of putting the kettle on to make a cup of instant coffee when the doorbell rings. When I answer it, there is Mark Dover standing on the doorstep.

'Good-morning!' he says. 'And don't look so surprised to see me. I told you I'd return your scarf.'

'Thank you,' I say. 'That's very kind of you, but you needn't have hurried.'

'Aren't you going to ask me in?' he says. 'Or do you have someone with you? Am I interrupting?'

'I'm sorry!' I say. 'No, I don't. Please come in. I was about to make a cup of coffee. Would you like one?'

'Yes please!' he says.

'Is instant OK?' I ask him, 'or would you like to wait while I make the real stuff?'

'I can happily drink either,' Mark says, 'but I'm not in a hurry so I'm more than happy to wait.' So I put the stuff in the machine and switch it on and we sit at the kitchen table, watching it trickle through, and I try to think of something interesting to say but he gets in before me.

'You're wearing your cassock,' he says. 'It suits you. I don't think that I've seen one on a woman before.'

'It's exactly the same as a man's,' I say, a bit tartly. 'That's because I do exactly the same job. I'm wearing it because I've been out on my job.'

'Whoops!' he says, making me feel churlish. 'Of course you do. I hadn't really given it a thought. But I must say, I've never seen a man in a cassock look as good as you do!'

137

He's smiling at me, and his smile reaches his eyes as well as his wide mouth. He really is a most disarming man, I can't be cross with him. And I have to admit I like compliments from men. Philip was very good at compliments; not flattery, but real compliments. Mark's, of course, might well be flattery. I don't know him well enough, do I?

'Perfect for the portrait!' he says.

I pour the coffee. We drink it, chatting about something and nothing, and then Mark says, 'I'm serious about the portrait. I've never painted a Vicar before.'

'I thought the idea was that you painted the person, not the occupation?' I say, frosty again. 'And would you want to paint me if I wasn't a priest?'

I have this feeling – oh, I daresay I'm over-sensitive – that he sees me as a sort of curiosity, a specimen he hasn't met with before, which is more than likely. There is only one other such specimen in the diocese, at the far end. It's a place known for not encouraging women priests. 'Inhospitable' would be a mild description.

'Actually, I would!' He's emphatic. 'I would indeed! And we can ditch the idea of the cassock and the dog collar if you don't like it. Or on the other hand you could think of it as making a statement if you wanted to. It *is* becoming, you know. A great combination of severity and femininity. It also has a certain sense of power.'

'As a matter of fact,' I say, 'I don't remember agreeing to have my portrait painted and now we're talking about what I'll wear!'

'But you will, won't you?' he says.

I don't answer, and then he says, 'Are you very busy? Am I keeping you from something important, a service or something?'

'This and that. Not a service.'

He looks at his watch, a Rolex.

'Well, it's around lunchtime. Would you like to come down to the pub and eat? The Ewe Lamb does a passable pub lunch.'

'But I'm not . . .' I begin, but he interrupts me.

'You do eat. You admitted that much the other day.'

'Of course! But . . .'

He has this habit, which could become irritating, of not letting

138

me finish sentences. 'So would it sully your reputation, a lady Vicar in a cassock to be seen in the Ewe Lamb lunching with a man?'

'Don't be silly!' I say. 'And please don't refer to me as a lady Vicar! Would you call Sonia Leyton a lady doctor? Or yourself a male painter, for that matter?'

'Sorry!' he says, raising both hands in front of him as if fending me off. 'Only teasing! Shall we go?'

So we do. I have fishcakes and Mark has shepherd's pie, both enormous helpings. We talk about this and that; television, films. Mark has seen all the latest and I haven't seen any of them, though Philip and I used to go to the cinema a lot, when he was well. Then we walk back to the Vicarage and Mark collects his car, which he'd parked outside. I don't ask him in.

I have to admit that when I let myself into the house I stand in front of the hall mirror and study my face with some intensity, pulling my hair this way and that, scraping it back from my forehead – does that make me look more serious – or is it better falling over my face? Wondering how I'd look in a portrait, should I decide to sit for it. There's conceit for you! There's the deadly sin of pride!

And then I walk through to my sitting room, pick up the phone and call my mother to talk to her about Becky.

'I'm concerned, love – of course I am,' she says, 'but I don't have a ready answer. I wish I did. It's good she's not quite as hostile to you, but I don't know what to say about the rest. Are you sure you shouldn't be going down to the school? The headmistress is a friend of yours, isn't she? I'm sure she'd be sympathetic.'

'It's partly because Evelyn's a friend of mine that I hate to bother her. I don't want to seem to be asking for special treatment. So I won't go down that road, at least not for a few more days,' I say.

'I wish I could come over,' my mother says, 'but I can't. Your Auntie Elsie isn't at all well and your Dad and me have promised to go to her first thing tomorrow. As you know, she's on her own, poor soul. Dad's quite worried about her.' Auntie Elsie is my father's sister, six years older than he is.

'It's all right, I don't expect you to come here again so soon,' I tell her. 'I just wanted to talk to you. I expect it'll sort itself out. It's perhaps only that it's taking Becky a long time to settle down. And give my love to Auntie Elsie!'

Becky is late home from school. This is most unusual. She's usually here well before four and now it's twenty past. Where can she be? I've been outside and looked down the road, but there's no sign of her. I don't want to phone the school just yet. There's probably some perfectly logical explanation and I don't want to embarrass her. And I don't really want to leave the house to look for her in case she hasn't taken her key – not unknown – and comes back to a locked door.

In Clipton she would sometimes go home with a friend, but she'd always phone me as soon as she got there – it was a rule. She'd tell me where she was and we'd arrange how she'd get home. But that can't be the reason now. Would that it were. So far my Becky doesn't have a friend who'd be likely to ask her back to tea. I wish she had.

Could she have been kept in? If so I'd have thought somebody would have phoned to tell me.

I decide I'll give it until half-past four and if she hasn't appeared by then I will definitely ring the school.

And now, it's twenty-eight minutes past and I'm looking out of the window, I see her walking up the road and I rush to the door to let her in.

'Oh, Becky!' I cry. 'Where have you been? I've been worried sick! Are you all right?'

'Of course I'm all right,' she says, pushing me away and making for the stairs.

I feel a sudden rush of fury. In the past half-hour I've gone through in my mind all the dreadful things I've seen on television, read in the papers. Everything, from a road accident to kidnapping, and worse, and here she is, as cool as a cucumber, no explanation, and trying to evade me.

'Don't you dare go up to your room!' I yell. 'I want an explanation! I was nearly out of my mind. Anything could have happened to you!'

140

'Well it hasn't,' she says sulkily. 'I just went down the village. Aren't I allowed to go down the village?'

'Of course you are! You know very well you are! But not when you're due home from school, not without telling me. Can you imagine how I felt?' And then I can't help it, and I burst into tears and she stands there, looking at me.

'Sorry,' she says.

'What did you go down to the village for?' I ask.

'To look at the shops,' Becky said. 'Of course I couldn't buy anything, could I? I've no pocket money left. Why can't I have more pocket money?'

This is a complete surprise to me. She's never grumbled about her pocket money before because she knows I give her what I can, and it's a reasonable sum. Not a lot, but reasonable, and she also knows she can earn more if she wants to by doing jobs around the house or in the garden. That's always an option, but Becky doesn't like domestic jobs so it's an option she seldom takes up.

'You can have more,' I remind her. 'And you know exactly how.'

And then to my great surprise she says, 'All right then, I'll do some jobs.'

I can hardly believe what I'm hearing.

'But don't ask me to do anything really horrible!' she says.

'As a matter of interest,' I say, 'what do you want more pocket money for?'

'That's my business!' she says, quite savagely. 'I don't have to tell you what I spend my money on. It's mine! Is nothing private in this house?'

And then she does run up the stairs to her room, and I let her go.

TWELVE

This weekend is not the best of my life, not by a long way. It starts badly on Friday morning, and quite by accident. When Becky leaves for school I clear the table and stack the dishes in the dishwasher and then I go upstairs to make the beds. At the weekends Becky makes her own bed but on schooldays I do it for her, and give a general tidy up, things like putting her dirty washing in the laundry bin, if she's forgotten to do it. But I don't move or rearrange other things no matter how bizarre they look, and certainly not personal possessions. This morning, however, there are some used tissues on the dressing-table which I clear away, and then I start to dust, which means I pick up her money box in the process. I don't give it a thought as I pick it up, my mind is elsewhere, and then it strikes me that it is very light, it weighs almost nothing.

Now Becky's money box is usually heavy, full of coins. She is not one of the world's big spenders, she's more of a saver, which was why on Thursday evening I hadn't been able to think why she was after more pocket money. I shake the box – it's nothing elaborate, just a painted wooden box with a hinged lid, no lock. I don't open it, I wouldn't do that, but I don't need to. There isn't the faintest rattle of money. It is definitely empty. I'm puzzled because I can't think of anything she's been buying – anything big, I mean, like a birthday present. It is strange.

142

However, I finish what I have to do and leave the bedroom, deciding, as I go to see to my own room, that I must try to get to the bottom of this, even if it means asking Becky a direct question or two.

She comes home from school, still looking pale and worried, not talking, but I wait until we're having tea before I say anything. We're having an early meal because I have the PCC meeting at the Vicarage that evening.

'So what are we going to do about this pocket money business?' I ask. 'I'd like to give you more but it's difficult. Two pounds fifty a week is the most I can manage.'

'Everybody I know gets more than that,' Becky says.

'How do you know?' I ask.

'Well they did in Clipton. No-one got less than three pounds and some of them a lot more. I expect this lot get more still!'

'Maybe their parents earn more,' I suggest, refraining from saying that most of them have two parents, both working. She doesn't need to be reminded of that. 'You know the clergy aren't highly paid. But you've always managed your pocket money very well; in fact I've been proud of you.'

She doesn't answer. How, I wonder, am I to get around to the question really in my mind: why is the box empty?

'For now, I might be able to let you have a little in advance,' I say. Then I put the direct question. 'How much money do you have left?'

She looks straight at me, and I at her, and I know she is reading me like a book. Then she jumps to her feet and screams at me.

'You've been looking in my money box! You have, haven't you? I can tell! That's terrible! It's foul! How dare you look at my private things? I suppose you've gone through my drawers as well?'

'I've done no such thing. And I have not opened your money box. I picked it up because I was dusting the dressing-table. I didn't need to open it, I could tell it was empty.' I speak as calmly as I can.

'You've got no right! You've got no business! What's it got to do with you?'

'Only that you've run out of money and you want me to help you out. I simply wondered why you'd run out. It's not at all like you.'

She hesitates for a moment, then says: 'I spent it when I was in Clipton with Grandma and Granddad. It's mine to do what I like with. That's when I spent it. And that's the truth and I hope you're satisfied!'

I'm not satisfied because I know it isn't the truth. No way would my mother let Becky spend her own pocket money. She takes the utmost pleasure in paying for everything. I've remonstrated with her more than once and she always has the same reply. 'Don't deny me, Venus! After all, she's my only grandchild!' and then I'm the one who feels guilty.

And then I am saved from thinking what to say next because Becky rushes out of the room and thunders up the stairs. My daughter could take a Master's degree in rushing out of rooms.

In contrast to that, the Friday evening PCC meeting seemed like a holiday, though Becky wasn't happy about it.

'I shall go to bed,' she says. 'I'm not staying around to talk to people. *Church* people,' she adds scathingly. 'And if they ask me stupid questions like, "And how do you like Thurston?" I shall tell them!'

'You can please yourself about going to bed,' I say. 'But don't even consider being rude to anyone visiting this house! Ever.'

But because I'm sorry for her, and I'm not keen on her being on her own all evening, undoubtedly moping, I move the small portable television from my bedroom into hers. She was actually and visibly pleased about this, the first light in the darkness for some time, so I think I shall leave it there permanently, though I shall have to put strict limits on how late she watches. I don't know why I haven't given it to her before now. It was bought for Philip when the time came that he had to spend a lot of hours in bed. I seldom watched it there myself, though in the months after Philip died I would be glued to it until the early hours of every morning simply because it gave me the illusion of bringing other people into the room. I hate sleeping alone, but now I

144

prefer to read a book, with Classic FM on the radio, until I fall asleep.

So on Friday evening Becky is up there watching 'Top of the Pops' before anyone arrives, which I know would be followed by 'EastEnders' and then switched over to Channel Four for 'Brookside'. But she will be temporarily happy, my little girl, and even temporary happiness is not to be sneezed at.

They arrive, sixteen members of the PCC, almost in one great rush. I serve them coffee and biscuits and then, after twenty minutes or so of chit-chat, we set to work. The agenda is short – the Sunday School and how to attract more teachers to it, the churchyard, the photocopier which is on the blink again and actually needs replacing by a more up-to-date one, and the inevitable gloomy report on the state of our finances from the Treasurer, which hits on the head all thoughts of a new photocopier. And then it is my turn to bring up the subject of the Tuesday evening Eucharist.

There's a bit of a murmur when I mention cutting it out, but only from one or two people.

'But it's been going a long time,' says a woman I know to be named Mrs Nathan. (I'm gradually getting to know people's names.) 'We're used to it.'

'Well, Mrs Nathan, we wouldn't be so much cutting it out as changing the time. I do propose a Tuesday morning service in its place,' I point out. 'That might suit you even better. Actually, I hadn't realized you came to the Tuesday evening.'

'Oh, I don't!' she says brightly. 'Tuesday is my bridge night, always has been. It's just that, as I say, the Tuesday evening's been going a long time now. It's sort of established. St Mary's is an old, established church, and people don't like change, do they?' She speaks kindly, as if to someone who doesn't know much about human nature.

'Indeed they do *not*, Mrs Nathan! I agree with you there!'

She looks gratified, but I haven't quite finished.

'As you rightly say, St Mary's is a very old church. I've been reading its history. Most interesting! Did you know – I expect you all did – that when it was first built there were no pews, not for a long time? People had to stand – except for the old and

145

infirm, there were a few benches around the walls for them. And it was lit only by candles for – oh, I don't know how long! Years and years! But I'm sure you know all that, and isn't it interesting to worship in a church with so much history . . .'

I know what I'm going to say next but Henry Nugent, who from now on I shall call the Blessed Henry, sees the way the wind is blowing and comes to my rescue.

'Yes, isn't it?' he says. 'And isn't it as well people made changes or we'd still be standing through the services, and groping about in candlelight! I believe there was a lot of opposition to putting electric lighting in the church – not to mention central heating!'

The Blessed Henry is well liked and much respected – I've discovered that – so people take notice of what he says and there is a lot of nodding of heads in agreement. As for me, I'd like to give him a big hug!

After that the dissension about Tuesday evenings fades away and it is agreed we should try the new time, so while acceptance is in the air I weigh in quickly with my ideas about baptisms, that they should take place in the middle of the ten o'clock Sunday Eucharist. There are a few uneasy looks, a bit of shifting in seats.

'But will people *like* it?' someone asks. I didn't know her name.

Richard Proctor speaks up. (Bless his little cotton socks, too!)

'They might well *prefer* it,' he says. 'Given time to get used to it. It sounds interesting, having the congregation take part. After all, we're not just giving the baby a name, are we? We're welcoming it into the church family. And if people don't like it then they're sure to say so. I've found people always ready to complain if there's something they don't like.'

'Anyway, it wouldn't be set in stone,' I say. 'If we try it and it's not quite right we can adapt it until it is.'

'We mustn't be afraid to try changes,' Henry says. Good old Henry!

'But what about babies crying in the middle of the service?' someone else says. 'Won't that be disturbing? And they will, won't they?'

'Oh, sure to!' I agree. 'So would I if someone poured water over my head three times in quick succession!'

'When a baby cries,' pipes up Miss Tordoff, Spinster of this Parish and our representative on the Deanery Synod, 'it's like a little prayer going straight up to God in heaven!'

True, I think – but there speaks a lady who has never been kept awake half the night by a squalling infant.

So you could say this part of my Friday evening is OK – I keep back my ideas on a music group and some new hymns for another time.

On Saturday morning after breakfast I go straight to my desk and write letters to the four people who are regulars at the Tuesday evening Eucharist. I want to announce it in church on Sunday and I think it only fair that they should know before then. The Blessed Henry knows who they are: the man is Herbert Butler, a retired school teacher; the two women in addition to Miss Frazer are a Mrs Ellen Kennedy and a Mrs Jane Morton, both widowed, both retired, though I don't know from what unless it was being wives. I don't think I would ever have wanted to retire from being a wife, and perhaps they hadn't either.

I phone Henry.

'If you know their addresses, then I'll deliver the letters myself,' I say to Henry.

'I do know them,' he replies. 'In any case they're on the electoral roll. But no need for you to deliver them. I'll do that.'

You can see why he's the Blessed Henry! Considering he didn't want a woman priest here, he's being very nice to me.

'That would be great!' I tell him. 'I do really want to go into Brampton for one or two things, including a couple of books I need to read before I sort out what I want to do for Advent.' In any case I don't fancy walking up Miss Frazer's path – though more likely she has a drive, not a path – in case she sets the dogs on me.

So by half-past ten he's been and gone and I'm ready to leave.

'I do wish you'd come with me!' I say to Becky. 'I'm happy to wait until you've finished your breakfast and got dressed.' She's only been up a few minutes. 'We could have a good look at the shops, any shops you like, and perhaps have some lunch. It would make a change for both of us.'

147

'I've told you, I'm not going!' she says. 'I hate Brampton!'

'No you don't!' I contradict. 'You enjoyed it when you went with Gran and Grandpa!'

She makes no reply to that, simply goes on eating her corn-flakes. It doesn't need to be said. She doesn't want to go with me.

'So shall you go out?' I wanted to know.

'I don't know what I'll do!'

'Well, don't go beyond the village. And make sure you lock the door and take your key with you.' I wonder if I should cancel my plans but I really need the books. I also wanted to go to Marks & Spencer's for some new underwear. When I looked in my knicker drawer yesterday morning I thought how disgustingly tatty every-thing looked. The white ones looked a sort of tired grey, the black ones were no longer deepest black, as if old age and long service had faded their strength, and all the lacy bits on every-thing looked as if they were about to fray. Philip wouldn't have approved of that. Nor would I have a year or two ago, but who cares about my underwear now?

'I shan't be long,' I say. 'Is there anything you'd like me to bring you?'

'No! And will you stop treating me like a baby?' Becky demands.

I would, I think, if you'd stop behaving like one. But she *is* my baby, and she's troubled, and I don't know how to help her because she's shutting me out. I just wish she had a friend she'd talk to.

'I'm taking my mobile with me,' I say. 'And I haven't switched the Vicarage phone through to it so you can get me if you want me for anything. Anything at all.'

She doesn't answer.

Nothing further goes wrong on Saturday. I find the books I wanted. I also buy extravagantly in Marks & Spencer's, not only lots of lovely underwear, but knee-high socks which are ideal under my cassock or trousers, and much easier than tights. And also several delicious-looking things from the food department including – for Becky's sake I tell myself, though I like them

148

every bit as much as she does – a couple of sherry cream trifles. I can't say they do a lot to lighten the atmosphere when we come to eat them: they don't, but we manage to keep a sort of truce. You can't argue while eating cream trifle.

And now it's Sunday. Sunday is the day I look forward to, and it never lets me down, but I don't feel like that today. I waken already dreading it. I'd heard nothing of Miss Frazer's progress from anyone. Henry phoned me to say he'd delivered the letters but not set eyes on any of the recipients. No news, I try to tell myself, is good news – but if I were to be honest I know my good news would be that she was still unwell and wouldn't be able to make it to church. But I can't pray to the Lord for that, can I? I can't even allow myself, deep down in my cowardly heart, to hope for it. 'Prayer . . .' I once read in some magazine or other which printed little moral sayings whenever there was a bit of space at the bottom of a page . . . 'Prayer is the heart's sincere desire, uttered or unexpressed.' So where does that leave me?

The eight o'clock goes well; I have the feeling it always will. Nothing exciting, nothing demanding, but no trouble, no trouble at all. Afterwards I hurry back to the Vicarage and do what I'd planned to do. A cooked breakfast: bacon, scrambled eggs and hash browns.

'I hope this suits you,' I say to Becky. 'We'll have this more often.'

She doesn't answer, but she eats steadily through it, leaving a plate as clean as a whistle.

'And now we'll have to get a move on or we'll be late for church,' I tell her.

'I don't want to go to church!' Becky says.

I stand quite still. I am clearing the table and my hands are full with dishes. If this has to be another battle, then it is one I'm not going to lose!

'That won't do,' I say. 'We are both going to church!'

'I won't go!' Becky says.

'Becky,' I said, 'over the last week you have been impossible! I've bent over backwards to please you. I think now it's your turn to please me. Get ready for church.'

I'm entirely sure, at this moment, why I'm being so insistent.

149

Did it really matter if she doesn't go to church? But somehow I think it does, and not just so that I can win the battle, much more because I know she's unhappy. I know there have been many times when I've rebelled against going to church, for a variety of reasons and sometimes for no reason at all. And not just when I was a child. Oh dear, no! Even since I've been ordained I've occasionally felt like that. Somehow, though, I've dragged myself there – and the miracle is that by the time I've gone through it, reached the last hymn, I've been healed. And other people have said the same thing to me about themselves.

I'm not totally certain what my motive for Becky is at this minute, whether to make her do it because she'd feel better in the end, or whether I'm just using an adult's power over a child.

'Please, Becky,' I plead.

'You can't make me!' she says.

'If you mean I can't physically drag you there, kicking and screaming, you're right. Though of course I could say if you can't please me in this, then I can move my television back into my room!' I tell her.

And then I hear myself and realize how horrid I sound. This is *really* using power! I also see Becky's expression change and I know I could win this one – the television is a great draw – but I won't do so.

'However, I won't do that!' I say. 'The television is yours. Moreover I will change my mind. If you don't want to go to church then I won't try to make you.'

So I don't. And I walk there on my own, heavy-hearted.

A little later I realize my unexpressed prayer is not to be answered, or maybe God is answering with a firm, 'No, Venus! How can you be so mean to a sick old lady?' Whatever. Miss Frazer has recovered sufficiently to be in church. I am not in the porch when she arrives so the first I see of her is when I am standing at the front, facing everyone, ready to take the service. She looks much as ever to me, though perhaps a little pale, tight-lipped, but what's new?

The service progresses; no hitch, no hold-ups. The hymns, the readings, the Gospel, the sermon. Standing there in the pulpit I reckon there are about the same number of people in church as on the previous Sunday, I don't seem to have lost anyone, or gained for that matter, but gains, if there are to be any, come slowly. Anyway, I chide myself, I shouldn't be thinking in terms of numbers, though it's my bet that most parish priests do so, even if not first and foremost. And even if we didn't, the media would rush to tell us, especially if the numbers were going down. That, and the misdemeanours of clergy, churchwardens, Sunday School teachers, are always good for a headline on an inside page.

Then, after the prayers and the consecration, I stand in front of the altar, ready to give communion, and I watch the congregation moving towards me in single file to kneel at the altar rail. Always a wonderful moment. Miss Frazer is amongst them. She drops to her knees halfway along the row – stiffly, she is obviously arthritic – and as I approach her, and see her cupped hands held high to receive the bread, I feel a sudden surge of happiness at the sight. God is good, I think. Praise the Lord!

'The body of Christ!' I say, making a slight move to place the bread in her hands.

At the very last second, before I can do so, and with a sweeping, circular motion, as if it's a movement in a dance routine, she waves her hands through the air and places them behind her back.

My spirits, which seconds before had soared, dive. I almost cry out but instead I take a deep breath and move along the line. Then I go back to the beginning of the rail and offer the chalice to each person in turn. Miss Frazer, whose hands are now in front of her again, as if ready to receive, closes her mouth firmly, shakes her head from side to side, and gives a repeat performance with her hands. I draw the chalice back, holding it out of harm's way, I continue smoothly along the line as if what she had done had hardly touched me.

The people on either side of her at the altar rail are well aware of what she did. How could they be otherwise since her sweeping movements threatened to knock their heads off? The people standing in line to take their places at the altar rail also witness this drama, as of course they were intended to. But except for the words which I speak quietly as I move along the line there is no

151

sound. No gasps, not even a sharp intake of breath. It was a performance entirely in mime, and no less dramatic for that.

I cannot tell you what this does to me. My heart is thumping. My whole body is shaking and I hold on firmly to the chalice trying to steady myself, trying desperately hard not to be filled with anger because this is neither the time nor the place for anger. If there is to be anger it will have to come later. So I continue with what I have to do, what it is my privilege to do, until everyone has been served and returned to their places, and somehow I get on with the rest of the service until the end when, facing the congregation, I give the blessing, reminding myself as I say the words that Miss Frazer must be included in this. It's God's blessing, not mine. It is also God whom she has slapped in the face; my God and her God, though she probably thinks I am the culprit. She has personalized God in the priest.

I give out the notices.

'There will be the usual meeting of the Bible class on Thursday morning at eleven a.m. in the parish hall.

'The Women's Group meets Wednesday evening when Mr Fallow will speak about his travels in the Alps. I am told he has some wonderful slides!

'Will those of you who so kindly deliver parish magazines every month please pick up your copies from the parish office on your way out.

'And on Tuesday we are experimenting with a change of service time. The eight p.m. Eucharist will, from now on, be moved to ten o'clock on Tuesday mornings. This has been agreed by the PCC and we hope, especially now that the dark evenings are here and the cold weather lies ahead, that those who attend this service will find the new time much more convenient.'

There! I think, I've got that out, and not a murmur! Probably no-one is the least bit interested, for there is no sign of the Tuesday-nighters, except Miss Frazer, who will already know all about it because she's had the letter.

I have no hope of escaping her as she leaves. I don't know whether I should say anything, or nothing at all, about the morning's episode. What *can* I say? The truth is, I don't know.

So I decide I will leave it to her. She will have no difficulty in finding the words, though what further words are needed on her part? Her actions have said it all.

Or one would have thought so, but this woman does not miss a trick.

She stands in the middle of the people who are leaving, some of them shaking me by the hand, some giving me a smile, some saying nothing at all, not meeting my eyes.

'Do not think,' she says in a voice which would cut steel at twenty paces, 'do not think that you will get away with this, Mrs Stanton, you so-called Vicar! You will not! I shall take whatever steps are necessary! Indeed, I have already taken steps!' With which she sweeps out of the door and limps away down the path.

I stand in my place at the door until everyone has left. I desperately need to be on my own and I go and sit in the Lady Chapel. I know I can't stay there long because I must put in an appearance at coffee, so after a few minutes I stand up again. I have stopped trembling, I square my shoulders, hold up my head and walk across to the parish hall. I don't know what, if anything, will happen, but I'm ready for it.

In the hall, people are sitting or standing around in groups, but then they usually are, that's nothing new. Nearest to the door there are half-a-dozen or so people at a table and a few more standing nearby. I do detect a slight falling off of their conversation as I approach, but then Walter Brown jumps to his feet, saying, 'Sit here, Vicar. I'll get you a coffee.'

I take his seat.

'Disgraceful!' Carla Brown says. 'Totally disgraceful! No point in pretending we're not talking about it, Venus, because we are! Some of us saw it all, and I reckon those who didn't have been informed. But we're on your side. That Frazer woman should be banned!'

There is a general murmur of agreement. Walter brings my coffee. 'Thank you!' I say to him, and then I say the same words to the rest of the group. 'I can't tell you how grateful I am for your support.'

'You have it,' Walter Brown says, 'but all the same I reckon

153

you should watch your back. Most people are going to be on your side, but not all. There'll be a few . . .'

'I'm prepared for that,' I say. 'I was long before I came to St Mary's. It happens. It's not going to get me down, I promise you – but most of all I don't want it to harm the congregation. I shall carry on as normal and I hope we all will. That would be the best thing we could all do.'

'I agree,' a woman says. 'But what if she does it again?'

'We'll face it when it happens!' I say.

'I suppose there's one in every church. A Miss Frazer, I mean,' Walter says.

He's probably right.

'I must go and have a word with the churchwardens,' I say. 'Please excuse me!'

I make a move to leave, and then I stop again.

'There *is* one thing you can all do,' I tell them.

'Done as soon as asked!' Carla says. I get the feeling she's bursting to go into battle – not what I want.

'So what is it?' someone asks.

'Pray!' I tell them.

THIRTEEN

On Monday morning when I go into Becky's room to waken her she is curled round in the bed with the duvet pulled up, leaving only the top of her head showing.

'Time to get up, darling!' I cry.

She emerges slowly, only her forehead and eyes revealed.

'I feel poorly,' she says in a weak, strained voice.

'Oh dear,' I sympathize. 'In what way poorly, sweetheart? You were all right when you went to bed last night, weren't you? You didn't say anything.'

'I was all right then,' she says. 'Now I have a headache and I feel sick!'

'When did it start?' I ask. 'Was it during the night? You should have wakened me.' I put my hand on her forehead. 'You don't feel as if you have a temperature, but I'll take it just in case.'

I fetch the thermometer from the bathroom cupboard.

'Well dear, your temperature's normal,' I tell her. 'Thirty-seven.'

'It can't be,' Becky protests. 'There must be something wrong with the thermometer. I tell you, I feel awful! *And* I've got stomach ache.' She pulls the duvet half over her head again.

'When did that start?' I ask.

'A few minutes ago,' Becky says. 'It's awful!'

'Oh, I *am* sorry, darling!' I say. 'Then you'd better stay right where you are. I'll bring you a drink of hot milk, or some juice. Which would you like? Or a cup of tea?'

'A cup of tea,' she says weakly. 'And some toast with Marmite.'

I nod. 'And I'll fill a hot water bottle. It'll help your stomach ache. I won't be long!'

Fifteen minutes later I take her tea and toast and the hot water bottle. She sits up in bed and I stay with her while she eats her breakfast.

'Do you feel better for that?' I ask, taking away her tray, shaking up her pillow.

'A little bit,' she admits. 'Just a little bit!'

'I'll ring the school secretary in a while,' I say. 'Tell her you won't be in today.'

'And perhaps not tomorrow,' she says in a weary voice.

'Oh, I expect you'll be all right by tomorrow,' I say cheerfully. 'We'll see! And I'm sorry, but I have to go out later. I have a funeral at half-past ten. Will you be all right?'

'I expect so,' she says. Then she turns away from me and snuggles down again under the duvet.

At half-past eight I ring the school.

'I don't think it's anything much,' I tell the secretary. 'But I'm keeping her in bed, just in case. And if it is a bug you don't want it spreading around the school, do you?'

'We certainly don't!' she agrees. 'Though there's no sign of anything at the moment, nor was there last week. I hope she'll soon be better.'

I look in on Becky to tell her I've rung the school but she appears to be asleep; at any rate I say her name and she doesn't answer, so it's a good time to say my Office. Like all priests, monks and nuns, and some lay people, I do this morning and evening every day. Prayers, a Bible reading, the psalm appointed for the day. It's as regular as brushing my teeth, though I hope not as mechanical, and I can do it almost anywhere, and indeed have. I can do it on a crowded train, on the bus. (I don't do it when I'm driving because I'd be a danger to the public. An even worse one than usual, Philip used to say.) I can do it in church, in the house or the garden; walking, sitting, kneeling, lying down.

156

It might sound like a chore but it never feels like one, partly because I know that I'm doing it in the company of others, everywhere, all around the world, even if not necessarily at that exact moment. So I go into my study and close the door behind me.

After that I get through a few chores in the house: change my bed, put on a wash, vacuum around the ground floor and then it's time to leave for Ronnie Leigh's funeral. I look in on Becky again but she's still asleep, so I write a note and leave it on her bedside table.

I spoke with the churchwardens before I left the hall yesterday. They hadn't seen the Frazer incident but they'd been told about it the moment they reached the hall. They were appalled, of course, but not all that surprised.

'She's been making her views known up and down the place since the minute she knew you were coming,' Henry said.

'The thing is,' Richard said, 'she's an influential woman.'

'Not quite as much as she thinks she is,' Henry put in. 'Financially, maybe. Not necessarily otherwise. She's just bossy!'

Richard shook his head.

'There are two or three people who'd follow her lead. We should watch out for them.'

'Well you do that,' I said. 'For the moment I'm going to wait and see what happens. When and if I think it's necessary, then I *will* do something. And don't worry that you think she's upset me. I can cope. I'm more upset at what she's done to God – but it won't be a first time for him, will it? He'll know how to deal with it.'

The funeral this morning goes according to plan, in fact it goes well, and one can say that of a funeral even though it's a sad occasion. There's a satisfaction in doing everything properly, giving the one who's died a good, and preferably loving, send-off. There are about twenty people present. Sometimes there might be fewer than half-a-dozen, which always saddens me, especially when it comes to a handful of people struggling to sing the hymns. 'Abide with Me' on the football terraces it is not!

Afterwards, standing around the grave in the bright autumn sunshine, Mrs Leigh introduces me to some of the mourners:

two men from the Thurston bowls club, one from the snooker club and a man who had been a colleague of Ronnie's before they both retired from working for Brampton Council. And Marilyn's husband, Brendan, of course.

'Little Garth wanted to come,' Mrs Leigh says. 'He's very upset about his grandpa, but Marilyn didn't want him to.'

'He's only seven,' Marilyn protests. 'I think he's too young to come to a funeral, even if it is his grandpa's! But Brendan doesn't agree with me.'

And I agree with Brendan, but this isn't the time, and perhaps it's not my place, to say so, but if she'd spoken about it earlier I'd have said that I think it's right for a child to be at a grandparent's funeral. Children accept more than we give them credit for. They also like to see things concluded, not just to feel that someone they love has vanished into thin air. But no way will I say that at this point.

'We've got refreshments back at the house,' Mrs Leigh says. 'We'd be very pleased if you'd join us, Vicar.'

'Thank you. That's very kind,' I reply. 'I won't, if you don't mind. My little girl's not well. I've left her in bed so I'd like to get back.'

'Oh,' Mrs Leigh says, 'I didn't know you had a daughter!'

That doesn't surprise me. A lot of people think the clergy, of either sex, live on another planet.

'Oh yes,' I say. 'Becky. She's ten. So I'll be getting along, if you'll excuse me.'

As a matter of fact, though I'm often invited, I tend not to go back to the house after a funeral. I think this is a time for family and friends to be together; to reminisce or – if there's been too much sherry flowing – to bring up old grievances. Where there's a will there's a quarrel. At any rate it's not the place for a stranger, which in this case is what I am; quite unknown to any of them in Ronnie Leigh's lifetime and probably unlikely to see any of them again.

'But don't forget, Mrs Leigh,' I say, 'if you want me for anything at all, even just for a chat, give me a ring and I'll be round!' I feel sorry for her. The whole thing will hit her much harder than it's doing at this moment.

Passing the church on my way back to the Vicarage I notice the door is open so I pop in to see who's there, and why. Sitting in a pew near to the back is a middle-aged man, deep in a book, which he puts down as soon as he sees me, as if I've caught him in some nefarious act.

'You must be the new Vicar,' he says – which is an easy assumption since I'm wearing my cassock. 'I'm Cyril Henfield. You won't know me because I don't come to church but I've been a voluntary verger for a few years now.'

'Then that's very good of you,' I congratulate him. And I mean it, though I'm intrigued yet again by these kind souls who would never come to a service here yet will give up several hours a month to do what would seem to be a boring job, presumably because of their love for the building. People are so attached to bricks and mortar – or, in this case, Caen stone. One day I shall ask one of them why.

'Have you had many people in?' I ask him.

'Not a single one!' he says cheerfully. 'But it's Monday morning. Not a busy time. That's why I was reading.'

Which he could presumably have done in greater comfort at home, I think.

'Well I won't stay, Mr Henfield,' I say. 'I just popped in to see if everything was all right. However, I can see the church is in good hands!'

When I arrive home – and I notice I'm beginning to think of it as home, even though it has hardly been a place of peace and harmony since we arrived – Becky is downstairs, in her dressing-gown, and watching television.

'Good gracious!' I say. 'You must be feeling better!'

'Not really,' she says wanly. 'It's just that I was bored.'

'But you have television in your room now,' I say. 'Why aren't you watching it there, keeping warm in bed?'

She sighs deeply.

'*Because*,' she says, as one speaking to an idiot, 'this one has cable and the one in my bedroom doesn't. Everyone knows all the best programmes are on cable. Who wants to watch BBC in the morning?'

For this I have given up my television!

'*Everyone* has cable in *every* room,' she informs me.

On Tuesday morning it's much the same. The same story from Becky. 'I still feel sick. I've been awake with stomach ache quite a lot in the night. I *definitely* can't go to school!'

I'm a bit uneasy about this. I looked in on her once or twice in the night and she was sound asleep, her bed covers as smooth as if she'd never stirred. But I'll give her the benefit of the doubt – for the moment.

'I'm sorry you don't feel better,' I commiserate. 'I'll ring the school, but I think I'd better take you to see Doctor Leyton when I get back from the Eucharist. If you wrap up well and we go in the car you won't come to any harm.'

'I don't want to see the doctor,' she grumbles. 'I'd be much better staying in bed. I expect I'll feel a bit better later.'

I'm sure you will, I think uneasily. Most likely when it's too late to go to school. I'm no longer worried about her physical symptoms, if indeed she has any, but I am concerned about this school business though I don't see how Sonia can solve that. So perhaps I'm the patient; simply wanting to share my problem? Either way, I shall ask Sonia to take a look at Becky. One can take children without making a previous appointment.

The ten o'clock service goes well enough. I am pleased to see that the three usuals from the Tuesday evening service are there, and I'm happy that since I know who they are I can address them by name as they leave. Mesdames Morton and Kennedy both give me a nod; Mr Butler offers me a wintry smile. There is also another lady, who on the way out introduces herself as Nora Whitfield. 'I would have come before,' she tells me, 'if it had been in the morning, but I don't go out much in the evenings.' So one gain, one satisfied customer. Miss Frazer isn't there and I don't know whether to be pleased or worried about that. Pleased in a way that she's not upsetting anyone else, but also slightly apprehensive, wondering why she's losing this opportunity of humiliating me.

As I walk down the path on my way back to the Vicarage Mrs Leigh is walking up towards me. 'Good-morning, Vicar,' she says in a quiet voice. 'I'm just going up to the grave to look at the

160

flowers. I didn't seem to get a chance yesterday. There were some lovely flowers.'

'There were indeed,' I agree. 'And how are you today?'

'Mustn't grumble,' she replies. I get the feeling that that's a phrase by which she lives her life. 'Was your daughter all right?' she asks.

'She's not a hundred per cent,' I tell her. 'I'm off to pick her up now to take her to the doctor.'

When Becky and I reach the surgery it's to be told that Doctor Leyton isn't available.

'She's been called out to an emergency,' the receptionist says. 'She mightn't be all that long, but who knows? Doctor Baines could see you if you don't mind waiting.'

'We could come tomorrow morning,' Becky chips in.

'No!' I decide. 'Now that we're here we'll wait to see Doctor Baines.' I know what's in Becky's mind. Stretch it out until tomorrow and that could be another day off school.

We wait twenty minutes and then it's our turn. Nigel Baines rises to his feet and smiles at us as we walk in. His smile is not just a twitch of the lips, it's one of those which takes up the whole face.

'Hello Venus!' he says. 'How are you?'

'I'm fine!' I say. 'It's Becky who's a bit under the weather.'

'I'm sorry to hear that, Becky,' he says. 'Supposing you tell me about it?'

Becky reels off her symptoms: headache, feeling sick, stomach ache. 'And I feel all hot,' she adds.

'Ah! Well, first of all I'll take your temperature,' he says – and does so.

'You'll be pleased to hear that that's quite normal!' he announces.

She is not at all pleased, but no way can she argue that the doctor must be wrong. He is not her mother.

He feels her pulse, peers down her throat, listens to her chest, nodding each time. 'No rash,' he says. 'Now tell me, whereabouts was this stomach ache?'

She looks a mite disconcerted. 'In my stomach,' she says.

161

'Sure!' he says pleasantly. 'Silly of me! So can you just point to where it was?'

She applies a finger vaguely to the middle of her abdomen. 'But really it was all over.'

'I see,' he says. Then he looks at her quite intently for a few seconds, and she looks steadily back at him, eyeball to eyeball.

'Very interesting,' he says. 'And I'll tell you what I'm going to do. I'm going to let you have a turn at being the doctor. *You* know how you feel. What do *you* think would make you feel better?' He looks at me. 'Sometimes,' he says in a serious voice, 'the patient knows the answer better than the doctor.'

It's her turn to hesitate. Then she says, 'Well, I think if I didn't have to go to school . . .'

He nods, considering her remedy carefully.

'I see,' he says. 'Now let's think. Tomorrow's . . . what?'

'Wednesday,' Becky answers.

'Wednesday. And on Friday half-term starts. That's a week off school, isn't it?'

Becky nods agreement.

'And what are you going to do at half-term?'

'I'm going to stay with my grandparents,' she says.

'Great,' Nigel says. 'I expect you'll enjoy that!'

She frowns. 'I wish I was going there for good!'

'Really?' He knows better than to ask why. Then he says, 'Well, I think it would be a good idea if you were to have the rest of today off school, and then go back tomorrow until Friday. I don't think it would do you any harm, and then you'll have a lovely week with your grandparents to get better. I expect they'll spoil you rotten, but no matter.'

She is a deeply disappointed girl. I could tell she thought everything was going her way, and now he's let her down.

'Have a good time,' he says. 'Perhaps I'll see you again when you get back, though I expect you'll be better before then.'

He walks to the door and holds it open for us to leave. Becky goes in front of me. He puts his hand on my shoulder and says, 'Be seeing you soon, Venus!'

Back at the Vicarage Becky goes straight up to her room, but when an hour later I call her down for lunch she comes down

162

and eats, though not quite as well as usual. When she gets up from the table she says, 'I'm going for a walk, down to the village.'

'A good idea!' I say. 'I'll come with you. I need a few things.'

She turns on me like a tiger.

'I don't want you to go with me!' she shouts. 'I want to go on my own! Why can't I go on my own? I'm not a baby!'

I raise my hands in the air. 'OK! OK!' I say. 'You do that! Have it your own way!'

While Becky is out there's a phone call from Elsie Jones.

'I met you at coffee a couple of Sundays ago,' she reminds me. 'I run the Brownie Guides. I'm sorry I wasn't in church last Sunday, I had visitors staying the weekend. Anyway, you said you'd like to drop in and meet the Brownies, so I thought I'd remind you Tuesday is the day. Do you think you might have time to come in this evening? Five o'clock – and it lasts an hour at the most. We'd be very pleased to see you there!'

I do a bit of quick thinking. I meant it when I told Elsie Jones that I'd visit the Brownies but as things stand at the moment I don't want to leave Becky on her own, though I know that in my job family can't always come first. Indeed, it often has to come last. Becky knows this too, it's something she's had to learn and it's been even harder for her since Philip died. Perhaps she might even ask – which she hasn't done so far, at least not out loud – with whom *does* she come first?

I wonder if, just for once, she'd come with me to Brownies? Not that I have any real hope of that.

'Fine!' I say to Elsie, 'I'll be there. I look forward to it!'

Becky is back within the hour. I hear her let herself in – she knows she must always take her key with her in case I'm out.

'Becky!' I call.

She doesn't answer and then, since my study door is open, I see her walking up the stairs to her room.

'I want a word with you, darling!' I tell her.

She stops halfway up the stairs.

'Just to tell you I'm going to the Brownie meeting. I wondered if you'd like to come with me? It only lasts an hour.'

'No thank YOU!' she says decisively.

163

The Brownies are milling around the hall, lively and bright in their brown jogging pants and yellow sweat shirts, with Brown Owl (alias Elsie Jones, but in her uniform of dark blue pants and sweat shirt looking full of firm but kindly authority). She introduces me to Tawny Owl, her second-in-command, name of Margaret Spratt.

'Nice to meet you,' Margaret says. 'I'm sorry I don't come to church, but I always seem to be busy on Sunday mornings!'

And then Brown Owl calls the little girls to order and they stand in a Brownie Ring around the toadstool in the middle of the hall and sing their Brownie song, which I know by heart – don't forget I'm the mother of a (lapsed) Brownie. When the song is over Brown Owl – in this habitat I find I can only think of her as Brown Owl; Elsie Jones belongs to a different world – introduces me.

'Now this lady – some of you will have seen her before – is our new Vicar, so I think we should give her the Brownie Guide welcome, don't you?'

They nod in unison, then at a signal from Brown Owl they all give me three claps; one above their heads and one to each side, and then we all give the Brownie salute; three middle fingers of the right hand, held at shoulder height.

'And will one of you tell the Vicar what the Brownie promise is?' Brown Owl asks. 'Perhaps you, Julia?'

If Julia doesn't know it I could prompt her.

'Lend a Hand,' she says in a clear voice.

Already my worries and cares have somehow dropped away from me and I have entered their world, a world of goodness and the right goals; of bright, shining innocence. And how long will that last, I'm asking myself cynically? And I'm immediately ashamed of my cynicism. A world which was once also Becky's, and I wish it still was.

The children break up into their Sixes and I wander around, talking to them, asking about what they're doing – which, let me tell you, is just about everything! Painting, clay modelling, writing, making small gifts to take home to their mothers. I end up with the Pixie Six, and I'm sitting beside a pretty girl with shoulder-length blonde hair who tells me her name's Melissa.

'How long have you been a Brownie?' I ask her.

'Five-and-a-half months,' Melissa says. 'I'm seven. Brown Owl says I can start working for my badges soon.'

'So which ones are you going to work for first?' I ask her. Becky has a large collection of badges which it had been my job to sew on to her sash – swimming, first aid, walking, art, and so on.

'House Orderly first,' Melissa says. 'You can do that at home. You have to dust your bedroom and make beds and things. And then dancing, because dancing is what I like best.'

If Becky had stuck to what she did to win the House Orderly badge, if she'd dusted her bedroom, then I wouldn't have found the empty money box, would I? But I don't know whether, in the end, that would have been bad or good.

The hour passes in a flash. We sing the Brownie closing prayer, I thank them for having me, and I go back to my Vicarage. Why does an hour spent with small children leave me feeling that the world is pure gold?

Alas, it's a feeling not to last! I'm back at home, in the kitchen. When I got back from Brownies Becky was downstairs, glued to television. 'I'll tell you what,' I said, 'I'll make a Welsh rarebit and we'll have it on our laps, in front of the TV. Would that suit you?' I know Welsh rarebit is one of her favourite meals.

She nods, which I take to mean thank you Mummy, that will be delightful.

So here I am, and I've no sooner started to grate the cheese than the telephone rings.

'St Mary's Vicarage,' I say. 'Venus Stanton!'

'Good!' a pleasant male voice says at the other end. 'I'm the Bishop's secretary. He'd like a word with you. Would that be convenient?'

'You mean now?'

'If you could.'

'Of course!' One does not say 'No' to one's bishop. What can he want? Is he going to pay St Mary's a visit? I doubt it, but it would be wonderful if he were.

'I'll put you through,' the secretary says.

'Ah, Venus!' the Bishop says. (If I were one of his male priests he'd probably call me 'Father'. As it is, he calls me Venus.) 'Are you well?'

'Very well, thank you, Bishop,' I say. 'I hope you are?'

'Thank you, I am,' he says – and then gets down to business. 'Now I don't want you to be worried,' he says, 'but I've had a letter from a Miss Amelia Frazer. You know her, of course?'

I should have guessed, shouldn't I? 'I have taken steps,' she said, didn't she? I didn't stop to think what steps she might have taken.

'Yes,' I say.

'Well then, you'll know she has a strong aversion to women priests, and that's what this is all about. More about that, I hope and believe, than about you personally.'

I am not too sure about that. I think she probably hates me personally but I can't help that. I don't reply, I wait for him to continue.

'I think we should have a chat, you and I,' he says. 'Much better than me writing to you, don't you think?'

'Whatever you wish, Bishop,' I tell him. I wonder if he's going to summon me to the Bishop's Palace.

But no, he isn't. 'I have to be in your area for a meeting on Friday,' he continues. 'Perhaps I could come and have a cup of tea with you?'

'Certainly!' I say. 'Would you like to tell me . . . ?'

'No,' he interrupts. 'I'm not going to bother you with the contents of the letter on the telephone. We can talk it through on Friday. And please don't worry. I'm sure everything's going to be all right!'

Which is more than I am, though I'm determined not to let it get me down.

'I've never met Miss Frazer,' he says, 'but there are those here who have. I shall have my secretary acknowledge her letter and I'll reply to it later, after I've talked to you. But please don't worry. I rang simply to make a time to see you.'

'Thank you.'

'Otherwise, everything all right at St Mary's?' he asks in a cheerful voice.

'It seems to be,' I tell him. 'I've just got back from Brownies.' Why would he want to know that, for heaven's sake?

'Good! Good!' he replies. 'Well, I'll see you on Friday.'

How can he ask if everything's all right when he's got a letter from Miss Frazer in front of him? But 'otherwise' he said, didn't he? And otherwise it is, at least churchwise. I doubt the Bishop is the one to talk to about my daughter.

I sit down for two minutes, to think, then I continue with the rarebit. It looks good when I serve it but neither Becky nor I eat much of it.

FOURTEEN

It's Wednesday morning and I'm seeing Becky off to school. To say she is unwilling is a total understatement.

'I think it's cruel of you to send me to school when you know I'm not well!' she storms. 'You're doing it just to get me out of the way!'

'I'm doing no such thing,' I say as calmly as I can. 'Why would I want you out of the way? You know Doctor Baines said you were well enough to go to school and I happen to agree with him. You can't stay off school just on a whim.'

But it isn't a whim, and I don't know what it is but I shall have to get to the bottom of it, though now is not the moment. We have to have a long talk – that is if Becky will take part in a long talk, if she'll confide in me, which she shows no sign of doing. When she comes home this afternoon we absolutely must try to sort it out.

I move to give her my usual good-bye kiss but she turns away and rushes out of the house. I stand at the window and watch her walk down the road.

Of course Becky is my chief concern but I have to admit that the Bishop's call is nagging at me, even though he sounded quite kind and has told me not to worry. But how can I help worrying? Who knows what Miss Frazer has said? And I can be sure, can't I, that she's slanted everything in her own favour and I'm the villain of the piece. I reckon she has influence, partly because she's been here so long and done so much, but also because of her financial contribution. No church, no diocese, can afford to sneeze at substantial financial support. They are all worried about money. Sometimes I get the feeling that it's the most important thing on everyone's mind. I wish I knew what line the Bishop was going to take. Will he reprimand me severely? But Miss Frazer was the prime mover, wasn't she? I just wish I didn't have to wait until Friday afternoon to see him.

Should I ever have come to Thurston, I ask myself? After all, they didn't really want me, I wasn't what they'd have preferred and I was well aware of that. But what else could I have done? There was no other opportunity for me in this diocese and I wouldn't have been in the front running in any other diocese. When it came to the crunch it was a straight choice between remaining at Holy Trinity and coming to St Mary's, Thurston. Perhaps I should have stayed put, not uprooted Becky from her friends, her school, her grandparents? I did think about it, long and hard. I did pray, I did ask the Holy Spirit to guide me, I did think in the end that I had the right answers. So here I am, and there's no going back on it.

But wait a minute, I don't want to go back on it! Here I am, and here I will stay, as long as need be! So pull yourself together, girl, I tell myself. Stop whinging! Get on with the job.

And it's in that new, fighting mood I decide I'll actually walk along to the church to say my Office. Saying it right here in the kitchen would be every bit as valid but I have this feeling I want to do it in the church. So off I go, taking my burdens with me but ready to cast them off.

I feel lighter after that. My problems are unchanged. The Bishop is probably going to give me a wigging, Becky is still bloody, but who said it was all going to be easy? No-one. I go into the parish office and do some jobs, including my letter for the November issue of the church magazine, and then I go home and I'm back in the Vicarage by noon ready to face whatever's thrown at me. I haven't been there more than ten minutes when the phone rings.

'St Mary's Vicarage,' I say.

'Good-morning, Vicar,' a rather pleasant, deep voice says. 'You won't know me. My name's Bob Chester and I keep the newsagent's in the village. I deliver your newspaper – or rather, one of my lads does.'

I've been in his shop – it's much more than a newsagent's, he sells stationery, a few paperbacks, children's toys, soft drinks, and a large selection of sweets and chocolates. I think he also sells milk, but then several shops in the village sell milk even though it has nothing to do with their trade. No-one need ever go without milk in their tea in Thurston.

'So what can I do for you, Mr Chester?' I ask. A wedding? A baptism? An advertisement in the parish mag? It seems it's none of these things.

'I wanted to talk to you,' he says.

'That's fine,' I tell him. 'My time's yours!'

'Not on the phone,' he says. 'There's people in and out of the shop and I'm short-handed so I have to be on duty myself.'

'So you'd rather come to the Vicarage – or do you want me to come to you later on?' I enquire.

'It would be better to come to the Vicarage,' he says. 'It's half-day closing, I shut up shop at one o'clock, so I could be with you soon after that.'

I agree with that.

'See you then,' he says. 'And don't worry!'

Why do people keep telling me not to worry? I know I've got a few things to worry about, but does it show in my face? And why would Mr Chester tell me not to worry? I don't know him, he doesn't know me. Is it a phrase people in Thurston use to each other, like the ubiquitous 'Take care!'?

At one-fifteen there's a ring at the door and there stands Mr Chester. I remember now having seen him in his shop. He's not very tall, he has a round, pink face – well, he's sort of rounded all over in a rather pleasant way – and he has wispy grey hair which at the moment is all over the place because there's a stormy wind blowing from the south-west.

I take him into my study and we sit in two chairs opposite to each other. Now I can see that he doesn't look a very happy man

170

and I wonder what it's about. It doesn't look like a wedding or a baptism. Could be a wedding with complications? In-laws at each other's throats? An awkward relative ready to throw a spanner in the works? None of that would be new.

'So what can I do for you?' I ask.

At first he seems reluctant to speak, and then he says, 'Well, it's about your daughter, Vicar.'

'My daughter? Becky? What . . .'

'I don't quite know how to put this . . .' he says awkwardly.

'She's at school right now,' I tell him.

'I know. Or I expected she would be. That's why I wanted to see you now, I mean when she wasn't here.'

I haven't the faintest idea what he's talking about, but suddenly I get an uneasy feeling, a horrible feeling, and I don't know why. Mr Chester fidgets in his chair. He doesn't seem sure how to go on – and then in the end he finds his voice.

'I'm afraid your daughter has been stealing from my shop.' He says it quietly, which somehow makes it more real than if he'd shouted it.

'Stealing? Becky stealing? Oh no, Mr Chester, Becky wouldn't steal! She can be all sorts of things, she can be naughty, but she'd never steal! Never!' The words are pouring out of me, my voice raised, and he keeps quiet until, because I don't know what to say next, I come to a stop.

'I know it must be a shock to you, Vicar, but I'm afraid it's true. You see I saw it with my own eyes – and not just once.'

I sit there, staring at him.

'There must be some mistake,' I say in the end. 'What do you think she stole?'

'I don't think, Vicar,' he says. His voice is gentle now. 'She stole chocolate bars.'

'Well, there you are then!' I say quickly. 'It couldn't have been Becky. There's some mix-up here. You see, she doesn't even like chocolate!' That's it, I'm thinking. He's got her mixed up with some other child. It's not Becky at all!

'I'd better tell you the whole story,' he says, sighing. 'I know it's Becky, because when she came into the shop the first couple of times she bought chocolate bars. I didn't know her, and I

171

know most of the children in the village, so I asked her name, like you do. "Becky," she said.' He points to a framed photo on my desk, one I took of her just before we left Clipton. 'That's her, isn't it?'

'Yes it is,' I agree. 'But I still don't understand, Mr Chester. Why would she buy chocolate bars when she doesn't like them? In fact chocolate brings her out in a rash. I would have seen if she'd had a rash. Mothers do.'

'I don't know *why*,' he says. 'But I can assure you she did. I was surprised because they cost around thirty pence each and she was buying two a day. That's a lot of money for a little girl.'

It's the word 'money' which does it, hits me hard. Money! Money box. An empty money box which shouldn't have been empty.

'Go on,' I say. I can hardly get the words out.

He hears the change in my voice. 'Well,' he says, 'for the first few days she bought them, and then after that she bought one and stole one. And then towards the end of last week she began to steal outright. My guess is she'd run out of money. I already had that thought when she bought one and stole the second one and I'm afraid I set up a little trap.'

'A trap? What do you mean?'

'Not for my sake, Vicar. For hers. I just knew she had to be stopped. I have a mirror fixed on the wall in the back room, for when I have to leave the counter. I only have to glance in it to see what's going on in the shop. Oh, I've had it there for years – you wouldn't believe what people try to get away with – and grown-ups quite as much as children. And I deliberately left Becky at the counter while I went out to the back room. So you see I saw her. Twice towards the end of last week, then again yesterday afternoon. She wasn't in on Monday.'

'She didn't go out on Monday. She wasn't well and I kept her at home.' I say it automatically. Everything is falling horribly into place, except *why*? Why would she do this? But there's something about Mr Chester himself, an air of integrity, which makes me believe that he's telling the truth, even if everything, except why, didn't fit so exactly.

I simply continue to look at him. I don't know what to say.

172

'I'm not going to do anything,' he says. 'Nothing at all. I just thought you needed to know. You're the one to deal with it, Vicar, not me. And I'm sure you'll know best how to do that.'

'I'm far from sure that I do, thank you,' I say. 'Of course I'll pay you for the chocolate.'

He dismisses that with a shake of his head.

'No way! A few chocolate bars don't matter. And let me tell you, Vicar, because I know, or I reckon I do, how you must feel, let me tell you that it's not the end of the world. It's not new to me after twenty-five years of selling sweets. It's happened before and it'll happen again.'

'But not to Becky!' I hope.

'No,' Mr Chester says. 'That's why I've told you. And now I'll be getting off, and we'll call it a closed book. I usually go to the wholesaler's on a Wednesday afternoon.'

I can hardly describe how I feel after I've seen him out and I'm left on my own. I feel sick, and my legs are trembling, but it's far worse than that. This is worse than twenty Miss Frazers. I sit down and put my head in my hands, trying to shut everything out, and then I hear the doorbell and somehow I know that it's been ringing a few seconds. I take a deep breath and go to open the door and there, smiling at me, is Nigel Baines.

'I was passing,' he says. 'Well, I was in the neighbourhood, so I thought I'd drop in, if that's all right?'

A few minutes ago I'd have said I didn't want to see anyone in the world, but looking at him I change my mind and realize that right now there's no-one I'd rather see.

We go into the living room. I sit on the sofa and he takes an armchair opposite to me.

'I knew you were upset about Becky,' he begins. 'There wasn't much more I could say in front of her so I thought this might be a good time.'

'You have no idea just how good!' I say. 'But before you go any further let me tell you something about Becky. Something I've found out in the last few minutes – though I'm not sure whether I *should* tell you. Perhaps it should be just between me and her. I don't know what to do!'

'If it will help,' Nigel says, 'then tell me. If you don't want to, then don't. But even if you choose not to tell me I think you have to do something about Becky. She's obviously deeply worried and disturbed. If you can solve it, then that's fine, but it shouldn't be allowed to go on too long, either for your sake or hers.'

So I tell him. I relate everything Mr Chester has said to me, and also about the empty money box, leaving nothing out, and he hears me out without interrupting.

'It's so unlike Becky!' I say at the end. 'Oh, she can be naughty, and awkward – especially since we came to Thurston. But she's always been honest, never told lies – and never, ever, did I think of her as stealing! A thief! My little daughter a thief!'

And then I can't cope with it one second longer and I burst into tears. He sits there, saying nothing, letting me cry my fill. Then when I stop, and I start searching around, unsuccessfully, for a tissue to dry my eyes and blow my nose, he brings out a clean, white, folded handkerchief from his pocket and hands it to me.

'Thank you,' I say, drying my eyes, trying to pull myself together. 'I thought it was only in old films that men took a snowy-white handkerchief from a pocket and handed it to the weeping female.'

He laughs. 'Hollywood to the rescue!' he says.

'Do you always carry a spare handkerchief?' I enquire, giving my nose a good blow.

He doesn't answer that. Instead he says, 'It's something to do with school, isn't it? I think we've both sussed that out.'

'I agree,' I say. 'But I don't know what.'

'Have you had a word with Evelyn Sharp?' he asks.

'No, I didn't want to bother her. I thought I could deal with it. Becky and I had a blip recently because someone told Becky her mother wasn't a proper Vicar, but I thought we'd sorted that out. I don't see how it can be anything to do with that. You might not know, but children of the clergy don't always have an easy time at school. They're expected to know things they don't know, sometimes even teachers expect that of them. They're expected to behave like saints instead of like normal children. And then they blame their parents for being in the job, and they become

174

rebellious. I knew this ages ago. My best friend at school was the daughter of the local Vicar. She was the most rebellious girl in the school, always in trouble of some sort.'

'That doesn't surprise me,' Nigel says.

'So at the moment Becky blames everything on me. It wasn't easy for her when her father died, and now I've made everything worse by moving to Thurston. So I've been asking myself, did I do the right thing, coming here?'

'And what answer did you give yourself?' he wants to know.

'That I did do the right thing. But now I have to talk seriously to Becky, and I intend to do that as soon as she gets home from school.'

Nigel nods agreement. 'And now, what about you? Becky apart, how are you getting on in Thurston?'

He's so easy to talk to that I find myself telling him about Miss Frazer and about the Bishop's impending visit. 'All to do with women priests!' I say. 'I'll get over it. At least you don't have that trouble in your church!'

'Not yet,' he agrees. 'But when the time comes – and I'm one of those who think it will – then we'll have it in spades!' He stands up. 'I'm truly sorry about all this, Venus, and I wish I could stay but I'll have to be off. I've several visits to make.'

'I'm afraid I've talked too much,' I apologize.

'No!' he says. 'And if you want to talk more, any time, give me a ring at home. Or I could come and see you. I'd be happy to.'

I go with him to the door, and I stand there as he walks down the path. Halfway down he turns round. 'I'm glad you *did* come to Thurston!' he says.

Becky will be home in twenty minutes and I'm thinking very hard about what I'll say to her, how I'll make a start on it. Will I say straight out, 'Becky, I know you've been stealing and I want to know why,' or will I say, 'Becky, I know there's something wrong and you've got to tell me what it is!'?

As it turns out, I don't try either of those approaches. She walks into the house looking so white-faced, so unhappy, that any anger there might have been in me fades right away.

'Darling,' I say, 'you look frozen! Are you all right?'

'You know I'm not all right,' she retorts. 'I told you I wasn't but you made me go to school.'

'Well we won't go into that right now,' I tell her. 'I'm going to make a cup of tea and toast some buns and then you and I are going to sit down and have a proper talk.'

She makes a move towards the door.

'And don't bother to go up to your room,' I say. 'I shall simply follow you.'

So I make the tea and she drinks it, and eats a toasted bun, and then I say, 'Now! I have some questions to ask you, darling, and I want the truth. Whatever it is, you're not going to get into trouble. I promise! So now are you going to tell me what all this is about?'

'I don't know what you're talking about!' she says sullenly.

'I think you do, but if not, I'll tell you.'

She says nothing.

'First of all,' I say, 'why have you been stealing chocolate?'

If I thought she was white when she came in from school, she's now three shades paler, and then within seconds she flushes red to the roots of her hair.

'I haven't!' she says. 'Whoever says so is lying!'

'I'm afraid not, Becky. Mr Chester himself told me. He came to see me this afternoon. He saw you do it. You've done it not once, but at least three times, haven't you?'

With that she rushes out of the room and up the stairs, but I follow her immediately and since there are no locks on the bedroom doors she can't shut me out. She flings herself face down on the bed and buries her face in the pillow. I sit on a chair at the side of the bed and stroke her hair, something she's always liked when she's been unhappy.

'Becky,' I say, 'I'm not going to punish you. I don't have that in mind no matter what you've done. I know there's something wrong and I want to help you. You're my daughter and I love you but how can I help you if you won't tell me what it is? Please, Becky!'

Then there's a silence, which probably lasts a minute but feels like ten, after which she says, her voice muffled because she's still face down, 'What will Mr Chester do?'

176

'Mr Chester will do nothing,' I assure her. 'He came to tell me because he thought I ought to know, because he didn't think you were the sort of girl to be stealing for no reason – and I know you're not. So please tell me, Becky!'

She's realizes of course – she's not stupid – that she's just as good as admitted to the stealing, so now we have another starting point.

'It's to do with school, isn't it?' I prompt her. 'That's why you were taking the chocolate. You were giving it to the other girls, to make yourself popular. Was that it?'

At that she sits up quickly and twists around to face me.

'No, it was NOT!' she flares. 'Who would want to be popular with that lot? I hate them! I hate them!'

'Then why?' I ask. 'Why did you do it? And who is "them"?'

'Because they made me. They said I was a goody-goody because I was the Vicar's daughter. I was a namby-pamby. I said I wasn't and they said I had to prove it or they'd find something worse to do.'

'And how had you to prove it?' I ask quietly.

'I had to steal two chocolate bars from Chester's every day for two weeks. I wasn't to miss a single school day or there'd be trouble worse than I could ever imagine.'

I feel the rage rising inside me. I have to take a deep breath and hold myself in check. I've never quite believed anyone who said that children could be downright wicked, but in this moment I do.

'And what would that trouble be?' I enquire.

'They didn't say. They said it would be awful!'

'So what did you do?'

'Well, I had the money I'd been saving in my box so instead of stealing I used that and I didn't tell them I wasn't stealing. It was the stealing part they wanted to make me do, it wasn't the chocolate.'

'And your money ran out, didn't it?'

'Yes. They wanted things like Mars Bars and caramel bars. It was about sixty pence a day. I tried to think of excuses for missing a day or two but they kept on at me.'

'And that was when you started stealing? But darling, why didn't you tell me?' I ask.

177

'What good would that do?' she says harshly. 'If you hadn't been a Vicar they wouldn't have done it, would they? That's why it started!'

Another stab to the heart, but this time it didn't quite go home. A bully is a bully is a bully. That's not my fault.

'They would have found some other reason if bullying a new girl was what they wanted to do,' I tell her. 'If you'd confided in me I'd have told you what to say, what to do.'

'Like what?' she says scornfully.

'Well, I would have suggested you should turn right around to them and say you were *not* a goody-goody, *not* a namby-pamby, that you didn't have to prove it to them or to anyone else. You are a person in your own right, Becky. Always stand up to bullies! Never give in to them!'

'I didn't know that, did I?' Becky says. 'I was afraid of them.'

'Of course you didn't, my love. And there's nothing bad about being afraid, you have to find the best way to deal with your fears, and that's not easy, even when you're grown up.' And at that moment, and in a way I resent her for it, Miss Frazer shoots into my mind, and I don't want her sneaking in on me when all my concern is for my daughter. And why has she shot into my mind? Because she, too, is a bully. And *I* have to stand up to *her*. And I will.

'Why didn't you tell Mr Beagle?' I ask Becky – and I'm also wondering why he didn't notice anything.

'Because he's still away,' she answers. 'His flu turned to bronchitis. We've had two supply teachers already.'

'Well,' I say, 'we'll have to tell Mrs Sharp because she's the Head and she needs to know, but I won't make a big fuss and I can tell you for certain that no-one is going to blame you. Now give me a big hug! And then tell me what you'd like best in the world for your supper and I'll cook it for you!'

'Fish-and-chips, from the fish shop,' she says without a pause.

FIFTEEN

As you can imagine, I didn't sleep much last night though Becky, bless her heart, seemed easier when I said 'good-night' to her. We'd had our fish-and-chip supper, she had had a warm bath, we'd read a bit of Harry Potter when she was in bed, and by the time I closed the book her eyelids were drooping and she was ready for sleep. We said prayers together – I gave her both a priestly blessing and a mother's blessing – and I left her.

Several things kept me wakeful. First and foremost was the thought of what Becky had been going through without me ever suspecting the cause. How could I have missed it? It wasn't that I hadn't cared – though had I, I asked myself, cared more about what was being done to me?

I thought about Mr Chester. What an understanding man he'd shown himself to be. After I've seen Evelyn I shall call on him, tell him what's happened, and at some point I'll take Becky with me so that we can iron out any awkwardness. I don't want her to feel she can't go in and out of his shop freely in the future.

I also thought about Nigel Baines. Right from the first meeting when he took me to the hospital Nigel's been so good, so helpful; he's easy to talk to. I miss Philip for a hundred reasons and one of them is that I don't have a man to talk things over with. That doesn't mean I don't value my women friends. Of course I do.

In spite of my disturbed night I was up early this morning, and now I'm seeing Becky off to school. 'It's going to be all right,' I assure her. 'Remember what we said. Say "No" to anything you think isn't right. And remember I'll be seeing Mrs Sharp this morning. I'm sure she'll sort everything out.' It's all very well, isn't it, for me to tell her to be brave? She's the one who has to face it. I had phoned Evelyn, told her I needed to see her rather urgently, but didn't say why and she didn't ask, so I'm seeing her at eleven-thirty.

I give Becky an extra big hug and this time she doesn't try to push me away.

There are six people at the ten o'clock. I know some of their names, but not all. The Blessed Henry and Molly Nugent; a Miss Carfax who is a retired teacher of music; Breda O'Halloran – who with a name like that and her broad Irish accent might seem more at home at St Patrick's. There's a couple whom I assume to be married because they look so comfortable together though they could be brother and sister, and a sixty-ish woman on her own with a thin, rather forbidding face.

They all go into coffee – Molly Nugent has been in earlier and switched on the coffee machine, so everything's ready, and we push two tables together and sit around amicably. I'm introduced to the couple – John and Mary Timpson – and to the single lady, who is not single in one sense since she's a widow. Her name is Josie Winter.

'I see Mrs Bateman's conspicuous by her absence,' Miss Carfax says.

There's a slightly awkward silence, which is broken by Mrs Timpson who says, 'Perhaps she has a cold. There's a lot of them about.' At this Josie Winter rushes in.

'Rubbish! We were all in church on Sunday, so we know why Mrs Bateman isn't here. Miss Frazer's forbidden it!' From which I gather that I'm not the only one who thinks of Mrs Bateman as Miss Frazer's satellite.

Then Josie Winter speaks directly to me. 'Everybody's keeping quiet for fear of upsetting you, but I reckon it'll do you good to know how many people are *for* you. Certainly everyone around this table. I can say that with certainty!'

'Thank you,' I say. 'I don't like a situation where people are for or against someone. It's not ideal to have people taking sides and I hope it'll be resolved before it spreads. But thank you very much for your support.'

Whatever I feel or think I don't want this to be made a major topic in the church. It's too negative. All my thoughts about St Mary's are positive, and I intend to keep them that way.

After that the subject is dropped. They don't (aside from the Blessed Henry and possibly Molly) know about my phone call from the Bishop, or about Miss Frazer's letter, and I don't propose to tell them. We go on to talk about the iniquities of the bus service to Brampton, the awful trouble in 'EastEnders' – I shall have to get Becky to bring me up-to-date on that, and possibly start watching it myself – and the imminent gas main repairs in the High Street which are going to upset every single person who goes through the village, either by car or on foot. 'And that'll no sooner be over,' Mr Timpson warns us, 'than they'll dig the road up again to do something to the electricity! I feel sorry for the shopkeepers.'

'You must excuse me,' I say presently, refusing a second cup of coffee but remembering to put my fifty pence in the basin for the first one, 'I shall have to go. I have an appointment.'

I sit in Evelyn Sharp's office, waiting for her to finish a phone call. All I want is to get on with what I'm here for, and now I'm relieved to hear, from the note in her voice, that she is winding up her conversation.

'I'm sorry about that, Venus,' she says as she puts down the phone. 'Nice to see you! How are you?'

'I'm fine,' I say. 'I've come to see you about Becky.'

I take a deep breath and plunge in, telling her everything I know, thread to needle, watching the changing expressions on her face as the tale unfolds. When I come to a stop, she looks at me for a few seconds without speaking. Her eyes are filled with compassion.

'Venus,' she says, 'I'm so sorry! I'm appalled! Both for you

181

and poor Becky. But I wish you'd come to me sooner, if only to say she was unhappy at school, even if you didn't know why.'

'You're right,' I say. 'I can see that now, but I suppose I thought I could deal with it myself.'

'I doubt you could, entirely,' Evelyn says. 'It's a school matter as well as a home one. And while it's true to say I'm appalled, I can't say I'm one hundred per cent surprised. It isn't the first case of bullying I've ever come across, either in this school or others where I've taught. The awful truth is that bullying is something which goes on to some extent in most, if not all, schools, and I think always has. And human nature being what it is I think it might continue. The plus side is that it's more recognized and reported these days. Parents and teachers have a better idea of what to look out for, especially if they work together.'

'I'm sorry I fell down on that one,' I say. 'I knew Becky was being very awkward, not like herself, but I put it down to other things – like moving from Clipton, leaving her friends. And of course her father's death.'

'Naturally you would,' Evelyn says. 'You shouldn't blame yourself for that.'

'There was the small episode of her being told her mother wasn't a proper Vicar,' I say, 'but I thought we'd dealt with that. We seemed to have.'

'What was that?' Evelyn says sharply. 'I didn't know about that.'

So I tell her. I also tell her about the supply teacher who had needled Becky, perhaps unthinkingly, on her first day.

'Mr Beagle would never have done that,' Evelyn says. 'In fact, if he hadn't been away ill I'm sure he would have noticed what was going on. Unfortunately, we've had two different supply teachers in less than two weeks and we'd have been up for a third if it hadn't been half-term next week. They do their best, of course, but they can't know what's normal behaviour for any of the children. They wouldn't know that Becky wasn't herself because they don't know what herself is. Anyway, Mr Beagle will be back after half-term, thank goodness.'

182

'I'm pleased about that,' I say. 'Becky very much liked what little she saw of him.'

'Good!' Evelyn says. 'And now I'm going to write down, while you're here, all the details you've told me, and perhaps ask you a few more questions. We have a set procedure for things like this – isn't it awful that we have to? – and I make sure that it's strictly observed. Actually, you know, bullying isn't just a case of children doing it to each other. It can be teachers doing it to children, or children to teachers. There seem to be no boundaries.' Then she says, 'Do you want Becky to be brought into this? Does she know you're here now?'

'She knows I was coming to see you this morning. I'd like her to know what you'd be doing but I'd also prefer it if it were to be kept as low-key as possible.'

'Oh, don't worry about that,' Evelyn says quickly. 'It will be! Now this is what we'll do.'

First of all she'd like to see Becky, while I'm here, and then she'll take the matter to a staff meeting. 'There's one this afternoon, after school. It'll be the last before half-term and I'd like to get things in place before then,' she says. 'All the staff will be asked to keep an eye on Becky, but she'll be given one special person to whom she can turn whenever she needs to. It won't be her own teacher. It could be another class teacher, or perhaps the school secretary. She's a very suitable person, and she has a daughter of her own. I'll think about that and let you know.'

She would also, she told me, choose someone in Year Five who would befriend Becky, and she thinks she knows just who she'll choose but, again, she'll discuss it at the staff meeting.

'If this works well, and it should,' Evelyn says, 'then it would be a good idea if you were to ask this girl to tea – or whatever. Something away from school.'

'I'd do that very willingly!' I promise.

'All in all,' Evelyn says, 'it could be an advantage that half-term's about to start. It will give Becky a break, and hopefully when she comes back, things will be different. And now I'd like to bring Becky in. I'm afraid I'm going to have to ask her to name the girls who've been doing this. At some point – preferably before they go off for half-term – I shall want to tackle them with it. I'll ask the secretary to get Becky from her class and bring her here. It's almost dinner break, so it won't be too noticeable.'

She picks up the phone and has a short conversation. 'OK,' she says. 'Well, why not catch her on her way into dinner?'

'Can you tell me,' I ask her while we wait, 'what sort of a child becomes a bully?'

'Not totally easy to answer,' Evelyn says. 'It's often a child with low self-esteem, not as academically gifted as the rest; or with a difficult home background, awkward family circumstances, a broken marriage for instance. But one can't be sweeping about that. I've known children with all those disadvantages who would never in this world turn to bullying. I've known one-parent families where the single parent does a heroic job, brings up children who'd be a credit to anyone. Judging what makes other people do things is an imprecise science, to say the least.'

'And where does the bullying take place?' I ask. 'I mean within your school?'

'Oh, seldom in the classroom,' Evelyn says. 'More often in the playground, or the cloakroom, or on the way to or from school.'

At this point the secretary arrives, accompanied by Becky, who looks pale and rather frightened.

'Hello Becky! Come and sit down,' Evelyn says in a cheerful voice. The secretary draws up a chair and places it right next to mine. I stretch out my hand and touch Becky's briefly.

'Your mum's been telling me you've not been having a happy time at school,' Evelyn says. 'I'm really sorry to hear that. I wish you'd mentioned it sooner, but there you are, you've done so now and I'm sure we'll be able to put it right. Let me tell you what we'll do, and see what you think of it.'

She chats to Becky person-to-person, as if she's really consulting her rather than just informing her what's been decided on her behalf. She tells her that there will always be one adult person to whom she can turn whenever she wants to. 'I think we'll call her your Mentor. Do you know what that word means?'

Becky shakes her head.

'It means "trusted adviser",' Evelyn says. 'And that's just what she'll be. You can trust her, and she'll advise you what to do. I'm not totally certain who I shall choose to do this, but it will be someone nice and friendly and it won't be your own class teacher. You'll be able to see her in private when you want to. Does that sound like a good idea?'

'Yes thank you, Mrs Sharp,' Becky answers.

'I'll let you know tomorrow who it will be,' Evelyn says, 'and of course, talk to your mother. I know she wants you to be happy.'

Then she tells Becky about someone in the class who will befriend her. 'It's something we usually do when we have a new pupil,' she says. 'If Mr Beagle hadn't been away it would already have happened. Now tell me, is there someone in the class you quite like, someone you think might make a good friend?'

Becky hesitates, but not for long.

'Anna Brent!' she says.

'Anna Brent! Now that's a good choice,' Evelyn says. 'I couldn't have chosen better myself! And I think I'll leave it to Mr Beagle to arrange this. He'll be back after half-term. I daresay the first thing he'll do is arrange for you to sit next to each other. And now, Becky, here comes the hard bit. I believe there were three girls in your class who made you do what you did, and I need to know their names. I'm not asking this for your sake, Becky, because I'm sure you're going to be all right from now on, but we don't want this sort of thing to happen to anyone else, do we?'

At this, Becky turns to me. She looks decidedly troubled.

'I think you must, love,' I tell her. 'Think of it as stopping what happened to you happening to someone else. I doubt Mrs Sharp will mention your name.'

'Of course I won't,' Evelyn says. 'They needn't know you've told me. I shall talk to them, tell them it must never happen again. I expect others in the class have an idea what's been going on, so it could be any one of them who gave the names.'

Becky bites her lips, twists her hands, then speaks in a voice which is only just audible.

'Jean Clough, Daisy Quinn, Cora White.'

'Thank you, Becky,' Evelyn says. 'And would I be right if I guessed Cora White was the ringleader?'

Becky gives a slight nod, but her face says it all.

'Right! Well don't worry about it any more. Have a wonderful half-term – I hear you're going to your grandparents – and I think when you come back you'll find everything's different. So give your mum a kiss, because she's been worried too, and then go and get your dinner.'

Friday. Not the day I've been most looking forward to because of the Bishop's visit, and I wish I could get it over with this morning instead of waiting until the afternoon. I spend the time doing odd jobs, and packing Becky's case for her visit to Clipton. I'm taking her tomorrow morning. She needs new knickers, not obtainable in the village, so I make a quick trip to Brampton and buy three pairs, and on the way back I stop off at the baker's and buy a Madeira cake in honour of the Bishop. I decide against their delicious cream slices as being (a) too festive for what might be a difficult situation and (b) too messy for a bishop to eat. Madeira cake is more suitable.

And now I'm back at home and I've been peering out of the window on and off for the last half-hour with nothing to show for it until this very minute when, lo and behold, a red BMW is drawing up outside the Vicarage. I never thought of the Bishop in a red BMW. Perhaps it's his one indulgence?

Keeping hidden, I watch him as he gets out of his car. He is tall, and he looks thinner than the last time I saw him, but then he was dressed in his splendid robes with a mitre on his head and now he's wearing a sober black suit enlivened only by a pinky-purple shirt and a whiter-than-white dog collar. His hair is thick, dark, but greying a bit. He has a pleasant, rather patrician, face. And now, since he's halfway up the path, I dash to the front door.

'Good-afternoon, Bishop!' I greet him.

'Hello, Venus!' he replies pleasantly, following me into the hall. 'How are you? Are you settled into the house yet? Is there lots to do?'

'Not too much,' I tell him. 'I'm doing it a little at a time.'

'Good!' he says. 'That's the best way. It took my wife and me several months to get everything sorted in the palace!'

But he's not here to talk about my domestic arrangements, or his, and we go into my study and sit ourselves down.

'Now, my dear,' he says, wasting no further time, 'what are we going to do about Miss Frazer, eh?'

I don't have any useful answer because I can only guess at what she's said. I'm waiting for him to tell me. 'I'd be glad of your advice,' I tell him. 'I'm not yet sure what her complaint is.'

'Of course you're not!' he agrees. 'And you need to know. Well, I had this letter from her – I shan't show it to you because that would be wrong – but without quoting her word for word I shall tell you what she said.'

I say nothing.

'First of all,' he says, 'she tells me of her – and her family's – long association with St Mary's, and with the village. She also points out that she has supported St Mary's in many ways, not least financial, but not only financial. She was active in the Sunday School and, though not a mother, in the Mothers' Union, and in Missionary activities. She was a long-serving member of the PCC, and she and her family have given a great deal, in money and in kind, to the church.'

He looks at me as if waiting for an answer.

'I'm sure all that's true,' I agree. 'I've been told that by more than one person. Her family have been great benefactors.'

'I think,' he says, 'that part of the problem is that she no longer has a hand in most of these things. I'm told – and though I don't know Miss Frazer myself there are a number of people at Diocesan House who do, or know of her – that she's no longer on the PCC, the Mothers' Union has closed down and I suppose younger people are now – quite rightly – running the Sunday School. So it has left her with not a lot to do, not as many spheres of influence – except financially, of course.'

I nod again, in agreement, though I'm not sure where he's going.

'But her chief difficulty, as I see it,' he continues, 'is that she is totally opposed to change of any kind. She will fight it tooth and nail. This is not unusual in the Church, is it? And with Miss Frazer the crux of the matter is that she cannot and will not accept women priests.'

'She made that abundantly clear to me,' I tell him. 'I don't see how I can change that.'

'You can't,' he agrees. 'Nevertheless, she thinks *she* can. What she wants, in short, is for you to be moved from this parish.'

I am horrified! I'm sure it shows in my face – I couldn't hide it if I tried. How dare she!

'Don't worry!' the Bishop says quickly. 'That's not going to happen. But I thought I must tell you so that you know where you stand with Miss Frazer. But that is *not* where you stand with me. Not at all! And before I reply to her letter I would like you to tell me your side of the story.'

'She hasn't told you?' I ask. 'She hasn't told you what she did, how she demonstrated what she thought of me . . . ?'

'I think not so much of you as of women in the priesthood,' he interrupts. 'But you happen to be in what she regards as her territory. So tell me.'

And I do. I try to tell it as unemotionally as I can, which is difficult. I'm aware that he's watching me intently. He pauses for quite a while before he replies.

'That is appalling,' he says. 'I'm sorry you had to go through that.'

'It wasn't the hurt to *me*!' I tell him. 'And it wasn't only the hurt to God. It was what was done to those others who observed it on the Sunday.'

'Yes. I understand that,' he says.

Then after a minute or so in which neither one of us says anything, he speaks.

'I shall write to Miss Frazer. I will do it tomorrow, I have a meeting this evening. I will not let you see a copy of the letter, that must be private to her, but I shall tell you now what I'm going to say to her. And you are at liberty to discuss this with your churchwardens, in confidence of course.

'First of all I shall thank her for all that she and her family have done for St Mary's. That mustn't be overlooked. And then I shall tell her that no matter what she thinks or feels on the subject of women priests, there is nothing she can do about it. It is the law of the land, and has been for more than ten years, that a woman who has the necessary qualifications and is of a suitable character can be ordained to the priesthood. I shall tell her how much I regret that she cannot come to terms with this. But she cannot change the law.

'I shall go on to tell her that your orders are entirely valid and there is no way you would, or indeed could, be asked to leave St Mary's on the grounds she puts forward. You are carrying out the job for which you were ordained and licensed and you are doing it here with my blessing and my full support.'

'Thank you,' I say.

'Then I shall suggest to her that if she is adamant that she cannot receive communion from you her best plan would be to attend a church where the priest is a man. There are churches in Brampton where she could go, and I would be willing to introduce her.'

'She doesn't want to do that,' I tell him. 'She did say so.'

'Then she must behave herself in St Mary's,' the Bishop says. 'As for the fact that she threatens to withdraw her financial support of the church, then I shall tell her that she is totally at liberty to do so, while thanking her for her support in the past.'

'I didn't realize she'd threatened that,' I say. 'I am sorry.'

'It's not for you to be sorry,' he says. 'The day the Church bases its judgements on money – desperately though it's needed – is the day it's lost.

'I shall also tell her,' he continues, 'and quite firmly, that if she does not wish to receive communion, then she should not come up to the altar rail. If she insists on coming to the altar, then she should not put out her hands to receive. Tell me, Venus, if someone knelt at the altar, indicating that they didn't wish to receive, what would you do?'

'Almost certainly I would place my hands on the person's head and give them a blessing,' I reply. 'I do that already, for people not yet ready for the sacrament, or who feel they're not.'

'Quite so!' he says.

'And that would drive Miss Frazer really mad!' I say.

'Indeed it would! So I shall tell her that if she wants neither communion nor a blessing then she should not present herself at the altar. I don't doubt that Miss Frazer was brought up on the Book of Common Prayer and there's plenty in that about

189

acceptable and unacceptable behaviour at the Holy Communion. I shall direct her to it.'

And then he smiles at me – a warm smile.

'Try not to worry,' he says. 'This is something you will learn to deal with. Unfortunately she is only one of many who hold the same opinion about women in the priesthood – and they are not all laity, as I'm sure you know perfectly well.'

'Oh I do!' I agree. Amongst the least welcoming people I have come across are not those in the church congregations but those I met in my training, and in the theological college. And they were mostly priests, or priests in the making.

'It will change,' he says. 'It might take longer than you want, things move slowly in the Church, but it will change. As for Miss Frazer, she's an unhappy woman, and you strike me as a happy one in spite of the sorrows you've had.'

'I am!' I agree.

He's obviously said all he has to say, so I ask: 'And now can I make you a cup of tea, Bishop?'

'That would be most welcome.' He stands up. 'I'll come and talk to you in the kitchen while you make it. I like kitchens. My wife and I tend to eat in the kitchen when we're on our own.'

So that's where we have our tea, and he eats a piece of Madeira cake with evident enjoyment, then he springs to his feet again.

'Reluctantly,' he says, 'I must be off. I would have liked to have talked to you about the parish, heard what your plans are, and so forth. I enjoyed being a parish priest. There is nothing in the Church more demanding or, in the end, more fulfilling. I never intended or wanted to be anything more – but there it is, one does whatever God seems to be calling one to do. But perhaps we'll speak another time. And do let me know – don't hesitate to ring me – if there's any more trouble on the Miss Frazer front. Do you see any as yet? Any sign of it spreading?'

'Perhaps a little,' I say. 'Though not much. I'm sure I can deal with it.'

'Yes,' he says. 'I reckon you can!'

He says a short prayer and gives me a blessing. 'And if your churchwardens want to discuss things further with me, tell

Henry Nugent to contact me. Remember, Venus, that you have the cure of all souls in your parish, those who persecute you as well as those who show you love. Try to go the extra mile, Venus, and do it with love. I will pray for you, you for me, and both of us for Miss Frazer. We must all pray for each other.'

I see him to the door, where he turns around and says 'Read Psalm twenty-seven.' Then he zooms away in his red BMW, not driving at all as I'd expect a bishop to drive. I know Psalm twenty-seven.

'The Lord is my light and my salvation:
Whom shall I fear?'

SIXTEEN

I am driving Becky to Clipton. It's a fine morning, sunnier and certainly milder than one might expect at this time of the year, and there's a nice sort of 'Saturday' feeling to it which I think must be due to the fact that I've settled the two matters which were really bugging me, Becky and the school business, and Miss Frazer, so I can relax. But no, it would be an exaggeration to say I've settled them. About Becky I do feel hopeful, I think that's going to be all right. Miss Frazer isn't so simple, but the Bishop is on my side, and that's great. As the psalm says, 'though war rise up against me, yet will I be confident'. So I'm feeling OK, but much more to the point, so is Becky and I hope it will last.

She is sitting beside me. The back seat is overflowing with her belongings, including several soft toys which normally live in her bedroom and which she was loth to leave, indeed her teddy bear, name of Blossom, is on the front seat with her. It might seem strange that a ten-year-old should be accompanied by an army of soft toys, but I didn't try to stop it. I know what a comfort they've been to her. She'll outgrow them when she's ready – though I know women years older than I am who are still attached to their teddy bears. In Clipton I met one who had taken one into a retirement home with her. She told me he was very happy there.

'When will we be there?' Becky asks. 'Will Grandma be in?'

'In about an hour,' I tell her. 'And of course she'll be in!'

'What if she's not?' she wants to know.

'Well, if she were to be out, then I have a key,' I say. 'But really there's no question of it.'

Evelyn Sharp phoned me last evening. 'Are you on your own?' she asked. 'By which I mean, is Becky with you?'

'No she's not,' I replied. 'I saw her off to bed about twenty minutes ago, though she won't be asleep because she's too excited about going to Clipton.'

'I'm glad it's half-term,' Evelyn said. 'Couldn't be better from Becky's point of view. Anyway, I'm ringing to tell you I've set everything in motion. We decided at the staff meeting – where by the way, everyone was sorry to hear about Becky – that the secretary – her name's Eileen Fawcett – was the very best person to be Becky's mentor, and Eileen is pleased to do that. We also reckoned that Anna Brent would be the perfect choice for a friend. She's a motherly little soul. I thought it best if I spoke to Mrs Brent, which I did. I didn't go into the bullying bit, I explained that Becky was finding it hard to settle in at school and we thought Anna could be a help to her. She was totally agreeable.'

'That all sounds marvellous,' I said. 'Can I tell Becky?'

'Of course you can!' Evelyn said. 'I also spoke to the three young bullies, gave them a piece of my mind, told them they'd be dealt with very severely if such a thing happened again, either to Becky or to anyone else, and that Mr Beagle and I would be keeping a sharp eye open. And we shall, but I think it will be OK. I wanted to give them a second chance before I did anything more drastic. I didn't tell them who had reported it except that it wasn't Becky – which it wasn't, because you were the one who told me. You might want to reassure Becky on some of this if she's still awake.'

'I certainly will,' I said.

So the minute Evelyn put down the phone I went up to Becky's room, and she *was* awake so I did tell her. We talked about it a little, but not much. Then I gave her a big hug, and left

193

her. Half-an-hour later I looked in on her and she was fast asleep, and somehow, even in sleep, she looked a happier child.

And now I have a tape on in the car and I'm singing along to it as I drive down the motorway. Ella Fitzgerald. I have old-fashioned tastes.

'This is yucky,' Becky complains. 'Don't you have anything better than this?'

'They don't come any better than this,' I say. 'You don't like it?'

'It's drear!'

I know what she means. Why should I expect her to enjoy 'Love Is Here to Stay'? Anyway, it's not true. If it's not fleeting in one way it is in another. 'Not for a year, but ever and a day'! I wish! And then I pull myself up sharply. Of course love is here to stay! Love itself will never die. Isn't that the bedrock of my faith? Isn't it what I stand up in the pulpit and preach about? And I don't mean only the love of God, I mean all kinds of love. Parents and children, men and women, friends. Of course it isn't going to die!

'When we're in Clipton,' I promise, 'you can choose a couple of tapes for the way back.'

'I thought Gran and Grandpa could bring me back,' Becky says. 'Then they could stay for the weekend – or a whole week!'

'We'll see what they say. They might be too busy,' I suggest.

'They're *never* too busy to do things!' she says. I know a rebuke when I meet one, though she mightn't have meant it as that.

Of course my mother is there when we arrive, it was never on the cards that she wouldn't be. I reckon she's been watching out of the window for us because she's down at the gate by the time I've switched off the engine. Becky, out of the car and on the pavement in a flash – so quickly that she actually leaves poor Blossom behind – is enveloped in my mother's arms. They walk up the path to the door hand in hand and I follow behind, carrying what I can from the back seat.

'Don't bother with that, Venus love,' my mother calls out. 'Dad'll do that. He'll be back in a minute; he's just gone down the road to post a letter.'

After which, follows a lovely day. Roast chicken for lunch, one of Becky's favourites, as my mother well knows; a trip into the town afterwards (and I buy Becky the promised tapes); potato scones for tea, and then soon afterwards I say it's time for me to leave. Dad's fussing about me getting back before dark, but in any case I never like to be out late on Saturdays because it's an early start the next day. Becky hasn't mentioned school, nor has anyone else. Everyone seems happy and contented. Could this, I ask myself, be the beginning of a new era? But perhaps too soon to start counting chickens.

Driving back, I wonder what I might do with the week ahead. Mum and Dad jumped at the chance of returning with Becky and staying for the weekend. 'We'll come on Saturday and stay until Sunday afternoon,' Mum said, 'or perhaps Monday morning.'

Meanwhile, apart from work commitments, I have seven whole days before me. Does it sound awful to say I'm almost pleased at the prospect of being on my own; not having the daily battles to get an unwilling Becky off to school, or the apprehension of what sort of mood she'll be in when she comes home? I suppose it does because she, poor mite, has had a worse time than I have.

And then it occurs to me that this could be the week I have the little supper party I'd vaguely planned. It's a bit soon after Sonia's but it's such a good opportunity, and maybe they won't mind. I can but ask. So for the rest of the journey, in my head I'm going through the guest list – which will be exactly the same as it was at Sonia's except that I know I ought to ask the Nugents (but will they fit in?) – and dreaming up menus which are within my capabilities.

When I reach the Vicarage, when I let myself in, it occurs to me that this is the first time I've returned to it after actually having been away. It's a pleasant feeling as I turn the key in the front door. It's mine, and I belong here.

I have not taken more than two strides into the hall before I realize that something is wrong! I don't know what, but there is a cold feeling in my body. For a moment I stand still, unable to move a limb. I'm frightened – and I don't know by what. And then I tell myself not to be stupid, and I take a step forward and with that I know what's wrong. The Madonna and Child which stands on a mahogany table in the hall, as it did in my previous home ever since Philip and I bought it on a day trip to Boulogne, is not there. Nor is the ceramic angel which Philip bought me when we were in Venice and which stands just behind and to the side of the Madonna. Since nothing else is ever allowed to clutter up this particular space, the table is now bare.

I have been burgled!

I feel sick to the stomach. Burgled is something which happens to other people and I never thought could happen to me. And when? When did this happen? I left home at ten o'clock this morning and now it's just after seven. Nine hours, almost all in daylight, though dusk has fallen now, and with that last thought real fear comes to me. Unless it was done in broad daylight it's happened very recently and – and this thought freezes me – he might still be in the house! He might be in the dining room behind that closed door two yards away! He might be upstairs in my bedroom and he might walk down the stairs at any minute, and I know with absolute certainty that the last thing in the world I want is to come face to face with him. I'm assuming it's a 'him'. I daresay female burglars are as thin on the ground as women priests.

I take a deep breath. My heart is thumping so hard that I think if he's still around he must hear it – and in any case he must have heard me come in by the front door. I wasn't quiet. But common sense – what bit I have left of it – tells me I can't just stand here doing nothing. I must make a move. I must telephone, first the police and secondly – who? Henry Nugent, of course! For a start, his is the number I know by heart and there's no time to start leafing through telephone directories, even if there was one handy. And Henry is my churchwarden and my friend.

The nearest phone is in the sitting room – my mobile is still in the glove compartment in the car. What if he's in the sitting room waiting? And this is the point at which I start to pull myself together. Common sense tells me that if he had been, he'd have made his escape through the window by now. It seems as though I've been standing here, doing nothing, for ever, though probably it's been a minute. I don't know. But now I take another deep breath and walk into the sitting room – and the burglar is not there though there are signs that he has been, but not escaped that way because the window is closed. I see at once that my new video recorder has gone, though not the television, which is probably too bulky or is too old a model to be worth stealing.

I pick up the phone and ring the police at once.

'Have you looked anywhere else in the house?' I'm asked.

'No,' I tell the lady.

'Then don't!' she says. 'Don't touch anything. Leave everything as it is. We'll be round as soon as we can.'

'When will that be?' I ask.

'As soon as we can,' she repeats patiently.

I suppose burglary is so common that it has to take its place in the queue, well behind injuries to life and limb, and when I'm in less of a dither I shall see the sense of that. For now, I telephone Henry and he assures me, without me having asked him, that he'll be with me immediately. While waiting for him I stay where I am, as advised by the police, though I no longer think the burglar is likely to be in the house. If he had been he'd have heard me speaking, have guessed I was on to the police, and he'd have scarpered. And wouldn't I have heard that?

I sit down, my legs are trembling, and while I wait, I look around to see what else might be missing from this room. Not a lot. Some videos and CDs, some knick-knacks. And then – oh what a shame – three rather nice pieces of old Bristol glass of which I was particularly fond. The theft of the glass sparks anger in me. I found all three pieces in an antique shop and I could hardly afford to buy one of them, let alone all three, but I did. And by now I'm convinced I'll never again see anything he's stolen and I find myself hoping that the glass will break into a million pieces before he gets it to wherever he plans to sell it.

True to his word, Henry is here in next to no time. Oh Blessed Henry! He has a key so he lets himself in. Naturally, I'd told him yesterday that I was taking Becky to Clipton and I'd be away for a few hours, but that was no reason for him to make a visit to the Vicarage.

'First of all,' he says, 'I'm going to go over every bit of the

197

house. Make quite certain . . .' He breaks off before he says '. . . that he's not still here. You'd better come with me, Venus. You'll know where anything's been disturbed.'

He's incredibly thorough. He looks in every room, every wardrobe and cupboard (as he opens each wardrobe door I find myself waiting for someone to fall out!). When it comes to my bedroom he, as with the other rooms, goes in first, then turns round as he says to me, 'It's a bit of a mess in here. And the window's open. Best to leave it alone until the police get here.' I peer around him and see the contents of my jewellery drawer – or rather the boxes in which my bits were kept – scattered on the floor. My instinct is to start looking, check what's missing, but he says, 'No, Venus! Let's do the rest of the house.'

So we go into the bathroom and he looks behind the shower curtain. He checks the glory hole under the stairs, and then we zoom upstairs again because he's forgotten about the loft. He's like a streak of lightning. Lastly, we go outside, for which I have to find a torch because by now it's quite dark, and check the garage and the garden.

'It's quite common to steal garden ornaments,' Henry explains. 'Or rather nice pots.'

It was in going around the garden that it became obvious where the burglar had got into the house. The gate which leads to the path up to the Downs was swinging open – I'm fussy about keeping it closed, and in any case there's a good, firm latch on it. (No wonder he didn't steal the television, I think, looking at the steepness of the path.) And on my side of the gateway, a yard into the garden, the light from the torch reveals a half-smoked cigarette lying on the ground. I bend to pick it up.

'No, no!' Henry cries. 'Leave it for the police!'

He turns and gazes earnestly at the back of the house, then pointing, he says, 'Aha! That's where he got in and out! That pipe's only inches from your bedroom window.'

Apart from the fact that he is sorry for me I think Henry is quite enjoying this episode. He finds himself in the middle of a TV script and, who knows, might well turn out to be the hero, the gifted amateur against the bungling police.

We are not to know for a while whether the police are bungling or super-efficient, since it is almost half-an-hour – we are back in the house – before the doorbell rings and Henry goes to answer it, returning accompanied by a young woman in uniform who looks as though she's auditioning for 'The Bill', only she's far too young to get the part.

'I'm Police Constable June French,' she says. 'Brampton Police.' And since she shows me her card I have to believe she's not too young.

'And this lady is Mrs Stanton, Vicar of St Mary's, Thurston,' Henry says, staying in the act.

'And your first name?' she asks me.

She doesn't turn a hair when I say 'Venus'. Not showing surprise is probably part of her training.

'So will you tell me what happened, and then I'd like to take a look around,' she says.

She listens carefully, writes it all down and then I take her round the house, Henry in tow. When she sees the state of my bedroom floor she says, 'Don't move anything! The Scene-of-Crime Officer will be here soon.'

'Ah,' Henry says, nodding, 'the Scene-of-Crime Officer! Well, we've sussed out where the burglar entered and exited!' A few minutes ago Henry said 'got in and out' but in his present role and in the presence of officialdom 'entered and exited' sounds better.

We go downstairs again. Constable French asks me to describe the things which I know to be missing, other than from the bedroom, and this I do. 'I can't think why a burglar should take a Madonna and Child and an angel!' I say. (A Christian burglar?) 'The Madonna was very distinctive, very modern. Made by nuns in a French convent.' And very dear to me, I would like to add, but I doubt she wants to know that.

'They can sell practically anything!' she says. 'It'll probably have found its way to London or Brighton by tomorrow morning.'

So much for my beautiful Madonna! The policewoman doesn't exude the faintest hope of my ever seeing it again.

The Scene-of-Crime Officer arrives, another woman, slightly more mature, taller and thinner. We go through the whole story and the guided tour again and she says if we'll leave her to it there are a few tests she'd like to make in the bedroom.

'You mean fingerprints?' Henry says. He would like to stay, but she politely shoos him off.

She comes downstairs ten minutes later.

'Well,' she says to Henry, 'you were right about the entrance and the exit! The intruder came in and went out by the window. I reckon he was disturbed, made a quick exit, probably when he heard your car draw up. You're lucky he'd left before you came in.'

They are intruders now, not burglars. It sounds more polite. 'May I intrude on you?' 'Excuse me for intruding, I'm here to steal your silver . . . !'

Henry nods happily. 'I thought as much!' he says.

'I've got two sets of prints from the window frame,' she says. 'Marigolds.'

'Marigolds?' Now Henry *is* confused.

'Rubber gloves. All the burglars wear Marigolds. They learn what to do and what not to do from the TV programmes. Marigolds leave prints, but they're all the same. Marigold prints.'

Henry takes her outside and shows her the open gate and the path to the Downs. She picks up the half-smoked cigarette and puts it in a plastic bag – and that's about it.

'We'll be in touch,' she says. 'We'll be giving you a crime number and we'll need a list of what's missing.' Then she adds, almost cheerfully, 'Even when you've done the list you're sure to find other things have gone! People always do. Please let us know!'

When she's left Henry says, 'Well, you mustn't stay here tonight, Venus. You must come home with me and Molly will make you up a bed.'

'Oh, no!' I protest. 'No, I mustn't do that! It's quite important that I stay here, in my own house. I'm not going to let this sod drive me out. He'd have won then, wouldn't he?' And he'd have won something more important than my Bristol glass and my Madonna, and whatever he's stolen from my bedroom, which I've yet to find out. I can't, at this moment, find the word for what he'd have won if I ran away, even for one night, but he's

200

not going to. I refuse to let him. I am determined not to be a victim.

'Well, I don't like to leave you,' Henry says, 'but if you insist. But promise you'll phone if you're the least bit uneasy. I'll be round at once. You know, Venus, what you need is a dog! No burglar would get past my Sukey!'

Sukey is an over-friendly golden retriever who enjoys company. She would be likely to lick the burglar's face as he climbed in through the window.

When Henry has gone I know that what I should do is go into my bedroom and tidy up the mess, check what's been taken. I can't do it. Not yet, not tonight! Nor can I sleep in my bedroom where my precious bits and pieces, or the boxes they should be in, are scattered on the carpet. The bed in the guest room is not made up and I'm too tired to bother with it, so I shall sleep in Becky's bed. I won't feel so alone in her bed. I'm so glad she wasn't here. I shall have to decide how to tell her without making her nervous.

I haven't been in bed more than ten minutes before the phone rings.

'It's me!' my mother says. 'I just wanted to know if you'd reached home all right. You usually ring.'

I am not going to tell my mother about the burglary; not now, and possibly not ever. I shall have to think about it.

'I'm sorry,' I tell her. 'Henry Nugent came soon after I arrived. He's only just left.'

'So you're all right?'

'I'm fine!' I say from the comfort of Becky's bed. 'Is Becky OK?'

'She's fine! She's just gone to bed. She was tired, so she's having an early night. Well, good-night, love. Sleep well!'

Ten minutes later the phone rings again. It's my friend Esmé Bickler, the woman with whom I was at theological college and who now has a living at the far end of the diocese. We keep in touch, though I don't see her often. I've resisted the temptation over the last week or two to ring her and have a good old moan.

'I thought I'd just ask how you were getting on,' she says now. 'Are you settling down? And what about Becky?'

201

'Teething troubles with Becky,' I admit, 'but I think she's going to be OK. She's with my mother right now, for half-term.'

'And the parish?' she asks.

'Interesting,' I say. 'A nice mixture of people.' I am not going to mention Miss Frazer nor, at the moment, am I going to mention the burglary. The truth is, fatigue has set in, or delayed shock or something, and I'm desperately tired. 'How about you? Is everything going well with you?'

'Mostly,' she says. 'I have one or two awkward customers. Well, one I'm especially worried about.'

I know she's going to tell me about it and Esmé is not the briefest of raconteurs, so I rearrange my pillows and lie back.

'It's sad, really,' she says after the preliminaries. 'This man is eighty, he's been receiving his communion every week, almost all his life, and now he won't because I'm a woman. "I'll no' tak' the Lord's Supper from a lassie!"' She gives a fair imitation of his Scottish accent.

'Oh dear! He sounds awful!' I commiserate.

'That's the trouble,' Esmé says, 'he's not. He's a very nice man, a sweetie, but he can't change and he won't discuss it. What makes it worse is that his wife's a regular communicant and she hasn't the least objection to me, so she comes every Sunday and he stays at home. I feel really bad about that. They've been coming to church together forever, or so I understand. Have you met with that sort of thing yet?'

'A little,' I say vaguely. I'm far too tired to want to mention Miss Frazer, nor do I want to remember that in a few hours from now I shall have to face her again.

'. . . Anyway,' Esmé says, and I realize she's been talking away and I've missed some of it, '. . . I won't keep you. We both have an early start in the morning, don't we?'

SEVENTEEN

When I open my eyes this morning the light is filtering through the curtains, but the curtains themselves are all wrong. They have blue and yellow flowers, with green leaves, on a cream background and I know they should be a pale turquoise colour, and not patterned at all. And then I realize that the dressing-table is not in its rightful place, and the painting of chrysanthe-mums in a vase, which should be on the wall facing me as I lie in bed, is missing. For years, wherever I've lived, that painting has been the first thing I've seen every morning. So where is it? Has it been stolen in the night?

It is the word 'stolen', not uttered, but sharp in my mind, which jerks me fully awake, and I realize I'm in Becky's bed, not in my own, and I remember why that's so, and that it's Sunday and I have a service at eight o'clock and the Mickey Mouse clock on the night table says it's already seven.

By now I'm fully conscious and I remember that I'd wakened a couple of times in the night and been horribly nervous, afraid of getting out of bed and going to the bathroom, which on the second occasion I badly needed to do, so badly needed that all the burglars in Christendom wouldn't have deterred me. I knew at the time that this was silly, there was no way the burglar was still lurking. Somewhere he would be fast asleep, probably dreaming of what he would do with my

203

belongings once he'd translated them into money.

I have personified the burglar. When I closed my eyes last night, before I went to sleep, I could see him quite plainly, standing there in front of me. I still can. He is medium-tall, say five feet ten, with thick, dark hair, slightly curly, badly cut. Shifty eyes. He has a swarthy skin and is in need of a shave. He wears blue jeans, a black polo-necked sweater and dirty white trainers. He's in his mid-twenties, and I could pick him out in an identity parade.

What rubbish, I tell myself now as I get out of bed! I have never – thank heaven – set eyes on him, nor has anyone I know. He could be a skinny sixteen-year-old blond dwarf – easier to shin up a drainpipe – in black trousers and a green anorak. Take your pick! But when I close my eyes again – just testing – it's the dark-haired one I see. He's possibly called Melvin, or maybe Fred.

Though dead tired from a broken night I shower, dress, eat a bowl of cornflakes and am in good time for the eight o'clock service. There are ten people present, everything goes normally and most of them say 'Good-morning' as they leave. They have no idea they are speaking to a woman who has been burgled and I have no intention of telling them.

When I return to the Vicarage to have my breakfast it feels strange, rather uncomfortable, letting myself in. I'm unsure. I stand still in the hall, and listen, but all I hear is silence. I had no idea that being burgled affected one like this. It's this horrid feeling of someone being in your space, touching your belongings, rifling through your drawers, and perhaps especially, I think, being in your bedroom, your private place. I still have to do something about the mess in the bedroom but that will have to wait until I get back from the ten o'clock. I can't face it yet. So I have toast and marmalade and make a cup of coffee. I'm missing Becky but I'm so very thankful she didn't come back with me yesterday.

It's spotting with rain as I walk back to church for the ten o'clock Eucharist, the crown of my week. This would normally be a time when I'd be looking forward to the next hour or two, but not today. It isn't the burglary, it's the thought that I shall come face to face with Miss Frazer and I don't know what she'll do. She won't have had the Bishop's letter yet, he can't have posted it before Saturday at the earliest and I can't kid myself that it's the most important thing in his itinerary. So what will she have in store for me? And how will I deal with it? I tell myself that in the world's view it's trivial, something to be brushed aside, but it's not so in mine and I don't think it would be for anyone else in my position. The Bishop didn't think it was trivial, did he? He didn't brush it aside. However, whatever she does I shall find the strength to meet it. I'm confident of that.

I am the first to arrive at the church but Henry and his wife follow soon after, and with them are Mrs Blamires and Miss Carson who are their near neighbours. It is clear to me from the word go that the burglary has been discussed. But then, why not? It's not a secret, nor has it any hope of remaining one. I can already see the headline in tomorrow's *Brampton Echo*. 'New Woman Vicar of Thurston Robbed!'

'Are you all right?' Henry asks. 'I phoned you earlier but you must have set off for the eight o'clock.'

'I'm fine!' I tell him.

'I told Henry he should have *insisted* that you came home with him, stayed the night with us!' Molly says. 'You shouldn't have been on your own!'

'You're very kind,' I tell her, 'but really I was OK.'

'You're very brave,' Mrs Blamires says.

'I couldn't have done it!' Miss Carson says. 'I'd have been scared to death!'

I shake my head. I know I wasn't brave; just bloody-minded. Anyway, they move on because by now there are other people coming into church, but I notice that they pause until the latest comers have caught up with them so that they can pass on the news. After which, I reckon, it will be related by the recipients to the pews in front and behind and soon everyone will be informed or, more likely, misinformed. It will be like the party game where the message is passed on by whispering into the ear of the next person and by the time it reaches the end it bears very little resemblance to the original. By the time it gets around all the pews there will have been rape and pillage in Thurston. So I must say something myself – which I do when I go up into the pulpit.

'Some of you,' I say, 'will have heard that there has been a burglary at the Vicarage. It happened yesterday when I took my daughter to Clipton to stay with her grandparents, probably when I was on the way back. As you can see for yourselves, I'm perfectly all right. I'm pleased to say I wasn't in the house at the time. A number of things were stolen and as yet I'm not sure exactly what, but in a way it doesn't matter and it has already taught me, in this very short time, that even some very nice possessions are not as important as I once thought they were. So be vigilant – perhaps I wasn't vigilant enough – but don't be fearful. If we let events make us fearful, then evil wins.'

Really, I think, I am preaching to myself. I can see Miss Frazer in her pew, though I hadn't seen her come in. Then I begin my sermon, based on the Gospel for the day, the two great commandments: love God, and thy neighbour as thyself. Anything which helps me to talk about love is a bonus for me. And then I suddenly realize, looking at the people in front of me, that these commandments aren't just for them. They're also for me. And the last face I see before I speak is Miss Frazer's. 'Thy neighbour as thyself.' It sure ain't easy, Lord!

When I step down from the pulpit the Eucharist continues as always. The great eucharistic prayer, the consecration of the bread and wine, the giving and receiving of the Peace (entered into with gritted teeth by those who like to keep themselves to themselves), the invitation to approach and partake of the communion. Miss Frazer comes out of her pew, the very front one, and stands for a second or two facing the altar. She does not bend her knee, as I expect she normally would before approaching, and I know that this is because she does not believe that what I am standing there offering these people is valid. In her eyes I am not qualified to consecrate. So what is she going to do? Almost everyone else is waiting for her to move forward, after which they will follow.

What she does – after a deliberate pause, and by no means quietly – is to turn on her heel and march – march is the exact word, but with a limp – down the aisle and out of the church. I give a small nod to the people in the front pews to start coming forward, which they do, except for one woman three or four rows back – I don't know her name – who follows Miss Frazer.

I carry on with what I have to do. One could say that I haven't been involved, as I was on the two previous occasions; but that would be wrong. I have been involved this time in front of the entire congregation. There might still be a few people here who don't know what Miss Frazer is up to, but very few indeed. Though not many have spoken to me about the previous episodes I guess that by now they are known to most. And most will see it as a personal affront to me and will have their own opinion about that – whether, for instance, in doing what I do I'm asking for it – but, as on both previous occasions, I see it as a rejection of the God I am offering, and it is no small thing, indeed it's a terrible thing, for a priest to know that she is the sole reason for a member of her congregation turning away from God.

When the service is over I stand at the door, as usual. Not much is said. I get smiles, but some people seem too embarrassed to say anything. And in the middle of all this Miss Frazer appears from around the corner of the church where she has obviously been lying in wait and lets off a torrent of abuse. The usual stuff: Whore of Babylon, an abomination unto the Lord, Traitor, Blasphemer . . . At which Henry Nugent steps in.

'Now, Miss Frazer, this won't do at all!'

'As for you,' she rounds on him, 'you are one of those who brought this woman here! Shame on you! And shame on the rest of you!' she says to the small crowd which is hovering around. 'You know not what you do!' And so on and so on, until she runs out of breath.

'But this is not the last of it,' she cries, turning back to me. 'I have seen to that! My voice is listened to by the powerful . . .' (I take it she means the Bishop rather than God himself) '. . . and you will not go unpunished!'

I look around everyone else there, they are rooted to the spot. I doubt if Sunday mornings at St Mary's are often as entertaining as this.

'Shall we go into coffee?' I say cheerfully.

They follow me as I move towards the parish hall.

'Who sups with the devil must use a long spoon!' Miss Frazer shouts after us.

Someone offers me a chair, someone else fetches me coffee, people come forward to sit by me. I am suddenly the flavour of the month, but not only, I discover, because I've been shouted at by Miss Frazer, but also because I've been burgled. The general feeling seems to be that no-one should have to endure both these trials so closely after each other.

'She'd no business to do what she did, say what she did . . .'

'Especially when you'd been burgled!'

'She's a stupid old bat!' Carla Brown says. 'She thinks she rules the roost!' For someone who says she doesn't often come to church Carla Brown is doing very well at the moment.

No-one has a good word to say for Miss Frazer; on the other hand no-one says they actually agree or disagree with her basic views about women priests. Their disapproval is of her manners. At the moment they are treating me as a woman who has been soundly berated and needs support. The question of the priest-hood doesn't come into it. However, I tell myself, they are being kind and friendly towards me and that counts for a lot. And, who knows, perhaps for most of them the sex of the priest doesn't matter? That would be a happy thought.

Miss Frazer, naturally, and wisely, has not followed us into coffee, and now I notice that Mrs Bateman isn't there nor, come to think of it, was she in church.

'Does anyone know where Mrs Bateman is?' I ask. 'Is she ill?'

No-one knows, though the general opinion is that Miss Frazer has forbidden her to come.

'And who was the lady who rushed out of church after Miss Frazer?' I enquire. 'I don't see her here.'

'Oh, that was Daisy Heston,' Carla says. 'She's a nurse. She always follows anyone who rushes out of church in case they're unwell. She's a sort of resident first-aider. She doesn't often come into coffee.'

So not, as I had thought, someone in sympathy with Miss Frazer's views, or not necessarily.

Should I pay a visit to Mrs Bateman, I ask myself as I walk home. But perhaps it would be better to let everything wait until I can assume that Miss Frazer has had the Bishop's letter. Will it be something she'll go and chew over with Mrs Bateman? I doubt it, if it's critical. Maybe she'll read her selected phrases, the polite ones which acknowledge what a wonderful support her family have always been to St Mary's. And then, quite deliberately, I put Miss Frazer out of my mind, and when I get into the house I dial Clipton.

'How's everything with you?' my mother asks.

'Fine!' I say. 'Absolutely fine!'

'Everything all right at church?'

'Great!' I tell her.

I don't say a word about the burglary. It can wait until I see her. I don't really know how much to tell Becky because I don't want to frighten her, also because she's had enough on her plate, but there's no way I can guard her from being ever left alone in the house, especially as it was possibly early evening when he came. I shall have to think about it and for the moment I'm thankful I'll have time to do that.

'So what are you going to do with yourself this week?' my mother asks.

'I'm considering having a small supper party,' I tell her.

'A good idea!' she says. 'Anyway, I'll put Becky on now.'

Becky tells me she's enjoying herself. 'I've been playing cards with Granddad,' she informs me. 'I won fourpence! We're going to the cinema tomorrow. We're having roast beef and Yorkshire pudding for lunch, and sticky toffee pudding. We had a cooked breakfast this morning.' Clearly her appetite is normal. 'We didn't go to church,' she adds with some satisfaction. We chat for another minute or two and then I say, 'See you on Saturday!' and we ring off.

And now I can't put it off any longer. I shall have to go up to my bedroom.

Two drawers are open. One contained nothing of value and he hasn't taken anything from it; the second drawer – he was lucky there – was my jewellery drawer. I keep it all together and, as far as I can, in small boxes, but now most of the boxes are scattered on the carpet, and horribly empty. He has quite clearly been disturbed because there are still things in the drawer and some of the boxes on the floor haven't been emptied. I think that, reckoning the house was unoccupied, he was taking his time to make a selection, until he heard my car on the drive. So he has left my pearls and at least I'm grateful for that, but he has taken a cameo brooch, set in gold, which was left to me by my grandmother, also a gold chain, some silver earrings, and a number of rings. He's not a knowledgeable thief because he's made off with two or three rings which were pretty, but of little value, zircons rather than diamonds, and left behind a diamond and amethyst eternity ring which Philip gave me when Becky was born. I'd hate to have lost that.

I now have the melancholy task of making a list for the police, and another for the insurance, of all that's missing – 'with as full descriptions as you can' the police said. So I do that, and then tidy the bedroom, putting the empty jewel boxes away in another drawer, though why I'm doing that I'm not sure because I have little hope that I shall ever see any of the contents again. First thing tomorrow I must inform the insurance company.

It's lunchtime, and I'm surprisingly hungry, so I cook myself an omelette into which I throw just about anything I can find in the fridge: bacon, potatoes, a few leftover vegetables, chopped chives and so on, and serve it with a salad and a glass of wine. After lunch I could go for a long walk, I'm free to do so, but there's something in me which doesn't want to go out, and then have to come back and let myself into an empty house. I shall get over this but at the moment, especially after doing the bedroom, I feel raw, defenceless. So I find a notepad and start planning the supper party I might, or might not, have one evening this week. Thursday would be a good day. And I will definitely invite the Nugents. They were so good to me last night, and again this morning.

There's no reply from the Nugents, so I ring the others in turn, Sonia first. 'I apologize for the short notice. It seemed a good opportunity. I'm on my own this week, Becky's with my parents.'

'Don't apologize,' Sonia says. 'I quite like short notice things –

I mean when they're pleasant. They're unlooked-for pleasures. And I'd love to come. And how *is* Becky? I meant to ring you but somehow I didn't get around to it.' Of course she doesn't know the half of what's happened, does she? So I put her in the picture.

'Oh, poor Becky! Poor you! I *am* sorry,' she says. 'But it sounds as though it's going to be all right now. Evelyn's very wise, isn't she?'

I agree with her, wholeheartedly. 'I want to phone Nigel now,' I tell her. 'Do you think he'd mind if you gave me his home number? Or I could wait until tomorrow and ring him at the surgery.'

'Oh, I'm sure he wouldn't mind,' Sonia says quickly. 'In fact it's probably better than ringing him at the surgery. It's 2746. He might just be out; he goes to the symphony concerts in Brampton and I think there's one on today.'

I call him and he *is* out. His voice on the answerphone is warm and friendly, just as if he were standing right there in front of me. I once heard my own answerphone message and I sounded awful, very toffee-nosed. I'm always meaning to change it. I leave a message, asking him to call me back, then I ring Mark Dover, who had given me his number.

'Venus!' he says. 'What a pleasant surprise. Are you ringing to tell me you're going to let me paint your portrait?'

'No,' I say, 'I'm calling to ask you if you'd like to come to supper on Thursday. I've invited Sonia and she can, and I'm about to ring the others. I'm sorry it's such short notice.'

'Don't worry about that!' he says. 'And I'd love to come, but on one condition.'

'Really? And what condition is that?' I ask.

'If I come to your supper you've got to promise you'll let me paint your portrait.'

'You're very persistent,' I say.

'I know! I don't give up easily. You can choose your own day and time, but you've got to say "yes".'

'I can't just arrange something like that on the spur of the moment,' I demur.

'Of course you can!' he contradicts me. 'But if you like you can

211

just say "yes" now and make a definite date when I see you on Thursday.'

'You're very persuasive . . .' I begin.

'. . . I know,' he says. 'Persistent and persuasive. Come on, Venus!'

I give in. 'I can only come for an hour or so at a time,' I warn him – but he interrupts me again.'

'Oh, we'll sort out all that on Thursday!'

I ring off. He's another one who has a nice voice on the telephone; not as deep as Nigel's, lighter, as is his conversation; almost teasing, whereas Nigel's voice is not only deep, it is warm, reassuring. I could do with a dose of Nigel's voice right now. Why does he have to be at a concert in Brampton? I wonder what time he'll be back?

I shan't tell the Blessed Henry Mark Dover is to paint my portrait. I'm not sure why. It's just that – well – he might not approve, he might find it frivolous, especially as I haven't been in the parish ten minutes. Not that it has anything to do with Henry.

I ring Evelyn – I did wonder if she might be away, it being half-term, but she answers the phone. 'We'd love to come,' she says. 'Have you heard from Becky?'

I tell her I've spoken with her and everything seems OK. Then I dial Henry's number and Molly answers the phone.

'Oh, what a shame!' she says. 'We'd have loved to have come,' she sounds as though she really means it. 'The thing is, we can't. We're out on Thursday, in fact it's a busy week all round.'

'I'm sorry about that,' I say, 'but some other time!'

These telephone calls have really cheered me up. Such nice people, sounding really pleased to be invited. And they've given me something to plan for. Now I only have to wait for Nigel. I ask myself how I will feel if he says he can't make it. The answer is 'disappointed'. Very disappointed. I should have waited to ask him first. In the meantime I get out the cookery books and pore over them, deciding what I'll do. I have far too many cookery books for one who doesn't entertain much.

Nigel phones me around half-past five.

'Venus!' he says. 'I've been meaning to call you for the last day or two. Is everything OK? I mean with Becky?'

So I tell him the rest of the story. He is horrified about the burglary. 'Why didn't you ring me?' he says. 'I'd have come at once.'

'But that wasn't what I was phoning you about,' I say. 'I was calling to ask you if you could come to supper on Thursday. Sonia's coming – and the Sharps and Mark Dover.'

'Thank you, I'd like to,' he says. 'I shall be on call that evening – we take it in turn. But then for that matter you'll be on call, won't you?'

'I will,' I agreed. 'But with any luck perhaps neither of us will be needed.'

'Amen to that!' he says. 'I'm sorry I wasn't in when you rang earlier. I've been to the concert in Brampton. They have them once a month. Their own orchestra, or sometimes a visiting one, and sometimes a soloist. Quite good, really! Perhaps you might like to go some time – that's to say if it's in your line. I don't know whether you like music.'

'Oh I do!' I assure him. 'My husband and I used to go to concerts – until he found he couldn't sit through them, that is. He played the piano himself.' He played the piano until near the end, but now it stands there silently since Becky has neither the desire nor, frankly, the talent, and I can't play a note.

There's a very short silence, as there sometimes is when I speak of Philip, and then Nigel says, 'Yes. Well, I look forward to Thursday!'

I realize a minute later that Nigel is the only one to whom I've mentioned the burglary. Never mind, it can wait! In any case I wouldn't have wanted to have given the details four times over. My idea is to put it behind me and get on with life.

EIGHTEEN

I have decided that in the next few days, between now and Thursday's supper party for which I must plan and shop and cook, and apart from the fact that I have a Deanery meeting in Brampton on Tuesday afternoon, a burial of ashes on Wednesday morning, a wedding couple the same evening, and a sick visit this afternoon, I am reasonably clear – until something else crops up, as of course it will. When I've been here longer and I'm better known my days will undoubtedly be considerably fuller. That's the way it goes.

I'm pleased to be doing the sick visit this afternoon, not pleased that the lady – her name is Bertha Jowett and she's eighty-nine and housebound – is sick, but pleased that a member of the ten o'clock congregation, Jean Close, asked me to visit. She apologized for asking me.

'I know you're busy,' she said, 'but it would make such a difference to Miss Jowett. She's never married, she doesn't have any family and about the only people she sees are the chiropodist, the milkman if she's up in time, the doctor occasionally, and me. I told her about you – well, she'd read it in the *Echo* when you first came – but I told her I'd met you and she was very interested. It's very good of you to say you'll visit.'

'It's not especially good,' I told her. 'I'll be pleased to do it. Actually, I have to thank you for bringing Miss Jowett to my notice. How would I have known otherwise?' Half the time the clergy are criticized for not visiting those who need them when it's because they simply don't know about the need.

'Would you like me to be there when you come?' Jean Close asked.

'Yes, I would, I think that's a good idea. If we go together it might be easier for Miss Jowett,' I said. 'When would be convenient?'

'Monday afternoon?' Jean Close suggested. 'About four o'clock. She'll have had her afternoon nap by then. By the way, she's not a churchgoer.'

'That's OK,' I said. 'You don't have to be a fully-paid-up member to get a visit from the Vicar!'

So that's where I shall be this afternoon. She lives in one of the small cottages behind the High Street. It is possible, and it's not unusual, that she has no friends because she never took the trouble to make them when she was younger. It's also possible that she's a cranky old woman. I shall find out. It seems that there's no sort of mechanism in St Mary's for visiting the sick or housebound, or for taking them for hospital appointments or to the hairdressers or whatever. It's hit-and-miss. We had a scheme at Holy Trinity and it worked well, so it's one of the things I shall put on my thinking list, though bearing in mind that possibly it's already being done in informal ways I don't know about and which work quite well. If it isn't broken don't mend it! And I mustn't assume, when I list my bright ideas, that nobody has had them before.

Jean Close picks me up at the Vicarage just before four and we walk down to Miss Jowett's cottage and ring the bell. We wait a while and I lift my hand to ring again, thinking that at her age she's probably hard of hearing, but Jean says, 'No! She can't move very fast. It takes her time to stand up and walk to the door and she hates it if someone rings again when she's halfway there.'

I get my first surprise when Miss Jowett opens the door. For no reason at all I'd expected someone tallish, and thin, and there she is, small and round, dressed in a long grey skirt and a bright red, shapeless top with a floral scarf tied around her neck. In her mop of frizzy, yellowy-white hair, which needs the attention of a

215

brush and comb, perches a multi-coloured butterfly clip. She leans heavily on a silver-topped stick. Then when she speaks I get my second surprise.

'Ah! Vicar!' she says. 'How kind of you! Do come in! Quite a pleasant day is it not, or at least it looks that way from my window.'

Her voice is far from musical, not in the same street as Rose Barker's, but it is sharp and clear, not at all the voice of an octogenarian, and her accent is impeccable, and undeniably upper class; every vowel pure, every consonant sounded. Moreover, in spite of her smallness and her untidy appearance, she has an air of total confidence and assurance which speak to me of years of being in command. I see her as being something high up in an Oxford college. Another of my flights of fancy, of course!

We follow her slow progress into her living room; small, square, with a deep windowsill, and a low ceiling, which presumably was once white, and is now a dingy shade of yellowy beige, which I take to be from cigarette smoke, as could be the unusual shade of her hair. The whole place smells of cigarettes, and indeed there is one just burning itself out on an ashtray. But the most striking thing about the room is its clutter. Every shelf, every surface, magazine racks, most of the chairs and a fair amount of the floor is crammed. But it is not everyday clutter. If clutter can be called intellectual, then this is. Books galore (some of them open), dictionaries, sheaves of typed papers, art magazines. The walls are crowded with drawings, etchings, paintings – most, to my eyes and at a quick glance, originals.

'Jean,' Miss Jowett says, 'be a dear and clear a chair for the Vicar!' True to type, she makes no apology for the mess. Jean clears a rather beautiful armchair by piling the things from it on to another chair, and then perches herself on a small vacant corner of the sofa.

'It's so good of you to come,' Miss Jowett says. 'Jean has told me about you. I can't say I've never met a Vicar before. When I was young they were in and out of the house all the time because my family was High Church – the whole works; High Mass, incense, confession, gorgeous vestments for every occasion. Not me though. I am a firm unbeliever. But, you see, I've not met a woman priest until now.'

This is when I realize this is not a 'sick' visit in the strict sense of the word. Miss Jowett is not ailing. She's a woman who's elderly, not mobile, and therefore housebound – but ill she is not. I think she simply wanted a change of company and thought a meeting with a species she hadn't yet met with would provide that.

'My father must be spinning in his grave at the thought of me having one in my house! He wouldn't have approved at all. Dear me, no!' She says this with a wicked little laugh. She has got the better of us all, Father included.

I realize I am being used for – well, for entertainment! I'm a novelty! For two seconds I bridle at that, I resent it. I am not in my job to be used! But as fast as I think the words in my mind, I realize I'm wrong. Of course I'm in my job to be used! That's what it's about, isn't it? Nor should I expect to choose exactly how I'll be used. I must take it as it comes. I don't mind being a novelty for God. Also, I think, with Miss Jowett involved it could be fun for me as well as for her.

Poor Jean! She's looking quite uncomfortable. Without saying it in so many words – except to throw in that Miss Jowett wasn't a churchgoer – she'd given me the impression that here was an old lady, lonely, disabled, waiting for someone of my ilk to cheer her up, perhaps even to set her feet on the right path while there's still time. Nonsense! Apart from spending it in one place, this lady has a full life. Books, newspapers, journals, pens and paper – and in the corner of the room there is a state-of-the-art music centre. No, as a female priest, qualities unknown, I am simply a diversion. What she doesn't realize is that she will be a diversion for me. I do spend a great deal of my time with Christians, or those who apologize for *not* being Christians. Miss Jowett is not going to apologize. No Siree! So it will be a change for me and I give Jean a reassuring smile.

After that, without many preliminaries, I mainly answer Miss Jowett's questions. 'Do you like the job?' 'What made you do it?' 'Do they give you a hard time?' 'How much do you get paid?' 'Do you *really* believe in the resurrection?' and 'Would you agree

217

with me that, since the grave clothes were found neatly folded in the tomb, when Jesus spoke to Mary in the garden he must have been stark naked? Not even a fig leaf, let alone a loin cloth!'

This is a point of view which has never been put to me before. Like many unbelievers, Miss Jowett has studied her Bible. Jean has gone bright pink. 'And Christians don't like nakedness, do they?' Miss Jowett continues. 'They're not at all keen on the body, are they? One wonders why?'

She says these things not at all offensively, in no way prurient. I reckon she would enjoy a real discussion, like 'What about the naked body in art?' or how many angels could one get on the head of a pin, and really, her original premise about Jesus in the Garden is most interesting, but out of deference to poor Jean I deflect it and answer 'What made you do it?' and 'How much do you get paid?' Much easier.

'Shall I make a cup of tea?' Jean asks brightly, seeing an escape.

Miss Jowett looks at the clock on the mantelpiece, and it strikes in a silvery tone as if answering her look.

'Five o'clock,' she says, 'a bit early really, but at this time of day I prefer a gin-and-tonic. What about it, Vicar? Will you join me? It would be pleasant to have company.'

So I do, though it's early for me. Jean has a glass of water. After which, it's time to leave. 'I don't want to tire you!' I say.

'I am a bit weary,' Miss Jowett confesses, 'but only in the body. The body lets one down. So tiresome! In the head I feel as fresh as a daisy! Will you see yourselves to the door? I hope you'll come again!'

'Oh, I will!' I tell her. And I mean it. 'I've enjoyed myself.' But what I can't understand, I'm thinking as we leave, is how Jean came to be friendly with Miss Jowett. They are as different as chalk and cheese. 'How did you?' I ask as we walk back.

'She fell one day, in the village,' Jean tells me. 'Tripped over a broken paving stone just outside the butcher's. That was in the days when she could walk down the High Street. I took her home and it went from there. I hope she didn't shock you, Vicar!'

What Jean doesn't understand is that very little shocks a priest.

A priest has heard it all before. In any case, such a thing was never in Miss Jowett's mind.

Jean and I part company when we reach the Vicarage. 'Thank you,' I say. 'It was a most interesting visit.'

Somehow, I am a little less apprehensive as I let myself into the empty house, partly, I think, because my head is full of thoughts, one of which is – why am I affronted by Miss Frazer's denial of my validity and not the least bit so by Miss Jowett's complete repudiation of my entire faith? I know – or almost certainly I know – that I will never change Miss Jowett's views, nor will she shake mine. That doesn't matter. We have respect for each other. I know when she describes herself as a firm unbeliever she's not attacking either God or me, and when I accept her unbelief I'm not criticizing her. This could be a firm friendship based on two entirely different points of view. I might, however, not always choose to have Jean accompany me.

It wants at least a couple of hours before I need think about supper, there's no reason to eat early when Becky's not here, so I really will get around to putting my thoughts on paper. I sit at my desk to do this. My thoughts are less likely to stray, or my intentions weaken, than they would if I got too comfortable in an armchair. So I take a new A4 pad and put a new cartridge in my pen, and in bold capitals at the top of the page I write 'THINGS TO CONSIDER'. I shall write down the ideas as they come to me, not bothering about whether they're in the right order. It will be a sort of one-woman brainstorming session!

And then, wouldn't you know, I, whose mind has been teeming with things which need to be done, should be done, might possibly be done, could no way be done (though what if . . . ?), am staring at a blank sheet as if both my brain and my right hand were paralysed. So I get up, go into the kitchen and make a cup of tea, take a ginger biscuit out of the tin, dunk it in the tea, and say to myself, 'Come on, girl! Snap out of it!' – and return to my desk and do so.

'New form of baptism.'

'Care for the sick – sick visiting.'

'Cleaning the church.'

'Music in church – new Music Group.'

'Redecorating Parish Hall.'

'Closer relationship with school.'

'Re-vamp parish magazine.'

'Closer participation with congregation on everything.'

'Sunday School – integration into church.'

'Financial repercussions (if Miss F. withdraws support).'

So there we are! Ten things to think about. That's a start. But not one of them I can instigate without having discussed them with the PCC. So my first point of call is obviously with the Blessed Henry and with Richard, though the latter will not be easy to pin down because he works such long hours out of the parish.

So I ring Henry.

'I've got one or two ideas I'd like to discuss with you and Richard,' I tell him, not mentioning that one or two is actually ten, and doubtless more will arise. 'I know you have a busy week – Molly told me – but do you think we could find a time?'

Friday appears to be the only time and he says he will consult Richard about this and let me know.

'Could you give me an inkling of what this is about?' he asks. 'Just tell me some of them?'

'Well yes, I can,' I say. 'I've made a list. But before I go into that, what it's really about is getting *everyone* together to do these things. I don't want the usual scenario – which might not be the usual one at St Mary's but certainly was at Holy Trinity – of a few people doing everything. I'm looking for a situation where almost everyone in the congregation is involved in one way or another.'

'My goodness, you're ambitious!' Henry says. 'That *would* be unusual! In all my experience . . .'

'I know!' I interrupt. 'But what's wrong with trying for something unusual?'

'So tell me what you've got on the list,' he suggests.

When I read them out – quickly, so as to make them seem fewer – he lets out a long whistle.

'Oh, Venus!' he says. 'Aren't you trying to bite off more than you can chew?'

'I don't think so. I'm not thinking we can do everything at

once,' I assure him. 'And some things are more urgent than others. For instance, I do have the feeling that Miss Frazer will withdraw her financial support . . .'

'Oh, so do I!' he breaks in. 'And it's no use pretending it won't make a difference.'

'I know!' I agree. 'So we have to allow for it, make plans to make good the shortfall, somehow.'

He reminds me that most of these ideas will have to go to the PCC – which I'm aware of. And I tell him I don't want things to drag on, I want to make a start. 'And I don't want it to stay with the PCC. It's particularly important it doesn't. I want everyone possible to be involved, so as soon as the PCC have given it the go-ahead . . .'

'If they do!' Henry says.

I ignore that. I'm not starting this off by being negative.

'I want a meeting of everyone, and I mean everyone,' I tell him.

'We'll have to see!' he says, soothingly.

I don't want to be soothed, I want to be backed up, encouraged, but I daresay, I think after he's rung off, I'll have to pace myself, if only because I won't be able to move too quickly. Sooner or later someone is going to remark about a new broom sweeping clean, and this remark is usually a complaint, but I've never found anything wrong in the idea of a new broom sweeping clean. What else is a new broom for? And I've no intention of doing everything at a crawl. The next PCC meeting isn't due for another six weeks and I certainly don't want to wait that long to start discussions, so when I see Henry and Richard on Friday I shall ask why we can't have a special meeting as soon as possible – next week, for instance.

It's now three o'clock on Tuesday afternoon and I'm at the Deanery meeting, which takes place in Brampton and is attended by all the clergy from the fifteen parishes in the Deanery, whether priests or deacons. When I was at Holy Trinity I went to the Deanery meetings. I didn't enjoy them much then and I don't suppose I shall today. I am the only woman here in what is, and I daresay will be for a long time, a man's world. But there's no

221

sense in moaning about that, and I'm not doing so. I knew what I was letting myself in for.

Everyone mills about before the meeting starts. They mostly know each other, they are all boys together. Bitchy remarks fly around – not about me, presumably about each other, about those who should be here and are absent, or about clergy higher up the ladder; about who might be promoted next, and whether they are worthy. They tell each other jokes, some of which are too *risqué* for me to repeat, though if I am standing close they tend to lower their voices on the punchline. They needn't bother. I'm a big girl now. I think it's a male thing, telling jokes. Actually, none of them are rude to me, unless you like to call ignoring me almost completely rude, and I expect that will change as they get to know me.

The Rural Dean – the boss man of this meeting, whom of course I've met before – introduces and welcomes me. He is a charming man. To be fair to them, one or two clergy did speak to me before the meeting started, and now a couple of others turn around and give me a smile of welcome. I must be careful not to get a chip on my shoulder about this man/woman thing. Poor darlings, it's probably just as hard for them!

We talk about services, we talk about the difficulty, sometimes impossibility, of getting cover when we're away for any reason. There just aren't enough priests to go round. And, inevitably, we talk about finance. Was there ever a church meeting, large or small, where finance wasn't on the agenda? I was never at one. It isn't that we're mad keen to do so – though one or two thoroughly enjoy it – but that we're always short of money to do the things we have to do if we're to keep going. There's a widespread idea among non-churchgoers that the Church of England is financed by the state. It comes out of taxes. Not so! Oh, most definitely not so! It is kept going by the people in the pews. It is kept going by jumble sales, church fairs, raffles, special collections. Imagine having a raffle to keep up with the running of Buckingham Palace!

When it's over the Rural Dean says good-bye to me – as do one or two others – says he's glad I could come and tells me he hopes to visit us in St Mary's ere too long.

222

I stay in Brampton for a while to do some shopping for Thursday's supper. I can't get everything in the village. When I get back to the Vicarage there's a message on the answerphone to call Cliff Preston, which I do.

'How are you?' he asks. I tell him I'm well, ask how he is. He tells me he's well, then says, 'A funeral next Tuesday, can you do?'

'Yes, as long as it doesn't clash with the ten o'clock Eucharist,' I say. 'Anyone I know?'

'No,' he says. 'Not a churchgoer. But a service in church and then the crematorium. Eleven o'clock all right?'

We mention the service sheets, which he says will be done by a local printer after I've given him the details. 'If we had a printer,' I say, we could do all the service sheets for weddings and funerals. We could make a bit of profit.'

'Well, why not do it?' Cliff asks. 'It sounds sensible.'

'It is sensible,' I agree, 'but I can't see the PCC voting to buy a printer. We haven't the money.'

But if we had a printer, I'm thinking, perhaps we could do our own parish magazine instead of paying for it to be produced. So after I've spoken to Cliff I go and add it to my list.

'Printer – service sheets, magazine: Source of income?'

The supper party goes very well. The food – you don't want to know the whole menu, do you? – went down well, and I'd chosen a nice wine, though most of them also brought a bottle of wine with them. This must be the way it is in Thurston. We found plenty to talk about, both through the meal and afterwards, around the table. I told them about the burglary, and they were both appalled and sympathetic.

'I've told her, she should have given me a ring,' Nigel said. 'I'd have been round here at once!'

'Me too!' Mark said.

What a lovely thought! Two men rushing to my rescue!

'I rang Henry Nugent,' I said. 'Poor Henry! I'm afraid I always turn to him.'

'Because he's your churchwarden,' Evelyn says, sensibly. 'Anyway, I'm glad Becky wasn't here.'

'So am I,' I agree. And that's all we say about Becky.

'Henry thinks I should get a dog,' I tell them.

'That's not a bad idea,' Sonia says. 'I'm sure Becky would like that, and you'd feel safer when you had to leave her in.'

'I had already been thinking about it,' I admit. 'Perhaps I'll do something.'

'Get a big one!' Mark Dover advises. 'Choose one which looks as though it'll tear a burglar to pieces the minute he sets foot!'

'Oh, Mark, do be practical!' I protest. 'How would Becky cope with a great big dog? If I do get one, she has to learn to take her share of looking after it. How would *I* cope with it for that matter?'

'No more difficult than a small one,' Mark says.

'Choose a small one which makes a lot of noise,' Evelyn suggests. 'Probably the noise is enough to frighten away someone who's up to no good.'

After this everyone gives their view of dogs they have known, everyone has a relevant anecdote, and then they decide what would be best for me. At a point when this conversation seems like going on for ever, Mark breaks in. I think he's had enough of dogs.

'Has Venus told you I'm going to paint her portrait?' he asks.

There's a short, surprised silence and I sense there's maybe a slight feeling that it's something which has been arranged behind everyone's back. I also have the feeling, I can't pin down why, that Mark Dover is possibly, though not to any great degree, *persona non grata*.

'It's not quite fixed . . .' I begin.

'Oh yes it is!' Mark says. 'You promised me! You can't deny it, and I won't let you off!'

He is flirting with me! I can't quite say how I know this, but I do. I know flirting when I encounter it. Perhaps it's something in the intimacy in his voice.

Do I want this? I'm not sure. I like Mark, I like him very much indeed. He's easy to talk to and he doesn't hold back. There's no reason why I should dislike it. I'm a woman, and it's a normal feeling for a woman to be pleased, or certainly not displeased, when an attractive man flirts with her. And I'm free to be flirted with. Not that one has to be free, not just for flirting. Philip knew

224

how to flirt. He flirted with most of my women friends, especially if they were pretty. It didn't mean anything, or nothing serious. It was me he loved. And when I say it didn't mean anything I'm not being derogatory. Flirting is pleasant. It oils the wheels. It lightens life.

Did I ever flirt when Philip was alive? I'm not sure. I doubt I was very good at it but it's a safe sort of thing, especially when one is secure in one's marriage.

Is it the fact that I'm a priest, and therefore supposedly inaccessible, which attracts Mark? Is that why he wants to paint me in my cassock?

But on my side the fact that I'm a priest doesn't mean that I don't have a woman's feelings. It doesn't mean that I'm sexless. I had thought when Philip died, that this was the end of all sexual feeling for me. Who other than Philip could arouse that in me? But Nature doesn't let go so easily. She waits – but she doesn't go away.

'So when?' Mark persists – and to keep him quiet I agree to Monday afternoon.

No-one leaves until after midnight, and then there is a mass exodus. When I close the door on my friends I feel elated, stimulated – and a little bereft – all at the same time: bereft because I'm left on my own, but then I remind myself that Sonia, Mark and Nigel are all going home alone, only the Sharps are a couple. Sometimes I have the feeling that the world is made up of couples, but it ain't necessarily so!

I say my night prayers in bed, which might not be entirely respectful to God, but I do say them with a thankful heart. It was a good evening.

225

NINETEEN

When the phone rings just after nine o'clock this morning it's Henry, to tell me that he's pinned Richard down and they'll both be with me this evening. Eight o'clock.

'Great,' I say. 'Thanks a million, Henry!'

I feel pleased with life. I shall spend as much of the day as I can in thinking out my plans and writing everything down, trying to anticipate every question Henry and Richard might put to me so that I can be ready with an answer. I shall banish Miss Frazer from my mind. I've already obeyed the Bishop and remembered her in my morning prayers and that's the sum total of what she'll get from me today. So, for the moment, I shall leave Miss Frazer to God. He'll make a better job of it – though I know, even as I think this, that what God will do is work through someone else. He has the knack of that. And perhaps it won't be me. I'm not sure I'd be the right person. Anyway, enough of that for now. I have exciting and very, very positive things to think about.

I am getting on nicely, I've made lots of notes, when, at ten o'clock, the phone rings again. It's the Bishop.

He goes through the preliminaries, like 'How are you?', 'Nice day, isn't it?', then he says, 'I've had another letter from Miss Frazer!'

'Damn Miss Frazer . . . !' I start to say, and then I remember who I'm talking to.

If he's heard me, and I'm sure he must have, he ignores it.

'A very angry letter,' he says. 'In reply to mine, of course. I couldn't expect not to receive one, could I? Anyway, I thought I'd better ring you, put you in the picture so you'd know what her latest is.'

'Thank you,' is all I can think of to say.

'As I said,' he continues, 'she's angry. I won't read every word to you, just give you the gist of it. She draws attention to how long she and her family have worshipped in St Mary's, how they've unstintingly supported the church – and she includes a catalogue of all the things the Frazer family have done over the years, which I must say is an impressive one. Not that I think one has to be grateful for evermore for things given. I expect she's one of those persons who give something and then continue to keep an eye open to see what's being done with it. When I was small I had an aunt like that. She'd give one a birthday present and then keep tabs on how it was being treated. I had to make sure it was on show every time she visited. But I'm digressing, and I mustn't.'

I quite liked his digression. It's difficult to think of such a senior bishop having once been a small boy with a difficult aunt.

'Miss Frazer tells me she has no intention of worshipping in another church,' he says. 'She will continue at St Mary's. "I will not be driven out" is the way she puts it. But no way will she take communion from a woman, a . . .' He pauses briefly, as if he was deciding whether or not to say the next bit, and then decides he will: '. . . "a so-called priest." And because I will not agree to have you moved she states that she is being deprived of her weekly communion.'

'I'm sorry, Bishop . . .' I begin.

'There is no reason for you to apologize,' he breaks in. 'You are not depriving her, I am not depriving her; she is doing it to herself. She is making the choice. A wrong choice, I believe, but hers to make. You are not responsible and you must not allow yourself to think that you are. I don't know what she will do. It would be better if she just didn't come to the altar – and I told her this in my previous letter. But you are to stand no nonsense

227

from her in your church and you mustn't hesitate to call on your churchwardens for help.'

'I will,' I promise. 'Let's hope it doesn't come to that!'

'And then there's the next bit,' he says. 'She goes on to tell me that in the circumstances she is withdrawing all her financial support from St Mary's, immediately. But that was to be expected, wasn't it? So don't worry too much about that either.'

'I'm sorry about it,' I say, 'but yes, I did expect it. In fact I'm already starting to think of ways to remedy it!'

'Good!' he says. 'Later on you must tell me what they are. It won't be easy. It was a large amount, as I'm sure you and everyone else is aware. I gather Miss Frazer was not one to keep quiet about her good works. However, I shall send a short reply to this last letter. I shall express my regrets, I shall thank her, yet again, for all she has done for St Mary's and I shall repeat that I have every confidence in you and there is no way at all you are likely to be moved.'

'Thank you, Bishop!' I say.

'Keep me in the picture,' he says. 'Tell Henry Nugent to ring me.' And then he gives me a blessing, at which I immediately feel better, and rings off.

Henry and Richard arrive together, right on time.

'I did wonder,' Henry says as we take our seats around the table, 'whether we should ask Rose Barker, as the PCC secretary. I thought it might be useful to have her take notes, but in the end I thought not. It is, after all, just an informal meeting to talk things over.'

I get a faint whiff of danger here. Does 'informal' mean 'not-all-that-important'? Because if it does I'm already in opposition, which is not what I wanted. Some disagreements I expect, but a fight – especially with my churchwardens – I don't want. But calm down, I tell myself. Stop putting too much emphasis simply on a choice of words.

'So you kick off, Venus,' Henry says. 'You tell us what you have in mind and we'll tell you whether we think it will work.'

'Especially if it will work in St Mary's,' Richard puts in.

'Remember, we know St Mary's, and with the best will in the world you don't, not yet. You haven't been here long enough.'

'I take your point,' I say. 'What I don't totally accept is that because a congregation – any congregation – hasn't done something in the past it will necessarily be against doing it in the future. It could be that they've never been asked, that the ideas have never been put to them. I would agree that probably most congregations don't move fast or far on their own. They prefer to be led. But once they are, even only initially, it's amazing what they'll do. Given the incentive, which is up to us.'

'Right!' Henry says. Do I detect a sigh? 'Let's go through the list and see what we think.'

'Fine!' I say. 'But it's not just this specific list I'm interested in, though everything in it could be important to some degree. It's about changing attitudes, getting as many people as possible to be involved, to take responsibility for their own church.'

'So let's get on with the list,' Henry repeats. 'Is there any special order?'

'Not as written,' I say. 'It was just as things came into my head. But some order's bound to emerge.'

'Finances will come into it,' Henry says. 'Especially if Miss Frazer opts out!'

At this point I stop to tell them about the Bishop's call. They are both appalled, not to mention worried about the financial aspects of it. I tell them I'm sorry and they're both decent enough to tell me it's not my fault. 'Let's face it,' Richard says, 'Miss Frazer is an unpleasant, bossy woman who if she doesn't get her own way will make trouble wherever she can. It's unfortunate that she has the clout to make financial trouble.'

We go through the list.

'New form of baptism,' Richard says. 'Well, that was mentioned at the last PCC meeting. There wasn't much opposition there. I think it's a good idea. So that shouldn't be difficult – at least not to try.'

'Redecorating the parish hall,' Henry says. 'No-one can say that's not sorely in need of doing. But whether we'll be able to do it now is another matter.'

'That's the kind of thing I mean,' I say. 'Or one of them. We get a working party together, men and women. Someone – I'll have to remember who – told me her husband would always get us paint and suchlike at a discount. We'd use the same method about cleaning the church, only that would have to be a regular roster.' I'd been amazed when I came to St Mary's to find that they paid a cleaning company good money every month to clean the church (rather indifferently at that).

'We've been cushioned by Miss Frazer's contribution for a long time,' Richard admits.

We continue through the list. Some things are controversial, some are not. For instance, the idea of a music group – guitars, a keyboard, various other musical instruments – is viewed with startled apprehension. 'People like the organ,' Henry says. 'They've always been used to it.' I point out that this isn't a meeting for making decisions right now on specific things. The only decision I want here and now is that we should have a PCC within the next ten days, and from that we should aim to have a meeting of as many of the congregation as we can persuade to come, so that I can put my ideas to everyone. 'And I hope you agree that we don't have to keep something going just because people are used to it,' I say.

I tell them I would like to have the meeting of the congregation in the Vicarage. 'I know it'll be a squash,' I say, 'well I hope it will be, and if it's not I'll be disappointed – but I think we'll get a better atmosphere than in the parish hall. I might have to borrow some chairs, and some cups or glasses, but never mind that now!'

It's ten-thirty before we break up. I go to bed in quite a happy frame of mind. And tomorrow, I'm thinking as I put the light out, Becky will be home.

I wakened this morning with the lovely feeling that something good was going to happen. And then I remembered. It's Saturday, and Becky will be coming back. I check the time; it's eight o'clock. I must have slept like a log. This is the first night I've slept at all well since the burglary. I feel great! I jump out of bed with more than my usual alacrity, and draw back the curtains. It's also – a bonus – a lovely day out there. Everything is washed in sunlight. It's too late for there to be any leaves left on the trees, except for one or two holly trees at the bottom of the garden, and the bay tree nearer to the house, but the bare, black, upward-thrusting branches of the sycamores, which are the most common tree around here – there's at least one in almost every garden – are outlined against a clear blue sky.

I know the main reason for my uplifted spirits is Becky but remembering last night's meeting with Henry and Richard is also a boost. They might well have dampened my enthusiasm, sent me away with my tail between my legs, but they didn't, and I'm so grateful for that. It's the first hurdle well and truly jumped. They'll get Rose Barker to round everyone up, to inform them it's a three-line whip.

I feel so good that I sing in the shower. 'Oh What a Beautiful Morning' followed by a bit of the Hallelujah Chorus, which is not easy to sing under running water!

After breakfast I go out into the garden. There are still a few plants in flower – dahlias, Michaelmas daisies, hardy fuchsias, the deep pink sedum, Autumn Joy, which I note will need dividing in the spring, and a few late roses – but most of the colour comes from berries and from the red-leaved plants which haven't yet shed their leaves. A *Rhus cotinus*, with its reddish-purple leaves now catching the sun, looks as though it's on fire. But why do gardens, at almost any time of the year, need tidying? This one certainly does.

Once again, I'm interrupted by the telephone. I almost always forget to carry the cordless one around with me so I have to go into the house. It's my mother.

'Actually,' she says, 'we're almost ready to leave. Would it be all right if we arrived for lunch instead of later, as planned?'

'Lovely!' I assure her. 'Any time you like.'

'Don't bother to cook,' she says. 'Something cold will be fine. Or perhaps some soup.'

'Don't worry, I'll think of something!' I tell her.

I already have, even while she was still talking. At the weekend Gander's sell really good quiches. If I get down there quickly maybe they'll have some left. I can heat them up and we can have them with a salad, or those little new potatoes one seems to be

231

able to buy all the year round. Fruit for pudding. So I leave the garden and set off for the village. I wonder, as I walk down the High Street, whether I might meet with Mark Dover; but I don't. Am I disappointed? I'm not sure. I don't meet with anyone else I know – except that I see Mrs Bateman a little way off, and I'm pretty sure she's seen me and that this is why she crosses to the other side of the road. I don't feel annoyed with Mrs Bateman, just vaguely irritated and rather sorry. Who would want to be in thrall to Miss Frazer? Little Mrs B. needs to be rescued.

When I get back I lay the table in the dining room, wash the salad and the potatoes, and still have time to skim through the *Brampton Echo* which I bought from Mr Chester – who asked after Becky because he hadn't seen her all week. I explained that she'd been with her grandparents. 'I'll probably bring her in later today,' I told him.

I only get the *Brampton Echo* when I happen to be in the village at the right time but now, reading bits of it, I wonder if I shouldn't put in an order to have it delivered regularly. It would keep me in touch with what's happening, or at least what's happening in the area. It's heavy on local news, though light on national and world affairs, unless it can give them a local slant. 'Brampton Man in Italian Car Smash!' It has crosswords, agony columns, sports news, astrological predictions (naturally, I check on my star sign, which is Virgo and therefore never very exciting. Virgos, it seems, are work horses and perfectionists), plus two long columns of births, marriages and deaths. I am skipping through these last when my family arrives. Oh, the joy of it!

Becky, who submits to a big hug, looks well, and much happier than when I left her last weekend. My mother says they've had a lovely week, Becky has eaten like a horse (no change there, then), and Dad doesn't say much but looks as contented as ever. He's a happy man, my Dad. Perhaps because he doesn't ask for much?

I'm aware that I have to tell my parents about the burglary, and at some point this weekend I shall have to tell Becky. I can't imagine it not being mentioned at school and I can't let her be unprepared for that. When Becky goes up to her room, not on

232

this occasion to hide away and sulk, but to re-instate her family of soft toys, I take the opportunity to tell my parents. My mother lets out a small scream, quickly stifled lest Becky should hear it. Dad swears at the idea that anyone should do this to his daughter.

'I'm OK,' I tell them. 'I'm absolutely OK. And I've got to get it over to Becky that everything goes on as before, so you'll have to help me. The last thing I want is for her to be frightened.'

When she comes downstairs I tell her.

I do it in an almost unconcerned manner. A sort of 'these things happen' tone of voice. 'He didn't go in your room,' I tell her. 'And I don't suppose he'll ever come back. It's not a house with a lot to steal!'

To my utter amazement she takes it entirely in her stride. It seems – why did I never know this? – that two girls in her school in Clipton had burglars, and to hear Becky talk it gave them some sort of status. My daughter is going to make capital out of this. My mother looks at my father with eyebrows which almost disappear into her hair. Dad looks unsurprised. Perhaps he knows Becky better than we do.

I don't prolong the subject because I have something better to say.

'I'm thinking of getting a dog!' I announce.

There's a stunned silence for a couple of seconds and then Becky gives a wild whoop of true joy. This is the first whoop of joy she's given since we came to Thurston and it's music to my ears.

'We have something to tell you, also,' my mother says when there's a short pause in the doggy fuss. 'I hope you'll be pleased, I think you will.' She pauses.

'So? What is it?' I ask. I can't imagine! A DVD player? A new car? Not before time if that's it.

'We've been talking it over for a while,' she says, 'but now we've made up our minds.'

'So when are you thinking of telling me?' I enquire. 'Or are you going to keep it secret?'

'Of course not!' she says, a bit sharply. 'What it is is that your father and I have decided that we're going to leave Clipton.

233

We're going to sell the house. There's nothing to keep us there now that you live here.'

I feel a sudden, horrible shock! What *are* they going to do? Where are they going? A villa in Spain? A house in France? I never thought of my parents as globe-trotters. I don't like it!

'Oh Mother!' I cry. 'Why? Where will you go?'

'Well, we thought we'd look for a flat in Thurston,' she says calmly, as if there was no other place in the world they'd think of going. 'That's to say, if you don't mind the idea. We wouldn't intrude, of course, but we could be on hand for Becky when you wanted it.'

'MIND?' I say. 'Whatever made you think I'd mind? I'm delighted! I just can't tell you . . .'

'It's fab!' Becky says. 'Wicked!'

I go to my mother and give her a hug, and then I do the same to my father, who so far hasn't spoken.

'Are you happy about it, Dad?' I ask. 'Tell me you are!'

'Of course I am! Why wouldn't I be? It makes sense. Anyway, I like Thurston.'

'He likes the Ewe Lamb,' my mother says. 'Home from home that'll be! We'll always know where to find him.'

'Did you know about this?' I ask Becky.

'Of course not!' she says. 'Wasn't I just as surprised as you?'

'Until we'd told you,' my mother says, 'we didn't tell anyone. You might not have liked the idea.'

'Oh, Mother, don't be daft!' I say. 'I think it's wonderful! I'm going to get the bottle of sherry out and we'll all drink to it!'

As it turns out, the sherry bottle is almost empty.

'Never mind,' I say. 'I shall nip down to the wine shop and buy a bottle of bubbly! This is really a special occasion!'

Saturday continues to be a very happy day indeed. We talk and talk. My parents decide that they'll put their house on the market as soon as they get back to Clipton on Monday, though Dad, being cautious, says, 'What happens if we sell our house before we find something in Thurston?'

'That's no problem, or not a big one,' I say. 'There's no reason why you shouldn't stay with me until you find somewhere of your own.'

Conversation about the proposed move – shall they start looking for a house in Thurston right away, or would it be better to wait a week or two, see how the land lies on selling the house in Clipton, and what kind of place should they look for in Thurston – a cottage, a flat, a house? – takes us through lunch and well into the afternoon. And then there's the question of the dog. As far as Becky is concerned it's a *fait accompli*. We have only to decide what sort we want and she's convinced it will be there waiting for us. We'll just have to bring it home. We're all agreed we should get one from the Dog Rescue Centre, partly because we have a particularly good one not far from Thurston, and partly because I'm not sure whether I'd be any good at training a puppy. Becky would like us to get in the car right now, and drive over there.

'It's not like that,' I tell her. 'We have to make an appointment. And *we* will have to be approved, it's not just a case of us choosing a dog. They'll want to know whether we're suitable to have one.'

'Of course we are!' Becky protests. 'I love dogs.'

'I know you do,' I agree. 'And I'm prepared to love the right dog. But there's a lot more to it!' And then I remember the books I have from the library, which I've not yet returned. 'Wait a minute!' I say to Becky. I go and fetch the books from my bedroom. 'Here you are! Read these. And then when we go to the Rescue Centre I'm sure you'll get points for that.'

She starts to read, avidly, but it doesn't keep her quiet because she keeps reading bits aloud to the rest of us. By evening Dad has had enough. It's not that he doesn't like dogs, it's not that he isn't interested in moving to Thurston, but there's a limit to what can be said at this stage, and he's reached it. So he takes himself off to the Ewe Lamb, Becky takes herself off to bed with the books and my mother and I watch television, which is its usual Saturday night rubbish.

I slept well last night, and now Sunday is here. I've done the eight o'clock and people are coming in for the ten o'clock. It wants only two minutes to ten, but there is no sign of Miss Frazer. Nor, as a matter of fact, is there any sign of Mrs

Bateman. When the church clock strikes ten I go in and take my place. If Miss Frazer has timed it to appear right now she could make a really dramatic entrance, but no, she doesn't. She doesn't appear and the service goes as smoothly as silk. Nor is she lying in wait when we leave the church. God is good!

I go into coffee. Miss Frazer is not mentioned to me by anyone and a surprising number of people go out of their way to be affable towards me, asking how I am, and if I'm feeling better. Someone says, 'Do sit down, Vicar! I'll get your coffee!' I can't think why this is until someone says, 'It happened to my sister and it took her ages to get over it,' and then I realize all this goodwill is lingering because of the burglary. How kind! How sympathetic!

It's while I'm waiting for my coffee that the church treasurer, George Phillipson, joins me.

'I phoned you yesterday morning but you must have been out. I didn't leave a message on your answerphone because, actually, I thought it was a face-to-face matter, and in any case I was going to be out myself for the rest of the day. I always go to visit my son on a Saturday. It's awful, isn't it?'

I'm confused, and I must look it, because he says, 'Don't say you haven't heard!'

'Heard what?' I ask.

'I was sure you would have. When I couldn't get you, I told Henry. It's Miss Frazer! I had a letter from her. She's written to the bank and cancelled everything!'

'That doesn't surprise me,' I reply. 'Did she give a reason?' Not that I don't know the reason.

He looks embarrassed. 'Well . . .' Then he hesitates.

'Come on George, you can tell me!' I say.

'Well, to tell the truth she said not a penny more would we get out of her while St Mary's allowed itself *to be led by a heretic*! I really thought that was a bit strong – I don't mean about the money, I'm thinking of what she said about you! Most uncalled for!'

I don't know whether to laugh or cry, or to beat my fists on the table! The lady certainly has a rare turn of phrase.

'She also said that this wasn't the end. I don't know what she means by that since she's chopped off every penny!' he says. 'What more can she do?'

'She'll think of something!' I say. 'But never mind, George. We'll also think of something. I'm sure there are lots of things we can do. We'll discuss it at the next PCC meeting.'

TWENTY

I see Becky off to school this morning after the half-term break. I can't say either of us is totally happy, but I pin my hopes on the steps Evelyn Sharp has taken and especially in her assurance that a close watch will be kept on Becky. Without sounding worried I remind Becky that if she has any problem at all she should seek out Mrs Fawcett at break time or dinnertime, and tell her about it. I also remind her, and this does seem to cheer her up, that Mr Beagle will be back today. I ask if she would like me to walk down to school with her but she will have none of that.

'Well then, have a good day!' I say.

She's a bit tearful about leaving her Grandma and Granddad but my mother says, 'Just remember, Becky love, it won't be long before we're living in Thurston. We'll be able to see each other every day then.'

My parents decide that before they leave for Clipton they'll walk down the High Street and take a look in the estate agent's window, just to see what's on offer and to get an idea of prices. Actually, it's my mother who decides. Dad thinks it's too soon. 'We should wait a bit!' he protests. 'See how we go with selling ours. It could take months!'

My mother raises her eyes to heaven.

'Oh, Ernest,' she complains, 'you are a wet blanket! In any

case we're only going to look in the window. We're not going to march into the office and buy a place on the spot! Are you coming with us, love?' she asks, turning to me.

'Try keeping me away!' I say. 'And cheer up, Dad! No-one's going to take any money off you just yet!'

Thurston is not a big village but it has two estate agents though I can't imagine how they can both make a profit because one sees very few 'For Sale' signs on houses around here. Obviously, we shall visit both of them. They are both in the High Street: Hanson's, opposite Gander's, the baker, is the first we come to, Trim & Parker's is a little lower down on the same side. They look more or less identical from the outside, smartly painted in black and white, large window filled with cards giving glowing details and colour photographs, every property a 'Des Res'.

Dad is shocked to the core by the prices. 'We'd never afford that, Mavis!' he says, even of the smallest property. 'It's outrageous! Daylight robbery!'

'Don't be silly, Ernest!' my mother says. 'It's all in accordance with what we get for ours. House prices have shot up!'

Hanson's window, however, reveals nothing quite small enough for them, at least not situated in the village, and they don't want to live far out so we walk down to Trim & Parker's and, alas, nor is there anything there which catches the eye.

'Why don't we go in and ask?' I suggest. 'I don't suppose everything they have is in the window.'

My mother is keen to do that; Dad isn't. I hold the balance so in we go. A charming young man who introduces himself as Rowan Trim flips through two card indexes. 'Something small,' he murmurs. 'Two bedrooms, in or near to the village. Well, I'm afraid it does appear there's nothing on the books at the moment which would fill the bill. But new ones come in all the time,' he adds (which I can't quite believe). 'Let me take your details and the minute there is something I'll put it in the post to you!' There follows a discussion as to whether it would be better to send the details to me or to Clipton, but in the end it's decided they should go to both.

'Oh,' says Mr Trim, as I give my address, 'then you must be the new Vicar! I have to confess I don't get to church often. Sunday is a busy day!'

On the way back we decide that we might as well give Hanson's a try, it's only fair, so we call in and there we go through exactly the same procedure except that Mr Hanson is afraid he doesn't go to church because he's in a football team which plays on Sunday mornings, and he can't let them down, can he?

Halfway back to the Vicarage I remember that I need a wholemeal loaf, so my parents go on and I return to Gander's.

'I saw you going into Hanson's,' Dulcie Gander remarks – and waits for an explanation. And since I reckon she has her ear to the ground at least as much as Hanson's or Mr Trim, I give it to her.

'I'll keep my eyes open,' she promises.

So now my parents have departed, my mother on a high, ready for anything, as excited as a girl. Dad is not so – or if he is he's keeping it hidden. It isn't that he doesn't want to come to Thurston, I know he does, but whereas my mother will revel in every last little arrangement, taking it all in her stride, Dad would like to go to sleep one night in his present bedroom and waken next morning in the new bedroom in Thurston, with everything, right down to his sock drawer, in the same place he's been used to in Clipton.

I do a few odd jobs, then I get ready to go to Mark Dover's for the first sitting of my portrait. I change into my cassock, put on a clean, white collar, fix two or three heated rollers in the top of my hair – I do want to look as feminine as possible and actually I would like to have had Sandra give me a blow dry but that might have been a bit over the top, so I do the best I can. Then I spend quite some time putting on my make-up to make it appear as though I'm not wearing any at all but am just radiantly healthy. Then I'm into my car, driving up the road, and ringing Mark's doorbell. He's a long time answering and I begin to wonder if I've got the day wrong, or the time, until in the end he opens the door.

'I'm sorry!' he says. 'I was out at the back, in the studio, getting things ready. Shall we go straight out?' He sounds very businesslike and I hope that's how he's going to be.

The canvas is already on the easel, and there is a rather nice chair with polished wooden arms, the seat and back upholstered in a dull red material, set up two or three yards away in which he invites me to sit.

'Would you like a cup of tea or a drink of water or anything before we make a start?' he asks, but I can tell by the tone of his voice that this is not what he wants me to do, he wants to get on with things. So I say, 'No, thank you.'

'Good!' he says. 'Now it's important that you sit comfortably, or you'll fidget. So take your time!' (But not too much of it, his tone of voice says.)

'How would you like me to sit?' I ask. 'Straight-backed? Relaxed? Bending forward a bit?'

'Just sit!' he says. 'You'll find it more comfortable if you sit back in the chair, and fairly upright. If you slouch to begin with you'll eventually find yourself sliding down.'

So I do as I'm told and I put a hand on each chair arm and I think I'm probably posed quite well. He looks at me critically, eyes narrowed, then he comes across to me, takes my hands from the chair arms and puts them together in my lap, the right one resting lightly on the left. Then he puts a finger under my chin and slightly tilts my head while turning it so that I'm looking to the left. But that's still not quite right. He does all this quite impersonally, as though I am a rag doll, not flesh and blood.

'I want you looking *slightly* to the left,' he explains, 'so that we get a suggestion of your profile – you have rather a nice profile, by the way! But though your head is turned a little I want your eyes to be looking directly at me. I find it very important in a portrait that the model has eye contact with me.' This, I think, as I fix my gaze on his rather beautiful dark eyes and he looks straight back at me, is not quite so impersonal, though perhaps he's seeing me merely as features and colours on a canvas.

'Right!' he says, 'I'll make a start. I'm going to block it in, get the position, get the angles and the proportions. About twenty minutes if you can hold it that long. If you can't hold the pose just give me a sign. I must say, Venus, you look very fetching in that cassock and the white collar! Did you join the priesthood to get the uniform? No! Don't smile,' his voice is suddenly sharp. 'If you smile you move your body. Hold it!'

I will hold it if it kills me! I will imagine that I have been turned into a block of stone, that there is no way whatsoever that I can move so much as one joint of my little finger, not even an eyelash!

'You've gone all rigid,' he says. 'Don't be rigid. It shows in your face. Be relaxed, but still!'

For the next twenty minutes he doesn't speak, and nor do I because I don't dare to. There is a pain in the small of my back which is killing me and an itch on the end of my nose which I would give a year of my life to be able to scratch, but eventually he says, 'There! That's fine! We'll take a break. I suggest you move around a bit.'

Miraculously, now that I've been given permission to scratch it, the itch on my nose has disappeared.

I drift around the studio, looking at the paintings and sipping a drink of water. There is no time for luxuries like coffee. Mark takes no break at all, he is busy mixing colours on his palette and making some adjustments to the canvas and he hardly speaks. All his concentration is on the job in hand. I rather like him in this mood.

'Right!' he says. 'Back to work?'

He comes and moves me around as he wants to – the rag doll bit – taking his references from the work he's done on the canvas, then he starts to paint again.

I sit still, not speaking for fear I should move the wrong muscle. What I do discover about sitting is that though one has to control one's body, the mind is free to wander everywhere, and indeed mine does. It goes from where my parents might find a property, to how is Becky doing at school, to Miss Frazer, to the Bishop, to last week's supper party – taking in Sonia, Nigel, the Sharps, and Mark himself – who is looking at me more intently than I've ever been looked at in my life, yet seeing, I presume, nothing beyond my outward appearance. I then branch

242

out and wonder how it feels to be the Queen, sitting for those endless portraits, and I wonder where *her* thoughts wander. Is she thinking, 'What will my family do next?'

The thought of family brings me back to Becky. I am anxious to see her after this first day back at school.

'There!' Mark says at long last, standing back from the canvas. 'I think that's it for today. You're free to move!'

I stand up and stretch myself. 'Can I look at it?' I ask.

'Yes,' Mark says. 'As long as you remember that it's only just begun.'

I'm impressed by it, as I always am by anyone who can take a brush and some paint, or a piece of charcoal, and make something come alive on a piece of paper or a canvas. I could never do that. I am also, in this case, intrigued by the way Mark sees me. It isn't how I see myself. Here is a woman strong and decisive – even though the work isn't far advanced, and so far there's not much colour in it, that's how it comes through to me. I don't dislike that but I hope, as it develops, he'll also see a softer, more feminine side in contrast to the starkness of the cassock and clerical collar which were Mark's choice. The Queen, of course, can choose an utterly ravishing outfit. I say as much to Mark.

'You have to believe me, Venus,' he says, 'you look as ravishing in your cassock as the Queen does in her ball gown!' Now that he's stopped painting he's back to his lay-it-on-with-a-trowel flattery.

'Stay and have some tea,' he says.

'I'm sorry, I can't, I have to be back for Becky,' I remind him.

'But you *will* be here Wednesday,' he says. 'We have to press on with it if I'm to put it in the December exhibition.'

'I'll be here Wednesday, and Monday next week,' I assure him. He has reckoned he could do it with three sittings.

'I'm looking forward to the exhibition,' Mark says. 'The catalogue will say "Venus", and they'll expect a nude goddess!' There is a gleam in his eye.

'Instead of which they'll get a clothed-from-top-to-toe, ordinary woman,' I put in.

'Not ordinary!' Mark says.

I don't need to set eyes on Becky when she comes home from school to know that she is a different girl, or, rather, she is my original Becky restored to me. I am in the kitchen, putting the kettle on, when the front door opens and she calls out.

'Mum! It's me!'

'I'm in the kitchen!' I shout – and I hear her hurried footsteps through the hall and then she's in the kitchen with me.

'Hello, darling,' I say. 'I'm making a cup of tea. Have you had a good day?'

And that's another thing I don't have to ask. It's there in her clear, bright face, the brightest I've seen her look since we came to Thurston.

'Yes,' she answers. 'Not bad!'

From my daughter, 'Not bad' is high praise.

'Anything special?' I ask. I'm dying to hear everything, A to Z, but to ask too much is to get to know nothing.

'Not really,' Becky replies, but there's a note in her voice which says otherwise. 'I'm sitting at the back now.'

I know that's good. If you sit at the back you can be trusted to behave yourself but if you sit at the front of the class you are under the teacher's beady eye. I would like to ask if the three troublemakers have been moved to the front and separated from each other but I'm not going to.

'I'm sitting next to Anna,' she says. 'Doggy said I should.'

'Doggy?'

'Mr Beagle,' she explains. 'Everyone calls him Doggy!'

'Does he know?' I enquire.

'I expect so,' she says. 'We don't say it to his face, of course!'

'I should hope not!' I say. 'So do you like "Doggy"?'

'Oh yes!' she says. 'He's cool!'

'Good old Doggy! And I hope he's quite fit again,' I say. If Cool Doggy had not succumbed to a chest infection life in the Vicarage might have been easier, but better late than never.

'Anna is going to be my best friend,' Becky announces.

'That's nice,' I say. 'Does she know? How do you know?'

'You just do,' she says patiently. 'Can I ask Anna to tea?'

'Of course you can!' I say. 'I'll have a word with her mother.'

'Can she come on Saturday?' Becky asks.

'Well,' I say, 'I do have something else in mind for Saturday . . .'

'I'd rather have Anna to tea!' Becky says quickly.

'What I have in mind,' I say, 'is to ring the Dog Rescue Centre and ask if we could visit on Saturday. Take a look around, find out more about it.'

'OH, MUM!' she cries. 'WOW! FANTASTIC!'

This is no calm, restrained response. She flings herself at me and I throw my arms around her, and we are both laughing.

'Perhaps Anna could come back with you after school on Friday?' I say. 'I'll call her mother. If the number's in the book I'll do it right now.' It is, and I do. 'That would be lovely!' Mrs Brent says. 'And if you like I'll collect her afterwards.'

I also phone the Dog Rescue and they give me an appointment for twelve noon on Saturday.

'I think you should take another look at the library books,' I say to Becky. 'We want to be as well informed as possible, don't we?'

Thursday evening is the time for the special PCC meeting. I've already consulted with the churchwardens and the treasurer and we've decided that this is the time and place to inform the other members about Miss Frazer's withdrawal of her financial support – together, at my insistence, with her reasons why. It will have a bearing on some of the things I'm going to suggest but I don't want the subject of Miss Frazer to dominate the meeting. We shall survive Miss Frazer and all her machinations. I want us all to be certain of that. Nor do I intend to let this meeting be dominated by finance. Far too many meetings are, and I have other things in mind which will have very little, if at all, to do with money but, more importantly, a lot to do with the life of the church.

So when we're all assembled and we've given due attention to talking about the weather – which is blustery and unpleasant so I thank them for turning out on such a night – Rose Barker hands out copies of a short agenda.

245

'Half-a-dozen items,' I say. 'One or two of them facts, one or two which have already been touched on briefly at the last PCC meeting, one or two new. Some possibly controversial, some not. What I want is a chance to let the whole of St Mary's congregation know what this new Vicar has in mind for our church in the months – and indeed in the years – ahead of us.'

They listen, so far, in a respectful silence, so far no shaking of heads in disagreement. I expect the latter will come, it would be too much to expect otherwise.

'There's no particular order of importance in the way these things are listed,' I tell them. 'Except for one, which will come first. What I want is for you as PCC members to have a chance to think about them before I put them to the congregation. But in the end I want everyone to feel they have a part in their church, that is not confined only to the PCC, important though you are, and we couldn't function without you. And I want us to consider not only what part St Mary's already plays in the community, but what part we think it could and should play.'

I have more in my mind, like what impact, if any at all, do we have on those who don't share our beliefs? Are we Christians just an inward-looking, pleasant group of people, content and cosy in our faith, happy with each other? Does the world outside the church know, really really know, what we're on about? Do they want to know? Do we have any impact, and does that matter? Well yes, it does, because one of the things the Gospels tell us is that we must give our faith to the world, and since the Gospels are what we try to live by, there's no get-out there. And if I don't think that's important, then what am I doing here right now? It's the foundation of my life.

'What we will do on this occasion,' I say, 'is to take the financial item first, because it will have a bearing on some of the other things on the list. George, as treasurer, will read you a letter he has recently received which will throw a new light on our finances.'

'Well, I'll just read the facts from it,' George says.

'No, George,' I say. 'Please read the whole letter. It gives the writer's reasons behind the facts.'

'I don't think . . .' George begins.

'*Please*, George!' I repeat. 'Cards on the table! If you don't want to read it, I will.'

So he reads out the bit where Miss Frazer has instructed her bank to cancel all her subscriptions to anything to do with St Mary's, and then he hesitates, and glances at me, and I give him a vigorous nod. He flushes slightly as he reads the next bit, lowering his voice, reading it too quickly, but such is the hush that no-one misses a word.

' "Not one penny piece more will St Mary's get from me while it allows itself to be led by a heretic, a woman masquerading as a priest of God." '

A murmur goes around the room; a murmur which is made up of sharp gasps, quick cries of indignation, and 'Oh!' and 'No!' I am thankful not to hear any cries of 'Yes! Yes!' but perhaps that might come later. And then I immediately tell myself not to start thinking like a victim. I am not a victim, nor will I ever go down that road. Miss Tordoff, in a voice trembling with emotion, is the first to speak up.

'That is *diabolical*,' she says, '*totally diabolical*! And I would like Madam Secretary to note my exact words in the minutes!'

'Which I will do with the greatest pleasure!' Rose Barker says.

I'm slightly surprised that this objection to Miss Frazer's words should have come from Miss Tordoff. She is a nice lady, not − so far as I know her − given to stating strong views. Moreover she is rather old-fashioned and in church matters, I would say, traditionalist. Exactly someone who would not welcome a woman priest. On the other hand she is a courteous, well-mannered woman, and it is perhaps Miss Frazer's rudeness which has provoked her, and that might be the attitude of quite a few people in St Mary's. I might not be their choice, but they won't go so far as to be rude to me. Well, I can live with that!

'George will give you the details of what Miss Frazer's decision will mean to us in hard cash, and he'll tell you that it's a considerable sum which covers several areas, both large and small. For instance, there is the annual children's outing at

Easter, and there's the children's pantomime visit at Christmas. Those are only two of the smaller things, but very popular I'm told. One has to say that Miss Frazer was extremely generous in many areas . . .'

'Well, we won't let those go!' someone interrupts. 'We'll find ways!'

'Of course we will!' I agree. I'm also pleased that they seem willing to move on from what's so personal to me, not to discuss it further.

We go through the other items on the list. Some are easy; for instance there had been a roster for visiting the sick and the housebound but it has fallen into abeyance. It is agreed that it should be revised. The proposed new place for baptism in the Sunday morning Eucharist is more or less agreed – but only for a trial period. I also raise the subject of early communion for children, another reform I would dearly like to bring in. As I expected, there is debate over this one.

'The Bishop is in favour of it,' I say. I am myself, but I think the Bishop's opinion will carry more weight.

'We were always confirmed at thirteen or fourteen, and we didn't receive communion until we were confirmed,' someone says. 'I think the children should wait until then, and make up their own minds!'

I wait in hope for someone to say what I believe, that at thirteen both boys and girls are a mass of surging hormones, mainly sexual, and they have so much on their minds that they're not able, or indeed inclined, to make up their minds about whether it's the time to be confirmed. Church doesn't figure large in their lives. But no-one comes forward with this view, nor do I make it right now. We'll discuss it later with more members of the congregation – which is exactly what I want.

The formation of a music group with the possibility of singing being led by youths on guitars or, God forbid, actually beating drums is a no-go area. 'And in any case what about Mr Blatchford?' someone asks. 'He's been our organist at St Mary's for thirty-five years! We can't let Mr Blatchford down!'

By the time the meeting closes, I have the feeling that it's all been worthwhile. We haven't leapt ahead, but we've taken steps.

And as they leave people say things like, 'Now don't you worry about Miss Frazer!' and 'Miss Frazer is a silly old woman, she thinks she can have everything her own way!' Not all of them, of course, but enough to cheer me up if I needed it. Lots to look forward to!

TWENTY-ONE

A large envelope from the Dog Rescue Centre comes in this morning's post and I think as I pick it up from the mat that it's as well Becky has left for school or I'd never have got her off. It's stuffed with leaflets, booklets and information sheets and there's no way I can resist starting to read them, ignoring the household chores, but reminding myself that this morning I have what you might call a post-bereavement visit I've promised to make.

Sometimes, if I feel the family – especially if it's the husband or wife of the one who's died – might be helped by a visit I'll go back, even if it's a while, after the funeral. I've had Mrs Leigh, widow of Maurice-known-as-Ronnie, in my mind. I'm not sure why except that I haven't seen her around and I did wonder how she was getting on. One of the things about going to church regularly, perhaps especially if it's in a village, is that if you miss a Sunday or two someone, often the parish priest, notices, and finds out why. You can call this nosey but I prefer to see it as caring.

But Mrs Leigh isn't a churchgoer. It was just that I had a feeling about her. So I phoned, said I'd be in her area on Friday morning, and should I drop in and say hello? She said yes, that would be very nice. So now, I also have an eye on the clock and quite soon I have to put the leaflets aside. Becky can read

250

them when she comes home from school. She's bringing Anna Brent to tea and I daresay they'll be happy to look at them together.

Mrs Leigh is once again looking out of the window, watching for me. I feel sorry about this. What it says to me is that there's not a lot going for her if a visit from someone like me, the Vicar she hardly knows, gives her such anticipation.

She's opening the door before I reach it.

'Good-morning, Vicar,' she says. She has a quiet voice, a rather shy manner.

'Good-morning, Mrs Leigh. Nice day!' I follow her into the front room.

'I've put some coffee on,' she says. 'Would you like a cup?'

'Oh, absolutely!' I say. 'I usually have one around this time but I left home in a hurry.'

I follow her into the kitchen. You don't get far from sitting on your own in someone's front room so, without waiting to be asked, I sit down at the kitchen table. She looks a bit surprised at this.

'So how are you, Ethel? How's it going?' I ask.

My use of her first name is also deliberate. It's what I do, unless I think it's likely it will offend, but that isn't often the case and I can usually suss it out beforehand. For instance, would I ever address the Honourable Miss Frazer as 'Amelia'? Never in a thousand years. But Mrs Leigh's face lightens a little at my use of her name.

'All right, I suppose,' she says. 'I get by. It's the little things, actually. Like having something to say, something not the least bit important, could be about the weather, or a TV programme, and there's no-one to say it to.'

'Yes, I know,' I agree.

She gives me a look.

'I'm a widow myself,' I tell her. I could also tell her, though I won't, that, from my experience, it doesn't get better. One learns to cope with the big things, it's the small ones which are one's undoing. But perhaps it won't be the same for her. I hope not.

She pours the coffee and puts a plate of home-made biscuits on the table.

251

'You're very young to be widowed,' she says.

I nod agreement. 'Not as many things to remember and miss as *you* must have after a long marriage,' I say. 'On the other hand, sadly not enough time to have so many memories to cherish.'

There's a short silence. 'How is Marilyn?' I ask. 'And Garth?'

'They're both well,' she says. 'Garth misses his Granddad.'

How long I should talk about the one who's died I always have to play by ear. To some it's a comfort to say a lot but others aren't yet ready to talk, so to discuss other members of the family is a sort of halfway house. We go on to talk about Garth, how he's doing at school and so on, and I bring in Becky and how she's doing.

'Tomorrow we're going to the Dog Rescue Centre,' I tell Ethel. 'We're thinking of adopting a dog. Did you ever have a dog?' There are no signs of it, no water bowl, no doggy toys on the floor. Everything is super-neat.

'No, we never had,' Ethel says. 'Ronnie didn't like dogs.'

We drift into idle chatter, nothing significant. I refuse a second cup of coffee and say, 'I suppose I must go. I have a hospital visit, and I must do a bit of shopping because Becky's bringing a friend home to tea.' It gives me great pleasure to be saying that last bit.

Becky is home soon after half-past three, bringing Anna into the house with what I can only describe as a proprietorial air, sort of showing off; partly showing off Anna to me, partly showing off the Vicarage to Anna. Anna is on the small side, very pretty, with fair, curly hair and a nice smile. I take to her at once. I give them both a drink of juice and a biscuit and then Becky takes Anna upstairs to her room.

'Tea about five o'clock,' I call after them. 'I'll give you a shout!' I've bought chicken nuggets. Ethel Leigh said Garth doted on them and I know Becky thinks they're food for the gods, so I hope Anna has similar tastes. And, I discover, she does. I'm glad I bought more than I thought I could possibly need! Then after tea I clear the table and bring out the leaflets from the Dog Rescue place and both girls are immediately immersed in them, choosing from the illustrations which dog they like best.

'It's not to say they'll actually have any of those when we get there,' I warn Becky. 'It's just to show the different breeds. And not all of them would be suitable for us.' But Becky is not even listening to that sort of talk. Anna is deeply envious. 'Though we have a cat,' she says. 'She's called Smokey.'

Then at half-past six Sally Brent arrives to collect her daughter.

'I've had a lovely time!' Anna says. 'Becky is going to get a dog tomorrow!'

Mrs Brent looks at me.

'At the moment it's a possibility, a strong possibility but by no means certain,' I tell her. 'We're going to the Dog Rescue Centre.'

'We have friends who got their dog there,' Sally Brent says. 'It worked out very well. They're quite fussy. They'll ask you a lot of questions to see if you're suitable to have one of their dogs.'

'Quite right, too,' I say. 'That's what I've been telling Becky. We can't just walk in and get one off the shelf!'

The Rescue Centre is on the coast a good twenty miles to the south of Thurston. Becky was up early, which is unusual for her on a Saturday, and is anxious to be off.

'There's no point in being there before twelve,' I tell her. 'They're closed until then.'

'Why?' she demands. 'Why don't they open earlier?'

'How do I know?' I ask. 'Don't you think it could be to do with the fact that they have perhaps seventy dogs to attend to – feed them, groom them and so on, all the things you'll discover, if we get one, one has to do for a dog? Why don't you go for a walk down the village?'

'All right,' she says reluctantly.

I can guess what she'll do there. There's a pet shop where she can gaze at the variety of leads, collars, winter coats, dog treats and toys which she would like to buy for the dog she hasn't yet acquired, and I've forbidden her to buy anything of the kind until something is settled.

★   ★   ★

Eventually she returns and we set off, and now we are nearing the Rescue Centre, which has been built on a spit of land which stretches out from the shore for about a mile from the small town of Dramwell, and is isolated from any built-up area, which I reckon is a good idea. It must at times be noisy. It is not quite twelve as we reach the entrance. Once inside we are in a clean, bright reception area where I give my name to the young woman behind the desk, whose badge identifies her as 'GRACE'. By the way, I have broken my usual Saturday rule and I am wearing my clericals because I think the sight of my dog collar might add a certain an air of responsibility.

'Ah, yes!' she says. 'Imogen is going to look after you. She'll be with you in a few minutes. Please take a seat!'

The few minutes extends to fifteen and Becky is impatient, though in fact there's a lot going on. A man and a woman with two children, round about Becky's age, come in, and a dog, a bit like a Labrador but not quite, is brought to them, already leashed.

'Look! They're taking it home!' Becky says.

There is a woman sitting on the other side of Becky who knows everything. There is one in every waiting room – doctor's, dentist's, Social Security, train stations. I sometimes wonder if they live there.

'No!' she contradicts. 'They're just taking it for a walk. You can do that regularly when you know which dog you're going to have but you can't take it home for a few weeks.'

There are two dogs in sort of open kennels at the other side of the room, so we go across and look at them. One kennel is occupied by a brown-and-black terrier. Her name is Floss, the card says, and she's eight years old. Bright-eyed, she watches everything in the room; no-one goes in or out, or crosses the floor, without Floss noticing them. I am suddenly choked by the fact that she might be watching for her owner, who never comes, but I say nothing of this to Becky. In the other kennel a white, fluffy dog – breed unknown to me – lies asleep. On his cage a card says, 'I'm Fred! I've got a new home!'

Presently, Imogen appears. She takes us into a small office just off the reception. We chat for a short time; she asks us several

254

questions: 'Why do you want a dog?' 'Have you ever had one before?' 'Do you have a garden? 'Do you have a car?' Then she gives us a form to fill in which has loads more questions. Everything is geared to whether I would be a suitable person to have a dog, and if I'm deemed not to be, then, I guess, we're not going to get one.

'So if you're a Vicar you'll have a fair-sized house, but we'd still want to make a visit, see where the dog would be kept.'

'You're welcome to come and see us,' I say. 'At any time.'

'Yes. And we do sometimes make follow-up visits after you've taken a dog,' she tells me. 'Not always. Now, the fact that you're a Vicar I suppose means that you'll be out of the house quite a bit?'

'On and off,' I tell her. 'I'm also in quite a bit.'

'And perhaps you could take the dog with you sometimes when you have to go out?'

'Oh, certainly!' I assure her. 'Not everywhere, but quite a lot of places.'

'And what about holidays?'

And so on and so on. It's very thorough and I realize it has to be done, but Becky is looking pale with anxiety. Fortunately, Imogen also notices this.

'Don't worry, Becky!' she says. 'All these questions have to be asked for the sake of the dog. We need to know it's going to be happy. But so far everything is going well, and I'm nearly through, after which I'll take you and your mum to meet some of the dogs. I'm sure you'll be helping to look after the dog, won't you?'

Becky's face brightens up no end at this. 'I'll take it for walks!' she says eagerly.

Imogen takes us off for a tour around the kennels. We see all kinds of dog, every colour and size, so many different breeds. We are very struck by two beautiful greyhounds.

'I expect they need lots of exercise?' I say.

Imogen shakes her head. 'Not true! Just short, sharp bursts is what they're used to. Apart from that they lie around a lot. I wouldn't advise one for you and Becky. Too big for a small child.' We pass on.

'And of course a good many of the dogs here are strays,' Imogen says. 'The dog wardens bring them in from the streets and we try to find their owners but we don't always succeed.'

We continue to walk around. Dogs climb up the front of their kennels to greet us; we meet dogs being walked by staff, everything seems relaxed, and far less noisy than I'd imagined. We see a kennel with half-a-dozen divine puppies and, naturally, Becky immediately wants one of them.

'No!' Imogen says firmly. 'Not suitable! Puppies need a great deal of time and attention and they need to be trained by someone who knows what's what and can be with them for most of the day. One day it might be suitable for you to have a puppy, but not yet. Do the two of you have some idea of what sort of dog you *would* like?'

'Not too large,' I say. 'And a nice temperament, as we're not used to dogs. I suppose rescue dogs can be difficult?'

'That's what most people think,' Imogen says. 'It simply isn't true. Occasionally there's a difficult one, but not often. And in fact we keep them for several weeks after they're brought in, so we have plenty of time to see how they get on with people.' Then she says, '. . . I wonder?' Then, 'Yes,' she says thoughtfully. 'She might be just the one!'

Becky is all agog. So am I for that matter.

'A dog came in earlier this week,' Imogen continues. 'A spaniel cross bitch. Small, but bigger than a Cavalier. She's not a stray, not by any means. She's a much-loved dog, six years old, but her owner, an elderly lady, has had finally to go into a nursing home. Missie is a healthy, good-tempered dog who's been looked after well. And now she needs another good home.'

'Oh!' Becky cries. 'Oh! Can we see her? Please!'

'Why not?' Imogen says.

Missie is black-and-white, with a glossy coat, drooping spaniel ears and large, lustrous brown eyes. She's lying on her bed, holding a soft toy between her front paws – a small teddy bear which looks as though it's had a lot of handling. When Imogen calls her name she stands up, the teddy bear still in her mouth, and slowly waves her rather beautiful fringed tail. And she moves towards us. It's that which clinches it!

256

'Oh! She's beautiful!' Becky cries. 'Oh, can we have her, Mummy?'

'Hold out your hand, Becky. Palm down,' Imogen says. 'Hold quite still!'

Becky does exactly as she's told and Missie walks rather slowly forward and licks the hand, just once. Becky goes pink with ecstasy. 'Oh!' she says. 'Oh!' At first it's all she can manage, and then she finds her voice and says, 'Oh, *please! please!* We can have her, can't we? She likes me, you can tell she does!'

I look at Imogen.

'I think it might be OK,' she says. 'But you know,' she continues, turning to Becky, 'you won't be able to take her for a few weeks. She's only been with us for a few days. There are all sorts of things to do. The vet will want to see her again, we'll have to check on her inoculations and that sort of thing.'

'When could we take her home?' Becky wants to know.

'You should say "*if* and when,"' I say. 'As Imogen says, it has to be decided.'

'Don't worry!' Imogen says. 'I'm pretty sure it will be. And you might not have to wait as long as you would if she was a stray. What we'll do is telephone you in a day or two. And if we say "yes" we'll expect you both to come to a training class. You need to learn something about dogs in general and Missie in particular. And when you do come, you can take her for a walk. In fact, once we've decided she's to be yours both of you can come and take her for walks as often as you like in opening hours. And in the meantime I do expect both of you to read all the information I'm going to give you about looking after a dog. It's extremely important. As I told you: remember a dog is for life! Will you do that?'

We both solemnly promise that we will.

'I'll tell you what!' Imogen says suddenly. 'Missie hasn't had her walk today. If I leash her up you can take her across the lawns and back.'

We do just that. Heavenly bliss! Imogen goes with us. Missie is very well behaved. In the end I have to drag Becky away and we go home. She spends the journey in bursts of talking fifty to the dozen alternated with longish periods of deep, wonder-filled silence.

We haven't been home more than ten minutes, just long enough to put the kettle on to make a cup of instant coffee, when there's a ring at the door, and when I go to answer it Nigel Baines is standing there.

'I had a visit to make in the village so I thought I'd look in. Is it convenient?'

'Absolutely!' I tell him. He follows me through to the kitchen.

Before he can say a word Becky says, 'We're getting a dog! She's black-and-white and she's called Missie. We took her for a walk and she licked my hand. We can't bring her home just yet and we shall have to go to a training class but we can take her for another walk next Saturday. I'm going to get her a new collar and a lead and she'll have a Lucky Dog disc from the Rescue Centre so that if she gets lost they'll know to bring her back to the Vicarage but she won't get lost because I'll be with her when she comes to live here!'

When she pauses for breath Nigel looks at me.

'All true!' I say. 'Or it will come true if they approve of us, and that does seem likely. Actually I was going to make some lunch when I got my breath back. We've only just come in. We missed out on lunch . . .'

'Oh! don't let me stop you!' Nigel says. 'I'll be gone in a few minutes. I just wanted to ask you . . .'

'I wasn't meaning you to rush off,' I say. 'In fact, I was going to ask if you'd like to have some lunch with us. Nothing special! An omelette, most likely. You haven't had lunch, have you?'

'No. I've had a busy surgery, and two visits even though it is Saturday. I was going to drop in at the Black Cat Café for something. They do meals all day. Why don't you both come with me. Please!'

'I'd like that best!' Becky says quickly. 'It's a lot better than omelettes. Also we could call in the pet shop on the way down and I could look at collars and leads. And toys. Imogen says dogs like toys, though Missie already has a teddy bear but I don't

258

suppose she'd mind having a few other toys as well. And we'll need dog biscuits.'

Nigel and I look at each other.

'Black Cat here we come!' he says. 'What do you like for lunch, Becky?' He seems at ease with her, but then I'd say he gets on with everyone.

'Chicken!' she replies. 'I expect Missie will like chicken.'

'Most dogs do!' Nigel says.

I haven't been in the Black Cat Café before. I suppose if it weren't for Becky being with us we'd be lunching in the Ewe Lamb but in fact the Black Cat is fine. It's small, wherever you sit you can see everyone else, and it's a bit old-fashioned; flowered wallpaper, checked tablecloths. Although lunchtime is almost over several tables are still occupied, the clientele mostly middle-aged, except for a couple with two children. Two or three customers recognize Nigel and speak to him briefly. I expect this happens wherever he goes in the village. What I'd like to ask him is, when he meets with a patient outside the surgery does he identify him or her by what's wrong with them? 'Ah, yes! Mrs-What's-her-name. Hiatus hernia! Mr Thingummy. Hypertension!' And although I don't see anyone I know from church I am still wearing my dog collar, and as women in dog collars are not thick on the ground I am noticed and it must be easy to work out who I am. So a certain amount of interest is being taken, especially, I imagine, since I am lunching with their doctor.

Luckily, roast chicken is on the menu, and we all three choose it. Becky, who either talks volubly about dogs in general and Missie in particular, or goes into a deep reverie at the thought of joys to come, eats well, emptying her plate.

'Did you say you called to ask me something?' I remind Nigel.

'Yes, I did,' he says – but doesn't continue.

'So?' I prompt him.

'There's a concert in Brampton tomorrow week. I wondered if you'd like to come? It's in the afternoon, so Becky could go with us.'

Becky looks horrified at the thought, but she has the perfect excuse. 'We might have Missie by then,' she points out. 'We're not supposed to leave her long at first.'

I shake my head. 'Darling, there's no chance we'll have Missie so soon.'

Actually, I would very much like to go to the concert. Classical music is my thing. I listen to it in the house but it's ages since I went to a concert. And apart from the music, I'd enjoy the outing. But Becky would hate it.

'Thank you very much,' I say to Nigel. 'I'd like that very much, but I'll have to see what I can arrange.' And then it occurs to me that perhaps Sally Brent would have Becky for the afternoon. I'm sure both Becky and Anna would enjoy that.

'When would you need to know?' I ask.

'Well,' he says, sounding a little bit embarrassed, 'actually I've already got the tickets. I took a chance. I do hope you'll be able to make it. Please do!'

'I'll let you know as soon as I can,' I promise.

TWENTY-TWO

I must say, I really enjoyed yesterday: all of it, the dogs, the lunch with Nigel, everything, but Sunday is still the best. Sunday is the day when all the people in my care – that's not quite true, I should say as many of the people in my care as wish to do so – come together to celebrate. It's the family day – by which I don't mean a family like myself and Becky, and occasionally my parents, but an extended family such as one might have on a special occasion, friends included and there to share a meal, which is what we do in the Eucharist. And it isn't just any old meal, it's a feast, a celebration.

Of course I don't decry those small weekday services attended by just a few devoted people. They have their importance, but the Sunday Eucharist *is* different. There is a diversity of people, of ages, the atmosphere is different. It isn't as quiet as some people might like, there's singing, there's more chattering as people come into church and leave it. There's more an air of – I think 'rejoicing' is the word – in what we're doing and if there isn't, we're getting something wrong – or I am. There's also the fact that gathering together on a day set apart is what Christians have been doing for two thousand years, and in St Mary's, Thurston we are a small but real part of that. That's a feeling at the same time both awesome and comforting.

A slight shadow over this morning is again what Miss Frazer

might get up to, but whatever form that takes I shan't allow it to darken the day.

So far, and the church clock has just started to strike ten, there is no sign of her. The usual stragglers are hurrying up the path and today, a yard or two behind the rest, is little Mrs Bateman. She is not – the Lord's name be praised – accompanied by Miss Frazer. I don't know why I think of her as 'little' Mrs Bateman. She's several inches taller than I am, and rather plump, though her voice is thin. It's just that she always seems as though she's in need of care and attention, but not getting it, and I can't give her it at this moment because Mr Blatchford is coming to the end of his organ voluntary which is a sure sign that I must now walk with some dignity up the aisle to the front of the church.

She comes into the porch with the other latecomers just as I'm about to move away and I see at once that she's in a real state! Her face is blotchy red and tear-stained, moreover she looks as though there are more tears to come. Quickly, I turn to one of the latecomers and say, 'Go up to the organ and tell Mr Blatchford to go on playing for another minute or two.'

'What do you want him to play?' the messenger enquires, helpfully.

'How do I know? Anything! It's not a request programme. Just tell him to keep on playing until he sees me walk up the aisle. The rest of you please go in! We're late.'

'Now, Mrs Bateman,' I say, I hope soothingly, 'you can see I can't stop for more than two seconds right now. So just tell me quickly what the matter is and then I'll spend as long as you like with you when the service is over.'

'Oh, Vicar!' Mrs Bateman cries – she is really anguished. 'Oh, it was dreadful! It's Miss Frazer!'

I take a firm grip on myself – after all, I am about to celebrate the Holy Eucharist – and drive away all thoughts, let alone hopes, that Miss Frazer might have suffered something unpleasant – not too unpleasant, nothing painful, just something which will keep her away from me.

'Well, tell me very briefly, and then go into church,' I say firmly. 'I'm sure Miss Frazer will be all right.'

'It's not her, it's me!' Mrs Bateman says, the tears starting to flow again. 'I went to call for her, I always do that, and when she came to the door she turned on me like a wildcat! She said the most terrible things! She said if it was my intention to go to church this morning then I was a traitor! "You are a tool of the devil!" she said. "But be sure your sin will find you out! Vengeance is mine, saith the Lord, and he will punish you as you deserve!" She said a lot more, I can't remember it all. At first I couldn't move, and then in the end I ran away as fast as I could. She was shouting at me all the time. Awful things!'

I am furious, but I mustn't show it. Not right now. I must keep calm.

'None of the things she said to you are true,' I say firmly. 'Neither God nor anyone else will punish you. You have done nothing wrong. Now dry your eyes, Mrs Bateman, and go into church. Sit quietly for a moment. I will pray for you very specially, though not by name because you wouldn't want that.'

'No! I wouldn't!' she says.

'We'll talk afterwards,' I promise. 'Just remember, you've done nothing wrong. It's not you.'

It's me, of course, I'm thinking as I walk down the aisle. Poor Mrs Bateman is taking the punishment Miss Frazer would like to heap on me. I shall have to think hard about this, and most of all I will have to pray. And I'm well aware that, even at this moment when, to put it mildly, my thoughts towards her are not charitable, I shall have to pray for Miss Frazer as well as for Mrs Bateman and myself. That's in the Gospels also. They're not always easy, are they? Do you wonder Christians sometimes get cross with God? He does ask some very difficult things of us! Love your enemies! Do good to them that persecute you! One thing is sure, I shall never make a saint.

The service proceeds as if nothing untoward had happened, though I keep an eye on Mrs Bateman.

When it's over it's my firm intention to collar her on her way out and to take her into the parish office where I shall do everything I can to reassure her, but unfortunately I am buttonholed by a woman who is anxious to question me about the arrangements for the British Legion (Women's Section) Annual Service which

I have never done before and she's clearly not sure that she can trust me with it – so Mrs Bateman eludes me. I decide she must have gone home, and if so I must visit her quite soon, but when I go into coffee, there she is, sitting at a table with four others and in full spate with her story. Carla Brown signals to me to join them and, as usual, orders Walter to get my coffee.

'Mrs Bateman has just been telling us,' she says dramatically as I sit down. 'Isn't it dreadful! That Frazer woman should have been drowned at birth! I know *you* can't say that, Venus, but me not being a true-blooded Christian, I can!'

There are two other women at the table whom I don't yet know, though I've seen them before in church. They look askance, more at Carla than at Mrs Bateman's revelations. I wonder where they stand?

'What am I to do, Vicar?' Mrs Bateman says. 'I want to come to church, but Miss Frazer has always been a friend, sort of . . . She was good to me when my husband died.'

'You mean you've always done as she's told you,' Carla Brown interrupts.

Mrs Bateman ignores her and looks appealingly at me, as if I can wave a magic wand.

'My dear,' I say, 'first and foremost you must realize that you have done nothing wrong, nothing at all. You must get that firmly into your head. But what you do about coming to church is entirely up to you. You mustn't come from pressure, nor must you stay away because of pressure. You are your own person.' But the truth is that that's what she finds it most difficult to be. She's one of those women who needs a prop. I expect that was the late Mr Bateman's role.

I look around the table.

'That goes for all of us,' I say. 'We must all make our own decisions. Even when we know the way it's up to us whether we take it or not. But if we do follow it then it should be done in love. Fear or coercion, or blind obedience, should have no part at all.'

Walter puts my coffee before me and I change the subject, telling them that I hope to have a parish meeting at which we can discuss where we think St Mary's should be going.

264

'I hope you'll all be there,' I say (I am touting this wherever I can). 'I want to have it in the Vicarage if I can squeeze everyone in.'

'That would be nice,' Carla says. 'I don't suppose anyone will mind being squashed.'

Neither Mrs Bateman nor the other two women have anything to say to that.

On Monday, it being my day off, I manage some gardening in the morning, and in the afternoon I go to Mark Dover's for my third and, presumably, last sitting. He's been working on the portrait since last Wednesday and it's a great deal further on than when I saw it then. In spite of the fact that quite a bit of the canvas is taken up by my black cassock, the painting glows with colour, even the cassock itself. I hadn't realized there were so many shades of black. I also reckon it's a bit flattering. Well, if that's how he sees me! But I'm not going to say that to him. Last Wednesday he was a bit silly. He paid me several compliments and when he'd finished painting he helped me from my chair – quite unnecessary – and put his arms around me. All right, only in a friendly way perhaps, though I thought for one second he was going to kiss me. I wriggled away very pointedly.

The awful thing was – and I don't know what came over me, or almost came over me – but, mixed with the annoyance, the episode gave me a feeling of fleeting, but distinct, pleasure. I was relieved that I had to hurry away because of Becky. If he tries it on today I shall be very sharp with him, and indeed with myself. And if he continues like this then there's no way I will go to his exhibition in December, not even to see my own portrait hung.

Fortunately, aside from the usual compliments, he doesn't try it on this afternoon. He asks me if I'll do another sitting next week and I tell him I can't possibly, I don't have the time. 'Things are really hotting up in the parish,' I say.

He roars with laughter at that.

'Oh, Venus, you are funny!' he says. 'Things hotting up in St Mary's, Thurston? Whatever do you mean? Are the choirboys being naughty?'

'If you ever darkened the doors of St Mary's,' I say, 'you'd

265

know we don't have choirboys. We don't even have a choir! But I *am* quite busy, laughable though you find that!'

'OK!' he says, holding up his hands and pretending to back away from me. 'OK, Venus! Don't be cross with me. And if you find you can spare an hour or two from your busy life, promise you'll let me know.'

'I promise,' I tell him.

On Tuesday, when I leave church after the ten o'clock Eucharist, I take it into my head to drop in on Bertha Jowett. No special reason except that she's housebound, we both enjoyed the previous visit, and it's not at all out of my way. I won't stay long, just say 'hello' and 'how are you?' – and I did wonder if she might be all right for things to read. She must have loads of time to do that, especially as she's too ridden with arthritis to do much else. She doesn't come to the door, she calls out to me to enter. She's in her chair, the gas fire's full on and she's sitting close to it. Is it my imagination or does she look a bit down?

'How are you?' I ask. 'Are you all right?'

'As right as I'll ever be!' She doesn't make it sound like a complaint, just a fact she must accept. 'Excuse me if I don't offer to make coffee,' she says. 'I'm a bit stiff today. Actually, I'm glad you've come. I've made a big decision and I want you to tell me I'm doing the right thing – though even if you say I'm not it won't change my mind.'

'Would you like me to make you some coffee?' I ask.

'Not yet,' she replies. 'Come and sit down. Listen to me first, coffee after.'

What she has to tell me certainly comes as a surprise. I'm not sure why, except she struck me on that previous occasion as a woman who was comfortably in control, and accepting of her own life.

The decision is this. She has faced the fact that she can no longer manage to look after herself, and the cottage, even though she has a woman who comes in twice a week to clean and tidy.

'It's beyond me! So I'm going into a retirement home,' she announces. 'I should have done it earlier but I didn't want to. I fought against it; but now I have to acknowledge that I can't continue as I am. There's so much I can't do. Getting upstairs to bed is a nightmare and there's no room downstairs for a bedroom. It's not only that, though. It's just – oh, well, so many things! There seem to be more of them every day. Now tell me I'm mad!'

'You're not mad,' I say firmly. 'You strike me as being as sane as anyone I've ever met. You do surprise me, though I'm sure you've thought it over very carefully. But where would you go?'

'Ah,' she says, 'that's where I'm lucky! There's a rest home just outside the village – the Beeches – have you been there yet?'

'Not yet,' I say. 'But I intend to.'

'It's well spoken of,' she says. 'I once visited someone there and I liked the look of it. The rooms are a good size and well-furnished, the bed doesn't somehow look like a bed. It looks more like a comfortable sofa. There's an en-suite shower which is easier for me than a bath. You can have your meals in the dining room, or served in your own room – or you can make a hot drink and cook snacks, there's a microwave oven. And if you get to the stage where you need it there's nursing care available, so you don't get chucked out! I sound like an advertisement, don't I?'

'It sounds pretty good,' I say.

'As these places go, it is,' she agrees. 'Expensive, of course, and I could only do it because I'll have the money from selling this place. But one of the problems is that they have a vacancy right now and they won't keep it open long: if I want it I'll have to get on with it. So that's what I've decided to do. I've no relatives to push me one way or the other. I can do what I like, I'm a free spirit!'

Bertha Jowett will always be a free spirit, I think. Confined to a room in a rest home, old, dependent, crippled by arthritis – she will still be more free than most people I know. But I wonder if the price for freedom is loneliness?

It's not until I've left that the full significance of what she's said sinks in. I'm back at home, making my lunchtime sandwich, when I realize that her cottage will be up for sale.

Pausing only long enough to look up her number in the book,

267

I'm calling her. She's a long time in answering and I realize that if she happens not to be sitting near it it takes her quite a time to get to the phone.

'Oh, Bertha!' I say. 'I know you said you'd have to sell your cottage. Do you have a buyer in mind?'

'Not a clue!' she admits. 'I've only just made the decision. Why? Do you know someone?'

'Indeed I do!' I say. And then I tell her about my parents. 'I haven't spoken to them, I thought I must make quite certain with you first, but really it sounds just the job. Is it OK if I get in touch with them?'

'Certainly!' she says. 'I'll have to get it valued, I've no idea what the selling price might be, but I could get that done without putting the sale with an estate agent. Save a lot of money!'

'Wonderful! I'll ring my mother at once, then I'll get back to you. Of course they'll have to sell their house.'

My mother is over the moon! Can't believe it! Tells me they've been to the estate agent in Clipton and he says their house should sell quite quickly, it's in a nice position and in good condition.

'When can we come over and look at the cottage?' she asks.

'I'll have to ask Miss Jowett, but I should think almost any time,' I say. 'I'll let you know.'

I'm about to get back to Bertha Jowett but before I can do so my own phone rings. It's Imogen at the Dog Rescue Centre.

'I reckon it's going to be OK about Missie!' she says. 'We think you'd be a very suitable owner. Of course you'll have to go through the usual preliminaries and I'd like to come to visit you. When could I do that?'

'The sooner the better,' I tell her. 'Tomorrow if you like. Could you come when Becky's home from school? She gets in just after half-past three.'

'That will suit me fine,' Imogen says.

I then ring Bertha Jowett and we fix for my parents to come over next Friday. 'That will give me time to get a valuation on the cottage,' Bertha says.

★   ★   ★

Mum and Dad will probably stay for the weekend, I'm thinking – and then I suddenly remember that on Sunday afternoon I'm hoping to go to the concert with Nigel – I must give him a ring – and if my parents are here Becky will be fine with them, I needn't phone Sally Brent about Anna. That can be another time. Nice things to look forward to! It should be a fun weekend.

I'm so eager to give Becky the good news about the dog that at half-past three I find myself watching from the window to see her coming up the road, and five minutes later there she is. She bounces up the road, brimful of health and happiness. What a change! I have my daughter back!

I rush to open the front door.

'Guess what!' I call out – I can't wait until she gets into the house.

She can read the good news in my face.

'The dog!' she cries. 'Missie!'

'Yes! Almost certain!' We hug each other on the doorstep and a woman I vaguely know by sight nods and smiles at us as she passes.

'Lovely day, Vicar!' she calls out.

'Wonderful!' I reply.

At Becky's request I give her every syllable of Imogen's phone call. 'So don't be late home from school tomorrow!' I warn her, though I'm sure there's no fear of that.

And then she's suddenly starving hungry so I make tea and toast some fruit buns and we sit down and talk about Missie; where she'll sleep, what she'll eat, what kind of collar we should buy – and I have to warn Becky that it will be a week or two before all this can come to pass. 'But we can take her for a walk on Saturday. We'll arrange the time with Imogen tomorrow,' I promise.

'And that's not all,' I add. 'I have a bit of good news about Grandma and Granddad.'

Her cup runneth over – and so, I have to admit, does mine.

'I'm going to phone Anna,' she says. 'I must tell her!'

'OK, but give me a minute,' I say. 'I want to call Doctor Baines. If I leave it until later he might be doing his surgery.'

Nigel seems pleased that I can go to the concert.

'It's a good programme,' he says. 'Rachmaninov's Second Piano Concerto and Sibelius's Second Symphony. There's a talented young pianist.'

'Wonderful! I love them both,' I tell him.

The visit from Imogen goes well. She likes the Vicarage, approves of the garden, which she says is happily not too formal and tidy to welcome a dog. This is the first time ever I've actually been approved of for having a less than pristine garden and I shall bear it in mind on those occasions, not infrequent, when I would rather read a book than mow the lawn or weed the borders. I arrange that we will be at the Centre on Saturday to take Missie for a walk, and Imogen says there is a training class earlier on the same day which she would like us to attend. Becky is totally excited. How will she ever sleep tonight?

Wednesday is the evening I set aside for wedding couples or for those seeking baptism for their infants. It's late in the year for weddings but this evening I do have one couple who would like to be married on a Saturday before Christmas.

'I'm starting a new job in Manchester before Christmas,' the groom, John Carter (who looks like a schoolboy but turns out to be twenty-six), explains. 'We think we've found a house there, but we'd like to be married and have our honeymoon before we settle in.'

'John doesn't live in the parish, but I do,' Jean, the bride-to-be, says. 'I'm afraid I don't go to church . . .' I wait for her reason for not going to church, hoping it might be something original, but even more interestingly, she doesn't give me one. 'But I wouldn't like to be married *not* in church,' she adds. 'I went to Sunday School.' And then as an afterthought she says, '. . . And I was in the Guides.'

They seem a nice young couple, sitting there holding hands. I go through the service with them, and we discuss practical things like the date and the time, the hymns, the organist, the brides-maids, who will give the bride away, if and where they may scatter confetti, and so on; and then, as always, I talk to them about marriage, which is not the same as talking about the

270

wedding. I talk to them about the life commitment of marriage. It's my firm belief, and I don't think I'm starry-eyed about this, that just about every couple who comes to me seeking to be married fully intends to make this commitment, in good faith, meaning every word of it. I can see it in their faces, in their eyes, and especially I see it later on when they stand at the altar making their vows. I am truly sad and upset when I hear of a marriage breaking down but it never lessens my belief that they meant every word they said at the time. If I didn't have that faith I'm not sure I could do this part of my job.

So I ask God to bless them and I tell them that if they have any further questions at all between now and the wedding they should feel free to ask me.

Soon after they leave I have an appointment with a couple who wish to have their baby baptized. They are not married, they tell me almost at once, a fact which I didn't know when I made the appointment but even if I had I would still have made it. Their baby girl is four months old and they very much want her to be baptized. I sense they have perhaps been pressurized into this by family (though if they tried to pressurize them into marrying then clearly they failed) but this turns out not to be so. It could be, and sometimes this is true, that they think that it is unlucky for the baby not to be 'done'. Something unspecified but awful might happen. I usually tell them that I'm not a witch doctor. But after a few careful questions to this couple I discover that it is their true desire to have the baby baptized for the right reasons.

Now I do know that there are clergy who will not baptize a child whose parents are not married, or, going even further, will not baptize a child whose parents don't go regularly to church. I can't possibly go along with that. It's my belief, I once naively thought it was the belief of all clergy, that baptism is a sacrament in which the child is given the grace of God. And if it is, who am I to withhold God's grace from a child because of what its parents do or don't do? So this couple, I think a little to their surprise, find that there are no barriers to their baby's baptism. I might at some point mention marriage to them, but that isn't what they're here for now.

271

When they've left I see Becky off to bed. She's a very happy girl. In fact it's been a happy day all round, except that I don't take any joy in Bertha Jowett going into a rest home. There is just an inevitability about that with which she seems to have come to terms. I must talk to her more about it.

TWENTY-THREE

I had a domestic day yesterday. I'd determined that after the ten o'clock I would go back to the Vicarage and do some housework, which is piling up on me. Perhaps, I thought, I should become more methodical and make myself do it every Thursday. I had to yesterday because my parents are due for lunch today and my mother appreciates a tidy house. If it were messy she'd set to and sort things out; not in a chiding way, she'd be cheerful about it, but I would feel guilty. I would quite like to have a bit of paid help in the house – domesticity and I are not natural partners – but it doesn't come cheap in Thurston and I have to watch the money.

The only good thing I can find to say about housework is that most of it can be done while thinking about other things. I've always done that. When I was a little girl my mother – I think it was for the good of my soul, she thought it was character-building – made me polish the silver once a month. All the cutlery and various other bits and bobs were laid out on the kitchen table in front of me and I sat there with my tin of magic wadding, which started out pristine pink and quickly turned black with use, and the soft yellow dusters which were kept for the silver, but actually I wasn't there – except in the flesh. I was away, I was in another world. It's easy to clean silver without giving it more than an occasional passing thought. I don't have much silver but fortunately it's a gift I can apply to most household chores.

It's important for a priest to spend time thinking, to empty the head of all the clutter which gathers there and to concentrate on the nature of more important things. I know I should set apart time to do this every day of my life but I don't always manage it. I say my Office but even that is sometimes more rushed than it should be. A priest should also spend time reading – not just reading the Bible, though that's of first importance, but other books, and the newspapers. I should know what's going on in the world, what's happening in politics, showing on television. Indeed I should be aware of anything which touches the lives of my parishioners. I need to be streetwise. Knowing what's going on in 'EastEnders' can often do more good than being able to read Greek. Mixed in with everything else, there's a lot of real life in the soaps.

I did take time from cleaning and thinking to ring Mrs Bateman, just to ask if she was OK – which she was, but pleased to be telephoned, though she had nothing new to report. I also had several calls myself about this and that, including one from Mark Dover.

'I have to come down to the village,' he said. 'Will you have lunch with me at the Ewe Lamb?'

I asked to be excused, said I was rather busy, in the middle of something I had to finish. I didn't tell him it was cleaning the bedrooms.

With part of me I wanted to go – for a start, I'm always ready to break off the housework – but I'm holding back on Mark Dover, partly because recently I find myself thinking about him, and about that side of my life in general. I have been wondering if there are stages in widowhood, and if so am I coming to the end of the first stage? It's not that I don't miss Philip, and no man could ever replace him. He was all I ever wanted in every part of my life, but sometimes now, from time to time when I see a man and a woman together, enjoying each other's presence, I wonder whether I want to spend the rest of my life as a woman on my own. I know I have Becky, but that's not for ever and I must guard against it becoming so. I must eventually let her go.

So at the moment, since I'm not sure where I am, or even where I want to be, I'm holding back even on what might be no more than a very nice, ordinary friendship. But I'm sure enough in the other part of my life. Being a priest is tremendously important to me. It deserves, and will have, everything I can give. How would any man deal with that? Philip did, but Philip was Philip.

That was yesterday. The Vicarage is now as clean and tidy as it's been since I moved in here. How long will that last? Mum and Dad will be here for lunch and I've arranged with Bertha Jowett that we'll be with her at two o'clock. She said that suited her. Like many old people she has lunch early, it's a landmark in the day, and two o'clock will give her time to have a little zizz before the three of us land on her. Becky asked if she could bring Anna home to tea because she wanted her grandparents to meet her new friend, and of course I agreed, so I have to be back for that.

When my parents arrive they are all excited. No, that's not totally true! My mother is as excited as a girl, can't stop talking and would like to set off right now to the cottage, never mind lunch. Dad is resigned.

'We've still heard nothing from the estate agents in Thurston,' my mother says, 'though we left home before the post came this morning.'

'There was nothing in my post,' I say. 'I suppose what you're looking for is difficult to come by.'

'Then let's hope it works out with Miss Jowett,' my mother says. 'It sounds the very thing.'

'The cottage is quite small,' I remind her. 'I did tell you.'

'I know. Small is what we want,' she says.

'We don't yet know what she's asking for it,' Dad says. 'It might be beyond us.'

'She'll be able to give you a figure today – at least I think she will,' I tell him. 'Though I've heard that houses actually in the village don't come cheap. There are so few of them.'

'Oh, I'm sure it'll be all right, Ernest!' my mother blithely says.

'That's what you always say,' Dad complains.

'And it usually is,' she replies, getting the last word.

At five minutes past two we ring Bertha Jowett's doorbell and wait while she makes her slow progress to the front door. I guess she hasn't left the door on the latch for us to walk in because she thinks my parents should be properly welcomed.

I make the introductions and we're invited to sit down, and she asks if we'd like a cup of tea and we explain we had one after lunch (my parents wouldn't think much of a meal which didn't end with a cup of tea). Then, since no-one seems prepared to start the discussion on what we've come for, we talk about the weather. A very nice day, but a real nip in the air, and the nights are drawing in, aren't they? Time passes so quickly, doesn't it? Before we know where we are it'll be Christmas, and then another New Year! We all nod in agreement with each other though I doubt very much that time passes quickly for Bertha Jowett. The years might but I doubt that the days do. I imagine they crawl.

There's a break, we all fall silent at once, and then Bertha says, 'Well! I'm sure you'd like to take a look around.'

Slowly, we make our way around the ground floor, Bertha with the aid of her stick. Small kitchen, but adequate. Needs new equipment. The back door leads out on to a flagged area, and then the garden, which is larger than I'd expected.

'I'm afraid the garden is somewhat neglected,' Bertha apologizes. 'I can't get to it.'

'Of course you can't,' my mother agrees. 'Ernest is very fond of gardening!'

'Oh! Then you might find this one too small,' Bertha suggests.

'I don't think so,' my mother answers on behalf of Dad. 'It's amazing what you can grow in a small space. Especially if you have hanging baskets. Ernest grew lovely little tomatoes in hanging baskets one year!'

There's another room at the back of the house which I suppose the estate agent would describe as the dining room. It would have to have a very small table and chairs, I'm thinking. A dwarves' tea party. 'Cosy' would be the agent's word.

There's an outside lavatory. 'Useful if you happen to be gardening,' Mum says helpfully. There's also a shed at the end of the garden. 'It's full of gardening tools and heaven knows what else,' Bertha says. 'I'd leave that as it is. You could throw away what you didn't want.'

That's the lot on the ground floor, except for the small hall and the living room, which I notice Bertha refers to as the drawing room. I expect she was brought up in a house with a drawing room.

'Would you mind if I asked you to go upstairs without me?' she says. 'It's a bit difficult. Just walk around and look wherever you want to. Open the cupboard doors and so on. Take your time!'

There are two double bedrooms, rather larger than I'd expected them to be; a landing with cupboards, a small bathroom, a lavatory. It's all very pleasant and surprisingly light, which must owe something to the fact that the walls and the paintwork, and most of the furnishings, are white.

That done, we descend the steep, narrow stairs which have an acute turn halfway down – no wonder Bertha finds it difficult to negotiate them – and rejoin Bertha in the living room.

'It's really nice!' my mother says. 'It's exactly what we want!'

Dad could kill her. She has left him no room to manoeuvre, no room to haggle over the price.

'Don't you think so, Ernest?' she persists.

'In the main!' he says. 'In the main!' He doesn't want to be at all rude to Bertha, that's not his way, but he prides himself on getting a good deal on anything, whereas my mother would rush straight in and pay up.

'You haven't yet told us what you're asking for the cottage, Miss Jowett,' he says to Bertha.

She immediately names the price. 'I had it valued and that's what the estate agent said I should get for it without any difficulty.'

'I see,' Dad says doubtfully. 'If you don't mind my saying so, it does seem a bit steep.'

'I know!' Bertha agrees amiably. 'That's exactly what I said to the estate agent. "It's what it will fetch," he said. He said I was probably out of touch with property prices, which of course I am, having lived here for years with no thought of moving.'

'That's exactly what I keep telling Ernest. Prices have risen!' my mother says, throwing another spanner in the works.

'You see,' Bertha explains, 'I have to get as much as I can for this house in order to pay the rest home fees. They're very steep. And who knows how long I might be there? Once one begins to be looked after, and well fed, one does tend to live longer.' She then tells us the story of a woman in the village, aged ninety-eight and in rapidly failing health, whose family found her a place in a private home for what was to be the last few months of her life, and she went on to live until she was a hundred-and-two, at crippling expense to her family. 'Though I hope I won't do that!' she added. 'Not that I *have* a family to support me.'

By this time my mother is ready to pay her the asking price plus a bit on top, and Dad can see this.

'Well, thank you for letting us see your house,' he says quickly. 'It's really very nice, but now we must go away and think about it.'

'Of course you must,' Bertha agrees. 'But I hope you won't think about it too long because if you don't want it I have to consider putting it in the hands of the agent. He says he could sell it quite quickly, which is what I need because – I don't know whether Venus has told you this – I have to say yes or no to the place in the home or I'll lose it. And places there are like gold!'

'Oh, it won't take us long!' my mother says with cheerful confidence. What she means is that she will sort my father out as soon as we get back to the Vicarage.

Bertha insists on seeing us to the door. 'Heaven knows,' she says as we take our leave, my mother promising to be in touch very soon, 'how I'm going to sort everything out – I mean furniture, possessions and suchlike. It's a bit like going to heaven – you can't take it with you!'

'I'm sure Venus will give you a hand,' my mother says, offering my services willy-nilly. She does still tend to think, when it suits her, that Sunday is the only day I work. But in fact, if I'm around I'd be happy to step in and help.

Back at the Vicarage my father puts up a fight but he has no chance, I suppose partly because I, too, am so keen for them to buy the cottage. Not that I need to say a great deal because my mother has all the answers. She reminds him that the figure for the cottage is in the same bracket as that being asked for their own house, which is likely to sell quickly.

'So there's nothing to worry about!' she says finally.

Saturday, and the visit to the Dog Rescue Centre goes like a dream. Becky would like her grandparents to go with us but I rule that out. I don't think it's fair to the dog or to anyone else, and I doubt the Centre would allow it. My parents agree.

'You can tell us all about it when you get back, and after that we'll wait until you bring her home,' my mother says.

We learn a great deal in the class: about a dog's routine – dogs need routine; regular meals, walks, bedtimes, toilet training. It sounds for all the world like having a new baby and I suppose it is. When we take Missie out for her walk she's a darling, so good on the lead, no trouble when we meet with other dogs. She's a friendly little thing also, and this thrills Becky, she answers immediately to her name and she's very affectionate. It almost breaks Becky's heart that we can't take her home with us there and then, but I promise we'll come again next Saturday.

'A whole week!' Becky wails.

Sunday again. The eight o'clock goes well, as usual. Same people, and I think I know all of them by name now, which is good. I would like to know why they don't go to the ten o'clock with most of the others but it's not something I will ask. If I did I expect there'd be as many different answers as there are people.

When I get home my mother has the breakfast all ready to serve – what luxury! – so I'm back in very good time for the ten o'clock and I do a few odd jobs in the parish office before I go into the porch to greet my congregation. As usual, I'm wondering if Miss Frazer will be amongst them, and if she is, what her attitude will be. Could it be possible that she has decided to give up on me and never darken the doors of St Mary's again? How would I feel about that? Would I feel I'd driven her away? If I have it's not what I've done, it's what I am, and I can't change that.

I suppose about a third of the congregation have arrived when I look down the church path and see people on the pavement at the other side of the lych gate accepting sheets of paper, leaflets I suppose, from a youth. I think nothing of this, leaflets are frequently thrust upon one in all kinds of places and they come regularly through the Vicarage letter box, offering to repaint the house at a bargain price or advertising a new Indian take-away in Brampton, though outside church on a Sunday morning is something I haven't experienced before. People are not stopping to read them. You don't, do you, when you have a leaflet thrust into your hand? You walk on. But as they are walking up the path I see one or two people starting to read them in what looks like a cursory way. And then two people stand still quite suddenly, and look at each other, and call out something I can't hear. Meanwhile the youth is still handing out the leaflets and now, it being almost time for the service to start, there are more people arriving and automatically taking them, and seeing those who are already reading them standing there as if transfixed, they too begin to read. I am mad with curiosity to see what intrigues them so, and since the two women who were the first to start reading theirs are almost at the church door I hold out my hand.

'Do let me have a look, Mrs Mayfield!' I say. 'Is something exciting going to happen?'

Mrs Mayfield is reluctant to give me the leaflet, so the other woman, Mrs Barrett, hands me hers.

'You're going to see it in the end!' she says as she hands it to me. It's a small sheet of paper, set out as you see it here.

My head spins and I feel sick. But way above that I am angry, oh, so very angry! And without stopping to say a word to anyone I run down the path. I run at such a speed that those still walking up, the stragglers, have to jump out of my way.

When I go through the lych gate and on to the pavement the youth is still there, still clutching a number of leaflets. I catch him totally unawares and grab at them, but all I succeed in doing is knocking them to the ground and he, startled – I am after all in my vestments and probably look like the wrath of God come to life – turns around and runs off. The leaflets, probably about a dozen, lie around on the ground and I start to pick them up.

WOMEN PRIESTS

So-called priests are **UNLAWFUL IN THE SIGHT OF GOD.**

The Holy Bible, the word of God, tells us that **GOD MADE WOMAN TO BE MAN'S HELPER. NOWHERE IN THE BIBLE IS A WOMAN ANOINTED AS A PRIEST!!**

WHEN WE FLY IN THE FACE OF GOD WE EXPECT TO RECEIVE HIS PUNISHMENT!!

THUS SAITH THE LORD!

"Because you have defiled my sanctuary I will cut you down! I will make you an object of Mockery!"

"The wrath of the Lord is upon you! I will punish you for your ways!"

"The heavens will reveal their iniquity and the earth will rise up against them."

WOMEN MASQUERADING AS PRIESTS MUST GO! THEY HAVE NO PLACE IN GOD'S CHURCH!!

God says, "I will scatter you to every wind!"

By this time someone has informed the Blessed Henry and here he is, helping me. If his face is anything to go by he also is in a state of shock.

'Oh, Venus . . . !' he begins.

'Don't say another word! Not one word!' I order him. 'I am going straight into the church and I'm going to do what I'm here to do, which is celebrate the Holy Eucharist.'

'You can't ignore this,' Henry says, waving a leaflet at me. 'Half of them have read it by this time and the other half have been told.'

'I shall say a very few words before I begin the service,' I say, 'and perhaps something in the sermon, but otherwise I shall carry on. The idea behind this is to disrupt and upset everyone. I'm not going to allow that to happen. I will not play into her hands!' There is nothing in the leaflet to say from whom it has originated, but I don't need a name or a signature. Nor does Henry. It is self-evident.

'It will have to be dealt with,' he says.

'I know. But not now. I will not allow it to take precedence. I intend to keep as calm as possible and I hope you will, too.'

I am already walking back up the path, at such speed that Henry can hardly keep up with me.

'Of course!' he says.

When I go into the church there is a buzz of conversation. I take a deep breath and walk at my normal steady speed up the aisle, and as I do so the buzz dies down so that by the time I turn round and face everyone there is absolute silence.

For a second or two I look around. I see my parents and Becky, all three looking distressed. I hadn't actually noticed them coming into church. Perhaps they were amongst the unlucky ones almost mown down as I rushed down the path. And as I look at the rest of the congregation I can't help thinking, 'Who is with me and who is against me?', but I dismiss that negative thought almost at once. I take a deep breath and find my voice.

'My friends,' I say, 'I'm sorry for what has happened. I'm sorry if it distressed you. I don't propose to go into it at this moment, we are here for another purpose. Later, at a time more suitable, and if we decide we wish to do so, we will discuss the whole matter between us.' I have little hope that it won't get around the village and there is nothing I can do about that.

And then I give the greeting of the Eucharist.

I raise my hands, palms uppermost, a gesture which takes in everyone present, and I speak in a firm, confident voice.

'The grace of our Lord Jesus Christ, the love of God, and the fellowship of the Holy Spirit, be with you all!'

The reply comes back, it seems to me, in full voice, loud and strong.

'And also with you!'

I've always felt that this is a greeting and a response which cannot be bettered. It's perfection. What more needs to be said? But it's at this point that emotion almost overwhelms me, I feel the tears pricking at my eyes, but they're mixed with tears of gratitude, and I don't allow them to fall.

I get through the service, of course I do. I'm in fighting mood, but this doesn't mean that I'm not sick at heart. At one point, when I see my congregation lined up in the aisle, coming towards me to receive the sacrament, I feel dizzy and I wonder if I'm going to pass out, but I don't.

Afterwards, I stand at the door as people leave, Henry standing beside me on one side and Richard Proctor on the other, both symbols of solidarity and support for which I'm grateful. Most people say nothing to me, probably they can't find the words, but several smile at me and some touch my hand, briefly. I reckon that most people have an innate sense of what's fair and what isn't and judge an attack of this nature to be unfair, perhaps especially because it's anonymous, though I reckon most people have no doubt about its source.

I go into coffee, make conversation, answer a few questions like, 'What are you going to do?' and, 'Where do we go from here?' by saying that I don't know and I will have to think about it. Carla Brown has no hesitation in saying in a loud voice, 'I could kill that woman!'

I have hardly finished my coffee when my family come across to me and my mother says, 'I think we'd better leave, Venus. I want to see to the dinner because, don't forget, we'll have to eat

283

early. You're going out this afternoon.' I had almost forgotten that I was going to the concert with Nigel. I'm not sure that I want to go now. Then I tell myself that music hath charms to soothe the savage breast – which mine is – so it might be the very best thing I could do.

TWENTY-FOUR

Nigel calls for me at two o'clock precisely. We have finished lunch and my mother has already cleared away. Surprisingly, and to my mother's pleasure, in spite of the tumultuous morning I ate and enjoyed my meal. Nigel knows nothing of this morning's events unless – and this is always possible – it's already around Thurston.

'Do come in and meet my parents,' I say.

My mother only has to say, 'Pleased to meet you, Doctor Baines,' for him to reply, 'Ah, Mrs Foster, you're from Yorkshire! I once lived there myself!'

I look at him in amazement. It hasn't affected his accent at all – though maybe I wouldn't recognize the finer nuances if it had. I've lived all my life in Sussex. Meanwhile my mother is smiling broadly at him.

'Well I never!' she says. 'Which part? It's a big county, isn't it?'

'Harrogate,' Nigel says.

'I was brought up in York,' my mother says. 'That's where I met Ernest. Not too far from Harrogate, is it?'

'No, it's not,' Nigel agrees.

I can see, and I think he can, that this conversation could go on a long time, my mother is deeply interested. She is ready to tell how and when she met my father, how they came to leave York, how many years it is since *she* was last in York. Once embarked upon it's a long story, and we have tickets for a concert in Brampton.

'Well, Mrs Foster,' Nigel says kindly, 'you and I must get together some time. We probably have quite a lot in common.'

'That would be lovely, Doctor Baines,' my mother says.

They sound like two expatriates in a foreign land.

'I'm all ready,' I tell him, standing there with my coat on.

He nods at me, then turns to Becky who until now has had no chance to speak even if she wanted to.

'Are you OK, Becky?' he asks.

'Yes!' she says. 'We're getting a dog! Her name's Missie and she's a spaniel . . .'

This could be another showstopper if Nigel allows it, but once again he's skilled at not doing so.

'Yes, I know,' he says. 'I used to have a spaniel. I must drop in when I have more time and tell you about her.'

'We'll have to be off now,' I say, 'or we'll miss the start of the concert. We'd be very unpopular, going in late!'

The concert is in the Corn Exchange, no longer used for its original purpose but adapted over the years for exhibitions, meetings and such, including a very pleasant concert hall. We are lucky enough to find a parking space in a nearby street, but we have to hurry to the Corn Exchange, arriving in the nick of time to take our seats before the concert starts. We have good seats, in the second row of the balcony, so that we shall have a good view of the instrumentalists who are tuning up – a sound I love. Then the conductor and soloist appear.

The Rachmaninov comes first – his Second Piano Concerto. 'The pianist's a great favourite here. Local boy made good!' Nigel whispers.

He is much younger than I expected, possibly in his twenties, small, shy-looking, and when he sits at the piano he seems smaller still; he doesn't look as though he'll have the strength to tackle Rachmaninov but when he starts, the chords quiet at first and then louder and louder, crashing, the strength is there all right; he is a different person, firm and sure, in total control. He and Rachmaninov seem made for each other. And when it ends, with all those runs and chords, there is complete silence, as if everyone has stopped breathing; and then, spontaneously, the applause breaks out, rapturous, tumultuous, one great eruption of sound.

In the interval after the first half of the concert when we leave our seats to stretch our legs in the corridor outside the hall, I turn to Nigel. 'So what are you going to tell me about Rachmaninov?' I ask.

'Oh, I expect you know anything I could tell you,' he says. 'It's not new.'

'On the contrary,' I say, 'I know next to nothing. It's a concerto I've always loved, and my mother says I'd love it even more if I'd seen *Brief Encounter*. "Magic!" she always says. "I don't know when I've enjoyed a film more! I cried buckets!"'

'I've heard people call it hackneyed,' Nigel says, 'but that's a word pretentious people use when something is enjoyed by the masses. I think it's sad that they can no longer allow themselves to enjoy something once it becomes popular.'

As we go back to our seats for the second half of the concert, the musicians are taking their places again for the Sibelius – his Second Symphony. When the conductor bows to the audience there's a ripple of applause.

I'm more familiar with Sibelius's 'Finlandia', which is played with great regularity on Classic FM, but listening to this symphony I do detect a similarity between the two works; they share a sombreness, and I wonder if it has anything to do with Sibelius being Finnish. I think of Finland as being dark and cold, eternal winter, with pine-covered hills rising from the shores of deep, ink-black lakes. As it draws to a close, it feels like the entire audience has been on a Finnish journey together. The applause is thunderous.

We leave, the two of us, hardly speaking – as if we don't have the strength for it – but when we step into the street and a blast of cold air meets us Nigel finds his voice.

'Shall we find somewhere to have tea?' he suggests. 'You don't have to rush back, do you?'

I don't, do I? And it would bring us back to earth.

The Brampton Arms has a tea room which is what I would describe as reluctantly open. Only one table is occupied and all a tired-looking waitress can offer us is toast and a slice of fruit cake, it being, she informs us, now out of season. So that's what we order. I didn't realize there was a close season for tea.

'Thank you for a wonderful afternoon,' I say to Nigel while we wait for the tea. 'It was marvellous. I enjoyed every minute!'

'So did I,' he says. 'Thank you for coming!'

I begin to tell him my thoughts on the Sibelius, and he nods. 'I know what you mean, when I first heard it it made me think of the English Lake District, lakes and mountains, sometimes stormy skies and lashings of rain. I used to walk there, or cycle, when I lived in the north.'

There's so much about Nigel I don't know, very little I do know, but would like to, though he's a man who doesn't talk much about himself. I wouldn't have envisaged him striding over mountains.

'As a matter of fact,' he says, 'Sibelius wrote this symphony when he was in Italy! It's supposed to be lighter than his other works.'

'You seem to be knowledgeable about music,' I say. And that's another fact I didn't know about him.

'Not really,' he says modestly. 'I don't play an instrument, except a few chords on a guitar. I wish I did.'

The kitchen has geared itself up to making a pot of tea and two slices of toast and the weary waitress serves it, plus a small dish of strawberry jam and the fruit cake. As far as two people can linger over this feast, we do.

'So what brought you to Thurston?' I ask when the subject of Sibelius is exhausted. 'I know you said you trained in London, and never went back to Ireland, but why Thurston?'

'Because of Sonia – and her husband,' Nigel says. 'We all three worked in the same hospital, in London, and then Sonia and Kit moved down to Thurston. Their marriage was rocky, they thought the move would improve things, but it didn't. I suppose it's difficult with one doctor in a marriage, and with two it's next door to impossible. At least it was with them. In the end he went to Australia. I understand he's doing well there.'

'Poor Sonia!' I say.

He nods. 'Fortunately for Sonia she's found someone else.

288

He's a lawyer. It seems to work well, though there's no talk of marriage, or even sharing the same house.'

'So which bit of this brought you to Thurston?' I persist. I'm interested in Sonia but much more interested in him.

'Sonia knew I was a bit restless in London so when Kit left she asked me if I'd like to join her here. I was also at the end of a relationship which hadn't worked, so I jumped at it. She's a good person to work with.'

In my romantic heart I'm thinking he could have married Sonia, they could have lived happily ever after, though I'm pleased he didn't or I wouldn't be here this afternoon. They could have spent Sundays doing the garden together instead of him going off to concerts on his own. Or with the widowed Vicar of a church which is not his own, any more than his will ever be mine, though we worship the same God. This is sad in the wider sense – I hate these divisions and I'm sure they're contrary to God's will – but at the moment I'm not thinking in the wider sense.

'Sonia had already met Ian before I came to Thurston,' he continues – answering the question I haven't asked. 'In any case there's nothing like that with Sonia and me. We're partners in the practice and very good friends.'

So, all these good friends around, all going their own sweet way!

In the car, on the way back to Thurston, Nigel says: 'I've just remembered something else I read about Sibelius. He said he always imagined life as a block of granite. Given a chisel of willpower, he said, and having the idea of what you wanted to do, you can carve out life according to your wishes.'

'It's an interesting idea,' I concede. 'I can see some truth in it, but the chisel, that's to say the willpower, would have to be strong and you'd have to know what you wanted from the block of granite, and have strength to wield the chisel.'

I can see it in my own life. I knew what I wanted to carve out of the stone: my priesthood, a long and happy married life, children.

'But life doesn't always allow you to get on with your carving, does it?' I say. 'You find awkward places in the granite which won't yield to your chisel, the chisel isn't sharp enough, or there's a flaw in the granite you can do nothing about.'

'And what then?' Nigel asks.

'Then I suppose you have to realize you can't carve out life exactly according to your wishes. I don't suppose Sibelius could all the time. You have to find a new design, adapt to what's within your power. Am I mixing my metaphors like mad?'

'I'm not sure,' Nigel says. 'It doesn't matter. I think you're right. But you have to keep chiselling away at the granite, don't you? You can't just give up, throw away the chisel.'

'Of course not,' I agree. 'Like I said, you have to adapt.'

'Sonia told me about your husband,' Nigel says after a minute or two, changing the subject – or not quite changing it because Philip certainly came into what I'd been musing out loud about Sibelius and his theory. 'I'm sorry. It must have been difficult for you.'

Difficult is too mild a word, but I go along with it and say, 'Yes, it was.'

Then for no reason that I can think of the Hon. Miss Frazer pops into my mind. Drat the woman, she pops into my mind when I least want her to! Now will the flaw in the granite block of my life, which she is, yield to my chisel, or will I be the one who has to adapt?

I'm tempted to mention Miss Frazer to Nigel – possibly he'll hear anyway – but instead I broach it in a roundabout way, not mentioning names.

'Do you have ups and downs in St Patrick's Church?' I ask.

He takes his eye off the road for a second and turns and looks at me, clearly surprised. And well he might be because what, as far as he can see, does that have to do with Sibelius and his block of granite?

'Oh, I suppose most churches do,' he says. 'I try not to get involved. A lot of people in the congregation are patients.'

'Well at least you won't be having arguments about women priests,' I say.

'Not a lot,' he admits. 'More about celibacy in the priesthood. That's a hot topic sometimes.'

'And what view do you take? Or shouldn't I ask?'

'It's no secret. I've grown up with the idea. My mother is Irish, a cradle Catholic and so am I. My father is a convert. My mother's view is that whatever the Pope says is right. If he'd said she should bathe in the river every night at midnight for the good of her soul, then I reckon she'd do it. Even so, I don't go along with celibacy. I also think it's at the root of the dwindling number of vocations to the priesthood.'

I decide not to talk about Miss Frazer. There's a short silence. And now we're turning into Thurston High Street and then we're at the Vicarage. 'Thank you, but I won't come in,' Nigel says in answer to my invitation. 'I have a load of paperwork to get through. But thank you for coming with me this afternoon. I've enjoyed it so much.'

'On the contrary, I must thank you for taking me,' I say. 'It was great.'

'We must do it again,' he says as he comes around and opens the car door for me to get out.

'I'd like that!' I say.

'He seems a very nice young man,' my mother says.

'He is!' I agree.

'How old would you say he is?' she enquires casually.

'I don't know. Possibly my age, or a couple of years older.'

'And he's never been married?'

'No.'

I can guess where this conversation is going. I know my mother.

She lowers her voice. 'You don't think he's . . . ?'

'Gay?' I supply the word over which she's hesitating. 'I wouldn't think so. But then how would I know? I haven't slept with him.'

'VENUS!'

She doesn't like things spelt out, and I'm a bit naughty. I do it on purpose. 'Why? Does it matter?' I asked innocently.

'You know perfectly well what I mean!' she protests. And of course I do. She's wondering if he's eligible. She worries about me remaining unmarried. She was very fond of Philip but she does like everything tied up in neat parcels.

291

'Why do you always think unmarried men in their thirties must be gay?' I ask her.

Her answer comes pat. 'Because they usually are!'

'Well, I don't think for a moment he is,' – and I'm not telling her he's had a relationship – 'but anyway, he's not eligible. For a start he's a Roman Catholic.'

'Oh dear!' she says. That puts him farther away than if he was coal black, an avowed atheist and a member – God forbid – of the Labour Party (though she thinks Tony Blair is a nice-looking young man and probably a very good father).

My parents leave for home after breakfast on Monday morning. My mother seems reluctant to go.

'I would like to take another look at the cottage,' she says.

'Why?' my father demands. 'You've looked over every inch of it. What more is there to see?'

'I know,' she admits. 'But when you think something might possibly be yours you want to keep looking at it! Before we got engaged I saw the exact ring I wanted in the jeweller's window and I went back at least six times to look at it!'

Dad gives her his 'I shall never understand women' look, but I can guess how she feels and I agree with her.

'Anyway,' he says, 'we need to get home, see what's happening about our house. We've got to sell that, remember.'

'We could call in the estate agent's on the way home,' my mother says. 'We have to pass the door.' And to this Dad agrees.

Later in the morning the Blessed Henry phones me.

'What are we going to do about yesterday's episode?' he asks. 'Have you thought about it?'

Of course I've thought about it, a hundred times, but I'm not going to admit that.

'Do you reckon we should tell the Bishop?' he asks.

'I'd much rather we didn't,' I say. 'That would be the sort of thing she'd like, giving it special attention. So my idea is to treat it as if it was a mere pinprick – unless, of course, it shows signs of upsetting the congregation. If it were to do that I'd think again.'

'Well, if you're sure,' Henry says. I don't think he's totally convinced. 'But if he should ring, I mean about anything, then I think we should tell him. Or if by any chance it gets into the *Brampton Echo*. You never know what gets into that, I reckon they have spies everywhere. And they'd make a meal of it.'

I agree to that also. 'But I don't want the Bishop to think I'm going to run to him with every little setback,' I say. 'Anyway, I'm not going to take it as a setback, I'm going to see it as a spur!'

'You're a brave lady,' Henry says.

'Also,' I say, 'I've thought of a way we can use this episode to our advantage. If we were to have this meeting you know I'm keen on with members of the congregation as soon as possible, I think what I have to say might strike a sympathetic note. One of the things we need to tell them is the effect Miss Frazer's withdrawal of her financial support will have, and I think that that, together with yesterday's behaviour, will galvanize people into doing what I want, which is moving forward in a very positive way. I think the congregation themselves might well come up with some suggestions about what we can do.'

'You're an optimist,' Henry says.

'I know!' I agree. 'I hope you are too!'

'Oh, I'll support you every step,' he assures me. 'So will Richard. But you need to recognize that there might be people who won't.'

'You mean there are those who will agree with Miss Frazer?' I ask.

'Possibly. When it comes out into the open.'

TWENTY-FIVE

This last week has been a full one, especially the last three days. On Wednesday my mother phoned me to say they'd had people to look at the house. 'A Mr and Mrs Dawson. A nice young couple with a toddler and a baby. They haven't been in Clipton long – well, strictly speaking they're not yet *in* Clipton, though he is because he's got a new job with the Council so he's travelling to and fro every day, which is why they want to buy a house as soon as they can, only they have to sell their house first and that's . . .'

I had to break in. I have no doubt my mother now knows everything there is to know about the Dawsons, she could do a 'This Is Your Life', but Wednesday is early closing day and I needed to shop in the village.

'Did they like the house?' I asked.

'Oh yes! They said it was exactly what they wanted. It was, as I've told you, simply a question of getting a buyer for theirs. We have someone else coming to view it tomorrow but I would like the Dawsons to have it. They're such a nice couple and you like to think of someone nice living in the house where you've been happy, don't you?'

'Well, it sounds as though it could be good news,' I said, 'but I'll have to go now, I have to do some shopping. Keep me posted, won't you? Shall I drop in on Miss Jowett and tell her?' Mum agreed that that would be a good idea.

I made Bertha Jowett my first stop and asked her if there was anything she wanted from the village. She said she'd like a brown loaf from Gander's and a packet of unsalted butter from the Co-op. I thought she seemed rather frail, also she had a niggling cough. When I returned with the shopping I made us both a cup of coffee and we each had a fruit scone from Gander's. Though I was wearing my leather jacket it felt really cold in her room and I suggested I should turn up the heat which she allowed me to do. I don't imagine that she can't afford to have the heating on, I thinks she just neglects herself. I'll feel easier when she's being looked after.

I wrote down my telephone number for her. 'Don't hesitate to give me a ring if there's anything you need,' I said. 'I'm always about in the village. It wouldn't be the least trouble.'

She was pleased to hear of some progress – if you could call it progress – on my parents' house and I promised to keep her closely in touch with things. I shall also not hesitate to pray about it – in my book we're allowed to pray about the little things as well as the big – but I didn't tell her this. I doubt she's a woman who would like to be prayed for, I'm not sure that God is allowed into any part of her life and I don't intend to ask her, but when I said 'God bless!' as I was leaving she didn't protest, or throw a cushion at me. She ignored me.

I went back to Mr Winterton's for some salad things and vegetables. 'How's your little granddaughter getting on?' I asked him. He said she was doing fine, so I said, 'Any more thoughts on the baptism?'

'Yes,' he said. 'We were discussing it only last weekend.'

So I suggested he should ask his daughter to give me a ring and arrange for her and her husband to come to see me about it. 'Wednesdays are best,' I told him, 'and this evening would be fine. But if that's too short notice, then whenever suits them.'

Back at home, Rose Barker phoned me.

'I've arranged the meeting you want for Thursday of next week, tomorrow week that is,' she said in her melodious voice. 'Seven-thirty, at the Vicarage. I must say, Venus, I think you're very brave!'

Whether that was because I'm crowding everyone into the Vicarage, or because I'm having the meeting at all, I wasn't sure. Anyway, will it be crowded? I don't know, do I? In terms of bridge, which I hear is a ruling passion in Thurston, we might not be enough to make up more than two tables.

And then in the evening, to my surprise and pleasure, but also to my chagrin because I've been neglecting her, my mother-in-law phoned. It was more or less a race between us to see who could get in first with apologies for not having been in touch with the other.

'It's been such a busy term,' Ann said. 'I've been working late most evenings and arriving home exhausted. I'm so sorry, Venus.'

'I'm sorry I haven't called *you*,' I said, 'and my reasons aren't as good as yours. I can't say I've been overworked and I can't say I've been exhausted. I think it must be because everything is new and I'm not quite organized. And then Becky hasn't been the happiest girl in the world, though she's fine now. Anyway, can you come over one weekend? I'd love to see you. It's a bit tricky for me to come to you. I'm too new to know where to look for cover for services.'

'Of course I'll come to you!' Ann said. 'No question!'

So we fix for her to come in ten days' time, Friday evening to Sunday afternoon, and I'm looking forward to it.

Yesterday Becky and I went to the Rescue Centre to see Missie and take her out for a walk. Well, it was certainly the highlight of the week for Becky. She's such a lovely little dog. She wagged her tail frantically when she saw us. 'She knows me!' Becky cried. 'Oh, Mum, she knows me!' I wasn't sure whether that was true, but who knows, it might have been.

The best news of all, however, came from Imogen.

'We've decided,' she told us when we returned from our walk, 'that you can take Missie home with you for good next weekend. Everything seems to be going well and there's no real need for her to stay here any longer. That's partly because she's a dog who's always been looked after, she's not a stray. Also, she's been well trained.'

'We're very lucky,' I said.

'So is she,' Imogen said, smiling. 'And the other reason is, frankly, we're short of room here. She'll make way for another dog. So you could pick her up next Saturday morning.'

That was yesterday. I don't think Becky has stopped talking about it since. It's her only topic of conversation. What a wonderful capacity a dog has for healing hearts!

So here I am, Sunday again. I've done the eight o'clock, which was, predictably, the same as ever. Nothing seems to ruffle them and if they have heard anything of last Sunday's to-do they showed no signs of it. I told them about Thursday evening's meeting. 'I do hope most of you will be able to come,' I said. 'Apart from the fact that I think you'll find it interesting, it will give me a chance, which I'd appreciate, of getting to know you better.' Whether they'll come or not I don't know. I think they're probably happy as they are as long as I don't rock the boat and perhaps some of them might come out of curiosity. Or perhaps concern about what changes I might make. My feeling is that they won't like change.

The ten o'clock congregation, as I stand in front of it to give them the opening greeting, is no smaller than it was last week, in fact it's perhaps marginally larger and there are some new faces. Have some come in the expectation of another 'happening'? If so, I hope they'll be disappointed – and since Miss Frazer isn't present I daresay they will be. I greeted little Mrs Bateman as she came in. I didn't ask her any questions and she gave me no information, which I hope means there was none to give.

Standing in the pulpit – which, by the way, I have plans to abandon any Sunday from now on in favour of preaching from the nave – I intend to make no reference to last Sunday's event in my sermon, I have better things to talk about, but at the end of the service when I give out the notices (and for my first time ever in St Mary's read some banns, for John Carter and his fiancée, Jean, who, as I told you, are going to be married here before Christmas) I tell the congregation about the meeting I've planned.

'It's very important,' I say. 'There are things to discuss and things to plan. I want you all to have your say. So please come! And if there's anyone who isn't here this morning, or indeed anyone you know who might be interested in what we hope to do at St Mary's, please invite them. Thursday evening, seven-thirty at the Vicarage. And if a couple of people would like to give me a hand with the refreshments I'd be grateful!'

When I go for coffee Carla Brown immediately offers to help on Thursday. 'Will you be wanting to borrow some of the cups and saucers from the hall?' she asks. 'If so, I'm sure Walter would bring them round to the Vicarage on Wednesday evening.' Carla, I've discovered, is very good at offering Walter's services, but he's an amiable man and never seems to mind. Now, he nods agreement. Trudy Santer also says she'll lend a hand, as does another woman whose name I must find out. I want to talk to Trudy. I have a guilty conscience because I've not yet discussed the Sunday School with her, as I promised to. Also, I have some ideas about it which I want to put to her.

'Thank you, Trudy,' I say. 'I'd be very grateful for your help, but aside from that would you be able to pop round to the Vicarage – or I could come to see you? We haven't talked about Sunday School – and I'm sorry about that. When would be convenient?'

She chooses Tuesday evening. She works part-time on the check-out at Marks & Spencer's in Brampton so daytime is a bit tricky. She has to be home to give the children (she has two daughters) their tea when they get home from school, and then there's her husband's supper and hers when he gets in from work, but she'll be free by eight o'clock.

'That's fine,' I say, 'but as it's in the evening will you mind coming to me, because of Becky? I won't keep you long.'

Becky has gone home. Coffee in the parish hall isn't her scene.

Just before people start to arrive on Thursday evening I say 'Good-night' to Becky, who has elected to retire to her room and watch television rather than mingle with whoever comes. I've seen her through bathtime and left her sitting up in bed in her pyjamas. I've also lent her my mobile phone so that if she wants to she can call Anna, though with warnings about very long calls, which she assures me she won't make. Becky is so amenable these days. I put it down almost entirely to Missie, but not totally since she continues to be very pleased about her grandparents coming to live in Thurston. I suggest that she might like to phone them also.

There are twenty-seven people in the Vicarage now, all somehow squeezed into the sitting room. Places to sit have been the problem. I have brought chairs from every room in the house, including the kitchen, plus the plastic garden chairs which had been put away in the garage for the winter; and when I run out of chairs I put cushions on the floor.

Carla, except when I manage to beat her to it, answers the door to everyone. Trudy Santer and the other lady who had offered to help (and whose name I've discovered is Violet Moore) serve coffee and biscuits. And now I want to get started on what we're here for. Well, I do and I don't. When it comes to the point I'm as nervous as a cat and for a second I ask myself why I ever decided to have this meeting. I could have sat back, dealt with the usual services, carried out weddings, baptisms and funerals as and when required, chaired the PCC meetings, and that would have been about it. Some worshippers might have left St Mary's, gone elsewhere, new ones might or might not have come, but as I'm not paid according to numbers I could have ignored that too. But what sort of a parish priest would that make me?

I could also have ignored Miss Frazer, right from her very first demonstration. Now *there's* a thought!

But I'm pretty sure that to hear about Miss Frazer is what some of these people are here for – certainly to talk about the leaflets. Is it possible that there's anyone who doesn't attribute those to Miss Frazer?

I have no agenda, except what's in my head, and this I've discussed with the churchwardens. I'm not sure they agree with everything, in fact I'm sure they don't, but they won't try to stop me saying it. There will be others, I'm sure, who won't agree with everything and I shall consider their views carefully. In the end, though – make no mistake – it's I who am parish priest and it's my responsibility to lead these people forward to the kingdom of God.

It's an awesome responsibility, frightening sometimes, but I

299

shouldered it willingly, and I would do so again. In some ways it is more important than my laid-down duties of taking the services, baptizing, marrying, burying. Important though those are, and they are my privilege to carry out and they must be done well, they are milestones. Living in the kingdom of God is an everyday thing.

'Good-evening!' I say. 'How very nice to see you all. I'm going to begin with a short prayer.' People are perfectly happy with prayers said in church, it's the right place, but less so with them said in a house, even though it's a Vicarage and a bit more holy than average, so there's a sort of slight shuffling; a moving of legs, easing of backs. When I've done it everyone is still, waiting for me to say my piece.

'There are several things to discuss,' I say, 'all with their own importance, but some more pertinent than others. Let's start with what I daresay has been on the minds of most of you, although I don't regard it as the most important of this evening's topics – so, last Sunday's leaflets. But not just the leaflets; things took place on previous Sundays which, to my mind, were far more damaging and more important. First of all, though, is there anyone here who has *no* idea who is behind these happenings?'

There's a general shaking of heads, but one woman says, 'But we don't actually *know* it was Miss Frazer, do we?'

It comes as something of a relief to have her name said out loud.

'We don't know one hundred per cent that Miss Frazer was responsible for the leaflets,' I agree. 'Though the opinions expressed on them were exactly the ones which she said to my face on my first Sunday here. She made no secret of her opinions.'

'I can vouch for that!' Carla Brown says fiercely. 'I was there, sitting at the same table. She was abominably rude!'

She would have continued, but I hold up my hand to stop her. 'That she was rude to me wasn't pleasant,' I say, 'but it's something women priests are used to. With regard to the leaflets, though my name wasn't mentioned, they were clearly aimed at me, though that matters far less than the fact that they upset some of you, and others in the congregation, and at the very moment when you were coming in to your worship.'

'But we don't *know* that it was Miss Frazer!' the first speaker repeats.

It's then that I get one of life's surprises!

'Oh yes we do! At least I do. I know for certain!'

It's Mrs Bateman speaking. All eyes immediately turn in her direction.

'How do you know?' the first speaker says. I don't think it's that this woman actually has anything against me. That isn't in the tone of her voice. I think she sees this as some sort of a debate where every point of view must be presented.

'I know because she told me!' Mrs Bateman says. Her voice, which had been surprisingly strong when she first spoke, now has a tremble in it.

'Then why didn't you tell Venus?' Carla Brown demands, turning round and glaring at poor Mrs Bateman. 'She could have done something about it.'

'Because she didn't say exactly,' Mrs Bateman replies. 'She said, "Just you wait until Sunday! If you're traitor enough to go to that so-called priest's church then you'll see her get her come-uppance. I've seen to that!" That's exactly what she said. I remember every word! I couldn't sleep for it!' Mrs Bateman looks at me, her eyes full of tears. 'I'm sorry, Vicar!' she says. 'It's all my fault! I should have told you! But you see I didn't really believe her, I told myself she wouldn't dare to do anything really awful. I suppose I didn't want to believe her! It's all my fault. I'm ever so sorry!'

She fishes in her handbag for a handkerchief and then dries her eyes. The room has gone quite quiet.

'That's all right, Thora!' I say. 'Don't upset yourself. Nothing was your fault, you did what you thought was best. And as I said, to my mind the leaflets were far less serious than the times when Miss Frazer deliberately turned her back on the sacrament. The leaflets were against me; the other occasions were against God.'

'But can't someone report about the leaflets, tell them our suspicions? She shouldn't get away with it!' It's another woman

301

who says this. It's interesting how much more vociferous the women are than the men.

And then the Blessed Henry speaks.

'The church can't officially do anything. It didn't take place on church land, it was on the public pavement.'

'And in any case,' I chip in, 'I wouldn't have wanted a complaint to be made. To draw attention to it would give it more prominence than it deserves. So let me tell you the rest of the story and then we can move on to something else.'

I've already noticed that there are two or three, not more, eight o'clockers in the room and I'd like to know what they're thinking. Is it 'Who would have thought that this kind of thing went on at the ten o'clock?' Will some of them be thinking how right they are to stick to the earlier service, and will any one of them rather envy the excitement of the later one?

'Miss Frazer,' I say, 'wrote to the Bishop about her strong objections to women priests. She asked that I should be removed from this parish forthwith.' There's a gasp from several of those present. 'The Bishop pointed out to her that I am legally a priest in the Church of England and that my ordination is every bit as valid as if I were a man. He told her that I had his full support and that there was no way I was likely to be asked to leave St Mary's. She threatened the Bishop with taking away all her not inconsiderable financial support of St Mary's unless I was removed and he, while thanking her for many years of such support, said that was a matter for her own conscience.'

I pause. There's another silence, which I break.

'I don't want all this to be the main subject of this meeting,' I say. 'It's truly not what we're here for. But if you do want to say anything, or ask a question on this subject, then please do so now, before we move on.'

If you had asked me before this meeting to write down the questions which would be asked about my priesthood, the observations which would be made, and to seal them in an envelope to be opened after the meeting, I would have been spot on. All I wouldn't have known would be who would voice them. I say 'them' though actually they would have boiled down to one

302

question, one observation. I know it by heart. And sure enough a woman puts up her hand to ask it.

'Jesus appointed only men as his disciples,' she says. 'He didn't appoint women to work with him. Surely this says that he thought women were unsuitable for such things? Surely he thought to use women was against the will of God?'

'It's an interesting thing about the will of God,' I say. 'You can take two people, equally upright, honest, thoughtful, equally learned and clever, both pronouncing on exactly the same subject, but with clearly divided views. One will say, quite sincerely, that what he believes is the will of God. The other one will say exactly the same about his belief. And you can extend that to two groups of people. So if they are both right then we're saying, aren't we, that God tells one group one thing, and the other something different? So don't we have to be rather careful in assuming that we have an exclusive knowledge of the will of God in anything?'

'That doesn't answer the question about Jesus only appointing men,' the same woman says.

'I know! And I'm coming to that. Many of the arguments against women being ordained as priests are based on what the world in which Jesus lived was like two thousand years ago. As you know, it was a Jewish world with its own ancient rules. Women had a very low place in life; for the most part kept in the house, not encouraged to have opinions, made to sit in a different place from the men in the synagogue, regarded as unclean when they menstruated. Did you know that at such times any bed a woman slept in, any seat on which she sat, was also rendered unclean, and whoever lay on that bed or sat on that seat would be contaminated until such places had been thoroughly washed, and left alone for a set number of days?'

There were a few sharp intakes of breath, a few squirmings in seats as I said all that.

'That was the world in which, as you rightly say, Jesus chose men as his disciples. It would have been unthinkable to do otherwise. But God isn't just for the world of two thousand years ago, he's also for today. Would you like to go back to that world?

Would you be content to live in the dark ages? Would you like not to be able to go out to work if you wanted, or needed to? Is this how you would like to bring up your daughters? Would you like them not to be educated? To think that their bodies were unclean? Do you actually think there should be one law for men and a different, and more restrictive one, for women? Do you see women as second-class citizens? And if not, why would you, hopefully not any of you here, but those like Miss Frazer and many others, see women priests as second-class priests – or not priests at all, even though the law says they are?'

I stop for breath, and also because I think perhaps I'm saying too much, getting carried away. I didn't mean to go on to this extent, on the other hand it needed to be said! Hopefully once and for all.

'Hear, hear!' Carla Brown says.

'Well said, Vicar!' Miss Tordoff says, thus surprising me once again. She is the woman who wouldn't object to babies crying in church. I reckon, if she'd been around at the time, she'd have been a militant suffragette.

There's one other thing I want to say because it's important.

'Yes, Jesus was a man,' I tell them. 'But more than that he was a human being. He embodied all humanity, not just the masculine, and still does. And all humanity embodies the feminine as well as the masculine.

'There's also another point which might interest you, possibly you might already have thought of it. If the Church is to base all it does in every detail on what was done two thousand years ago, then there are other things which need to be looked at, because they don't fit in. For example, at the Last Supper, when the Holy Communion was instituted, Jesus gave the bread and the wine only to his disciples – men – presumably because, in keeping with the custom of the times, they were the only ones there. Are we saying, then, that women should be excluded from taking communion? Did Jesus mean it only for men? I've never met anyone who said *that*, but a totally different kind of logic is applied to women as priests. Though perhaps not by you here, or not all of you.'

There's a murmur of agreement from the majority, but silence from one or two. That's about what I expected, and what I shall have to live with.

'If I sound as though I'm against men,' I tell them, 'that's far from the truth! I like men, but I have no desire to take the place of a man, or be like a man. All I want is to be your priest, for which I have been ordained and appointed; to serve you in every way I can, and for that I need your support. And I am a priest of God, not just of the Church. My authority comes from God, which is above the authority of man.

'And now,' I say, 'shall we move on? We have a number of things to discuss, in fact if you're to get home to your beds tonight I think we might just have to outline some of them, and discuss them in detail later.

'The first thing I need to tell you is that Miss Frazer has indeed carried out her threat to withdraw all her financial support of St Mary's. This is no small thing. She has been most generous to St Mary's over a long period and the lack of her support will mean there'll be many things which have always been done that we'll no longer be able to do, unless we can find the money elsewhere. But I'll leave George Phillipson to fill you in on the details. As our treasurer he has all the figures.'

George does just that; clearly spelling it out, leaving no doubt about the effect Miss Frazer's action will have, but also underlining the folly of depending too much on one person. No-one will say it out loud but I suppose we are all aware that, since she has cut St Mary's out of her will, we also stand to lose a sizeable lump of capital at a later date. However, I am not going to go around in sackcloth and ashes because of this.

TWENTY-SIX

The meeting goes on until ten-thirty, which is way past midnight by Thurston standards, but we accomplish a lot. Or, rather, we talk a lot about what we mean to accomplish in the future, some of it in the very near future. I read out a long list of what I want us to achieve. I reel off the list, purposely not waiting for immediate comments on any one thing. I hear a few gasps as I go through it and I'm well aware that some of my ideas will be, to say the least, controversial and one or two might never see the light of day, but it's cards on the table time for me and I reckon if I give my whole list (so far!) then we should at least get some of it through.

'I'm aware it's quite a basketful,' I say, 'and no doubt you'll have other things to add, so should we deal with what we think is most important first? And what that is I leave to you to suggest. Tell me what *you* think it is!'

There are a few people who remain mute; there are always those who stop at the point where they might possibly become involved and I do wonder why they come to such a meeting, unless it's to keep a rein on those who might be too enthusiastic. There is no doubt, however, what it is those who do have something to say put at the top of the list, and that is the pantomime visit for the children.

'We can't let the children down!' Miss Tordoff said. 'Jesus always looked after the little children!'

'Also it's their reward for coming to Sunday School for weeks on end,' Violet Moore adds. I could think of better ways of putting it, as if Sunday School is an obstacle race you have to get through before you get a prize, though I think, in some cases, it's seen like that. At Holy Trinity we had rather a good outing for the children every year and it was amazing how many children came to Sunday School for a few weeks before it was due to take place, and melted away like snow in summer soon afterwards.

'We should get on with booking it,' Carla Brown says. 'It's November already. And the pantomime's always popular. It's *Cinderella* this year.'

'Which is a great favourite,' someone says, 'though I'd have liked *Puss in Boots*. You don't often see *Puss in Boots* these days!'

There is a diversion while the merits of favourite pantomimes are discussed, *Mother Goose*, *Aladdin*, *Jack and the Beanstalk*, etc., which is brought to an end by Carla Brown who says, 'Well, whatever we all like, *Cinderella* is what we'll get in Brampton!', and our Treasurer throws a spanner in the works by saying, 'And how do we propose to pay for it? The church can't run to it, and that's a fact!'

I break in here.

'I don't, ever, want us to get the idea that finance is the most important thing at St Mary's,' I say. 'That's a long way from the truth. If, at the moment, it's taking undue prominence then we mustn't let that continue. We're not in the church to be fund-raisers! We're here to carry out the gospel, you as well as me. But we have to meet our obligations. We have to keep up the church building in repair, both to use it and to hand it on. We also need money for teaching, for reaching out to others. You might not think that paying for treats for the children falls into this category, but I think it does. It's all part of it.'

'Can't the parents pay for their own children?' a bold soul suggests. And that does cause a protest! Elsie Jones (she of the Brownies) sitting on the front row turns her whole body around and glares at the man who had the temerity to make the suggestion.

'The parents have *never* been asked to pay for the pantomime!' she says. 'The church has *always* paid!'

What she means is that Miss Frazer has always paid. I can see this being a recurring situation.

'Then the church must pay this time,' I announce. 'And we'll have to raise the money quickly. May I have some suggestions?'

Several are offered. Unfortunately nothing new or original. I have lived through them all before.

A bring-and-buy sale, everyone to supply items suitable for Christmas presents; a wine-and-cheese party, a raffle – or why not a weekly raffle? A coffee morning, a bridge evening, a cake sale. A sponsored swim is ruled out because of the time of the year, even though it would take place in Brampton swimming baths where the water is heated. A stall in the parish hall every week at coffee time is suggested – selling preserves, pickles, gingerbread and the like. Apparently we have a lady in the congregation who is famous for her gingerbread, people will queue for it. I notice, as I always have, that people will work hard to do these things, will give and will also buy, but no-one ever has the temerity to say, 'Couldn't we all put in a fiver, or whatever, and save all the work?' That is *not* the way it's done, not in any church I've ever been in. You give of your labours, you profit from the fruit of other people's labours, the money is raised and honour is satisfied. I also have to admit that a good time is usually had by all, and people do get to know each other.

So a small group of people is formed to coordinate these ideas and make sure that, for instance, a coffee morning with home-made biscuits, a cream tea and an evening wine-and-cheese do not all happen on the same day. In the meantime George Phillipson, though a mite grudgingly – he doesn't like paying out – will lend the church's money so that we can make the booking before all the seats are sold out.

'I will put a few lines in the parish magazine to say, quite briefly, and without mentioning Miss Frazer's name, that the money for this year's pantomime treat is not forthcoming,' I say, though I have little doubt that the reason will get around. 'But that we will be having fundraising events which I hope everyone will support.'

'That should do the trick!' the Blessed Henry says.

'And then,' Miss Tordoff adds, 'as soon as Christmas is over we must start to think what we'll do about the Whitsun event. The children do so enjoy that!'

Dear Miss Tordoff! I wonder if she would have liked to have had a husband and six children – and by what mischance she didn't.

The time is flying by. Everything takes that bit longer than one thinks it will because there are always byways to explore, though there's nothing wrong with that. These good people in my sitting room, and indeed the rest of St Mary's congregation who aren't here this evening, have a right to know what I have in mind, and to have their opinions listened to. I want my congregation with me rather than me going full steam ahead, leaving them behind. On the other hand, what I don't want is for us to stand still, to have no progress in the faith at all. And I *am* here to lead.

I look at my watch. 'There's no way at all we're going to be able to talk this evening about all the things I've mentioned,' I say. 'Some of them will have to wait for further meetings. They're all important, but for now I'd like to mention two matters from the list which in terms of time need to be dealt with, soon.'

This is when I see one or two others look at their watches.

'I won't be lengthy,' I promise. 'The first is the Sunday School. I've been talking with Trudy and we've agreed that the Sunday School children need to be brought more into the church, to feel part of it, so she and I will work something out about that. Also, Trudy does need more help. So will you think about that, and pray about it.'

In fact, Trudy came to the conclusion, when we talked on Tuesday, that she would carry on a bit longer if she could get more help, and more ideas about what to do.

'The other important thing,' I tell them, 'is baptisms – and it's important for me to mention this now because we have two baptisms coming up soon. To put it shortly, I would like baptisms to take place at the ten o'clock Eucharist, in the presence of all of us, preferably with the parents and godparents making their promises to the congregation, not just to me. I've seen it done, it's quite simple, and it works. The words we use will be the same, and I shall baptize in the same way. It's really a bringing of the child into the whole assembly of the church rather than doing it in an empty church in the middle of the afternoon. It's already been mentioned to the PCC, but I'd like to hear what you think.'

There are various opinions; one thing I'm enjoying is that people here – well, most of them – aren't afraid to speak up. Now, one or two ask whether people would still be able to have the baptism at the usual time on Sunday afternoon, privately, if that's what they prefer. I say yes, of course. I won't force people to have it in the ten o'clock service, but I've never thought of baptism as being a private affair. As far as I'm concerned it's a case for public rejoicing. There are the expected remarks about the babies crying in church – people are obsessed, and not just at St Mary's, about children making the least sound in church – and I hope Miss Tordoff will come up with the observation she made at the PCC about crying babies, but she doesn't.

All in all, they seem to think it reasonable, as did the PCC, that I should try out this new form, at least for a period, always providing the parents are agreeable.

And then we decide that we really must call it a day.

'But before you leave,' I say, 'I want you to be sure about one thing, and that is that I will do everything I can at St Mary's to serve you. If there are any advantages to my being a woman in the job – by which I mean advantages to you – then I offer them. If there are disadvantages because I'm a woman, then I'll do my best to make up for them. If any of you have doubts on this subject, or are troubled by it, then don't hesitate to discuss it with me, privately if you like. I promise to listen. And I will need your help, and particularly your prayers. And remember that there is the priesthood of the laity. We are all priests.'

That was yesterday. This evening, about an hour ago, Ann Stanton arrived. It's so good to see her. And in her I see Philip again; the same clear blue eyes, the same direct look. And her voice too; low pitched for a woman. We hugged each other with genuine pleasure.

'You're looking well,' she said as I took her up to her room. 'I hope you've got lots to tell me?'

'Oh, I have!' I said. 'Come down when you're ready. We'll have a drink and I'll give you a run-down. What would you like, tea, coffee, gin-and-tonic?'

'Tea,' she says, 'for now. Where's Becky? I thought she'd be home from school. Is she settling down?'

'Very much so. She's found a friend, Anna, and that's where she is at the moment. She'll be home soon.'

I go downstairs to make the tea. The phone rings just as I'm pouring the boiling water into the pot. It's my mother.

'How are you?' I begin – but she has no time for that.

'It's happened!' she cries. 'We've had an offer on the house! The Dawsons! Exactly who we wanted! We've just heard from the estate agent.'

'Oh fantastic! That's wonderful!' I feel every bit as excited as she sounds. 'Is it an acceptable offer? Did you have to come down a lot?'

'Not a great deal,' she says. 'Dad reckons it's a fair one, but you know your Dad. He says he'll let them have his answer tomorrow. Why not at once, I asked him, but he said it didn't do to seem too eager.'

'I'm really delighted for you, and for us!' I say. 'Shall I let Miss Jowett know?'

'Oh yes!' my mother says. 'Tell her we'll be in touch very soon.'

Ann comes into the room.

'Ann's here,' I tell my mother. 'I did say she was coming for the weekend? Would you like a word with her?'

I leave them talking to each other while I go back into the kitchen. After a couple of minutes Ann joins me.

'Your mother said to say good-bye to you, she has things to do. She's really excited, isn't she?'

'If I know my mother she'll have half the house packed by this time tomorrow!' I say. 'But it is good news, and it's been very quick.'

311

Becky arrives. She's pleased, as always, to see Ann. They get on well, though there isn't the same degree of closeness between them as there is between Becky and my mother. That's easily explained. Until now my mother has lived closer to us and since she doesn't go out to work, as Ann does, she's had more time to spend with Becky. I immediately tell Becky the good news about the house and she's overjoyed. 'Gran will be able to see Missie nearly every day!' she says.

'Missie?' Ann questions.

So all that has to be explained, which Becky delights in doing. 'And from tomorrow she's ours to keep for ever! We have to pick her up at twelve o'clock!' she ends her breathless recital.

Two minutes later there's a ring at the door and when I go to answer it there stands Nigel Baines.

'I found the photographs of my dog,' he says. 'I told Becky I'd let her see them. Is she in? Is it convenient?'

'Yes to both questions,' I say. 'How kind of you. Do come in!'

He does so, and I introduce him to Ann.

'We were going to have a gin-and-tonic in a minute,' I say. 'Can you spare the time to join us?'

'Thank you, I can,' he says. 'I don't have a surgery this evening because I've just come from an afternoon one. We stagger them so that most people can find something which suits them.'

I serve the drinks, he shows the photographs to Becky. He has a way of talking to her as if they were both the same age, and as the subject at the moment is totally dogs they have plenty to say.

'I want to take lots of photographs of Missie,' Becky says, 'right from the minute we bring her home!'

'What I could do,' Nigel offers, 'is bring my digital camera tomorrow . . .' He breaks off to speak to me. 'Sorry, Venus! You've probably got one of your own.'

'Not a digital,' I tell him. 'Just the usual roll-of-film one.'

'What I was going to say,' he continues, 'was that when you got back from the Rescue Centre we could take some photographs with my camera and I could take them home and print them right away on my computer. But perhaps you have other plans? I wouldn't want to break in . . .'

'No, we haven't!' Becky cries. 'We haven't at all. Oh, that

would be super! Oh, we can, Mum, can't we! I could take them to school with me on Monday morning to show to the others!'

There seems to be only one answer to that. Even so, I turn to Ann. 'Is there anything special you wanted to do this weekend?' I ask her.

'Nothing at all,' she says agreeably. 'I came here to be with you and my granddaughter. I've no ambitions beyond that, except now, of course, to include Missie!'

'Then thank you,' I say to Nigel. 'You've turned up at exactly the right time.'

'In that case,' he says, 'to go one further why don't I take you to the rescue place. My car's bigger than yours' – his glance clearly includes Ann – 'and it's Sonia's turn for Saturday surgery tomorrow. We can take the photographs from the minute Missie's handed over to you. A record from Day One.'

'Fab!' Becky shouts.

And then the doorbell rings again.

I can hardly believe it when I see Mark Dover.

'I was going to phone,' he says pleasantly, 'but then I needed to come down to the village so I decided to see if I could catch you at home. And I've been lucky!' He is more or less past me and into the hall, I don't quite know how. 'Have you had dinner?'

'Not yet,' I tell him.

'Then how about . . . ?'

'I have visitors,' I say. And since he's already in the house I add, 'Come and meet my mother-in-law!'

He does a double take when he sees Nigel, who is sitting on the sofa beside Becky. 'Surprise, surprise!' he says.

'Hi!' Nigel says. 'You're almost a stranger these days. What have you been doing with yourself?'

'Working,' Mark says.

'Good! Anything special?' Nigel asks.

'Very special!' Mark gives me a look which somehow hints at a secret between us. It annoys me because it makes me look like a conspirator, which I'm not.

'Very special?' Nigel queries. 'Are we allowed to know what?'

313

'If Venus doesn't mind,' Mark says.

'Certainly not,' I say. 'Why should I? Mark has been painting my portrait. Mark makes it sound far more important than it is.'

'How thrilling!' Ann says – and for a split second I feel annoyed at her choice of words. 'What did you wear, Venus?'

'My cassock! Very ordinary.'

'You looked anything but ordinary. And I hope you're not saying the painting is ordinary.' Now it's Mark's turn to sound peeved. 'It's one of the best things I've ever done. What's more, it's finished. That's what I dropped by to tell you. I thought you might like to come and see it. Perhaps tomorrow?'

'How wonderful!' Ann says. 'I'd love to see it! I'm here for the weekend, is there any chance I could come too?'

'We have a very full weekend,' I say to Mark. 'I'm not sure that we can fit it in. We have to collect our new dog tomorrow and we won't be able to leave her on her own, not so soon.'

'Couldn't we go before we collect the dog?' Ann suggests. I don't know why she's being so persistent.

'If it would help, we could call in on the way to the Dog Rescue,' Nigel says, thus neatly including himself in the party. 'We pass quite close to your place, Mark.'

This is not at all what Mark had in mind, I'm certain of that, but he's a civilized person, so are we all, so he can do nothing but agree, and we settle on ten o'clock.

'Only we mustn't be late for collecting Missie!' Becky says anxiously.

'I promise we won't be, darling!' I say.

I give Mark a gin-and-tonic, and we all settle down to inconsequential chat. It doesn't take me long to see that neither of the men is going to leave before the other one does so. It's strange, I think, that I hadn't noticed this – perhaps antipathy is too strong a word, but there's something between them – when we all had dinner together. In the end Becky solves the problem.

'I'm *starving*!' she says dramatically. 'When are we going to eat, Mum?'

'Oh dear! I'm terribly sorry!' I say, looking at the two men. 'I would like to ask you to stay to supper but I can't. It's lamb chops, and I only have three!'

So off they go, Nigel repeating that he'll pick us up at nine-thirty in the morning. 'Please don't be late!' Becky says.

After supper, Becky, with unusual willingness, takes herself off to bed. I know what her theory is, I've used it myself: the quicker she goes to sleep, the quicker tomorrow – and Missie – will come. I clear the table, everything into the dishwasher, then Ann and I settle down with a second glass of the rather nice claret we'd had with the lamb. A present from Ann.

She and I are never short of things to talk about and our shared grief has brought us closer together. I do love her and I know she loves me, and now, as always when the two of us are together, we talk about Philip, particularly about the happy times we've had. A 'do-you-remember-when' session. Then we switch to the subject of my work, and how it's going in Thurston. Ann is interested in everything to do with it, though I can't bring myself to mention Miss Frazer. Before we know where we are it's well past midnight and I say, 'You've had a long day, Ann. I don't want to keep you up. You must be tired, and I know I am.'

'Yes,' she agrees. 'I think I'll go up.' There's a pause, and then, hesitantly, she says, 'You know, Venus, there's something I want to say to you.'

This sounds rather formal. I'm puzzled.

'What is it?' I ask.

'I've been thinking a lot about you recently and it seems to me – I hope you don't mind me saying this – I think you should get on with your life, start looking forward.'

'But I am getting on with it, I am looking forward,' I say. 'I have all these plans I've just been telling you about. I'm going to be very busy indeed.'

'I know, love,' she says, 'and that's great. But I'm not just thinking about your working life, I'm thinking about your personal life. Oh, I think about mine too! I just work hard, and enjoy it, go home – and do exactly the same thing next day and most days. But you're young and I'm not. You still have a long time to live.'

'That's what Philip thought. It isn't always true,' I say.

'I know that too,' Ann says. 'But we have to live as if it is true, and more often than not it is. Oh dear! I'm not putting any of this very well! What I mean is . . . Oh, Venus, I must just come out with it! What I'm trying to say is, don't think because Philip's no longer here you can't have a man in your life. I know how you loved him, and that you'd always have been faithful to him, but what we promise when we marry is that we'll be true until death parts us. And death has parted both you from Philip and me from my lovely Jim.'

'But you didn't marry again,' I point out.

'I know,' she says. 'Perhaps I should have, but it's probably too late for me. It's not for you, though.'

'It's not anything I've ever had in mind,' I tell her. But in the same breath I know that that isn't entirely true. Oh, it's true about re-marrying, I've never thought as far as that, not at all, but haven't I recently felt the longing for something and someone, recognized the stirring of my own sexuality? Wanting someone close? And the answer to that is, 'Yes, yes, and yes.'

'What made you bring this up now?' I ask Ann. 'It wasn't . . .'

'It wasn't the sight of two men both vying for your attention,' she says, smiling. 'Diverting though that was, and it didn't surprise me. No, it was something I've been thinking a lot about and I'd decided that this weekend I'd say it to you. You see, what I also want you to know, in case you've ever thought otherwise, is that I would never be any kind of an obstacle to you. I love you as if you were my daughter, and I'd be happy and glad for you – I mean if you were to find new happiness. Don't forget, Venus, you're not only a priest, you're a woman, and an attractive one too! I don't think you realize how attractive you are.'

There's a silence between us. I think neither of us knows what to say next, where to take this conversation. In the end, I speak first.

'Thank you. I'm glad you said that, I'm glad you feel that way. However, I have nothing and no-one in mind. And when, and if, I do have, you'll be one of the first to know.'

'Thank you,' she says. 'And now I really will go to bed. Good-night, love!' She gives me a hug and a kiss.

As she reaches the door I call after her.

'By the way, Ann, I'll expect you to be equally up-front with me if you decide to do something of the kind! No sudden elopements!' Then I'm laughing, and so is she.

TWENTY-SEVEN

At half-past six Becky is standing by the side of my bed, already washed and dressed, hair combed, shaking me awake.

'Come on, Mum,' she says. 'It's Saturday!'

'Becky, go away,' I say, pulling the duvet over my head. 'No way am I getting up before seven-thirty! I'll be down then, and not a minute earlier. And you are not to waken Ann. I hope you haven't already.'

'Oh, Mum!' she begs. 'Come on! Nigel's coming soon!'

'Not for three hours,' I tell her. 'Now just *GO*!'

Reluctantly, she does, but I'm wide awake now, so I get up and shower, and go downstairs to make breakfast and Ann appears soon afterwards.

'I don't want any breakfast,' Becky says. 'I'm not the least bit hungry!'

I face her fair and square.

'Becky Stanton,' I warn her, 'if you don't eat at the very least a bowl of cereal then I shall go and collect Missie on my own! You are not leaving this house on an empty stomach!'

There's no answer to that, is there? So she eats a bowl of Coco Pops. Sometimes I'm ashamed of the power we wield over our young, except, I usually tell myself, we do it for their own good. It's still only eight o'clock and Nigel isn't collecting us until nine-thirty. Lucky Nigel! He'll be having a lie-in.

Ann clears the table while I go back to my room and say my Office, adding a special prayer for Becky and Missie, and what we're undertaking today. I haven't much doubt that having a dog will change our lives; restrict them in some ways and hopefully enhance them in others. Meanwhile, Becky assembles the things we have to take with us to the Rescue Centre – or I should say re-assembles them because she did it all last night. Now all she does is check them out and place them right by the front door. Dog lead, water bowl and a screw-top bottle of water in case Missie should be thirsty, and a squeaky toy in case she should get bored. Dog treats, a cushion for her to sit on in the car, though I suspect she will spend most of the time on Becky's lap.

Nigel arrives fifteen minutes early and spends the time showing Becky how his camera works.

'It looks dead easy!' she says. 'Can I take a picture of Missie myself?'

'Sure!' he says. 'It is easy.'

We pile into Nigel's car and arrive at Mark's house on the dot of ten. 'Don't forget,' Becky says as I ring the bell, 'we absolutely must be on time for Missie.'

Mark takes us straight through to his studio and there, on the easel, is the finished portrait. Me, in all my glory!

There's a gasp all round. It really is – how shall I describe it? – arresting, I think would be a good word. Not because of the subject, after all it's just a woman in a black cassock, but because of the sheer skill and proficiency of the painting.

'Wow!' Nigel says.

'It's wonderful!' Ann cries. 'Quite wonderful!'

Nigel looks at Becky. 'Well?' he says. 'And what do you think of your mother's portrait?'

'Wicked!' Becky says.

I have learnt that 'wicked' is the highest form of approval, and actually she sounds genuinely enthusiastic.

'It's *so* like you,' Ann says. 'You look as though you could step down from the canvas!'

I would like to think it was like me. The woman in the painting has clear, unblemished skin, her hair is thick and bouncy, not too tidy, her brown eyes are clear and shining. If her figure isn't

319

perfect, if she needs to lose a few pounds, it doesn't show under her cassock. Yes, it would be great to think it was like me, but I think it flatters me. Not that I'm complaining.

'You're right!' Nigel says to Ann. 'It's remarkably lifelike.'

Mark has said nothing so far, but he does look gratified. 'Thank you,' he says.

'I didn't know there was so much colour in a black garment,' Nigel says.

'That's what most people think,' Mark replies, 'but it's not true. The more you look at something black, the more variations of shade you see.' And then he turns to me. 'So what do you think of it, Venus? You haven't said a word so far.'

'I think it's wonderful!' I say. 'I do really! But I have to say, I think it's flattering.'

He's not totally pleased by that.

'I don't paint portraits to flatter,' he says, rather sternly for him. 'If I did I could easily get more commissions, probably from Lord Mayors or elderly chairmen of public companies. I paint what I see, though not only what I see outwardly. I like to think I paint the whole person rather than just the outside and the trappings.'

'Well, I do think it's lovely!' I say. It sounds inadequate.

'Thank you,' Mark says. 'It's important that *you* like it. You were a perfect subject, as I knew you would be. I reckon it will be the focus of the exhibition. I shall certainly give it pride of place!'

'You're having an exhibition?' Nigel asks. 'Where and when?'

'In December, in London,' Mark answers.

'Great!' Nigel says. 'We'll all come on the first day!'

I feel a bit sorry for Mark. Once again it's not what he'd planned. But he's a step ahead.

'Fine!' he says. 'Tell me how many and I'll see you get invitations. Of course I shall be taking Venus to the preview. You will come, won't you?' he asks me. 'You promised. There'll be a bit of a party. People will enjoy meeting the model.'

What can I say? He hadn't said a word about a preview party. 'Of course I'll come,' is what I do say. 'But I hope you'll explain that I'm not entirely a model, dressed up – I'm a real live priest!'

He insists on going into the house to make us coffee. 'Come in when you're ready,' he says. While he's gone we look around at the rest of his paintings, which I've already seen.

'He's very talented,' Ann says.

'Yes,' Nigel agrees. 'I'd no idea. Actually I haven't known him all that long and I've never seen his work before. It's good!'

This is generous of him because when it comes to the London visit Mark has pipped him to the post.

Becky pulls at my sleeve. 'Mum, if we've *got* to drink coffee we'd better go and do it or we'll be late for Missie!'

'No we won't,' I assure her. 'We have plenty of time.' Nevertheless we move back into the house and stand around in the kitchen with our coffee until it's time to leave.

At the Rescue Centre Nigel and Ann are asked to wait in Reception while Becky and I are taken behind the scenes by Imogen. Becky, I feel sure, has thought that all we will have to do is put the lead on Missie, and depart. Of course it's not so. We do go to Missie's kennel, which she shares with a fox terrier, and Missie does recognize us and barks a welcome while Imogen puts her on the lead, but there is more to come before we are free to go. We return to Imogen's office where we're invited to sit down. 'There are one or two things I want to say to you,' Imogen says. I'm not sure that Becky, at this point, wants to hear any of them, but we are not in charge; not yet.

Imogen checks through the list of things we need to have to welcome Missie home, and of course we can't be faulted on that. Missie will be a well-provided-for little dog. We're given diet sheets, and a sheet of handy questions and answers about her health, the date when her next booster will be due, a form or two for me to sign, and so on.

'Give her a small meal when you get her home,' Imogen says. 'She's not had one today so she'll be ready for it and it will help her to settle. Also, I would like to pay you a visit in about a month's time to see how everything's going. I'm sure it will be all right, but I want to make certain.'

'Of course,' I agree. 'We'll be pleased to see you.'

All the time we've been talking people have been in and out of the room to say good-bye to Missie. 'She's a great favourite,'

Imogen says. 'We shall miss her very much. That's the trouble with this job. You get fond of the animals and then you have to part with them!'

'Do you ever adopt them yourselves?' I ask.

'Oh yes!' Imogen says. 'Most of the staff have one or more dogs they've taken from the Centre. Sometimes because no-one else has chosen them.'

Then she rises to her feet, bends down and gives Missie an affectionate cuddle, and says, 'There you are, then! She's all yours! Look after her, Becky!' Becky is flushed with emotion and can't answer but I promise that we will.

'I'll see you to the door,' Imogen says.

When we see Nigel and Ann waiting for us in Reception Becky immediately remembers about the photographs.

'Can we take one just outside the door?' she asks. Then she turns to Imogen. 'Please will you be in it?'

'I'll be delighted,' Imogen says. 'And could we have one of Missie on her own? I'd like to put it up in the Centre. In fact, it might even find a place in our magazine! Who knows?'

We go outside. Nigel takes Becky with Missie, Becky with Missie and Imogen, with me, with Ann, then Imogen takes one of all four of us with Missie in the middle. At last we go out and get into the car, Ann and Becky in the back seat with Missie on a cushion between them, me in the front with Nigel. Everyone waves and Nigel sets off down the drive. No sooner have we turned into the main road than Missie is lying on Becky's lap. I lean across to look at them through the driving mirror and there's a lump in my throat. It's one of those moments I wish so hard that Philip was here to experience.

When we get back to the Vicarage Nigel nips out, opens the rear door and carefully lifts Missie out. Becky follows swiftly, and takes the lead from him. I am marching to the front door, key in hand.

'Straight through and into the garden!' I order. 'She'll want to pee!'

Let off the lead in the back garden, she immediately runs round a couple of times in large circles, then dashes off into the far corner and does a pee, which seems to take for ever.

That done, Becky, standing on the lawn, calls out, 'Missie! Missie!'

Ann, Nigel and I stand amazed while Missie runs straight back to Becky, jumps up once, then sits immediately, at attention, in front of Becky. Becky is too moved to say a word, then she recovers and kneels down on the grass to give Missie a hug.

'I'm going to feed her now!' Becky says. So we all go back into the house and, remembering that we haven't had lunch, I heat some soup and make sandwiches for all of us. 'I'm not going to have mine until Missie's had her dinner,' Becky says, though I know she must be hungry. I needn't have worried. Missie polishes off the food in her dish in no time at all.

'Can I phone Anna?' Becky asks. 'Can I ask her to come round?'

'Well, all right, you can,' I say, but doubtfully. 'But she mustn't stay long and you mustn't invite anyone else. I don't think that would be fair to Missie. She's in a new home with new people and I think she needs time to settle down quietly.'

'I'd say you're right,' Nigel says. 'I'll be off too. I'll print the photographs on the computer – make a few extra copies – and will it be OK if I bring them round tomorrow, when I get back from church? Say around noon?'

'Fine!' I tell him.

When he's left Ann says, 'What a nice man he is! Do I take it he doesn't go to St Mary's?'

'That's right. He goes to St Patrick's. He's RC,' I say. 'Actually, Ann, what I should do now is go to see Bertha Jowett – I told you, didn't I, she's the lady with the cottage Mum and Dad hope to buy? I think she'll be pleased to have the news about their offer. And if I went now, you'd be here with Becky and Missie. I think it's a wee bit too soon to leave them. I could give her a ring, of course, but she doesn't hear well. I won't be long.'

'Take your time,' Ann says. 'I shall read the newspaper. Too chilly to go in the garden.'

Before I leave I give my mother a quick call to check that all's going according to plan, and it is. 'Dad's accepted their offer,' she says. 'They've already had a word with their solicitor. It doesn't look like there'll be any delay.'

Bertha Jowett is having her lunch; it's there on a tray, half-eaten. Baked beans on toast. She sees me glance at it.

'I'm rather fond of beans on toast,' she says.

'So is my daughter,' I tell her.

'It's quite nutritious, you know,' she says, defensively.

'Oh, I know!' But I'm wondering how often she has a bit of something on toast instead of cooking herself a meal, and how much variety she gets. The only sign of fruit, for instance, is a seriously wizened apple in a dish on the sideboard. But at least when she goes into the Beeches she'll get three square meals a day.

She can read my mind. 'I've never liked cooking,' she admits. 'And shopping's quite difficult. But I manage very well. Except that I can't get around much I'm really quite healthy. Now you young people are always getting colds, but not me! I practically never have a cold!'

'Good!' I say. My theory is that anyone as old as Bertha Jowett has met with so many germs over a lifetime that they've developed an immunity to most of them. 'And when it comes to shopping, as I've mentioned before, it's dead easy for me to do that for you. Just pick up the phone and I'll call in while I'm doing my own shopping. And, of course, Mr Winterton would deliver fruit and vegetables any day.'

'I know.' She sounds bored. I'm sure people of my age are always going on at the elderly to eat more sensibly and I can tell it's time I changed the subject.

'I came to bring you a bit of good news!' I say – and give it to her.

'Oh, but that's wonderful!' she says. 'Are you *sure*?'

'It seems pretty certain,' I tell her. 'I spoke with my mother just before I left home. It seems the people who want to buy my parents' house already have the money in hand, so there isn't a long chain. I don't see why it shouldn't go through quite quickly.'

'That's marvellous!' she says. 'Do you think I might just

possibly be able to move by Christmas? I'm sure I shouldn't say it to you, but I hate Christmas. I don't mean the church bit, though that's not for me, but everything else!'

'That would be quite quick, I imagine, but it might be possible. I expect it's what everyone involved would like. I know my parents would.'

'Well I shall live in hope,' she says, 'and in the meantime I'll make a start at getting ready.' She looks around the crowded room. 'I don't know what I'm going to do with this lot, and every room in the house is the same. And I won't be able to take much with me. They do let you take a few of your own things, but not many.'

Nor do I see how she's going to cope with it. It's horrendous!

'Would you like me to ask around, see if I can find anyone who'd come for odd days and give you some help? I can't think of anyone offhand but I'm sure there must be someone in the church.'

'I'd be grateful,' she says. 'And of course I'd pay them, though I can't afford a lot. And I'll start doing a bit at a time, perhaps clearing out one drawer a day. Oh dear! I don't look forward to that!'

I know what she means. Drawers, wardrobes, cupboards are full of memories, especially when you're as old as Bertha Jowett. It will be like saying good-bye to bits of her life.

'Well, let me know if there's anything I can do, I mean apart from finding someone to help you. And I'll keep you in touch with every bit of news from my parents. I should think they'll be over here for the weekend before long.'

Sunday – and we discuss what's to be done about Missie. We're agreed in thinking that we can't leave her alone while we all three go off to church.

'Though very soon,' I tell Becky, 'we'll start to leave her in the house for a short time each day. She must be trained to stay on her own. I expect she is already; she just has to get used to this house and to learn that we'll always come back to her.'

'I would willingly,' Becky says with enthusiasm, 'stay with her this morning while both of you go to church!'

'I'm sure you would!' I say, 'but since there are three of us here today we'll try to work something out.'

In the end it's agreed that Ann will come with me to the eight o'clock while Becky stays with Missie, and then Becky and I will go to the ten o'clock Eucharist, after which I will go to coffee, which Becky flatly refuses to consider.

'While you do that,' Ann says, 'Becky and I will take Missie for a walk on the Downs.'

I can see that, for as long as it takes, life is going to be filled with plans for who goes where and when. Becky knows that for some time she won't be allowed to take Missie out for a walk on her own. The Centre was firmly against that. 'Becky must be accompanied by an adult,' Imogen said, thinking of the dog, but in any case I wouldn't like my ten-year-old to be walking over the Downs with no other company than a small dog.

To my surprise Ethel Leigh turns up at the ten o'clock. 'I thought I'd like to come,' she says.

'I'm pleased to see you,' I say. 'How is Marilyn?'

'All right,' Mrs Leigh says. 'Missing her Dad, and Garth is missing his Granddad.'

'I hope you'll stay for coffee after the service,' I say. 'I'll get someone to go with you and then I'll join you later.' If Carla Brown comes – and she seems to be making a habit of it – I shall ask her to look after Mrs Leigh. She will know how to put her at her ease. Besides, I've discovered that Carla Brown likes to be given something to do.

Mrs Bateman is here, but there's no sign of Miss Frazer and neither Mrs Bateman nor I mention her. Otherwise, everything seems as normal. One or two empty places. Miss Carson, and her friend Mildred Blamires, are not in their usual pew near the front. Possibly they're away together for the weekend. Afterwards I join Ethel Leigh and Carla – and a few others – for coffee. Ethel Leigh is quiet, a bit timid, and doesn't say much. I can't judge whether this is her usual self; I've only met her in bereavement. The first weeks and months of widowhood are terrible to live through, especially if looking after a partner through a long illness has not only exhausted you, but cut you off from friends.

It's also possible that Ethel Leigh had a marriage which concentrated on her husband and didn't include many friends. She had that air about her the first time I met her, and certainly there were very few friends at the funeral. I won't mention it to her now, in front of the others, but I'll have a word with her when I get a chance.

I'm back at the Vicarage just before noon. Becky and Ann have had a lovely walk with Missie. 'She was ever so good,' Becky says. 'We met some other dogs and she liked that.' For now she's fast asleep in her bed.

Nigel arrives with the photographs, which we spread out on the table. They're wonderful. 'Fantastic!' Becky says. We discuss who will have which. Ann chooses one showing Becky, Missie and me. I choose one of Becky and Missie in the garden to send to my parents and a similar one for myself. 'I'll give one to Anna,' Becky says, 'and I'll take the rest to school to show them. I think I'll give one to Mrs Fawcett!'

I'm pleased to hear her say that. Eileen Fawcett, as her mentor, helped to see Becky through a tricky time and I'm glad Becky has remembered that.

'Would you like one?' she asks Nigel.

'I've taken the liberty of keeping one back for myself,' Nigel confesses. 'I can print more if you need them.'

'Which one have you chosen?' Ann asks.

'Becky and Venus, with Missie,' he says.

We look at the photographs all over again, and then I say, 'I really must get on with the lunch!' and ask Nigel if he'd like to join us. He's been so kind.

'Thank you, I would,' he says. 'But I can't. I have two hospital visits to make and I should do them right away, before families start visiting.'

When I see him to the door there's an envelope lying on the mat. I hadn't heard the letter box, which I usually do, I suppose because we were all cooing over the photographs. I pick it up and, when Nigel has left, I take it into the kitchen. My name and address are handwritten, nice, neat writing which of course I don't recognize. I am alone in the kitchen when I open it.

'Dear Mrs Stanton,' it says.

It occurs to me that 'Mrs Stanton' is a name by which no-one in Thurston has so far called me. It's been 'Vicar', or 'Venus'. I read on.

We are sorry to be writing this letter, but we have thought about it and discussed it between us and we have decided there is only one decision we can come to. We are therefore writing to tell you that, although we have both worshipped in St Mary's Church for many years, we can no longer do so. This is not against you personally, though we believe you to be misguided and indeed deeply wrong, but is because we cannot accept any woman as our Vicar and Parish Priest. It is against all we hold sacred, all we have ever been taught, and indeed against the will of God. We do, in fact, agree in principle with what Miss Frazer has publicly said, as, we think, you will find many others also do, though we would not have expressed our beliefs in the same manner. We are letting you know, therefore, that from today we shall attend St Saviour's Church in Brampton. We shall miss St Mary's and our friends there very much indeed.

   Yours sincerely,
    Emily Carson
    Mildred Blamires

TWENTY-EIGHT

There are four chairs at my kitchen table. I sit down, almost drop down, on the nearest. I have to because my legs feel like cotton wool and I'm trembling from head to foot. The letter I'm still holding is shaking in my hand. I start to read it again from the beginning, though actually I don't need to. It's all there, as if it's been photographed on my brain. Certain words stand out . . . 'deeply wrong', 'cannot accept', 'against all we hold sacred', 'many others also do'.

The fact that, though it pulls no punches, it has no appearance of having been dashed off in a temper but, rather, having been written after careful thought and deliberation, and with a degree of politeness, somehow makes it seem worse. There is nothing of Miss Frazer's frenzy in this, no personal vilification, no threats. No way can I dismiss it as the ranting and raving of two extreme women. Indeed, reading between the lines I can imagine it's been written with some degree of reluctance.

Ann bursts into the kitchen, bright and breezy, full of life.

'I'm sorry, Venus!' she says. 'We've been putting Missie through her paces. I can see she's going to be a real time consumer! Now, what can I do to help?'

And then she looks at me. 'Venus, what is it? What's wrong?' she asks.

Without speaking, I hand her the letter. As she starts to read it she also sits down. When she's finished, she looks up. 'Oh, Venus! Oh, my love!' She sounds truly distressed.

And then I find my voice. I had hoped it would be a calm voice, I don't want to go over the top, but it isn't. I'm aware of a slight feeling of panic, which isn't like me. I rush my words.

'It had to happen, didn't it? Why was I so foolish as to think that Miss Frazer would be the end of it? Of course she couldn't be! So what next?'

And have these two women done this independently, I ask myself, or has Miss Frazer got at them? And how many others have they discussed it with? Right now I feel there's a conspiracy going on around me. Oh, that's irrational, I know! And I realize I'm tipping over into self-pity, which I hate and it's not like me, but for the moment I can't control it.

'How many others have they discussed it with?' I go on. 'And who are they? How will I know?'

'If any,' Ann says reasonably. But I'm not sure that I'm open to reason.

She stretches across the table and puts her hand on mine.

'Calm down, Venus! This isn't like you. You were always the fighter, that's one of the things Philip loved about you.'

'I'm sorry,' I say, quietly now. 'I'm being stupid, aren't I? But it was so unexpected.'

'I know,' Ann says. 'I'm sorry. Perhaps the best thing is to consider what you'll do, if anything.'

I agree. 'I can't simply do nothing,' I say. 'For one thing, I must reply to the letter. And certainly I must tell Henry Nugent. He has a right to know.' I glance up at the clock on the wall. 'But I won't do it this minute. Molly will be ready to dish up lunch.'

'And perhaps lunch is what we should get on with,' Ann says.

'Oh Ann, I don't feel like eating!' I protest.

'I daresay you don't, but Becky will,' Ann says. 'And in fact so do I. It smells delicious!' It's true. There's a shoulder of lamb roasting in the oven. 'And you mustn't let Becky see you eating nothing, she'll wonder why. Anyway, you'll feel better after you've eaten. One usually does. So now let's get down to it. Tell me what I can do to help!'

I take a deep breath and pull myself together, and make a

swift, silent prayer straight to God. 'Sorry to pester you, Lord, but HELP!'

'You're right,' I say to Ann. 'I concede! So if I see to the vegetables, deal with the meat and make the gravy, would you lay the table? And open a bottle of wine. And naturally, not a word about the letter when Becky's around. I'd rather she knew nothing about it. She's already had a bad time because of my job. I don't want any more of that for her.'

'That won't be difficult,' Ann says. 'All Becky can think about is Missie!'

'Then let's keep it that way,' I suggest. 'In fact, I think I'll give Henry a quick call now, ask him if he can come here this afternoon. I'll do it from my bedroom in case Becky should come in. And perhaps, if you're not in a rush to leave, you and Becky could take Missie out for another walk while Henry's here?'

'No trouble!' Ann says. 'Do you want me to lay the table in the dining room, or shall we have lunch in the kitchen today?'

'Why not the kitchen?' I say. Normally when I have a visitor we would eat in the dining room, which is particularly pleasant because it overlooks the garden, but at the moment – ridiculous, I know – I favour the warm familiarity of my kitchen. Besides which, I remind myself, Missie has her bed in the kitchen and it will please Becky not to be parted from her.

Ann sets about her chores, I make the brief phone call to Henry and then return to the kitchen and get on with the rest of the cooking.

'You see,' I say – I've got over a bad moment but I'm unable to keep off the subject – 'I don't know, do I, that they haven't already written to Henry. I didn't ask him, it was a very quick call. It would be natural for them to do so. He's churchwarden and they've almost certainly known him a long time. Or, for that matter, *have* they told a load of other people what they intended to do? Why would they go off not saying anything to their friends? I did notice they weren't in church this morning. No-one said anything about that at coffee, but then I didn't get around much because I knew Nigel was coming to the Vicarage with the photographs.'

Ann interrupts. 'Shall I make some mint sauce?' she offers. I

331

think she's trying, no doubt for my own good, to make me change the subject.

'Yes please,' I say. 'And there's a jar of redcurrant jelly in the fridge.'

We get through lunch, chatting about inconsequential subjects. At one point Becky offers Missie a titbit from her plate and I rush in with a stern reminder that she is NOT, not now, not ever, to feed Missie while we are at the table. I deal equally sternly with Missie, saying BED! fiercely while pointing her towards it. To my astonishment she obeys me instantly. Becky is amazed by my success but I realize that this dog already knows what she should and should not do. She was trying it on.

'You must never let her get away with anything naughty,' I tell Becky, with all the wisdom of one whose only knowledge of dog training comes from the books I borrowed from the library.

When lunch is over and the table cleared Ann says, 'Well, Becky, what about it? I reckon Missie has earned another walk, don't you? Shall we go on the Downs?'

Through the window I watch them climb the hill at the back of the house. It's a lovely, sunny day, more like spring than the end of November. Above the Downs there are fluffy white clouds in a blue sky. Missie, off the lead now, is running to and fro beside them, covering twice as much ground as Becky and Anna. So much energy for a small dog! Then Henry arrives.

I take him into my study, sit him down, and without more words hand him the letter. I watch him while he reads it. He reads slowly and deliberately, as if he's digesting every word, then when he's reached the end he puts it down on the small table in front of us, and looks at me. His face is serious, which is oddly pleasing to me. I feel less as though I'm making a mountain out of a molehill.

'I can hardly believe it,' he says. 'Not of those two! I've always thought of them as nice women, never a minute's trouble. Not given to sounding off about anything. Never saying much, in fact. Certainly nothing controversial. They've been coming to St Mary's for years.'

'And I suppose they have lots of friends in the congregation?' I ask.

He nods. 'Oh, I'd say without a doubt!'

I'm sure he doesn't intend it, but with every word he's rubbing it in that I am the cause of all this. And he's right, isn't he? I am.

'As I said, they're two very nice women,' he adds.

If he tells me once more how nice they are I shall scream, or burst into tears. I'm not sure which.

'So they're likely to have discussed this with several people in church?'

He looks at me as though that was a thought which had never entered his head. It's not like Henry to be obtuse.

'Well yes, it's possible,' he admits reluctantly. 'But what I wouldn't have thought possible, or even likely, is that they'd have done anything nasty, they're not the kind to spread gossip, for instance.'

'It wouldn't be nasty from their point of view, or even gossip,' I point out. 'If you'd been attending a church for a long time and then decided to go somewhere else, without moving house, you'd naturally tell your friends the reason why, wouldn't you?'

'I suppose so,' Henry says. 'So what are we going to do?'

If I'd ever thought he was going to come up with a solution I now know I was wrong. On the other hand, nor am I. There isn't one, at least not a satisfactory one.

'There's not much to *be* done, is there?' I say. 'Miss Carson and Mrs Blamires have a perfect right to go elsewhere, and to hold the opinions they do. Their opinions are hurtful to me, but nothing new. It will be the rare woman priest who hasn't heard them before – and who also doesn't think they're based on prejudice. So, Henry, I shall write a nice polite answer to their letter, in fact I shall wish them well at St Saviour's, and I shall do nothing at all about the others at St Mary's, not unless they wish to bring it up with me.'

'I think you're very wise, Venus,' Henry says. 'After all, we don't know, do we, who these others are or whether, even if they're friends of Miss Carson and Mrs Blamires, they hold the same opinions?' I'm sure he's relieved that I've taken it on the chin, and don't propose to go into battle.

We discuss, briefly, whether we'll tell the Bishop but decide we won't unless something worse happens. After all, we agree, people leave their churches and go elsewhere for all sorts of reasons. It's a free country. So it seems that that little problem's solved – except that I know it isn't, and I wonder if it ever will be, at least in my generation of women priests. And of course for me it isn't a 'little' problem. Not at all. But it's one I always knew I would have to deal with, and I *will* deal with.

I see Henry to the door, he pats me on the arm, and leaves. I return to the kitchen and while I'm tidying up after the meal I do some thinking. It's interesting how doing routine domestic jobs – stacking or emptying the dishwasher, making beds, peeling potatoes, ironing, dusting, is conducive to thinking; the body doing one thing, the mind elsewhere. I know, I tell myself, that I can't win everyone to my side. It's inevitable that I'll lose some, and why not? Not even Jesus kept everyone, so who am I to think I can do better? Get real, Venus! No, this is something I will have to learn to live with; and I am already learning, but it's not as easy as it sounds. It's not simply a case of logical thinking. However, I am strong, so I will. I must go forward without stopping too often to look over my shoulder.

Eventually, Ann, Becky and Missie return from their walk, the human contingent flushed pink with fresh air, Missie taking great gulps from her water bowl before collapsing on to her bed and falling immediately into deep sleep.

'Everything all right?' Ann asks me.

'Thank you, yes,' I reply.

'Good!' Ann says. 'Then if you don't mind I'll go up and pack. I don't want to be too late getting home.'

'I'll be making a cup of tea,' I say. There's no opportunity to say anything else because Becky is there, but when Ann eventually leaves, with promises to visit again before too long, she says, 'Please ring me! And promise to think over what I said, and I don't mean about the church.' I promise I will.

It's a quarter-past nine now. Becky and I took Missie for another short walk before both of them went to their separate beds. I'm thinking of buying a second dog bed for the sitting room so that Missie can be with us in the evening if that's what she'd like – and certainly I would like it – but for now she's fast asleep again

334

in the kitchen and I hope Becky is likewise in her bedroom. Perversely, although for the last few hours I've wanted to be alone, I now feel bereft and I sorely need someone to turn to.

Esmé Bickler, I think suddenly. Esmé will understand. She is probably in the same position, or if not at the moment then at least she's vulnerable to it, so I dial her number. No immediate reply but I let it go on ringing and eventually the answerphone kicks in. 'Sorry,' Esmé's voice says, 'there is no-one available to answer the phone at the moment, but in case of an emergency please dial . . .', and it gives a number which might or might not be that of Esmé's senior churchwarden. No point in me phoning him! 'Otherwise,' the voice continues, 'please leave a message after the tone.' So I do. 'Venus here,' I say. 'Thought I'd catch up with you. Another time, then. Bye!'

I'm really disappointed, though I've never been one for exchanging confidences, for needing someone to talk to about the things which really mattered. After all, I had Philip, didn't I? Who could wish for more? But the bottom line is that I don't have Philip, he's *not* in the next room, and at this moment I do have this need. But who else can I talk to about what's on my mind? Not my parents, I don't want to upset them. Not anyone at St Mary's, it's not something I want aired in the church, quite the reverse at the moment. Miss Carson and Mrs Blamires are, according to Henry, and I feel sure it's true, nice women and well liked; it's not like the Miss Frazer situation which actually gained me some sympathy. This would inevitably lead to people taking sides and I can think of few things worse than that for a church congregation. No, it has to be someone not involved, which is why the Blessed Henry isn't the total answer. But who do I know well enough to phone in the late evening, and who do I know who won't reckon I'm as mad as a hatter?

And then I think of Nigel Baines.

Can I? Can I do this? While I'm considering it I look up his number, which I suppose means I've decided that I can. There are two numbers, one of which I recognize as the surgery, so I will ring the other one. But what if I lose my nerve the minute he answers the phone? And the answer to that is obvious; I will ask him some question or other about doggy photographs. Make it up.

So I tap out his number, and he answers at once, as if he'd been standing by the phone.

'Nigel Baines.'

'It's Venus. I'm sorry to phone you at this time of the evening.'

'Are you all right?' he asks quickly. 'Are you ill – or is Becky?'

'Neither of us,' I say. 'It was just . . . oh dear, I shouldn't have rung you so late!'

'It's a quarter to ten,' he says. 'Hardly the middle of the night! What can I do for you?'

'It's nothing, really! It was about the photographs . . .' And then I realize I'm being completely silly and I say, 'No, it wasn't! It wasn't about the photographs at all! I just . . . Well, I just wanted to talk to someone and it's not something I can talk to anyone in the church about and not to my parents because it would upset them. And Esmé Bickler wasn't at home . . .' And then I run out of words.

'Who,' he asks in a gentle voice, 'is Esmé Bickler?'

'She's a priest,' I tell him. 'We were ordained at the same time. But she wasn't at home. So then I thought of you.'

'And what were you going to say to Esmé that I now hope you're going to say to me?' Nigel asks.

So I tell him. I tell him everything, including all the Miss Frazer episodes, at which he's horrified, and he understands my feelings, because from his own standpoint he recognizes the enormity of her behaviour at the Mass, perhaps more than some of those at St Mary's would have recognized it. What they saw was her rudeness to me and, bless their hearts, that was why they gave me their support.

He also realizes why the case of Miss Carson and Mrs Blamires – though it arises from the same cause, their antipathy to women priests – is different, and in a way more hurtful to me. He also sees the trouble it could cause, the divisions.

'Would you like me to come around to see you now?' he asks.

I hesitate. I would like it, it's a lovely, comforting thought, but in the end I say, 'Thank you, but I don't think so. It's not that I don't want to see you, and it's very kind of you, but I'm not sure it's a good idea.' I'm thinking that once we started to talk it could be very late indeed before he left, and he picks up on my thinking.

'OK,' he says. 'So tell me what you think you'll do?'

I tell him exactly what I've told Henry.

'I think that sounds the best thing,' he says, 'but don't do anything tonight. Sleep on it, and in particular, don't write the letter tonight. Leave it until tomorrow at the earliest. And as you don't want me to come around this evening, will you have lunch with me tomorrow? I have a surgery in the morning but I'll be through before lunchtime. We could drive out somewhere, away from Thurston.'

'That would be wonderful,' I tell him. 'Thank you very much – but I can't!'

'Why can't you?' he asks.

I remind him about Missie, and the fact that Becky will be at school. 'As you well know, Missie only came here yesterday,' I say (though right now it seems like a month ago). 'I can't leave her alone yet.'

'Then how about taking her with us?' he suggests.

'No. I don't yet know how she'd be, left in the car. And we wouldn't be able to take her into the restaurant.'

And then I have another idea, and I think, why not? And I hear myself saying, 'You could come to lunch here, if you liked! It's my day off. I'd be very pleased to see you.'

'That would be fine,' he says. 'I'd enjoy that!'

'Come about one,' I say. 'Thank you for listening to me this evening, I'm sorry to have troubled you.'

'Don't be silly, Venus!' he says, rather impatiently. 'It was no trouble at all. And now pour yourself a brandy before you go to bed, and sleep well. Doctor's orders!' He hesitates, then says, 'In fact, I'm not sorry Esmé Bickler wasn't at home!'

Becky is reluctant to go to school this morning, though thankfully not because of anything wrong there, simply because it means leaving Missie. 'She'll be perfectly all right!' I say. 'I'll look after her. I'm quite capable of doing that! How about me bringing her down to school this afternoon? I'll meet you at the

337

school gate and we'll take her for a walk.' Naturally, Becky loves that idea. She'll be able to show Missie off to all her friends.

'Can Anna come with us for the walk?' Becky asks.

'As long as her mother knows, and agrees,' I say.

I feel better than I expected to today, though still troubled about the letter, to which later on, and not until after I've seen Nigel, I will reply. I slept reasonably well, which might have been the brandy but I'm sure was mostly because of the phone call to Nigel. I'm glad I plucked up the courage to call him, and now I'm looking forward to lunch, though I haven't yet decided what I shall give him. I had also hoped to pop round to see Mrs Leigh this morning but I'd forgotten that it would mean leaving Missie. Although I'll have to leave her for a spell tomorrow morning because there's the Tuesday Eucharist. It's a bit like having a baby in the house.

I wonder if, this morning, I could take her with me? I won't do it without asking, Mrs Leigh might not like dogs, or she might be one of those people who are truly allergic to them. I have her number from the funeral details, so I give her a ring.

'Oh, hello!' I say. 'I'm likely to be around your way this morning and I wondered if I might pop in and see you? Nothing special, just a chat!'

'That would be very nice,' she says.

'The only thing is, I've got a new dog. She's only been with us since Saturday and I don't like to leave her yet. Would it be all right if I brought her with me? She's a small spaniel, very well behaved. She's not a puppy and her previous owner must have trained her very well. But do say "No" if you'd rather not, and I'll fix some other time.'

'You're very welcome to bring her,' Mrs Leigh says. 'I like dogs!'

I arrange to be with her around ten to ten-thirty. I shan't stay long because I have to think about lunch, but I have this feeling that I want to be certain she's all right. There was something in her look . . . I know from experience that there's this period, a little while after the funeral, when you can feel very down. I think that might be why Ethel came to church yesterday. It takes time to settle to being on one's own, and sometimes one needs a bit of help. I know Ethel has her daughter, but Marilyn has a part-time job and Garth is at school.

She's very welcoming in her quiet way, makes a fuss of Missie, which Missie clearly enjoys. The coffee is ready and she serves a plate of custard creams with it.

'Can I give the dog a bit of biscuit?' she asks.

'I'm sure Missie would love that,' I tell her, throwing my rules out of the window.

We talk of this and that; her daughter, her grandson, the weather, and then she says, 'I do miss Ronnie! It's not that we ever talked a lot, he was a quiet man, but he was always there. And I had to do things for him, make meals, keep the house nice, and so on. Now I don't feel as though I've anything to do.' There's a pause, then she says: 'In fact, I wondered if I might find a little job. I don't have all that many skills, but I can cook and I can clean, and I suppose I could serve in a shop. Not a full-time job, of course; just an hour or two a day, or a few half days a week. I wondered whether I'd put a card in the post office window?'

'That sounds a good idea,' I say. 'Why not try it? And in the meantime if I hear of anything I'll mention your name.'

'Thank you,' she says. 'That would be great.'

At eleven o'clock I say, 'I'm sorry, I'll have to leave now. I have someone coming to lunch and I still have to shop for it. Perhaps I'll see you on Sunday? Or whenever.'

'Thank you for coming,' she says. 'You've cheered me up. And I shall think seriously about getting a little job. I'm sure it's what Ronnie would have wanted, though he never wanted me to go out to work as long as he could earn the living. He was very old-fashioned that way.'

I've decided to make a lasagne for lunch and it's while I'm standing at Joss Barker's counter, watching him weigh out some nice lean mince – I have had to tie up Missie outside for the moment – that the thought comes to me. Two thoughts, actually both on the same subject.

First of all, why don't I work out whether or not I can possibly afford to have Ethel Leigh give me a hand in the Vicarage for two or three hours a week – which from my point of view would be heavenly bliss – and, secondly, couldn't she be the one to give Bertha Jowett a hand, clearing things out, packing things up, cleaning, whatever was wanted? Bertha is going to have to have help, there's no way she can do it herself. I suppose she could afford it and in any case it's only a temporary job but it would get Ethel outside her four walls. I don't have time to see Bertha this morning but perhaps I could go later today. I'm quite pleased with both ideas, I think as I call in at Winterton's for some salad things, where once again I tie Missie up outside. It will be much more convenient when I can leave her at home while I shop. On the other hand, she is clearly enjoying it all. She's getting a lot of attention from people who've not seen me with a dog before.

'Would Sunday week be all right for the christening?' Mr Winterton asks. 'My daughter's going to phone you.'

'Absolutely fine!' I tell him. 'I'll keep the date free, but ask her not to leave it too long.' I'm hoping that the parents will agree to be the first to have their baby's baptism at the Eucharist. I think they might, Mr Winterton and his family are well-known and liked in the village; they're outgoing people, I think they'll be taken by the idea.

I am busy making the lunch, I have laid the table in the dining room, the lasagne is in the oven, when the phone rings. It's Esmé Bickler.

'I'm sorry I wasn't in,' she says. 'We had a parish retreat this weekend. I didn't get back until late last night. How are you? Did you ring for something special?'

I had already decided that, since I spoke with Nigel at the moment when I most needed someone, and I'd decided how to deal with it, what to do and what not to do, that I wouldn't take it any further. If Esmé rang me back, which I expected she would eventually, I'd ask if everything was all right with her, and if it was I'd keep quiet. Sometimes it makes things worse if they're spread too far. Of course if I asked her, 'How are things with you?' and she said, 'They're awful!' then I might change my mind, we might pool our difficulties. As it happens, she doesn't.

'I just rang to say "hello",' I tell her. 'Is everything going OK?'

'Fine!' she says. 'How about you?'

340

'Also fine!' I tell her. It is possible we are neither of us telling the exact truth, but in fact I feel better for not going into the whole story yet again. I feel that what I have to say I can say to Henry and to Nigel. I already feel stronger for deciding how to deal with it.

We chat for a while, this and that, and then the doorbell rings and I say, 'Lovely to talk to you but I'll have to go. I have someone coming to lunch.' We ring off, promising to visit each other as soon as we possibly can. And I go to let Nigel in.

TWENTY-NINE

I'm so *pleased* to see him standing there. There is a comforting familiarity in the sight of him, and yet there's something new. Not visibly new, he's the same tall, thin man with the same unruly red hair, and when he says, 'Hello, Venus! Am I too early?' it's with the same attractive Irish accent, but it's almost as if I'm experiencing all this for the first time. And in a way I suppose I am because when I first met him, at the surgery and then at Sonia's dinner party, I don't remember him making a strong impression on me, not even when he took me to the hospital. He was just a pleasant, kind man. And when he took me to the concert it was much the same. But now it's different, he *is* closer and I think it can only be because I turned to him when I was down, dispirited, vulnerable. I still don't know what gave me the nerve to do that, actually to phone him, but I'm glad I did. And thankfully I don't feel the least embarrassment about that today. I feel at ease with him.

'Not at all too early,' I tell him. 'I was on the phone to Esmé Bickler, that's why I was a bit slow getting to the door.'

'Ah,' he says, 'the invisible Esmé Bickler! Shall I ever set eyes on her?'

'I expect you will,' I say. 'We plan to meet, but no time fixed. Like me, she's single-handed. It isn't easy to leave one's parish.'

He hands me a bottle of wine and then follows me through to

the kitchen. I've laid the table in the dining room but I still have one or two things to do to the meal.

'Can I help?' he asks.

'Yes, you can open the wine,' I say, pointing him in the direction of the corkscrew. 'We can have a glass while I'm making the salad. I don't usually have the luxury of wine at lunchtime.'

'Nor me,' he admits. 'I usually do my visits straight after surgery but I'll do them later in the afternoon today.'

'Is it a busy time of the year for you?' I enquire.

'Most times are busy,' he says. 'Perhaps after Christmas and most of January are the busiest, especially with the old people and particularly if the weather's bad.'

He opens the wine and pours it, then he sits at the table with his while I sip mine in between chopping the chives and washing the watercress. 'Mmm! Nice wine,' I say. 'Now all I have to do is make the dressing . . .'

'Let me do that!' he interrupts.

'OK,' and I direct him to the olive oil, the white wine vinegar and the mustard and he sets to work; then while he tosses the salad I take the lasagne out of the oven. It looks good – golden and crispy on top, which is how I like it. We move into the dining room.

Nothing, so far, has been said about last night's phone conversation, though this is the reason why he's here, and I'm not sure that I want to plunge into it. I'm enjoying these untroubled minutes and, almost as if we had a pact between us to do so – which we haven't – we keep off the subject right through the meal.

'Whereabouts in Ireland do you come from?' I ask him.

'County Clare,' he tells me. 'From Quilty, a fishing village on the coast. My mother still lives there. I visit her when I can. Gatwick to Dublin is only an hour's flight. I hire a car at the airport and drive west. Have you never been to Ireland?'

I admit I haven't.

'Oh, but you should!' he says. 'You'd like it. It's wonderful – especially the west, but I suppose I'm prejudiced!'

'One of these days I will!' I say.

343

And so it goes, chit-chat, chit-chat throughout the meal, no awkward pauses. It's a warm and comfortable feeling. In fact it's not until we're drinking our coffee that he mentions last night, and all he says is, 'Well, are you feeling better? And have you written the letter?'

'I've drafted it,' I say. 'It's very polite.' And I get up and fetch it to show to him.

He reads it. 'Masterly!' he says. 'So what now?'

'I shall carry on as usual,' I say. 'If there are any repercussions about this, anything more from Miss Frazer – which I daresay there's bound to be – but if there's anyone following Miss Carson's and Mrs Blamires's lead, then I'll deal with that, as seems best, when it happens. I'm not going to go looking for trouble. I'll deal with whatever comes, *as* it comes. There's loads of things I want to do in the parish. I had a meeting and I've given people some of my ideas. There seems to be a fair amount of goodwill, so I shall hang on to that and just go ahead wherever I can!'

'Fine!' Nigel says.

'Do you have factions at St Patrick's?' I ask. 'I mean, for instance, do you have those who think the Pope is way above God himself, as opposed to those who don't approve of him?'

'Oh, I expect so!' Nigel says. 'Though I reckon any differences which surface are mostly about smaller things. What's gone wrong with the heating, does the church hall need repainting? Everyday stuff. I don't think we get around to discussing God or the Pope. What we're constantly doing is scratching around for money, as I suppose you are. And we don't even have a rich Miss Frazer to come to the rescue!'

'Nor do we, any longer!' I remind him. 'Thanks to me!'

'Now don't you go down that road, Venus!' he says firmly.

'I won't,' I promise. 'But isn't it silly that here's St Mary's and there's St Patrick's, both in the same village, both with the same needs, both professing the same faith, both with good, decent people – and there's this deep uncrossable chasm between us? It really is too silly for words!'

'It's not just silly,' he says, suddenly sharp. 'It's a sin. It's a sin against the gospel, it's a sin against God. It's a sin against each other. It drives us apart! Every Sunday morning you go off to your church, I go off to mine, both of us to worship the same God and in almost identical words. We all eat the bread, we drink the wine – in two separate buildings. What sense does that make? The devil must be laughing his head off!'

I've never heard him sound so fierce – but why would I have, I hardly know him? – then suddenly I wonder if it was something like this which caused the rift in the relationship I know he once had. Were he and she irreconcilable because of their different beliefs?

'I agree with you,' I say. And then I change the subject.

'We're planning to take the Sunday School children to the pantomime in Brampton,' I tell him. Really, I don't know why I'm telling him this! It's just something to say. 'If we can raise the money, that is. It's *Cinderella*.' Then I hear myself saying, 'Why don't you come with us? Be my guest? That would be very ecumenical, don't you think?' I'm smiling now, and so is he.

'It surely would,' he says. 'I might well do that! I'll have to look at dates and times.'

'Let me know,' I say. 'We have to book the tickets quite soon.'

He looks at his watch. 'I must push off,' he says. 'I don't want to, but I've a few visits to make and then I have an evening surgery. Thank you, Venus, it was great!'

'Thank you,' I reply. Then I add, 'Thank you especially for last night.'

I see him to the door. He puts a friendly hand on my arm for a second, and then leaves.

I reckon now I just about have time to phone my parents to see how the sale's going. I had hoped to do that and then go round to see Bertha Jowett, put her in the picture. I expect she's anxious for news, but I've promised to take Missie to meet Becky from school, haven't I? So Bertha Jowett will have to wait.

Mum says everything's going fine. She and Dad have told the solicitor they're keen to be in the cottage for Christmas, so will he get a move on. 'Of course we said it more politely than that,' she tells me, 'you have to when you're talking to a solicitor, don't you? But Dad was surprisingly firm! Anyway, he said he thought we could just about manage it.'

'That's wonderful!' I say. 'Do you reckon I can tell Miss Jowett that?'

'Well, you can tell her exactly what I've told you,' Mum says. 'In any case she'll need to start getting things together, won't she? Not to mention getting rid of things, poor lady. That's the hardest part – and I'll have a bit of that myself. There's no way we can take everything from this house to the cottage, is there?'

That's for sure. My mother is a hoarder!

'What bothers me,' she continues, 'is that there'll be no time for me to clean through the cottage, or I shouldn't think there will be, before your Dad and I move in. And from what I've seen I'm sure it needs it. Still, never mind! We'll have to do it when we're in there, won't we.'

'I'll be able to give you a hand,' I say. 'And I think I've found someone to help Miss Jowett to pack up and so on. If she agrees, and I expect she will.'

'Oh, good!' Mum says. 'And I think you'd better pop in at the estate agents and tell them we've been suited.'

'I'll do that,' I promise. 'Sorry, Mum, I'll have to ring off now. I'm taking Missie down to the school to meet Becky and then we're going for a walk.'

'That's nice,' she says. 'I'll be able to do that sometimes, once we're living in Thurston.'

Missie is fussed over like mad at the school gate, and she enjoys every minute of it. She's a very sociable dog. Becky, of course, is in seventh heaven. It seems as though the ownership of Missie – because Becky does see Missie as *her* dog – has raised her status sky high. Together with Anna, we have a lovely walk over the Downs and we can let Missie off the lead there because she's very good at coming back the minute she's called. We come off the Downs by another route and we walk down the High Street to the estate agents. By now, dusk is falling, so we drop Anna at her house and return home. No chance at all of going to see Bertha Jowett. That will have to wait until tomorrow.

What I *do* do is write the reply to Miss Carson's and Mrs Blamires's letter, much as I've drafted it. I'm polite, as indeed I'm sure they tried to be in theirs. 'I shall miss you both,' I write, 'as will all your friends at St Mary's. I wish you well at St Saviour's. I hope you will be happy there.' Then when I sign off I write, 'God bless you both!' Perhaps they'll accept a blessing from me, even though I'm not a proper priest!

'I want to put this letter in the post,' I tell Becky. 'If I walk down to the post office there's a late collection there. Will you be all right?' (It's now dark.)

'Oh Mum!' she protests. 'Of *course* I will! I'm not a small child! Besides, I've got Missie!'

I'm not convinced that Missie wouldn't give a warm welcome to whoever decided to come into the house, nevertheless I go to the post. It's with a heavy heart that I hear the envelope plop into the letter box. I'm praying that it will be the first and last of its kind.

On Tuesday morning I leave Missie alone for the first time while I go to celebrate the Eucharist. Then, when it's over, I nip back to the Vicarage where she greets me as effusively as if I've been gone for a week. I take her into the garden. 'Do a nice pee-pee, then!' I say, and she duly obliges. 'And now I'm going to leave you again, but only for an hour. I have to go to see Miss Jowett!' I expect people who live alone, with only an animal to converse with (though 'converse' is the wrong word, Missie has said nothing), talk like this all the time. Then on the way to Bertha Jowett's I call in at Gander's to buy a couple of jam doughnuts. Bertha seems really pleased to see me.

'Well, any news?' she asks as we sit down.

'A little,' I say. 'I phoned my mother yesterday. It's all going ahead and they're very set on moving by Christmas. The solicitor says it just might be possible, providing there are no snags. Would that suit you?'

'Down to the ground!' Bertha Jowett says. 'I really would like to be in the Beeches by then. Christmas would be a good time to start there, don't you think?'

'I'd imagine so,' I agree. 'They probably get up to all sorts of things. And there'll be special meals and so on, won't there? I expect you'll get a slap-up Christmas dinner!'

'Rather nice!' Bertha says. 'I haven't had one of those for some

347

time. Who wants to cook a turkey for one? Would you like a cup of coffee?'

'I would,' I say. 'Especially as I've brought some doughnuts. Shall I make it?'

When we're drinking our coffee and eating our doughnuts – deliciously light and very jammy – Bertha says, 'It's so good of you to come to see me, to take all this trouble!'

'It isn't any trouble,' I assure her. 'Anyway, this morning you could say I came on my mother's behalf.'

She nods. 'Partly, I suppose, but the first time you came here it wasn't for any reason. You just came to see me. I can't think why except that Jean probably dragged you here.'

'She brought me. I didn't have to be dragged,' I say. 'After all, I *am* the Vicar. So apart from wanting to meet you – and I don't get all that many chances to meet a dyed-in-the-wool atheist – I am in a way responsible for you. I have the cure of all the souls in this parish. That's my responsibility.'

At that, Bertha sits up straight.

'Well, young woman,' she says. It's the way she says 'young woman' with all the authority of a head of college putting down a first-year student who has shown herself too big for her boots – 'Well, young woman, you certainly have no responsibility for me!' she says with extreme firmness. 'No-one has responsibility for me! I am responsible for myself! Always have been. Beholden to no-one, that's me!'

I always find that a slightly sad phrase. It's one I hear, too often, when I do a bereavement visit before a funeral. 'What was he like, your Dad?' I will ask, trying to get a picture from the sorrowing, middle-aged daughter. 'Oh,' she'll say, 'he was a very upright man. Independent. Looked after himself when Mum died. Didn't ask for help. He was a proud man, he was beholden to no-one!' There's also always pride in the daughter's voice when she uses that phrase, but I feel sadness. There's no warmth, nothing there either for the won't-be taker or the would-be giver. And right now, as Bertha Jowett uses the words, undoubtedly with pride, I feel she's shutting herself away, closing doors.

'Now I don't wish to be rude,' she says, 'you've been kind to me, but I am *not* one of your lot! I am not a soul you need to save! I thought I'd made that quite clear on your first visit.'

'Oh, you did! You did!' I answer. 'Crystal clear! And I promise you I haven't any plans to convert you. I won't come the heavy hand . . .'

'It wouldn't work if you did!' she interrupts.

'But I'm not just here to look after the Christians. Long before I came here some of my most interesting friends – I hope I can call you a friend? – '

'I had hoped so!' she says.

' – were atheists. We're both positive, you see. I know by faith, you know by conviction. We're both sure we're right. You must admit that's interesting? But in the space between us there's a great army of "don't knows".'

'Then you'd be better off concentrating on them,' Bertha says.

I contradict her. 'Oh, not necessarily! You stimulate me. You sharpen me up. I can't get complacent with you around. Besides, you would never bore me!'

'Well, thank you,' she says, a bit grudgingly, as if she's not sure she believes me. 'Just so long as we both know where we stand!'

'Of course! And sometimes,' I say, 'the atheists are nicer than the churchgoing Christians, but swear you'll never tell anyone I said that!'

'I won't,' she promises. 'And don't you think I don't know it. Don't forget I grew up with churchy folks!'

There's a pause, then she says, 'Oh dear! I do truly want to move out, I've got my mind around to it, but I just don't know how I'm going to deal with all this!' She waves a hand around the untidy, crowded room.

Being really wicked, I say, 'I'll pray for you!'

She is up in arms at once. 'Don't you dare! I forbid it! If there's one thing I can't stand it's being prayed for!'

'Too late, Bertha!' I answer. 'I've already done it. What's more, I reckon I've got the answer!'

'I don't believe you,' she says, giving me a dirty look.

'Then listen to this,' I say.

I tell her all about Mrs Leigh, about her circumstances, about the fact that she wants a part-time job. 'She feels a bit lost without her husband to look after,' I say.

'That's exactly what comes of depending on other people,' Bertha says with very little sympathy, 'you don't know how to be yourself.' Nevertheless she is interested in the prospect of Mrs Leigh's help and I promise to bring Ethel to see her.

'What about tomorrow morning?' I suggest. 'I'd say you can't start too soon.'

She gives a deep sigh. 'Very well,' she says. 'I suppose you're right. I just hope she's not a do-gooder!'

'Not in the least,' I assure her. 'More in need, at the moment, of having something good done to her.'

Striking while the iron is hot, when I get back home I phone Ethel Leigh.

'Miss Jowett thinks it could work well,' I tell her. 'Would you be free to see her tomorrow morning? I'd go with you if you like.'

'Oh, I would like,' she says. 'You'd know what to say.' She's clearly nervous at the prospect. I hope Bertha doesn't frighten her to death.

'I haven't discussed hours or rate of pay, anything like that,' I say. 'That's up to the two of you, but I think Miss Jowett will be fair.'

So we arrange to meet at ten-thirty at the lych gate.

When I put the phone down I wonder again whether I can afford to have Ethel Leigh to help me, and in the end I reckon I could afford a couple of hours a week. The going rate for housework in Thurston, so I've been told, is five pounds fifty an hour. I reckon I could manage that if I cut back on something else, which I'd be willing to do. I would get her to do the jobs I hate most – clearing the rubbish, washing the kitchen floor – and what bliss to have someone else make the beds, if only once a week! So I shall ask her about that when I see her tomorrow.

There is a bench on either side in the lych gate and when I get there Ethel Leigh is already sitting there, waiting for me. We set off at once.

350

'I'm quite nervous,' she says as we walk along. 'I haven't had a job, let alone an interview, since I was married. My husband wouldn't have it.'

'And what did you do before then?' I enquire.

'I worked in the Co-op,' she says.

'Oh, you should be all right!' I say brightly. 'And remember, Miss Jowett needs you as much as, or perhaps more than, you need her. You might find her a bit sharp spoken at first, but it's only her manner. She's all right, really.'

Bertha Jowett is agreeably polite to Ethel. I recognize it as the one-must-always-be-polite-to-one's-servants variety of politeness, which was no doubt instilled in Bertha when she was a child and has remained, though it's probably many years since she had even a maid-of-all-work. Ethel, however, does not recognize this particular brand of politeness as being different from any other, so all is well. And to be fair to Bertha, she is not being condescending, she isn't a snob. She is doing what comes naturally.

'Well, Mrs Leigh,' she says, 'it will be very much a case of sorting things out. A few things, though not many, I'll be able to take with me, some will undoubtedly have to be thrown away or given to a jumble sale, and some, I'm sure, can be sold. I might get a good price for a few nice pieces.'

'I couldn't do that bit!' Ethel says nervously. 'I mean I couldn't sell things. I've never done that – except at the Co-op!'

Bertha, who doesn't know of Ethel's previous work experience, looks a bit fazed by this. 'I don't think the Co-op . . .' she begins, but I jump in and rescue both of them.

'You must have a valuer for some of your nice things,' I say. 'Perhaps they should go to auction? If there isn't a good one in Thurston then I'm sure there will be in Brampton.'

'You're quite right,' Bertha says. 'That's what I shall do. But they'll need cleaning up, the furniture polishing and so on.'

'Oh, I can do that, Miss Jowett!' Ethel says with her first show of confidence.

'Good!' Bertha replies.

'I must go,' I say. 'I'll leave you both to it, making your arrangements, I mean. By the way, I think there's someone at St

Mary's who has a large attic where she stores things for the jumble sales. Shall I find out for you?'

'Please do,' Bertha says. 'I can probably fill it!'

Ethel looks somewhat apprehensive as I take my leave, as if she's nervous about being left alone with Bertha Jowett. Well, she'll have to get over that, won't she?

When I get home there are two messages on my answerphone, one from Evelyn Sharp, the other from Mark Dover. Fortunately Evelyn says, 'Now don't panic, Venus! Nothing dire has happened to Becky – in fact she looked the picture of health when I saw her in assembly. Just phone me when you have a minute.' Mark says, 'Sorry not to catch you in. Give me a ring.'

I choose to call Evelyn first.

'I just wanted to say how pleased we are with Becky,' she says. 'She seems to have settled down really happily now. Is that your impression or is there anything you're still anxious about?'

'Nothing at all!' I say. 'She's a changed girl. And I can't thank you enough for what you've done, I mean all of you in school. She's so happy. There's Anna—'

'And the dog!' Evelyn breaks in. 'That's a great success, I hear. Well I'm glad all's as well with Becky as it seems to be to us.'

She doesn't linger on the phone, she's a busy lady. She says we must get together again soon, then rings off.

Now for Mark Dover. I can guess what he wants me for. Two weeks from now it's the exhibition in London and he'll want to make arrangements. I'm in two minds about whether I want to go. Of course I want to see the portrait hung – who wouldn't – but I wish I was going with the others – and Mark of course – instead of to the private view on the previous evening. Which reminds me that I shall have to make arrangements for Becky.

THIRTY

So much has happened since the morning I took Ethel Leigh to meet Bertha Jowett. Everything suddenly started moving, as though someone had turned on several switches at the same time. There was Mark Dover, reminding me about the London preview. We will travel up by car, he said, and afterwards he will take me out to dinner, so we will be back late. Becky and Missie and both to stay with the Brents. Heavenly bliss for Becky! A sleepover with Anna, *plus* Missie. What bliss!

And then, that same evening, following my conversation with Mark, a couple arrived at the Vicarage to make wedding arrangements. You will not believe this next bit but I assure you it's true. The conversation went like this:

Bride-to-be: 'About bridesmaids . . .'

Moi: 'Yes. How many are you thinking of?'

Bride-to-be: 'Three, actually. My sister, my best friend, and my dog.'

Moi: 'Sorry, I didn't quite catch that. For one moment – ha ha! – I thought you said "my dog"!'

Bride-to-be: 'I did, Vicar. She'll be the sweetest bridesmaid! She's an apricot poodle. Oh, don't worry, she's a very good little dog, well-mannered. She won't do anything she shouldn't. She's very well trained! She wouldn't even bark. I'd just adore to have her there and I think she'd really add something to the wedding!'

'She certainly would!' I agreed. Otherwise I was temporarily lost for words.

'In fact my colour scheme will be white and apricot,' the bride-to-be said, 'but that's not why I want to include Trixie. Do you have a dog, Vicar?'

'As a matter of fact, I do,' I told her. 'A small spaniel.'

'Ah,' she said quickly, 'then you'll understand!'

I didn't. I still don't. 'I'm not sure . . .' I began.

'There aren't any rules about bridesmaids, are there?' she interrupted. 'I mean about how many? Because if so . . .'

I could tell she would without a second thought ditch her sister or her best friend in favour of Trixie.

'Not about how many,' I said cautiously. In fact, to the best of my knowledge, nor are there any rules about whether brides-maids should be human or canine. It never came up in my training and I doubt if it often comes up in what we refer to as real life. And I'm sure there's no rule about bringing a dog into church because I've known people who did. 'It's just, well, rather unusual at a wedding,' I said.

'I know!' she agreed happily. 'I think people will like it!'

The groom said nothing, just smiled at her fondly. She will be able to twist him around her little finger, get whatever she wants.

'Do you think perhaps if your mother brought Trixie in on the lead, if she stayed with her for the ceremony . . . ?'

She pouted, rather prettily. 'I had rather hoped . . .' she said.

'Let's leave it for the moment, think it over!' I said, taking the coward's way out. 'Right now we've got other things to settle.' Why didn't I just say, 'No way, José!'? I don't know. If it had been a horse there'd have been no difficulty.

On the following Sunday we had the Wintertons' baptism, new style, at the Eucharist. It went well, and certainly, the family told me afterwards, they were very pleased. They felt supported by the involvement of the congregation, and without a doubt the congregation were interested. There's something special about welcoming a new member in baptism, and it certainly struck a chord when the baby cried like mad as the water was poured over her head. There were several sympathetic 'oohs' and 'aahs' from the ladies. Conversely, Mr and Mrs Mortimer didn't fancy a similar baptism for their child. It seemed too public for them, so I was happy to baptize baby Joseph on the following Sunday afternoon in the presence of only family members. I won't push people into something they don't want.

Miss Carson and Mrs Blamires have been conspicuous by their absence, though nothing has been said directly to me, except by Carla Brown, who said, 'Silly twits!' I think everyone else was being tactful. Then last Sunday the twin sisters, Joyce and Alice Dean, were missing. I asked about them at coffee. 'Are they ill?' I enquired.

There was a rather embarrassed silence from the people around the table, then a brave soul said, 'I'm afraid they've followed Miss Carson and Mrs Blamires to St Saviour's, Venus. But don't worry!'

I'm not exactly worried, but it would be untrue to say I don't care. Of course I do.

'On the other hand,' Trudy Santer said, 'Mrs Marshall has come back. She's been here the last two Sundays.'

'Mrs Marshall?' I still don't know everyone in the congregation and in any case not everyone comes every Sunday.

'She left a while ago. She didn't get on with the previous Vicar,' Trudy said. 'Nothing serious that I know of. I reckon he was a bit sharp with her, probably with good cause, but she wouldn't like that.'

'Par for the course with the clergy,' I said. 'One mustn't ever disagree, or criticize. It's not the thing.'

'Anyway, I reckon she's giving you a trial period,' Trudy said.

Ethel Leigh is now helping at the Vicarage from nine o'clock to twelve noon every Friday. I can't afford it, but it's heaven. If there are economies to be made I already know it won't be in this direction. I would fast from food and drink for a day a week rather than part with Ethel, now that I've experienced the magic wrought in the house during those three hours. Not content with cleaning the rooms and polishing every surface until I can see my reflection in it, she gathers up all the bits of ironing she can lay hands on, and deals with them.

She tells me she's getting on all right with Bertha Jowett,

though 'We're making progress' is about the limit of her description because she isn't a gossip, but the tone of her voice tells me there's a great deal more progress still to be made.

Mum phones me almost daily, itemizing what she's dealt with. The best glass and china has been washed and packed into the tea chests the removal people have obligingly let her have in advance; the bookshelves have been sorted through and several volumes given towards Holy Trinity's next jumble sale – about which Dad is not madly happy since he hates parting with books, even the ones he's read and is unlikely ever to read again.

Occasionally he takes over the phone from Mum. 'Your mother's in her element,' he told me. 'Packing everything she can lay hands on. We'll be lucky if we have a plate to eat our dinner from or sheets to sleep in for at least a week before we move!' All the same, I think he's as happy as she is.

And then, ten days ago, Richard Proctor stunned us all, or at least everyone in St Mary's, by the announcement of his engagement to a woman he's met in the course of his work. No-one suspected a thing, not even the Blessed Henry (so the latter told me). The feeling is that the fiancée, who lives in Kingston-on-Thames, has never so much as set foot in Thurston, at least not with Richard, or someone would have seen them.

The day after that news broke Nigel called in the afternoon with a CD he'd promised to lend me – Schubert, whom I like very much. Schubert knows how to write a good tune.

'Have you heard about Richard Proctor?' I asked him.

He had. I wasn't surprised. That's Thurston for you.

'They're to be married in Kingston,' I informed him. 'So at least Richard will be spared the embarrassment of deciding whether he could go through a wedding taken by a woman priest – though I don't think he has any personal animosity towards me. Indeed, I hear I'm to be invited to the wedding!'

'Good for you!' Nigel said.

'Should he move away from Thurston to live,' I continued, 'then I'll have to have a new churchwarden. So I'm looking around.' In fact I'm asking myself, 'What about a woman?' – though I'm not asking it out loud. I doubt St Mary's has ever had a woman churchwarden.

At that point Becky came in from school, to the usual ecstatic welcome from Missie. She and I have fallen into the pattern of taking Missie for a walk straight after school every day, not stopping to have tea because it gets dark so early.

'Are you ready?' she asked me the minute she came through the door.

I explained to Nigel why I'd have to shoo him out and he said, 'Why don't I come with you? I've finished my visits and it's my evening off from surgery.'

He and Becky talked twenty to the dozen as we walked over the Downs. 'I'm staying two nights with Anna next week,' she informed him. 'Anna's my best friend.'

'I know!' Nigel said.

'Mum's going to London twice. She won't be home till late.'

'I know that too,' Nigel said. 'I'm going with her.'

Becky turned to me, surprised. 'I thought you were going with Mark Dover.'

'One day with him, the next day with me, and some other friends,' Nigel said.

'Why?' Becky asked. 'Why don't you all go together?'

'That's precisely what I've asked your mother!' Nigel said.

I chipped in. 'Nigel, you know perfectly well why I'm going twice!'

'I don't like Mark Dover,' Becky said. 'I don't think he likes children!'

'That's rude,' I told her. 'And also, you should say "Mr Dover".'

Nigel winked at her.

'Am I supposed to call you Mister?' she asked him.

'Definitely not!' he said. '*We're* friends!'

Ten days ago I did the trip to London with Mark. I wore the same outfit I had bought for that first dinner party. I loved it. It didn't matter that Mark had seen it before; I wasn't out to impress him. He picked me up in the afternoon, shortly after I'd delivered Becky, Missie, and a couple of teddy bears to the Brents'. Becky didn't give me so much as a backward glance when I left and I suppose I should be happy about that.

357

'She'll be fine,' Sally Brent said. 'We'll look after her!'

I was sure they would but, perversely, I would have liked Becky to show the teeniest bit of emotion on leaving me, even a tenth of what I felt about parting with her, though probably mine was compounded with guilt.

Mark drove fast and furiously up the motorway, undoubtedly breaking the speed limit until, reaching London, the traffic slowed him down.

'I know people aren't due to arrive until around seven,' he said, 'but I want to make quite certain that everything's in order before they do.'

It was about all he did say on the journey, which surprised me. I'd expected him to be his usual chatty self, totally in command of everything, but I sensed he was nervous. Thinking about it, I supposed that was reasonable. He was offering his work, openly displaying it, for all to see, to approve or criticize – or even show no reaction at all, which might be worse – without any explanations, any declaring of intent. It had to speak for itself, there was nothing more he could do, and I wondered if his usual brimming-over self-confidence had temporarily deserted him. At the beginning of the journey I chatted, until I realized that my place was to keep quiet – which I did.

The gallery was in one of the streets off Piccadilly, that area which seems to be awash with works of art. It appeared unprepossessing from the outside, with a small window in which one of his paintings, on an easel, was the sole display, but inside it was unexpectedly spacious with paintings and small sculptures not only on the ground floor but in galleries on two floors above. Mark had the whole of the gallery on the first floor, which, he said, was quite the best position.

The gallery owner, Paul Threlfall, a dapper little man with receding hair and a ready smile, came forward and greeted us with a quiet enthusiasm – it wasn't, I thought, a place where one would ever speak in loud tones – and Mark introduced me.

'Ah,' Mr Threlfall said, 'the lady of the portrait! I hope you like it. We think it's rather special!' Then he turned to Mark. 'Everything's in order,' he said. 'I think you'll be pleased with the hanging. We've had quite a bit of interest. I've given out a few

358

invitations, apart from your own list, to clients I thought would be useful.'

'That's fine!' Mark said. 'Are the caterers here?'

'They are,' Mr Threlfall assured him. 'They're very competent.'

We followed him up the stairs to the first floor.

The first thing I saw – and I would have even if I hadn't been looking for it – was my portrait. It was in the centre of the long wall, immediately opposite the door by which we entered, the perfect place. Mark had told me it would have the place of honour but I don't think I'd ever believed him. Here, hung where it was, it glowed with life and colour. The three of us stood together, just inside the room, looking at it.

'It's great, isn't it?' Mr Threlfall said. 'I hope you like it.'

'It's lovely!' I said. 'It really is!'

Mark said nothing, but he looked pleased, and a little more relaxed, though I knew it wasn't just my approval he wanted, but that of the real critics who would see it later.

'I do think it's the best thing you've done,' Mr Threlfall said. 'And now I'll leave you to it. I expect you'll want to look around. Let me know if anything doesn't suit you, though I'm sure it will.'

Look around was what I did, while Mark went to speak with the caterers and then to the madly attractive young woman with a haircut to die for who was there to be at the desk just inside the door where she would give out catalogues and deal with queries – hopefully from would-be buyers. Mark came back to me and said, 'I'll be with you as much as I can, and I'll introduce you to people, but I might have to neglect you a bit.'

'That's OK,' I assured him. 'I expect people always want to talk to the artist.'

'That's true,' he agreed, 'though in this case I think they might also like to talk to the model. Do you mind?'

'Not at all,' I told him.

And then people began to come in, ones and twos to begin with and then more and more, and the champagne flowed and the canapés were offered and the room was alive with chatter from a surprising number of people. It was clearly a success. Mark was here, there and everywhere. He introduced me to several people whose names I immediately forgot, and a few people spoke to me, having recognized me from the portrait. I took a look at the catalogue while Mark was away from me, checking the price against my portrait. Two thousand pounds, so there was no chance at all that I could ever buy it.

'You don't look a bit like a Vicar!' an elegant, elderly woman said to me. 'But then you're a new species, aren't you? I've never met a woman priest before! A strange subject for a portrait!'

I don't suppose she meant to be offensive. It just came naturally to her.

After a while, a time of eavesdropping on a lot of chat which went on around me as people stood in front of the paintings making what sounded like quite clever remarks as if they knew what they were talking about, and what seemed to me a fair amount of champagne had been drunk – I had two glasses myself, not to mention several bites to eat to soak up the alcohol – the visitors began to leave. Mark appeared at my side.

'They'll be gone soon,' he said. 'Then we can leave. I've booked a table at a restaurant in Jermyn Street I think you'll like. Just the two of us.'

I hadn't expected this. I don't really know what I'd expected; I'd supposed that a few of Mark's arty friends would be joining us. I realized, however, that in spite of the nibbles I was quite hungry. I never eat much lunch and it was past my supper time so I was happy at the thought of food, though less so at the 'just the two of us' bit.

It was without doubt the most upmarket restaurant I'd ever been in; exquisitely furnished, though in a rather ornate French style – but why not, since it *was* French. The maître d' greeted Mark by name. 'I've reserved your usual table, Mr Dover,' he said. It was in a corner, from which we could see everything, or would have if the lighting had not been on the dim side of discreet. One waiter from a myriad of them brought me a menu one could happily spend half a day reading, which showed no prices, and from which I finally chose a sole.

'A good choice,' Mark said. 'And I shall have the same. It's always delicious here.' I had an aperitif, though Mark said no to that. 'Since I'm driving,' he explained, 'though I will have a glass of wine. Their Chablis is good. Do you like Chablis?'

'Oh yes, I do!' I told him, but not adding that it was something which didn't often come my way.

The sole was grilled to perfection. The waiter brought it whole to the table then proceeded, with infinite skill, to take it off the bone for me. I felt pampered. It reminded me of when I was a little girl and my mother would probe delicately through my cod or haddock, searching out the hidden dangers so that I wouldn't choke on them. In real life I have to do it for myself.

But this was not real life, I told myself as the sole was followed by a creamy meringue confection, accompanied by a glass of champagne, which went straight to my head. Really, I thought, Mark Dover is quite nice! Perhaps I've been unfair to him? I also wondered how he could afford a lifestyle which took in regular visits to this restaurant. I'd thought that artists were mostly impoverished. Perhaps he sold dozens of portraits at two thousand pounds apiece? Or perhaps he had inherited wealth? I also wondered who sat with him at his 'usual' table.

He ordered coffee and we were sitting there drinking it when he suddenly bent forward, stretched across the table, and covered my hand with his. My first reaction was to pull away, but almost at the same time I thought how silly that would be. It would make the gesture seem more important than it was. Play it cool, I told myself!

'Venus,' he said, 'do you know how beautiful you are?'

That was when a shiver of apprehension went through me, partly because I didn't know what to say. It's a long time since anyone told me I was beautiful – even Philip didn't use such extravagant words – but what woman anywhere wouldn't like to be told she was beautiful? I wasn't sure whether I liked it, or not. Nevertheless, I withdrew my hand from under his, though gently.

'Thank you, Mark,' I said. 'You exaggerate, of course!'

'No I don't,' he said. 'And it's time someone told you just how attractive you are!'

At that moment the waiter came to pour more coffee, which I refused. 'I really ought to be getting back!' I told Mark.

'Why?' he asked. 'You don't have to clock in, do you?'

'Not exactly,' I agreed, while searching for an excuse. 'But I am more or less on call. I might be needed.'

It was a lame excuse, and I think he thought that. Nevertheless he said, 'OK Cinderella! I'll get you home before midnight strikes!'

He paid the bill, we left, and went to pick up the car. As we walked along Piccadilly he took my arm and held me closer than need be, so that I wondered what the journey back to Thurston might be like. I needn't have worried. Before we left London the rain started, a heavy, misty rain, and the traffic was thick even at that time of night, so that he had to concentrate on his driving. We didn't talk much.

When he drew up at the Vicarage, well after midnight, he opened the car door for me and said, 'Are you going to invite me in for coffee?'

'No,' I said. 'It's much too late for me. But it was a lovely evening, I really do thank you – and the portrait is wonderful. I wish I could afford to buy it.'

'I'm not at all sure I want to sell it,' he said. 'Just one thing, Venus, don't let's, because the portrait's finished, lose touch with each other. I wouldn't like that at all. There's still a lot going for us.'

'Of course we won't lose touch,' I assured him. 'It wouldn't be easy to do that in Thurston even if we wanted to, which I don't.'

'Right!' he said. Then without another word he took me in his arms, kissed me on the mouth, then turned and got back into his car and drove away.

Afterwards I lay in bed and thought, would I like to be seduced? Would I, if I were really honest? I recognized that, had I been agreeable, this would have been Mark's plan.

It was a difficult question to answer. Yes, I'm a priest, and I'm the mother of a ten-year-old daughter – but I'm a woman and my body has all the instincts of a woman, which need no more than a touch for them to catch fire. If you were to ask, would I like sex back in my life, then the answer is yes, I would.

That's my body speaking, and the body is powerful (especially fuelled by champagne and wine, I reminded myself), but when they have to the mind and the spirit can beat the body – and in this case they have to. Besides, I don't think Mark, charming and attractive though he is, would be the man for me.

I put out the light, turned over, and eventually – but not quickly – I went to sleep.

I was on the phone to Sally Brent reasonably early next morning but Becky and Anna had already left for school.

'She's absolutely fine,' Sally assured me. 'She and Anna get on so well together, and of course having Missie is a bonus. I think I'm probably going to have to get a dog!'

'Thank you for everything,' I said. 'I'm afraid I might be home quite late again this evening so I won't call you then. Shall I come in the morning and collect Missie?'

'Not unless you specially want to,' Sally said. 'I'll pick up the girls from school and bring them and Missie back to you. Is that OK?'

I told her it was fine. I think Sally will turn out to be a good friend.

Next day's trip to London was quite different. Sonia wasn't able to go because she and Nigel couldn't both leave the practice, but Evelyn Sharp and her husband made up a foursome. We, that's to say Evelyn, Nigel and I, left as soon as school was through and went by train from Brampton, meeting Colin, who had had business in London for the day, at Victoria. We made straight for the gallery – Mark wasn't there as I'd thought he might be. The beautiful girl, hair still super – I wondered where she had it cut and what it cost – said he had just slipped out, she didn't know when he'd be back. The portrait was extravagantly admired, even by Nigel. 'I'd no idea Mark Dover was so good,' Evelyn said. 'It really is wonderful.' I caught Nigel looking at the price in his catalogue, though he said nothing. He wouldn't be able to afford it, not on a doctor's pay, and why would he want it?

Afterwards we had a Chinese meal in one of those small streets close to Piccadilly Circus. It was very different from the previous evening, about which I said little or nothing to the company I was with. It was crowded and noisy and the service was slow, but the company was good, we found plenty to talk about, and the whole thing was a success. I fell asleep on the train back to Brampton. Nigel had left his car in the station car park. He dropped off Evelyn and Colin first, then took me home to the Vicarage. Again, it was after midnight but I thought that if Nigel mentioned coffee I would ask him in, but he didn't. He simply came round, opened the car door, walked with me to the door and waited while I fiddled with the lock, which is always dodgy, then gave me a kiss on the cheek, and left. 'A wonderful day,' he called out as he walked back to the car. I wondered if my neighbours heard any of this, and what they thought of their Vicar, returning two nights in a row after midnight.

THIRTY-ONE

It's amazing how quickly the time flies by between the end of summer and Christmas. I suppose it always did, especially in the church because the last four weeks before Christmas are Advent and we're looking forward for reasons additional to presents and family and friends and shopping, but I've never noticed its passing as keenly as I have this year. Perhaps it's because I've never in the past had so many responsibilities, large and small, some of them sole responsibilities about which only I could decide. In former years I've had someone, like Philip – especially my dear Philip – with whom to share them or, not nearly as agreeable as sharing, someone telling me what to do without allowing me any freedom in the doing. The Reverend Humphrey Payne springs to mind. Now, though I have two churchwardens to keep me in order (they have the right, in fact the duty, to report me to the Bishop if they think I'm neglecting my duty), I am really Head Girl of the parish, with everything that entails.

It was no surprise to me, therefore, when the morning after the visit to London everything began to hum. My first call, straight after breakfast and before I'd even had time to phone Sally Brent to ask about Becky, was from Cliff Preston.

'Have I got work for you!' he said. I thought he sounded gleeful, as gleeful as his job allows him. 'Two funerals. They both came in yesterday when you were living it up in London.'

Did the whole parish know I'd gone to London? And if so, how?

'And a third more or less in the bag,' he continued.

'What do you mean, in the bag?' I asked.

'Pending File. NYD,' he says, a bit offhand.

'NYD? What on earth . . . ?'

'Not Yet Dead,' he says patiently. 'In this case the lady is in intensive care, still alive, but from what I hear it can't be long.'

I'm somewhat shaken by the sound of the Pending, NYD file – would I want to be in it? And yet I know that no funeral director I've ever encountered is more caring, more sympathetic, than Cliff. He takes so much of the weight off the shoulders of the bereaved – and I suppose to do this he has to have a firm business nature.

'I'm sorry,' I said. 'Are they anyone I know?'

'You know the first one,' Cliff said. 'It's Cyril Henfield. He was one of your vergers, wasn't he?'

'Oh, Mr Henfield! Yes, he was. One of those who didn't go to church but helped to look after it. A nice man! I didn't even know he was ill.'

'In a manner of speaking, he wasn't,' Cliff said. 'At least not until he had a heart attack and died more or less on the spot. The other was a Mrs Bulmer. Lives in the parish but I didn't know her. I gather she'd been ill a long time.'

'Right!' I said. 'Give me the details and I'll ring both families this morning. And what about the lady who's in intensive care? If she's one of my parishioners I must go to see her.'

'A Mrs Carson. Lives in Anderby Drive,' Cliff said. 'Her daughter Emily – spinster of uncertain age – was the one who notified me.'

I realized at once, I recognized the address, that the daughter must be the Miss Carson who, with Mrs Blamires, left St Mary's for the greener pastures of St Saviour's. And of course I knew I must go and visit her mother, and from what Cliff said, the sooner the better. Whether I would be welcomed by daughter Emily was another matter. Possibly, I thought, she had her own ideas about visits by women priests to the sick and dying. Nevertheless, there was no way I wouldn't do it and I decided not to phone Emily beforehand. After all, if either of the two needed me it would be Mrs Carson.

I made some phone calls, first to Sally Brent who said Becky had been fine, they'd enjoyed having her, and Missie, and she'd seen the two girls off to school this morning. As agreed, she'd meet the girls from school and bring Becky and Missie back to the Vicarage. I'm so looking forward to seeing Becky – and Missie of course.

I phoned the Henfield and the Bulmer families and made arrangements to pay bereavement visits, the Henfields this evening and the Bulmers tomorrow morning. Then I set off for the hospital.

I supposed if I'd stopped to think I'd have realized that Emily Carson was likely to be there, and she was, but I would have gone anyway. Emily was sitting at the bedside. She looked surprised to see me, but nothing more than that. Mrs Carson lay as still as if she was already dead, eyes closed, face a yellowy, waxen colour. There was a purple bruise on her temple. Her breathing was almost imperceptible, not moving the bedcovers.

'I'm so sorry,' I said to Emily Carson. 'This must be very sad for you. I came as soon as I heard, but if you'd rather I didn't stay, rather I left you alone with your mother, then of course I'll leave right away.'

She shook her head.

'No,' she said. 'Please stay! I know Mummy's going to die and . . .' she hesitated, then forced the words out, 'I'm frightened! I don't know what I'll do. You see, there's only ever been Mummy and me. My father left us when I was very small.'

'I'll stay with you as long as you want me to, Emily,' I said, using her first name deliberately. 'I won't leave you.'

To me, it was all there in the way she said 'Mummy'. Like a little child. I wondered if she had ever been allowed to grow up, to be herself, or had she taken her father's place? 'There's only ever been Mummy and me.' I've seen it happen. It's cruelty of the worst sort because it's disguised as love. See how devoted I am to my child! On the other hand, is it cruelty if the perpetrator doesn't recognize it as such? I don't know. But how could anyone not know it was deeply selfish?

I sat there a long time. We didn't talk much, and when we did it was about Mummy, how attentive she had been, how they had done everything together. 'We neither of us ever wanted anyone else,' Emily said. I could have said that want and need are two different things, but it was neither the time nor the place and it was too late anyway. I did wonder how Emily had managed to form a friendship with Mrs Blamires and if that would stand her in good stead when her mother died.

Nothing was said about Mrs Blamires, or what had led them to decide to leave St Mary's. I suspected that Mrs Blamires had been the leader in this and that Emily had meekly followed after. Nevertheless, it was going to have to come up at some time in the near future. Mrs Carson was going to die very soon, she would probably have expected to be buried in St Mary's churchyard, or to be cremated and her ashes buried there. What would Emily's attitude be towards me as a woman priest doing either of these things? Were burial, and perhaps baptism, seen as minor rites with which I could be entrusted, whereas preaching and teaching, and celebrating the Eucharist, were not? Of course Mrs Carson could be buried at St Mary's with another priest officiating, and I was sure I could find a suitable male to do it. This, I decided, was what I would offer Emily when the time came, but not now.

The time wasn't long in coming. Mrs Carson died an hour later – I was still there, in the middle of saying some quiet prayers – without ever opening her eyes again, or giving any sign that she knew Emily was present. I finished the prayers, and then the surprise came. I had expected Emily to fall to pieces on the spot, to be a soggy mass of tears, or near hysteria, but she didn't, she wasn't. She was silent for a minute, then she stood up and, looking down at her mother, she took a very deep breath. It seemed as if she had breathed new life into herself. The nurse took her away to the office. I followed behind and waited in the corridor, and then I took Emily home.

'Can I ask someone, perhaps a neighbour, to come and stay with you, at least for the rest of today and for the night?' I asked. She said no, she'd be all right, she'd make a few calls, including one to Mrs Blamires. She was quite calm and seemed as though she had gained strength from who-knew-where? Death can have a strange effect on people and I've seen this kind of thing happen before. It was as if Emily took on a new persona. Perhaps it wasn't new; perhaps it had been waiting. She was very grateful to me, she said, and she'd get in touch later. She did so the next day. Her mother, she said, had wanted to be buried at St Mary's. I interrupted her. 'I know your difficulty about women priests,' I said. 'It will be quite easy for me to find someone else who will do the funeral in St Mary's.'

'Thank you, but no,' she said. 'My mother was never a churchgoer but she had nothing whatever against women priests. I'm sure you'd be the one she'd want. She had a low opinion of men.'

It was lunchtime when I got back to the Vicarage. After my sandwich I phoned the Blessed Henry to bring him up to date with my news and to see if he had any for me.

'Anything more about Richard?' I enquired.

'Only that he'll almost certainly be leaving Thurston,' Henry said. 'It makes sense, really.'

After that I did some paper work, including taking a good look at my diary. Enquiries and bookings for next spring and summer are coming in fast and furious. I have a wedding at three o'clock next Saturday and although Mr Blatchford knows he is playing the organ for that I must give him a reminder because he's a wee bit forgetful. Well, that's my excuse for being neurotic about wedding details, worrying beforehand that something might go wrong or be overlooked. Once it starts, once the bride walks down the aisle to Mr Blatchford giving his all at the organ, I'm OK. I've heard nothing more from the bride-to-be about the doggy bridesmaid and I'm lying low, hoping that some friend or relative will talk sense into her.

Then the phone rings and it's Esmé Bickler.

'Hi!' she said. 'How's everything?'

'Fine! Busy, but OK.'

'I wondered if you'd seen a letter in *The Times* yesterday, about women priests?'

'No. I was in London yesterday. In any case, I don't get a newspaper every day,' I told her. 'So what did it say? Who was it from?'

'Well, that's the thing,' Esmé said. 'It was from nine men, as far as I know most of them priests and three of them bishops!'

'So tell me the worst,' I said. I wasn't sure I wanted to hear it.

'That's just it, none of it was the worst. They were on our side and they were calling attention to the way we've been treated in the last ten years, but particularly how we've almost entirely been ignored for promotion, with very few women, however well-qualified, in senior jobs, right through the country. They pointed out that women priests are about the only female workers in the country who have no redress in law against discrimination. It wouldn't be tolerated, they said, if it were a racial matter.'

'Too right it wouldn't!' I agreed.

'There's a lot more,' Esmé said. 'It's a long letter. I'll tell you what, I'll get a photocopy and send it to you, shall I?'

'Please,' I said. 'It's interesting, though what good it will do, who knows. Especially in this diocese!'

'It points that out also,' Esmé said. 'I mean about the wide differences according to where you serve. Oh well, we soldier on! Any trouble at your end?'

'Nothing much. Not everyone is nice, but most are. I've had a few depart because they couldn't cope with me. On the other hand I've gained one or two. I try to take it is my stride.'

'Me too,' Esmé said. 'Well, nice to talk to you and I'll send you a copy of the letter.'

The really big blow-up will come, I thought as I put down the phone, when – if ever – we get the first woman bishop. It's already about to be debated and voted upon in the Scottish Episcopal Church. There's no reason why women priests can't be bishops, it's the natural progression, exactly as it is for the men. There are men in high positions in the Church who believe the time has come for this to happen, but once again the opposition is lining up. They have said that they will not accept a woman bishop and that whoever she ordains to the priesthood or whoever she confirms, this will never be valid in their eyes.

Don't think from all this that I've set my eyes on becoming a bishop. I would never be suitable. I don't have those gifts. What I love is parish life, all the minutiae of it, even when it frustrates me. I love the daily contact with the people. But there are women who would be eminently suitable to be bishops. They see the larger picture.

Oh boy! What fun and games it will be when the time comes!

An hour or so later Sally Brent arrived with the girls and Missie. I invited Sally and Anna to stay for tea with us but Sally said no, they couldn't because Anna had a ballet class. Becky hasn't yet requested ballet lessons and she's not a child who's always asking for things but I'm sure this one will come and how will I say 'No', even though I can't afford it? I want her, within reason, to have everything her friends have. On the other hand, right now she did have another request.

'You know I'm going to the pantomime after Christmas?' she began.

'Yes!' I agreed. The fundraising for the pantomime has gone well. We booked the seats and the coach in the faith that it would, and it went even better than we expected. I'm told there'll be enough money for ice cream in the interval. 'So?' I asked Becky. I knew there was more to come.

'Well, can Anna come?'

'That's difficult,' I said. 'The outing is for the children who go to Sunday School. Anna doesn't. She doesn't go to church.'

'I don't go to Sunday School,' Becky pointed out.

'No, you don't – though I think you should. You might even enjoy it. But you're coming to the pantomime because I'm the Vicar and I'm going, and you're my daughter. I wouldn't leave you at home, would I?'

She didn't seem entirely happy about this explanation. I could see she was thinking hard about it. In the end she said, 'Well, if me and Anna both came to Sunday School between now and Christmas, could we both go?'

'Becky!' I said, 'you really don't go to Sunday School just to qualify for the treats!' But even while I was saying it I knew that wasn't true. It's common practice and every Sunday School knows it – and puts up with it.

'Well, Nigel is going, and he doesn't go to St Mary's!' she said it with an air of 'get out of that if you can'.

I had invited Nigel a week or two ago to be my guest, partly

371

because he had invited me to go to a performance of the Messiah in Brampton, actually next Wednesday evening, with a group from St Patrick's. I'm all for the two churches doing things together. (It means Becky going to the Brents again, but Sally seems happy enough about that and it's good for Becky.) Also, for the pantomime, there was no restriction on adults going because they all paid for themselves. I explained that to Becky but it didn't wash. 'You could pay for Anna,' she said. 'I'll put something towards it from my pocket money.'

I gave in. 'Very well,' I said. 'I'll give Trudy Santer a ring and ask if she can possibly get us another ticket. And of course,' I said, seizing my chance, 'you and Anna might like to start going to Sunday School together, though we'd have to ask Anna's parents whether they agreed.'

'I didn't mean I didn't want Nigel to be going to the pantomime,' Becky said. 'He's nice. But I wanted Anna as well.'

In the evening my mother phoned, absolutely over the moon. 'Everything seems to be OK,' she said, 'in fact we've provisionally booked the removal for the week before Christmas! Friday December the twentieth. There now, what do you think of that?'

'Marvellous!' I said – and it is marvellous. The only thing is, and I shan't mention it to my parents, it will be all hands aloft in the church, every day something happening: the school carol service, a Christmas concert by a visiting choir, the church to decorate, etc. – and I will be involved in all of them. There's a deanery meeting, also, and without a doubt one or more funerals will come up in that very week. Sod's law! Nevertheless, I repeated that it was marvellous, wonderful, and I was delighted.

'Will you tell Miss Jowett as soon as you can?' Mum said. 'Oh dear, I do hope there won't be any hitch about her moving into the home!'

'That bit's OK,' I said. 'By now she can't wait to be off, and the place is waiting for her. Getting her stuff out of the cottage will be the difficulty, but Ethel Leigh has done a wonderful job in helping her to sort things. Between them they've got rid of a mountain of stuff already, so I'm sure the rest will be dealt with. Don't worry about it!'

I went to see Bertha Jowett the next morning, quite early, but Ethel Leigh was already there, beavering away. Bertha was delighted.

'You'll have to have the cottage totally cleared,' I warned her.

'Oh, I will,' she said firmly. 'I'll just need help to get some of my bits and pieces to the Beeches; and as for the rest, it can go on the council tip for all I care!'

She's full of bravado, but it's a big step and I wonder how she'll feel when the time comes? Anyway, busy or not busy, I shall make it my priority on the day she moves to spend as much time as possible with her.

'And if there's one clear day before your parents move in,' Ethel Leigh said to me, 'I'll manage to clean right through the cottage.'

'That would be great,' I said. 'And perhaps you'd be able to give them some time afterwards, help them to settle in? I expect there'll be a lot to do.'

'I'd be glad to,' she said.

The Christmas season is never quite complete to me without hearing, and preferably being present at, a performance of the Messiah somewhere or other, though it seems to me that it's not done as often as it used to be. Certainly my parents say that when they were younger you couldn't get away from it at this time of the year – every venue, from the local chapel to the grandest concert hall, gave it. 'And very varying standards they were!' Mum said. 'Though all in their own way enjoyable.' It was my parents who once took me to a memorable performance in the Albert Hall, but my favourite remained the one I went to at university, when the audience could join in and sing along as they wished. I say 'remained' because it has now been surpassed by the one I went to in Brampton last Wednesday with Nigel and the group from St Patrick's. I couldn't say that it was the best ever, musically. Possibly not, though the soprano soloist and the chorus were exceptionally good and the words came over as if I was hearing them for the first time. But it wasn't just the performance, there was something about the atmosphere of the whole evening. As if the whole world was right and everything was in its proper place, and it wasn't until Nigel took me home afterwards that I realized fully why that was.

'You will come in for coffee, or a drink?' I said to Nigel when we reached the Vicarage.

'If you hadn't asked me,' he replied, 'I would have invited myself!'

We went straight through to the kitchen. 'Since it's been such a lovely evening,' I said, 'shall we open a bottle of wine?' I stood with my back to him, facing my small wine rack.

'Not yet,' he said. 'There's something I have to say first.' Then he put his hands on my shoulders, turned me around to face him, and took me in his arms. It was the first time since Philip that anyone has ever kissed me or I have ever kissed anyone, at least like this, because this was a lovers' kiss, long and sweet. I had no thought of Philip then, only of this man here, who was holding me as if he would never let me go and whom, I knew, I never wanted to leave. It was as if I had come home after a long journey, had reached the only place in the world I wanted to be. I didn't think all this at the time. There were no words. The words which describe my feelings have only come to me now in the telling. Then it was all feeling, but oh!, it felt so right.

Was I surprised? It was certainly sudden, and yet it didn't feel sudden, and no, I wasn't surprised. It felt inevitable, as if I'd known inside me that one day it would happen.

Eventually Nigel released me, but only to hold me at arm's length and look at me. 'Venus,' he said, 'I love you. I think I have ever since that first evening when I drove you to the hospital. Please tell me you love me!'

'I do,' I said. 'I don't think I quite knew I did until this evening, but I know now.'

We kissed again, hungrily, as if we could never get enough of each other, and then again he broke off and let me go, though I didn't want to go.

'Will you marry me, Venus?' he said.

'I will!' I said. 'Oh yes, I will!'

'Then we'll open the bottle of wine and celebrate that!' Nigel said.

'I'm sorry it's not champagne!' I apologized. 'If I'd known . . .'

Between us we chose the best bottle of red I had, though it was nothing special except to us, for whom it was the finest wine ever to come from the grape. We toasted each other, we drank out of each other's glasses, we kissed with the taste of wine on our lips. Then he raised his glass again and said, 'To the future! Yours and mine, together for always!' I repeated his words. 'To the future!' and then reality hit me.

He saw the look on my face. 'What is it? What's wrong, my darling?'

'You do know it's not going to be easy?' I said. 'We're already divided, you and I. We're divided by what we each hold most dear.'

Nigel shook his head. 'I know what you mean, but nothing's going to keep us apart. I won't let it!' he said.

'It's not as simple as that,' I said. 'If we were both lay people we could do what we liked. You are, and you can. I'm a priest. Once a priest, always a priest. My priesthood is mine for life. There are things I can't do.'

'What things?' he asked. 'I don't understand!'

'I can't just say I'll marry you, and get on with it. I must have the permission of my bishop. I don't know what he'll say when I tell him I want to marry someone from your church.'

'But we're the same faith!' Nigel protested. 'We've talked about this before. Our churches might be divided – more fool them – but you and I follow the same paths.'

'Not entirely,' I said. 'Oh, Nigel, I wish we did! But we don't and we won't. You won't give up what you hold dear and I won't give up being a priest. We're divided by two churches which both preach the same love of Christ as their central theme.'

'I'm not going to give you up as easily as that,' Nigel said.

'No, nor am I you!' I said. 'I'll phone the Bishop tomorrow and ask to see him as soon as possible.'

'I'll go with you,' Nigel said.

'If the Bishop agrees,' I said. 'I daresay he'll want to see me on my own, first. I really don't know. It's all outside my experience.'

He took hold of my hands. 'Venus, I love you, I always will. And you love me . . .'

'And I always will!' I added.

'So we'll let nothing and no-one come between us. And now we'll drink the rest of the wine and then I'll go home – though I don't want to leave you, I never want to leave you again.'

'And I don't want you to,' I said. 'You must know that.' I would have liked to have led him up to my bedroom there and then. 'But you have to go, my love, and the sooner the better.'

THIRTY-TWO

Nigel phoned me next morning before he started his surgery. It was a call in which we reassured each other that what had happened the night before was not a dream, it was all true, that come what may we were engaged to be married.

'I'd like to keep it to ourselves until I've spoken to the Bishop,' I said. 'Except that as it concerns the Bishop I think I must also tell Henry Nugent. But no-one else – and Henry is very discreet. I shan't even tell my parents or Becky.'

'And I suppose that means I can't tell Sonia,' Nigel said. 'I've seen her briefly. She said, "I don't know what it is, but you look like the cat that's got the cream!" But whatever you say, my love. Personally I'd like to broadcast it far and wide! I'm just so happy!'

'Me too!' I agreed. 'But I must speak to the Bishop first. We don't want to start by doing the wrong thing, do we?'

'I suppose not,' he said. 'But you will ring him soon, won't you?'

'Of course!' I assured him. 'I think around ten o'clock. I don't want to interrupt his breakfast, do I? In any case he's quite likely to have an early service.'

'I'll ring you straight after surgery,' Nigel said.

It had been hard not to say a word to Becky before she left for school, and then when my mother phoned just after I'd spoken

377

to Nigel – more details of the move – it was even more difficult. I managed it only by putting Nigel completely out of my mind, at least for those few minutes.

When, on the dot of ten, I phoned the Bishop I was put through first to his secretary.

'I'm sorry,' he said. 'The Bishop's on retreat. He'll be away for the next three days. Is it something I can help you with, Mrs Stanton?'

'I'm afraid not in this case,' I said. 'It's personal, not parochial.'

'I'm sorry!' he said. 'As you will know, I can't interrupt his retreat except for something very urgent. Would you describe it as that?'

'I don't think so,' I told him. 'To me, but perhaps not to the Bishop. I'll ring later in the week.'

'I'm terribly disappointed,' I told Nigel when he phoned, which he was doing, he said, the very second he'd seen his last patient out of the door.

'Can I come and see you later this afternoon?' he asked.

'Of course,' I said. 'But bear in mind that Becky will be there and I can't tell her yet. It would be impossible to expect her to keep it to herself.'

'Do you think she'll be happy about it?' Nigel asked anxiously. 'I do want her to be.'

'I'm certain she will,' I assured him. 'She's very fond of you.'

'All right then, my darling,' he said. 'I'll see you later and I'll try to hide my feelings, though it won't be easy.'

'Nor for me either,' I said.

I badly wanted to tell Ann about all this, perhaps Ann more than anyone else. I wanted to be sure that she knew I was not deserting Philip, or being in any way disloyal to him. Philip would always be an important part of my life. Apart from having been my much-loved husband he was Becky's father, wasn't he? I would always want Becky to acknowledge that, and to remember him. We live as long as we live in someone's memory, which is the way my great-grandmother lives for me. Though she died when I was seven my memories of her are sharp and clear.

Nigel came as arranged, and was there when Becky arrived home from school. As always, they seemed pleased to see each other and I hated the fact that I couldn't give her the good news there and then. She had a glass of orange juice and a biscuit and then, as usual, went up to her room. 'I have something to ask you,' Nigel said when she'd left us. 'Would it be all right if I told my mother? I hate not to do so. And as she lives in Ireland and the only person she can contact in England is me, I don't see what difference it would make. I hate this secrecy!'

'Of course you can tell your mother,' I agreed. 'And I don't like the secrecy either, but it's only for a few days, until the Bishop is back. I have the feeling that he'll see me quite soon after that.'

'He's in for a surprise,' Nigel said.

'Will your mother be surprised?' I asked. 'And will it be pleasantly or not? She's a Catholic . . .'

'In a way she'll be disappointed you're not Catholic,' Nigel said, 'but she'll be so pleased I'm to be married that I reckon it will outweigh the disappointment. Anyway, she's basically a nice woman, she's not going to hold it against you personally. I'm not expecting her to be prejudiced. So you're happy for me to phone her this evening?'

'Of course! And tell her how much I'm looking forward to meeting her. For my part,' I said, 'and I've only thought of this in the last hour or two – I really would like to tell Ann. I feel she has a right to know, apart from the fact that I want her to. There's no way she's going to disapprove.'

'Of course you must tell her,' Nigel agreed. 'And you and I haven't talked much about Philip, have we? The way he'd feel. I do want you to know, my love, that there's no way I'm going to think I'm taking his place.'

'That's all right,' I said. 'You're not. You couldn't. Philip was Philip and he had his own place which no-one can usurp. But you wouldn't need to take his place. You'll have your own place in my life, unique to you. And I won't ever be holding anything back from you.'

He left soon afterwards; he had a string of visits, he said.

People complain that doctors never visit these days but I know that isn't true.

Later on – I waited until Becky had gone to bed – I phoned Ann. She was so gracious, so pleased for me – and I have to say she didn't seem the least bit surprised. 'It's wonderful news, Venus darling,' she said. 'And I'm sure it'll work out just fine with the Bishop. There must be lots of Anglican priests who've married Catholic women. I don't see the fact that yours is the other way round makes any difference. Anyway, promise you'll let me know what he says – and as soon as you can.'

Two or three days later – it was a Friday morning so Ethel Leigh was zooming round the house with the vacuum – the phone rang and when I answered it was George Phillipson, which was unusual because apart from PCC meetings he doesn't have a great need to talk to me, he does most of the financial stuff with the churchwardens.

'Surprise, surprise!' he said. 'I've had a letter!'

Now that would be the least surprising thing in the world to me, and I'd have thought to most people. Letters, packets, unsolicited catalogues, book offers, invitations to win large sums of money, drop through my letter box and thud on the floor every day except Sunday, most of them to be consigned within minutes to the waste paper bin. So what was it about George's letter? I almost said, 'So what!' but drew it back because he was speaking again.

'From Miss Frazer!' he announced.

My heart dropped like a stone. I've always thought that was a fanciful phrase, but no, it was exactly how I felt, as if there was a heavy weight inside me. I had been so happy; Nigel, Ann, everything going well with Becky, my parents coming. The sky was blue. I should have known it couldn't last.

'I'll read it to you,' George said.

'Please don't bother,' I said sharply. 'I'm sure it's the usual abusive stuff and I've had enough of that, thank you.' But I knew of course that I'd have to listen to it.

'It is a bit abusive,' he admitted, 'but not entirely.'

'Go on then! Let's get it over!' I said.

He began to read.

' "Dear Mr Treasurer," ' (Only Miss Frazer would address George as 'Mr Treasurer'.) ' "The enclosed cheque for four hundred pounds is to take the children of St Mary's Sunday School on their annual trip to the pantomime. As you doubtless know, my father did this for many years before he died and since his death I have always made it my responsibility. I would not wish the wrong and sinful views and actions which, alas, now prevail in St Mary's to deprive the children of their treat. They are the innocent ones. Please let me have a receipt.

' "Yours faithfully, Amelia Frazer." '

'So what would you like me to do, Venus?' George asked.

'What I would *like* you to do,' I said, 'is to tear the cheque into very tiny pieces and return it to her by registered post!'

He laughed – and then was immediately serious.

'I can't do that,' he said. 'Four hundred pounds is not to be sneezed at!'

'I would do more than sneeze at it,' I said, 'I would spit on it – after I'd torn it to bits!'

'It *is* for the children,' he pointed out. 'Why should they miss out?'

'They're not missing out,' I said. 'They're already booked to go to the pantomime.'

'So what am I to do?' he asked again.

'Write her a short note. Thank you very much but the pantomime is already taken care of. Say that if she wishes we will put the money towards the children's summer outing. If she would rather we didn't do that, then we will be happy to return her cheque. Don't bother to give her my love!'

'OK,' he said. 'And if she doesn't ask for it back we'll ring-fence it for the children.'

And then I thought I was being rather nasty, and very un-Christian. There is that thing about turning the other cheek, isn't there? The Gospels are full of bits like that which prevent you doing what you'd really like to do. Very frustrating! So I said, 'Don't make it as rude as I sound – and you'd better tell Henry, see what he says.'

'Four hundred pounds is four hundred pounds,' George said. There speaks a treasurer!

By coincidence, I was in the village that afternoon, buying fruit in Mr Winterton's – I asked about what I always call *my* baby and was told that she was doing exceptionally well, already teething. 'When my Becky was a baby,' I told Mr Winterton, 'every child in the neighbourhood cut their teeth before she did. I thought she was going to grow up a toothless wonder!' And then in the middle of this fascinating conversation little Mrs Bateman came into the shop. I hadn't seen her for two or three Sundays; sometimes she comes to church and sometimes she doesn't, and when she doesn't I reckon she's probably at St Saviour's. So when I do see her I don't mention her absences because I don't want to embarrass her. While I was still talking to Mr Winterton, though not still about teeth, she bought a small head of lettuce and two tomatoes – and somehow we found ourselves leaving the shop together. Good manners demanded that we stood together on the pavement for a minute or two's chat.

'How are you?' I enquired.

'I'm very well,' she said, 'but I'm worried about Miss Frazer . . .' She broke off – she must have noticed my unreceptive face – then she continued. 'I really am worried,' she repeated. 'She has a nasty cough and she's lost such a lot of weight. I've told her she should see Doctor Baines but she won't!' (Miss Frazer must be in an awful dilemma about the doctors in Thurston; one a woman and the other a Catholic.)

'I'm sorry to hear that,' I said – which was true, I don't take any pleasure in even the Miss Frazers of this world being ill. 'I doubt there's anything I can do for her, though. I'm sure she wouldn't like me to put her on our prayer list for the sick!'

Mrs Bateman agreed that that wouldn't be a good idea, sighed heavily and went on her way. Poor little Mrs Bateman! And why had I suddenly wanted to say to her, 'By the way, I'm going to be married!' I suppose because I want everyone to know. Anyway, I resisted it.

★   ★   ★

Then three days later the Bishop himself phoned me.

'I hear you want to come and see me, my dear,' he said. 'I hope everything's all right?'

'More than all right, Bishop!' I said. 'The fact is' – I rushed the words – 'that I want to be married!'

'Well now, isn't that splendid!' he said. 'So yes, you must come and see me, tell me all about it. And who is the lucky man? Do I know him?'

'I don't think so,' I said. 'He's the doctor here – well he's one of them. The thing is . . .' I hesitated, and he noticed it.

'What is the thing?' he asked.

'He's not of our church,' I told him. 'In fact, he's a Roman Catholic. He goes to St Patrick's. His name is Nigel Baines. He's a very nice man!'

'I'm sure he is, or you wouldn't be wanting to marry him, would you?' he said. 'And I expect you'd like to see me as soon as possible, so what about the day after tomorrow? Let's say eleven o'clock. Would that suit?'

'Oh yes! Thank you!' I said. 'Shall I bring Nigel with me?'

'Not this time,' he said. 'Come on your own this time.'

I didn't know whether that was a good sign or a bad one, but I was pleased I wasn't going to have to wait too long.

The first thing I did was to ring Nigel. I knew it was surgery time and I shouldn't do so, and indeed the receptionist said, 'Is it an emergency? He has a patient with him at the moment, so I can't put you through unless it is.' I had to admit that it wasn't. Very important in my eyes, but not top ranking in the larger life of Thurston – none of which I said.

In spite of the fact that the Bishop had been so pleasant on the telephone, and had also been kindness itself over the Frazer affair, driving to the Palace two days later I was a bundle of nerves. What if . . . ? I kept asking myself. What if he says 'No'? What if he says I haven't been in my post long enough – if he says I have to wait a year, or even longer? What if . . . ? In the end I told myself to stop it, to pull myself together. Looking at my watch – yet again – I realized I was too early, so instead of going straight to the Palace I parked close to the cathedral, and went in. It was quiet, dimly lit, just a few people wandering around and two middle-aged women manning the bookstall, without a customer in sight. I found a quiet corner and knelt down. I don't know what I said in my prayers, I'm not sure I said anything but then one doesn't have to. After a few minutes I left, got back into my car and drove the short distance to the Palace.

'The Bishop is on the telephone,' his secretary said. 'He won't keep you waiting more than a few minutes.' He gave me the latest copy of the cathedral quarterly magazine to look at and I turned the pages without taking in a single word. Less than five minutes went by before I was shown into the Bishop's room. He rose to his feet and held out his hand.

'Now sit down, my dear, and tell me all about it, all about this man you want to marry!'

So I did.

'Well, he sounds a very nice man,' the Bishop said. 'Did you know him before you came to Thurston?'

'No,' I admitted. 'But very soon after. I met his partner in the practice on my first Sunday at St Mary's, and then Nigel very soon afterwards.'

'So you've known him a little less than three months?' he said. 'It's not long, is it?'

I had to admit that. 'But we've seen each other often and I am quite sure of my feelings – and so is he, as he would tell you if he was here.'

'That's not impossible,' he said. 'I fell in love with my wife at first sight, and she tells me it was mutual. Of course we had to wait to get married, I was a very young curate then! She was in the choir.'

Greatly daring, I said, 'But it worked. For you, I mean.'

'Oh yes!' he said. 'And I'm pleased to say it's still working. We shall be celebrating our fortieth anniversary in January. But you would also have disadvantages we didn't have. We were of the same church whereas you and your doctor would not be able to worship together, except on certain occasions, and not at the Eucharist. That will be sad, though I'm sure you've both thought about it.'

'We have!' I said. 'We've discussed it more than once. We

both think it's nonsense that our churches are divided, but we would live with it.'

'Yes, it is nonsense,' the Bishop agreed, 'but it's much more than that, it's a sin against God. That's why I am never, other things being equal, against an Anglican marrying with a Roman Catholic. It's a beginning of unity, and from small beginnings . . .' He broke off and I rushed in!

'Does that mean . . . ? Are you saying I can marry Nigel?' I could hardly believe it.

'Oh yes!' he said. 'But you have to realize, and you're a sensible woman so I'm sure you will, you will have more difficulties than if you were two lay people. You are a priest, now and for always. Never forget that.'

'I wouldn't!' I said. 'Not ever!'

'But,' he said, 'you must wait a little longer. Three months will not do – I would say that whatever the circumstances.'

'How long . . . ?'

'I can't say at this moment,' he said. 'I would like to meet Nigel, I must meet him. You must wait at least six months, perhaps longer, I don't yet know. It will be my duty to keep watch over you, you are in my pastoral care and I have your welfare at heart. I hope you believe that. But the time will soon pass. You might not think so now, but it will!'

'And,' I took a deep breath, 'can we be engaged?' I asked. 'Can we tell people that we hope to marry?'

'Of course you can, my dear!' the Bishop said. 'I think you'd burst if you couldn't! He can buy you a beautiful ring and you can wear it with love, and because I know how women enjoy planning for weddings I shall tell you a few practical things which you must take into account and weave into your plans.

'You should be married in the Anglican church – I myself will marry you – but Father Seamus from St Patrick's, whom I know well, should be invited to take a prominent part in the service, which I'm sure he'll be pleased to do. Then there is the question of where you and your husband will live and I'm afraid there's no choice for you about that. You must live in your Vicarage. As you probably know, as the incumbent of St Mary's you must live in the house provided and you must not spend more than ninety nights in any one year away from that house. What will Nigel think about living in your Vicarage?'

'I don't think there'll be the slightest difficulty about that. I haven't seen his flat but I doubt it would be big enough for the three of us. In any case, I wouldn't want to uproot Becky again.'

The Bishop nodded. 'Quite right! You must consider your daughter at all times. Does she get on well with Nigel?'

'Very well indeed,' I assured him. 'There's no doubt about that at all. They're good friends already.'

'Then have a word with your young man about when he can come with you to see me, and let me know. And now we'll have a cup of coffee and you can tell me how everything is in the parish and how you've settled in.'

I went back to Thurston a very happy lady, and immediately phoned Nigel, who was over the moon with the news.

The following week came the day – Wednesday – when Bertha Jowett was to leave her cottage and move into the Beeches. She was to go in the morning, to allow her all day to settle in before bedtime, so on Tuesday afternoon I'd spent time with her, helping her to sort out which personal items she would take with her. It couldn't be many, there was a limit to how much her room at the Beeches would hold. I was to take her there while Ethel Leigh stayed at the cottage until the rest of Bertha's things, which were mostly going to charity shops, had been collected later that day.

When I arrived Bertha was sitting there, wearing an ancient fur coat, musquash, and a felt hat. I had never seen her in outdoor clothes before. I'm not sure she ever went out in the cold weather. She looked enveloped by them. Ethel helped me to put her things into the car, and when the last item had been packed it was time for Bertha and me to go. At the front door, before she stepped outside, she stopped in her tracks, turned around, and gave a last look at the house she was leaving. Her eyes went everywhere, floor to ceiling, as if she was taking photographs to be imprinted on her mind. She said nothing, nor did anyone else speak. Then she gave a loving pat to a small table which stood in the hall, waiting to be collected, and we left.

It was no more than a seven-minute journey to the Beeches. The bell was answered, almost as soon as it had finished ringing, by the Matron herself.

'Ah! Miss Jowett!' she said pleasantly. 'So here you are then! Come in at once, out of the cold. Someone will bring in your things from the Vicar's car. I expect you'd like a cup of coffee?'

'Thank you,' Bertha said. 'You're very kind.'

We followed Matron into Bertha's room, which was at the end of the ground floor corridor. It was a pleasant room with a French window looking on to the garden, and a single bed made up with a floral cover and a couple of cushions so that at the moment it looked like a sofa. There was an armchair, a kettle, teapot and crockery on a small table, a dining chair, shelves, drawers, a built-in wardrobe cupboard and, sensibly not too far from the bed, a door which led to what the brochure described as en-suite facilities. Really, at a quick look, the room could not be faulted, but I wondered what was going through Bertha's mind as she looked around this space which from now on would be her domain. Whatever it was, she said nothing and the silence was broken by a young woman bringing in Bertha's belongings from the car.

'Thank you, Maggie!' Matron said. Then she turned to Bertha, who was sitting in the armchair, now looking rather pale. 'I'll leave you to unpack your things,' she said. 'And I'll see to some coffee for both of you. When you've emptied your suitcase Maggie will take it and store it in the locker room for you.'

When she left, and Maggie had gone back to the car to bring in more belongings, Bertha said, quite sharply, 'I can't see me needing my suitcase again!'

I busied myself unpacking her things – half-a-dozen favourite books, a pack of cards, a Scrabble board (I decided that I would drop in from time to time and have a game of Scrabble with her. I had no doubt she'd beat me at it). Then followed a porcelain figurine, a china dog, and after that came the box with the photographs. Bertha delved into it to show me a faded sepia one of her parents – 'Taken in the 1920s,' she said. 'I was two.' She stood there, wearing an ankle-length white dress and a little white cap with a frilly brim, between her mother and father.

387

There was a photograph in a silver frame of a handsome young man in air force uniform, with pilot's wings, about which she said nothing. All these things, and several more knick-knacks, she scattered around the room. She will make it really untidy in no time at all, I thought, and then it will seem more like home.

I stayed as long as I could and when it was time to go, greatly daring, I gave her a hug and a kiss. She seemed surprised, but not cross. 'I'll be in fairly soon to see you again,' I said. 'And Ethel is coming tomorrow to report on how the rest of the move went. And don't forget, a lady comes regularly to change your library books for you. If there's anything else you want, give me a ring. There's a mobile telephone.'

I went outside and got into my car. As I drove home tears trickled down my cheeks.

THIRTY-THREE

I am standing in the church porch at eleven forty-five p.m. on the twenty-fourth of December, greeting people who are arriving for the Midnight Mass. Since this is Christmas Eve I am allowed to call it the Midnight Mass, but if I were to describe the Sunday morning Eucharist as the ten o'clock Mass, there would be rioting in the ranks and possibly complaints to higher authorities, even as far as the Archbishop of Canterbury. Complaints have been made to His Grace for much lesser suspected misdemeanours by clergy, like 'How much annual holiday is our Vicar actually allowed?' But never mind that now. This is the season of goodwill and I am filled to the brim with it as I see these people, many of them known to me, others total strangers whom I shall possibly never see again unless they are around next Christmas. I love them all, even those who, having refreshed themselves first with the Christmas spirit available in the Ewe Lamb, breathe fiery fumes over me.

The Blessed Henry has been here for ages, with his lovely Molly and their grandchildren. He, and a posse of helpers, are handing out service sheets and finding places for people to sit – the church is already two-thirds full and there will be the usual rush at the last minute, which will include Ann, my parents and Becky. Vicarage families countrywide, possibly worldwide, are known for being amongst the last to arrive, as are most people who live closest to the church. Richard Proctor is not here since he is spending Christmas with his lady love in Kingston-upon-Thames. And alas for me, nor is Nigel as he has gone to Ireland to be with his mother for Christmas, though even if he were in Thurston he would be at St Patrick's, where I suppose they are likewise streaming in through the door.

Here is Sonia coming up the path.

'I suppose with Nigel being away you're on duty all over Christmas?' I say.

'Afraid so,' she says. 'We take it in turns at holiday times, and it was mine to be on. You must excuse me if my mobile goes off in church, though I hope it won't!'

'I hope so for your sake,' I tell her.

She'd been so pleased to hear about Nigel and me – 'Though I saw it coming, right from the first,' she said. 'You're so right for each other.'

I've been touched, since we've let it be known we were to marry, by how many people were pleased for us. There were so many good wishes, from both St Mary's and St Patrick's, and if there are those whom the news doesn't please at least they've kept quiet about it. When the time comes for the wedding I think we'll have a packed church. I just wish I knew when that would be, but I'm trying to be patient. I had a nice Christmas card from the Bishop, as indeed I did from so many of my parishioners; far more than I expected.

Carla Brown comes in with Walter. 'Happy Christmas, Venus,' she says, giving me a hug. 'Don't the Christmas trees look wonderful!'

They do indeed, which is because a small group of men have been toiling all afternoon, setting up the ten-foot trees, one on each side of the door, climbing up ladders, draping lights, and dashing down to the shops for replacement bulbs which should have been noticed as being spent when the trees were taken down last year, but never are in my experience.

'They certainly do!' I agree with Carla. 'And just wait until you see the flowers in the church. Eric and his band of ladies have been hard at it for ages. They're so clever!'

I went to see Bertha Jowett this afternoon. The Beeches was all

390

trimmed up too, with a Christmas tree in the hall and paper chains all over the place. It's the second time I've been this week and today I thought she looked a little more settled. The wary, apprehensive look had left her eyes, as if nothing had turned out quite as badly as she'd expected.

'It all looks very festive,' I said to her.

'Oh it is!' she agreed. 'They've got quite a few things planned. Carol singers coming in this evening, though I don't have to be present if I don't want to be. And of course a real Christmas dinner tomorrow. Turkey and all that. I never had a turkey. It would have lasted me until Easter. When I wanted to celebrate I would have a nice fillet steak and a bottle of claret.'

'I shall see you tomorrow,' I told her, 'though only for a minute and I don't know at what time. In between services I shall be bringing communion to those who can't get out. Not just here, all over the village.'

'Include me out!' she said. 'I want none of that!'

'Oh, don't worry!' I told her. 'I'll include you out all right. I shall just put my head around the door, say "Merry Christmas!" and vanish!' I shall, though she doesn't know it, give her a small present, a book of quotations I found which I thought would suit her.

I'm looking at my watch. Seven minutes to twelve. Time my family were here. Becky is a very happy bunny at the moment; delighted about Nigel and me – though at one point, when I was saying good-night to her, she said, 'But we won't forget Daddy, will we?' I promised her that we wouldn't, not ever. She's also been pleased this week because she was chosen to be Mary in the school's nativity play. I don't know who was responsible for that but it was a wonderful boost to Becky, even though a couple of girls did tell her it was only because she was the Vicar's daughter, which I flatly contradicted. 'The Vicar's children are just who they *don't* normally choose!' I said. Anyway, she did it well, as did all the children. I sat with the other mums and dads. We sang 'Away in a Manger' – not my favourite carol. Whoever said of a baby 'no crying he makes' was way off the mark. All the mums shed a few tears, as we do at nativity plays, while the dads blew their noses hard.

391

Ethel Leigh is here in church. She did wonders with the cottage in the short time she had before my mother and father moved in, and she was no end of help to them on the day itself, so much so that Mum has asked her if she'll come regularly, a half-day a week, which Ethel was very glad to do. 'It's not just the money,' she said. 'I've got Ron's pension and the Widows, and the mortgage is paid. It just gives me something to do, and company. I don't have to talk to the walls!'

And here they are, the last of the stragglers, including my family. Missie, whom Becky would dearly have liked to have brought with her, has been left in sole charge of the Vicarage!

I say 'hello' to them, then go quickly into the vestry and put on my chasuble and stole, the beautiful white ones embroidered with gold, worn especially for the festivals of Easter and Christmas; worn to the glory of God. Before I leave the vestry I say my short prayer and then I walk slowly up the aisle, behind the servers. Everything is so beautiful. The whole church is lit by white candles: candles on the altar, candles in the sconces on the end of the pews, candles on the lectern, on the windowsills, everywhere! The flowers are another of Eric's miracles. We are singing 'Once in Royal David's City' and it is as beautiful in my ears, sung by this hotchpotch of a congregation, which we are, old and young, good singers and terrible ones, and Mr Blatchford, belting it out on the organ, as anything which comes out of King's College, Cambridge every Christmas Eve. Yes, the church is well and truly crowded. There are people standing at the back. And when, at the point in the service when I face the congregation and, holding up my arms, say, 'The Lord be with you!' the response 'And also with you!' comes over about as loud and as heartily as anything you will ever hear in the Church of England.

I pause for a matter of seconds, and look at them. How I love them! And then what flashes into my mind are the ones who are not here. I don't mean Nigel or Philip, but Miss Frazer, Miss Carson, Mrs Blamires, little Mrs Bateman – and a few others – and I am truly, truly sad and I miss them. And, without in the slightest way wishing to put myself up higher, because that's the very last thing on my mind, I wonder how God feels when we turn away from him. And all that takes no more than a second or two and we are back on course again.

When it's all over – though there'll be a Eucharist at ten in the morning – I hand over to Henry who will see that everything's put away properly, that the beautiful silver chalice, which was given by a worshipper in this church in the seventeenth century and has been in use here ever since, is locked in the safe, and that the church door is securely locked, and I walk home with my family. My mother and father are staying at the Vicarage over Christmas. The cottage isn't yet organized enough to be comfortable, and in any case I think they are both due for a rest.

It's a fine, dry night, with a high, starry sky. It's cold, and I suspect there'll be a frost before morning. Back at the Vicarage, greeted as ecstatically by Missie as if we had been away for a week, Ann elects to make sandwiches while my mother brews a pot of tea. 'I doubt you've had a proper meal all day, Venus,' my mother reproves me. 'I know you!'

She is right about one thing and wrong about the other. I have a hearty appetite and eat well and regularly (including the wrong things) but today is one of those exceptions when I literally haven't had time. And there's another thing: this has been an emotional evening, and for me the aftermath of emotion is that I'm extra hungry, so I'm standing beside Ann and I'm wolfing down the sandwiches as fast as she can make them.

Becky, who is more or less falling asleep on her feet, decides she'll go to bed and have hers brought up to her. She would like Missie to go upstairs with her but Missie is not to be parted from this unexpected influx of company at this strange hour, not to mention the smell of ham sandwiches, so she refuses to go. My father decides, Christmas now officially having begun, that he will celebrate with a glass of whisky as a chaser to his cup of tea and the rest of us think that's a good idea and choose our various tipples, brandy for Ann and me and sweet sherry for my mother. In the end, I am too tired to finish mine and, after wishing everyone a happy Christmas yet again, I take myself off to bed.

I am dropping off to sleep when the telephone rings. I pick it up, wondering how anyone could be so unkind as to call me out in the early hours of Christmas morning.

It's Nigel!

'I thought I wouldn't ring earlier,' he says, 'in case you'd all gone on to some wild party after church! How are you, my love? How did everything go?'

'Fine,' I say.

'What are you doing now?'

'I'm in bed.'

'I wish I were there,' Nigel says.

'I wish you were!' I say. 'I can hear a lot of noise at your end. What's happening?'

'There's a bit of a party going on,' he says. 'They came back here after Mass. I reckon my mother's invited half of Quilty because I'm here. I feel like the prodigal son. Goodness knows when they'll all leave. I'll ring you tomorrow when it's a bit quieter, but my mother would like a word with you now. OK?'

'Sure!' I tell him.

'I'll put her on.'

'Hello, Venus!' she says. 'I just wanted to wish you a happy Christmas.' She has the loveliest, softest Irish voice imaginable. 'I'm so looking forward to meeting you. Whatever else, I'll be over in England for the wedding – whenever that is.'

'That's great!' I say. 'And I wish I could tell you when it's to be. Perhaps in June if all goes well. You can be sure I'll let you know the minute I know. And if there's a friend or a relative you'd like to bring with you . . .'

'Thank you,' she says. 'I might well like to bring my sister, Veronica. Nigel's very fond of his Aunt Veronica and 'twould be company for me on the way. Also, she's never been to England.'

We chat a little longer, about this and that, and then she says, 'I'll say good-night to you, and once again a happy Christmas, and now I'll put Nigel back on the line.'

'She sounds nice, your mother,' I say to him.

'She's a bit of all right,' he agrees. 'The two of you will get on famously.'

We say our lengthy good-nights and then I ring off. I am so

happy, but oh, how I long for him to be here! But three days from now he will be, I remind myself.

So that was Christmas, my first in my own church. It was wonderful, and now it's over, and here we are on New Year's Eve, at the theatre and in the process of taking our seats for the pantomime. They're good seats, in the circle, but at the moment there's a lot of discussion going on between the children about where they will sit and, in particular, who they will sit next to. The whole evening will be enhanced if they can sit next to their best friends and I understand that because I am going to sit next to Nigel, with Becky on my other side, and on her other side she'll have Anna. Yes, we did manage to get an extra ticket. My parents are here – Ann isn't because she had a long-standing invitation to a New Year's Eve party elsewhere. It did occur to me that I'd have liked to have invited Bertha Jowett, but by then all the seats were taken. In the event, a small party from the Beeches will be going to a matinee and Bertha, if she wishes, can join them. She might do that, she told me, though the ballet or a good murder play is more to her taste.

We are now all seated, more or less amicably I hope – at any rate there are no protests. We all came on the same coach, which dropped us at the door and will pick us up when the show's over. We arrived earlier than we expected which means that now there is time, and a good view from our seats, to watch all the other arrivals, something I've always enjoyed doing at the theatre. Becky is talking to Anna and Nigel is chatting with my parents, who are on his other side. There's a buzz all around me and I'm aware of it – and then suddenly I'm not aware because my mind has gone off at a tangent and, except that I can feel the warm comfort of Nigel and Becky on either side of me, I'm not really here. Part of me is back in the last few months I've spent at St Mary's, and at the same time part of me is in the future, with what will happen, to me, to all of us.

I know now, quite surely, that I'm in the right place. St Mary's, Thurston, is where I want to be and where I believe I'm meant to be. I haven't done everything well, I'm very aware of that. Sometimes I've been too outspoken, not tactful, or I've made changes too quickly. There are people who like me, and I thank God for them, and people who don't. I'm sure there are those who haven't yet made up their minds about me. And of course there are the ones I've lost by being who and what I am, and who, I've faced the fact, I will not regain. I remind myself that Jesus, who did everything well, who was without sin, didn't keep everyone and still doesn't. So who am I to complain? Who do I think I am that everything should go perfectly for me?

And there I draw a line over my thoughts about what has happened and think about what's to come in this new year, or what I hope is to come, because I don't know, do I? But I have faith that many of the things I dream about and plan for, things large and small, will happen. When I come to next year's pantomime, for instance, it will be with my husband!

And then I'm switched back to the present, to where I am, because the musicians have crept into the orchestra pit, and they're tuning up their instruments, which must be the sound which has brought me back. Nigel turns away from my parents and back to me, and takes my hand in his. Then the lights go down and the curtain comes up and we sit back and wait to have everything unfolded before us.